Praise for the novels of Joyce Lamb

TRUE COLORS

"Fast paced and gripping. The story is dark and twisted . . . The romance is sizzling and satisfying. It's easy to empathize with the characters, and the action makes this a perfect weekend read."
—*RT Book Reviews*

"Will hold you spellbound. [It's] splashed with just the right amount of romance, [and] you will keep turning the pages to see where the unexpected twists and turns lead next." —*Fresh Fiction*

TRUE VISION

"Lamb knocks it out of the Chicago ballpark with this fast-paced romantic mystery. Combining paranormal elements, a carefully crafted mystery and a powerful romance, *True Vision* has something for everyone. Readers will be looking for the next book in the trilogy as soon as they finish reading this one."
—*RT Book Reviews*

COLD MIDNIGHT

"Impossible to put down! A spine-tingling whodunit constantly keeps you on the edge of your seat with scenes that will make your toes curl . . . Joyce Lamb is a highly talented writer who knows how to write a captivating suspense novel." —*Manic Readers*

"Tension runs high throughout the entire story and the drama is terrific . . . Well crafted and intriguing."
—*Huntress Book Reviews*

continued . . .

"The interaction and emotion between the characters [are] very entertaining . . . This is a page-turner."
—*Night Owl Reviews* (Top Pick)

"An enjoyable romantic police procedural."
—*Midwest Book Review*

FOUND WANTING

"Top-notch suspense . . . Believable characters in an action-packed plot will enthrall readers. Like Tami Hoag and Iris Johansen, Lamb weaves the textures of romance and suspense together in a satisfying read."
—*Booklist*

"This wonderfully written story is a must read for any fan of romantic suspense! Joyce Lamb is a master storyteller . . . Don't miss out on one of the best novels ever written!"
—*Romance Junkies*

"Fast-paced suspense, full of twists and turns and nonstop action . . . To find out the many other fabulous nuances of this story, you'll just have to go and grab yourself a copy!"
—LoveRomances.com

CAUGHT IN THE ACT

"Page-turning suspense and a rewarding romance make for a riveting read."
—*Booklist*

"Captures readers' interest from the opening pages."
—*Romance Reviews Today*

"Full of shocking twists and turns . . . A wonderful novel that achieves the perfect balance between the romance and the mystery."
—LoveRomances.com

TRUE SHOT

Joyce Lamb

BERKLEY SENSATION, NEW YORK

THE BERKLEY PUBLISHING GROUP
Published by the Penguin Group
Penguin Group (USA) Inc.
375 Hudson Street, New York, New York 10014, USA
Penguin Group (Canada), 90 Eglinton Avenue East, Suite 700, Toronto, Ontario M4P 2Y3, Canada
(a division of Pearson Penguin Canada Inc.)
Penguin Books Ltd., 80 Strand, London WC2R 0RL, England
Penguin Group Ireland, 25 St. Stephen's Green, Dublin 2, Ireland (a division of Penguin Books Ltd.)
Penguin Group (Australia), 250 Camberwell Road, Camberwell, Victoria 3124, Australia
(a division of Pearson Australia Group Pty. Ltd.)
Penguin Books India Pvt. Ltd., 11 Community Centre, Panchsheel Park, New Delhi—110 017, India
Penguin Group (NZ), 67 Apollo Drive, Rosedale, Auckland 0632, New Zealand
(a division of Pearson New Zealand Ltd.)
Penguin Books (South Africa) (Pty.) Ltd., 24 Sturdee Avenue, Rosebank, Johannesburg 2196,
South Africa

Penguin Books Ltd., Registered Offices: 80 Strand, London WC2R 0RL, England

This is a work of fiction. Names, characters, places, and incidents either are the product of the author's imagination or are used fictitiously, and any resemblance to actual persons, living or dead, business establishments, events, or locales is entirely coincidental. The publisher does not have any control over and does not assume any responsibility for author or third-party websites or their content.

TRUE SHOT

A Berkley Sensation Book / published by arrangement with the author

PRINTING HISTORY
Berkley Sensation mass-market edition / December 2011

Copyright © 2011 by Joyce Lamb.
Cover art: *Woman Holding Gun* by Joshua Sheldon/Getty Images;
Empty Street by Carlos Hernandez/Corbis.
Cover design by Annette Fiore DeFex.

ISBN: 978-0-425-24492-0

BERKLEY SENSATION®
Berkley Sensation Books are published by The Berkley Publishing Group,
a division of Penguin Group (USA) Inc.,
375 Hudson Street, New York, New York 10014.
BERKLEY SENSATION® is a registered trademark of Penguin Group (USA) Inc.
The "B" design is a trademark of Penguin Group (USA) Inc.

PRINTED IN THE UNITED STATES OF AMERICA

10 9 8 7 6 5 4 3 2 1

ACKNOWLEDGMENTS

Thanks to:

- Grace Morgan, who always looks out for me.

- Wendy McCurdy, a super editor.

- Katherine Pelz, Kayleigh Clark and all the myriad professionals at Berkley, who do some truly top-notch work.

- Julie Snider, whose artistic talent continues to blow me away.

- Mary G., who asks great questions and frequently makes my day.

- My wonderful friends and family, who are unfailingly supportive and enthusiastic despite my "I'm in my head right now" moments and who no longer blink when I say stuff like, "This would make a good murder weapon."

CHAPTER **ONE**

Zoe was dead.

Dead.

Sam closed her eyes and gritted her teeth against the throb of pain in her shoulder.

Focus, damn it, she thought. It's what you're good at. What you're trained to do.

Soldier on. Accomplish the mission. Get to the cabin. Hunker down. Hide. Get warm. God, she couldn't wait to get warm.

Blinking cold rain from her eyes, she squinted into the growing dusk, trying to get oriented. The cabin was around here somewhere. She was sure of it.

Unless she'd gotten herself lost.

No. She wasn't lost. She knew where she was going.

Just like you knew where you were going when you ran away from home fourteen years ago?

Don't think. Focus.

She peered through the rain running in rivulets over her forehead and into her eyes. She couldn't see a damn thing. Just towering trees decorated in gold and orange and red. The same coppery red that spattered her Nikes and the leaves squishing underfoot. Her feet were cold and wet, just like the rest of her. At least she still shivered, the body's way of creating its own warmth. But she'd been shivering for so long and so hard that she should have generated enough heat to warm a small house. If she didn't find the cabin soon, she was toast. And not the warm, golden brown kind.

She was probably toast anyway. No way was he going to let her go. He'd hunt her down like an animal. Have her shot down like they'd shot down Zoe—

She battled back the wave of grief that tried to steal her breath and forced herself forward, one foot in front of the other. Don't think, don't think.

But she couldn't help but think.

Zoe was dead. Her closest friend.

Don't go there, she thought. *Don't* go there.

Then she saw it. The Trudeau family cabin. Materializing out of a copse of amber gold and dark orange trees. An honest-to-God log cabin.

A rush of much-needed warmth spread through her blood. Almost home. As close to home as she'd gotten in a decade. Wouldn't it be cool if her sisters and parents waited for her there? Alex and Charlie and Mom and Dad.

She pictured the cozy living room with its stone fireplace and polished wooden floor, the big, overstuffed couch with the red-and-black-plaid blanket draped over the back. She imagined that blanket draped around her shoulders, imagined sinking into the poofy cushions and drifting off, wrapped in the familiarity of home away from home.

She found the key in its place, tucked into a cleverly carved notch three feet up from the planks of the porch. Her half-frozen fingers fumbled with it, missed getting it into the lock the first three tries. Hot tears streamed through the cold rain on her face.

Stupid, so stupid. Crying *now*, after everything that had happened, after so many years of not crying. N3 operatives didn't cry. N3 operatives carried on.

But Zoe, poor Zoe.

Her hands trembled as she finally nailed the lock and heard the tumblers squeak open. The door swung inward, and she all but tripped over the raised threshold into dust-choked air and a musty odor that didn't smell at all like the cabin she remembered. Where was the scent of fresh-chopped wood? The hint of fabric softener that spoke of clean sheets on big, soft beds?

She dropped her dripping bag on the floor and pushed the door closed, her arms and legs leaden now, weighed down by her sodden denim shirt and jeans. All she had to do was make it to the couch and get the blanket, and she'd be warm in no time.

But her knees buckled, and as they hit the floor, pain seared through her shoulder. A burst of light flashed the world bright, and she flinched. A deep, quaking rumble vibrated the worn wooden floor under her knees. Thunder.

On the next flash of light, she noticed the pink water pooling near her left knee.

Oh, yeah. She'd been shot in the shoulder. Funny how she couldn't feel it anymore.

In fact, she couldn't feel much of anything. Maybe that should alarm her, but somehow it didn't.

It figures, she thought. Make it almost home, and it wasn't going to matter.

She was still going to die alone.

CHAPTER **TWO**

Mac Hunter squinted against the rain slashing the windshield and hoped he was going the right way. He had no clue at this point. No street signs for miles, just this crappy, pothole-ridden road that kept going. Thank God for four-wheel drive, or his back end would have sunk into three feet of mud by now.

A streak of lightning made the towering trees pressing in on all sides look menacing against the night sky. Why had he let Alex and Charlie talk him into a week by himself in the middle of the Shenandoahs with nothing to do but brood? He didn't need to get away to get his act together. He was fine.

Okay, yeah, he was a little burned out, and, yes, he'd started drinking more than he should. But it wasn't like he was downing shots at the local bar every night then stumbling home at two in the morning with no memory the next day of how he got there. He wasn't sneaking drinks at work from a bottle stashed in a bottom desk drawer. He wasn't slipping out at midday for a three-martini lunch. The Trudeau sisters seemed to think a few drinks after a stressful day meant he was veering onto the off-ramp to alcoholism.

He supposed he could see their point. His father had drunk himself to death, after all. But that was why Mac had always tried to be careful about his alcohol intake. Not so much lately, though. So, yeah, maybe he did need someone to slap him upside the head. Maybe he was lucky that Alex and Charlie had staged their version of an intervention before more serious measures became necessary. They wanted to stop the self-medicating drunk before he became an alcoholic. He had to appreciate the depth of their friendship, whether he agreed with them or not. Every man should have friends like his.

Finally, he saw it.

The dark clouds of the storm lightened, and there sat the Trudeau family cabin, nestled among tall trees dressed up in the golden colors of fall. He suddenly wished he knew what kind of trees those were, but he had no idea. Some people knew plants. Mac Hunter knew inverted pyramids and how many picas in an inch. He knew how to write a story hook that'd pique your interest, even if it was about nothing more exciting than a city council meeting. He knew nut graphs and hammer heads and how to get a shooter to the scene of a fire in less than ten minutes. But trees? The closest he came to knowing anything about trees was that the newsprint he spent his days filling with stories and photos started out as trees.

With a relieved sigh—because now he wouldn't have to drive the hour back down the mountain to find a crappy motel for the night—he parked the Jeep Commander and stepped out onto the soft, squishy ground. As rain pelted his leather jacket, muddy water oozed up around his loafers. He should have put on his new Gore-Tex hiking boots when he'd stopped for supplies, but he'd shrugged off the threatening clouds, too eager to get to the cabin and crash. The flight had been long, picking up the rental SUV a hassle. The cherry on top of his shit sundae: an unrelenting thunderstorm the entire way up the mountain, at times so fierce the windshield wipers couldn't keep up with the deluge. So far, not a fun trip.

On the porch, he found the notch exactly where Charlie said the key resided. Three feet up, a handy little nook. But there was no key.

His heart thumped. Maybe he was destined to spend the night in a ratty motel after all. But, with his luck, the road he'd just put behind him would have washed out by now, trapping him.

He stuffed his hand into his front pocket and retrieved the new Swiss Army knife Alex had given him for the trip. Maybe he could pick the lock.

After a few seconds of fumbling with the knife, trying to figure out which tool to use, he gave up. Before beginning the wet slog back to the truck, he tried the door, just in case the universe took pity on his pathetic soul.

The knob turned.

He pushed the door open and blinked several times as his eyes tried to adjust to the gloom inside. Alex had told him a lantern sat on a table right by the door. All he had to do was pop in some batteries and he'd be good to go until he could get the generator going. Batteries, of course, that still sat with the rest of the supplies in the back of the Jeep.

He sprinted back to where he'd parked, figuring his shoes were ruined anyway, and it was kind of liberating to splash through the mud puddles like a kid.

Batteries in hand, he stepped into the cabin while ripping into the packaging. Within a minute, he cranked the light on and, eager to see where he'd be spending the week, held up the lantern.

And just about dropped it.

CHAPTER **THREE**

Earlier the same afternoon

Zoe, you have to calm down and tell me what's wrong."

"They did it to me, so they might have done it to you."

"Done what? You're not making any sense." Sam tried to guide her friend out of the entryway and toward the sofa. She'd arrived home in DC less than an hour ago, relieved to drop her bag by the door and start shedding the persona she'd worn for the latest assignment. She'd gotten as far as shrugging out of the denim shirt she'd worn as a jacket when Zoe started pounding on the door.

"Come sit down and talk to me," Sam said. "I'll pour us some drinks."

"No!" It burst out of her, and Zoe covered her tear-streaked face with shaking hands. A wild sob quickly followed. "I can't . . . I can't . . ."

Seriously concerned now, Sam pulled her weeping friend into her arms and held her tight, smoothing her hand over Zoe's quaking back. "It's okay. Everything's going to be okay."

She didn't even know what was wrong, but it seemed like the right thing to say. At the same time, her alarm grew. This was *Zoe*. Stoic, ramrod-straight-posture, I-didn't-cry-at-*Bambi*-as-a-kid Zoe Harris. She never cried, rarely even showed much emotion. What the hell had happened while Sam was undercover in San Francisco?

"No, it's not all right," Zoe said and pushed her back with surprising strength. "Everything will *never* be okay. He betrayed us, Sam. We trusted him, and he betrayed us."

"Who? Who betrayed us?"

"Flinn."

Sam's stomach did a flip. "What?"

"I'm pregnant," Zoe blurted.

More shock had Sam shaking her head, denying herself the leap to conclusions. "You and Flinn?"

Zoe's blond, spiral curls bounced as she violently shook her head and stalked into the living room as though she couldn't stand still. "No! Never."

Zoe sank onto the sofa and dropped her face into her hands as stronger sobs tore out of her. "I don't know when it happened. I . . . he must have . . . must have drugged me or something. I don't . . . remember . . ."

Drugged her? Sam's heart took off at a sprint as she thought of the night a month and a half ago when she'd suspected Flinn had drugged *her*. But she'd decided then that she was wrong. The days of being strapped down and forced to endure experiments designed to test the limits, and extent, of her abilities were over. Weren't they?

Zoe raised her face to Sam, her brown eyes red and puffy. "He's using me as an . . . as an . . ." Her breath started hitching, and fresh tears poured down her reddened cheeks. "As an . . . *incubator.*"

Sam's stomach rolled with dread. She knew when she needed backup and never hesitated to make the request. As soon as she picked up the phone, though, Zoe clamped iron-strong fingers around her wrist and twisted until Sam winced. Before she could think to create an empathic block, memory that wasn't hers crashed over her.

"Why would you do this? What kind of sick bastard does this?"

Flinn pats my shoulder. "It's going to be okay, Zoe. Just hear me out."

"Why should I listen to you? You're the one who did this to me!"

"You're part of something vitally important, Zoe. Something that's going to change the world. You were chosen—"

"Fuck you!" I shove him back, but it's not enough. If my

Glock was within reach, I would kill him. "I'm not some breed mare for you to use to grow super spies!"

Sam fell out of the empathic memory as Zoe jerked her up close so that they were nose to nose. For the first time since she'd come weeping through Sam's front door, Zoe looked coherent and deadly. "Do you get it now?" she hissed. "Did you *see?*"

Sam resisted the instinct to try to break Zoe's grip on her wrist. They were both combat trained, both knew the moves and countermoves for incapacitating an attacker. But this was her friend. She knew Zoe's intention was not to hurt her.

Sam relaxed her muscles and waited until the taller woman's shoulders sagged. Regret added to the emotional chaos of her expression as Zoe dropped Sam's wrist and took a step back. "God, I'm so sor—"

Her brows arched sharply, and shock wiped the despair from her eyes.

The wet splat against the front of Sam's shirt had her flinching back and glancing down to see a thick spray pattern of red against the white backdrop of cotton. It took a second to register.

Blood.

Sam lunged toward her friend. As she tackled her friend to the floor behind the sofa, she felt a tug of pain burn through her left shoulder. Too late. She'd let the enemy take her by surprise.

She scrambled to her knees and pressed shaking fingers to Zoe's neck. That was when she realized trying to find a pulse was pointless: Her eyes were open and empty.

Sam fought down the nausea and grief and forced herself to remember her training. The sniper who had just killed Zoe no doubt waited patiently for Sam to come into view so he could take a second kill shot.

She had to *do* something. Move.

A ticklish feather-stroke down her arm drew her gaze, and she watched the thin stream of blood tracking over her forearm. Numbness spread from her shoulder into the hand resting palm up on her thigh.

The sound of breaking glass snapped her out of her paralysis, and she slithered across the slippery hardwood floor toward her bag, toward her SIG. With cold, hard—comforting—metal pressed to her palm, she flipped over onto her back and fired one shot into the chest of the intruder tearing toward her.

He dropped about a yard from her feet, crumpling into a heap, and she kept the gun aimed at him. She didn't so much as breathe until she saw his fingers go lax on the trigger of his weapon.

She crawled to him, forcing herself to focus, to do her job, to not think about Zoe, and used both hands to shove him over onto his back. She trained her SIG on him, hyperalert to the tiniest twitch. In head-to-toe black, a balaclava obscuring his features, he looked like any other assassin. Yet, something about him seemed familiar.

She yanked off the balaclava and sat back on her heels with a startled gasp.

She knew him.

He wasn't a fellow N3 operative, but he was part of the team, one of three men Flinn called "the muscle."

And Flinn had sent him to kill Zoe, to kill Sam.

Disbelief lightened her head. Betrayal tightened her lungs.

She had to run.

CHAPTER **FOUR**

The present

Frustrated, Mac Hunter hunched over the steering wheel and glanced at the wet, dark-haired woman unconscious in the passenger seat. She hadn't so much as whimpered when he'd wadded a clean T-shirt and stuffed it between her denim shirt and oozing shoulder to help staunch the bleeding. Then he'd bundled her up in the red plaid blanket from the sofa and hustled her into the Jeep, careful to protect her shoulder from too much jarring. He'd turned the heat on high, conscious of the wet-dog smell of the blanket's old wool while he'd navigated the rutted road back toward Skyline Drive.

Now, the rain drumming against the roof of the SUV drowned out the wild pounding of his heart as he watched the frothy, muddy water surging past the front bumper. Just as he'd feared: The storm had washed out the road.

He had no choice but to turn back.

He executed a tight T-turn, praying the Jeep's wheels wouldn't get bogged down. Four-wheel drive could handle only so much.

Back at the cabin, he carried the woman through the torrents of rain for a second time. Inside, he kicked the door closed and settled her on the sofa. After cranking the lantern to its brightest setting and positioning it on the table next to the couch, he knelt by her side and smoothed soaked hair off her forehead. Her skin felt cool under the heat of his palm, her dark eyelashes stark against her pale complexion.

He fished his cell phone out of his jacket and checked again for a signal. None. "Of course," he muttered. "That would be too easy."

Alex had rattled off something about cell signals here, but he'd already forgotten what she'd said. He hadn't planned to make any calls from here, anyway. Not that a cell signal would help much. He doubted anyone could manage to get anywhere near this cabin tonight with the road washed out.

Okay, first things first. He had to get the woman dry. Then he'd crank up the generator to heat the chill out of the air and help warm her up.

A trip with the lantern into the cabin's only bedroom turned up a white and blue quilt. In the bathroom, he grabbed a couple of thick towels and a first-aid kit then stood there staring at his own pale face in the mirror. His red-rimmed eyes looked wide and hollow, and the rest of him looked more than a little bedraggled. So much for a relaxing week of destressing.

He carried his bounty back to the living room and dumped it all on the floor next to the sofa. After a deep, fortifying breath, he stripped her down to practical white cotton underwear as efficiently as he could.

"Just so you know, I'm keeping my eyes to myself," he said in a low, soothing voice. If she regained consciousness now, he didn't want her freaking out on him.

Still, he couldn't help but notice how lean she was. Not skinny but toned with clearly defined muscles. Yet she had distractingly feminine curves.

The lethal-looking blade strapped to her ankle gave him as much pause as the realization that a bullet had most likely passed completely through her shoulder, leaving behind twin entry and exit wounds. Given the other scars he glimpsed, it apparently wasn't the first time she'd been shot.

Terrific. Stuck on a mountain in a rainstorm with an unconscious fugitive. Obviously, she'd been on the run, too desperate to get away from whomever had hurt her to seek medical treatment. Maybe that person or, God help him, *people* were still after her. Any second now, commandos would bust down the door and turn him into a bloody pulp with their big honkin' guns. If she hadn't been limp as an overcooked noodle with lips rapidly turning blue, he might have backed out the door and pretended he'd never made it to the cabin.

Instead, he lifted her upper body and slid the quilt underneath, then maneuvered it under her legs. When she was completely covered, he slid his hands under the quilt, holding his breath as his palms glided over the satin skin of her thighs to her hips.

"Don't wake up now, don't wake up now," he chanted as he worked her underwear down her legs and off then dropped it to the floor with a rain-soaked *thwap*.

Next, he leaned over her and wriggled his hands behind her bare back to fumble with her bra clasp. This close, he noticed that her skin smelled of fall rain and some kind of floral soap. And blood. His stomach turned, but then the clasp yielded, and he divested her of the last piece of sodden clothing. "Mission accomplished. Now let's get that shoulder taken care of."

He quickly cleaned the bullet wound, thinking perhaps the sting from the antiseptic pads he found in the first-aid kit might rouse her, but she didn't move even an eyelash while he worked. After he'd taped gauze to both the entrance and exit wounds, he noted she didn't seem as pale as before, and the bluish tint to her lips had given way to a healthier, rosy hue.

For a moment, he wondered about the color of her eyes. With that ebony hair, he imagined a dark, dark brown, almost black. Mysterious and deep, the kind of eyes a guy could fall into headfirst. Dangerous eyes for a dangerous woman.

Pushing to his feet, he shook his head at his own foolishness. Instead of wondering about eye color, he should worry about how she'd gotten shot in the shoulder. For all he knew, the cops would be beating down the door by morning, maybe even arrest him for harboring a fugitive. Not that he'd had any choice. A washed-out road made sure of that, and he couldn't very well just let her bleed, or freeze, to death.

He'd done the right thing. Now all he had to do was wait until morning. He'd get her to the hospital, let the medical professionals deal with contacting the cops then get back to why he'd come here in the first place: relaxing.

He took the lantern and headed out into the cold rain to figure out the generator.

CHAPTER **FIVE**

Flinn Ford hated the rain, especially the kind of cold rain currently dripping into his collar and down his back.

His walkie-talkie squawked at his belt, and he lifted it, hoping for some good news. He desperately needed good news. Everything that mattered had gone FUBAR in a matter of days.

"Talk to me."

"We're not getting anywhere near her tonight. The storm's taken out the road."

"What about on foot?"

"There's a river surging down the side of the mountain, sir. Only way we're getting over it is to be airlifted. Requesting that kind of help will get the attention of the boss. You want that?"

Flinn scowled at the mention of Andrea Leigh. He didn't want the FBI assistant director getting wind that something was up, especially considering she had no idea about the project. That stupid fruitcake Zoe shouldn't have known about the project, either, and now she'd dragged Samantha into it.

Deke and Tom had assured him they'd made the mess at Samantha's apartment look like a burglary gone bad, but damn it all to hell, he was fucked. He could live with losing Zoe. That screwed-up bitch had been nothing but trouble from the start. But with Zoe dead and Mikayla reassigned in Afghanistan, Samantha held the only key to making his plan work. He'd be damned if he'd let her slip away from him.

"Hello? You there, boss?"

Closing his eyes, Flinn listened to the time bomb ticking in his head. He had to find a way to get to Samantha before it was too late. But how he went about it had to be as under the radar as the act that had started this rolling thunder of a disaster.

He depressed the "talk" button. "What about approaching through the woods from the other direction?"

A brief pause, then, "That'd take time, but it could be done."

"Then do it."

Holstering the walkie, he leaned his head back and let the rain wash over the angry, burning heat in his face.

"I'm coming to get you, Samantha," he murmured.

CHAPTER **SIX**

Mac Hunter settled in front of the cold fireplace with a groan. His muscles ached and his head pounded. His hopes for a cozy fire had gone up in smoke when the wood he'd dragged inside had done nothing more than steam and sizzle when he'd tried to light it.

The generator hadn't cooperated, either, so he'd rummaged through kitchen drawers with the battery-operated lantern in hand until he'd collected several candles and some matches. Now, tiny flames flickered throughout the room, giving it a comforting glow that belied the chill in the air. Rain continued to hammer the roof, and occasional thunder purred in the distance. If not for the unconscious woman bundled inside the heavy quilt in the other room, the atmosphere would have been exactly as he pictured it. But with a fire. And perhaps better lighting.

Instead of curling up under a blanket with the latest Dean Koontz novel, he snapped open the wallet he'd fished out of the soaked bag he'd found by the door. He had to squint in the dim light to study the driver's license. The shining waves of ebony hair and lively blue gray eyes didn't look anything like the pale, sopping-wet woman he'd stripped over an hour ago.

Claire Hogan. 1235 Rhode Island Street, San Francisco, CA 94107. Blue eyes. Black hair. No restrictions.

An organ donor. He smirked a little at that. Considering the scars he'd seen, he couldn't imagine her insides had escaped unscathed. Who'd want a liver that had been lacerated or a heart nicked by a knife?

Next, he pulled out a company ID, surprised to see she worked for Biomedical Research Corp. in San Francisco. The controversial company, which conducted stem-cell research, had been in the news lately after one of its scientists had gone missing. The words *"Research Assistant"* were printed in bold, black letters under Claire Hogan's name, right next to a picture of the woman in the other room. In the photo, she flashed a dazzling smile that totally contradicted her current, wounded state.

Since when did biomedical research assistants get shot? And how had she gotten from San Francisco to this remote cabin in the Shenandoahs?

And, damn, but that smile looked familiar.

Recognition washed over him, and he pushed up from the sofa and ambled over to the fireplace mantel and a collection of Trudeau family photos. He had to move a candle to get a good look, but it wasn't tough to spot the similarly stunning smiles beaming from a photo at least fifteen years old. Teenage versions of the two Trudeau sisters he knew well—Charlie and Alex—flanked a teenage version of the woman he'd put to bed. The three young women shared the same prominent cheekbones and full lips, the same wavy hair in varying dark shades. The girl in the middle, however, was taller and thinner than the other girls, her features somewhat sharp. She also had soulful blue eyes rather than brown. Even so, Mac would have bet money that she was Samantha, the oldest of the Trudeau sisters. That explained how she ended up at this cabin. It belonged to her family.

"Where's my bag?"

He turned, surprised to see her wrapped in a quilt and leaning unsteadily against the frame of the bedroom door. Her now-dry hair hung in soft waves around her face, softening cheekbones that had looked severe before. The softer look did nothing, however, to lighten the dark circles under eyes that were a far more intriguing, and arresting, shade of blue steel than he'd gleaned from the photo.

"Uh, hi," he said, and smiled to reassure her. "How're you feeling?"

"My bag?"

A shiver shimmied up his spine at the husky rasp of her

voice. Jesus, that voice alone could make a man fall head over heels in lust. "I hung it in the bathroom to dry with your clothes."

Interesting that she asked for her bag before she asked about her clothes. All he'd done was retrieve her wallet from said bag before hanging it from the showerhead. Privacy and all. Maybe he'd have to rethink that.

"Get it and my clothes," she said.

He was certain she would have retrieved them herself if she hadn't been leaning so heavily against the frame of the door. "You probably shouldn't be out of bed."

"Get them. Now."

Okaaay. Not a polite request but a harsh demand. Guess this wasn't the time to bust her on the fake ID. "I was kind of in the middle of something, but since you asked so nice . . ."

She didn't respond, pressing back against the wall as he eased by her. In the bathroom, he ignored the bag dangling in the shower, gathered her jeans, denim shirt, ruined T-shirt, underwear and bra and gingerly carried the cold and clammy bundle back down the hall.

She'd slipped to the floor, paler than before, the quilt bunched around her shoulders and her head resting back against the door frame. He wondered how she planned to get dressed when she couldn't even remain standing. And where did she plan to go anyway?

He set the pile of clothing at her feet then straightened. "You're Samantha, aren't you? Samantha Trudeau?"

Her gaze snapped up to his face, sharpening anew. Everything about her—despite the cocooning cream-and-blue quilt and the nakedness underneath—screamed suspicion and danger. So unlike Charlie and Alex.

"Did he send you?" she asked.

He cocked his head, thrown. "Did who send me?"

"I don't have the energy for banter."

"Uh, this isn't banter. I'm pretty good at that."

"Just answer the question."

He slid his back down the wall until he sat on the floor, forearms resting on his knees. Maybe he would seem less threatening if he weren't towering over her. "No one sent me. Well, unless you count Charlie and Alex, who pretty much shoved me out the door with the directions. You're their sister, right? You look like them, and"—he gestured over his shoulder toward the fireplace—"I saw your picture on the mantel."

She stared at him, her confusion clear. "Who are you?"

"Mac Hunter. I'm an editor at your dad's newspaper in Lake Avalon."

"What are you doing here?"

"Before I found you unconscious and bleeding on the floor, I was on vacation. You?"

She rolled her wounded shoulder and winced, then shifted her legs so that they stretched out before her, bare toes tipped with red polish peeking from under the quilt's edge. Cradling her injured arm against her stomach, she gave him a curious look that didn't appear all that genuine. "How are my big sisters these days?"

He noted the way she watched him, quietly assessing. "You're testing me."

"It's a simple question."

"Not really. You see, you're not the only Trudeau sister to take a bullet in the recent past. Your *younger* sister Alex took one in the chest several months ago, so the question may be simple, but the answer isn't."

If possible, her ashen complexion went whiter. "But she's okay, right? Charlie told me she was okay."

He hesitated. If he withheld the information, maybe she'd answer *his* questions. But cruelty wasn't his style. "She's fine. Charlie, too. And also younger than you, by the way, so they're not your *big* sisters, as you called them. Do I pass?"

She used her free hand to push herself up so that she sat straighter. The only indication that moving hurt was the deep crease between her narrowed eyes. "That was an easy one. If Flinn sent you to take me back, you'd be prepared."

"Who's Flinn?"

When she met his eyes, her expression stony, he tried another question: "Is he the one who shot you?"

She repositioned herself yet again, her brow furrowing. When the quilt drooped off one shoulder, she managed to salvage her modesty at the last instant. "I need some dry clothes."

"I can help you with that, but first I need to know what's going on. Are we in danger here?"

Her lips tightened, as though she'd decided not to answer.

"I have a right to know," he said. "Seeing as how the road's washed out and I'm stuck with you here."

"We should be fine."

"Are you sure?"

"Yes."

"I'd like to know how you're sure. You've been shot, and I'd like to avoid the same fate."

"I wasn't followed, and no one knows about this place."

"So you're on the run. This Flinn wouldn't happen to be a U.S. marshal, would he?"

"I'm not a fugitive, and there's no one-armed man."

He smiled at the nod to *The Fugitive*. Dangerous and mistrustful, but she still had a sense of humor. That made her considerably less threatening. "I have a T-shirt I can spare," he said as he got to his feet.

Before he could turn away, she asked, "Alex is really okay? After being shot, I mean."

Her voice, low and worried, bore no resemblance to the commands she'd issued earlier. So the woman had a soft spot for her kid sister. He could relate to that.

He gave her a reassuring nod. "She had a rough time, but she pulled through it." He didn't think Samantha had the strength at the moment to hear about the serial killer who'd kidnapped Alex and almost killed her. Later, maybe. For now, he'd keep the mood light. "She's in love now. Kind of sickening, really."

"Sickening?"

"You know. Puppy-dog eyes. Cute nicknames. Holding hands every second of the day. Goofy shit like that."

"Oh. I wouldn't know."

His gut tightened as her slight, weary smile faded to a

battle-worn hardness that looked an awful lot like resignation. The visible shiver that followed snapped him out of the moment. "Okay, well, I'll get you that shirt."

As he rummaged through his duffel by the front door, he heard her moving around behind him. He turned, black T-shirt dangling from one hand, to find her on her feet, uninjured shoulder braced against the door. Apparently she didn't trust him enough to let him out of her sight.

He held up the shirt. "Think you can handle getting it on or do you want some help?"

"I can handle it."

But she didn't reach out to take it, as though she feared leaving the support of the door. He angled his head toward the bedroom behind her. "Put it on the bed?"

She nodded. "The clothes on the floor, too."

He bent to scoop up the bundle. "I hope you don't plan to try to put any of this wet stuff on. You'll make yourself sick."

"Don't worry about it," she said, and shifted to give him room to pass, pressing back against the door a bit too defensively.

"Jesus, lady, I don't have cooties." But when he deposited the T-shirt on the bed and the wet clothes on the bedside table, his annoyance vanished. Blood spotted the white sheets.

He faced her and paused, struck by her bone-white complexion. She'd started to shiver harder, the circles under her eyes more prominent than before. Sheer will alone seemed to keep her upright, yet she watched him with such wary eyes that it saddened him. It must suck to live with so much distrust.

"I should check your shoulder."

Her features softened, as though his concern touched her. But the softness quickly hardened again, and she shook her head. "It's fine."

"I'm not going to hurt you, you know. You can trust me."

Tears filled her eyes, making their blue a stark contrast to the black of her hair. Before anything could overflow, she said, "You should go."

"Go? Oh, you mean into the other room so you can change."

He walked out into the hall. "You're probably hungry. I've got some groceries out in the truck—"

"I mean go, as in leave. We can't both stay here."

"Like I said, the road's washed out. Otherwise we'd be on our way to the ER. And, frankly, you shouldn't be alone in your condition."

"I can take care of myself."

"I'm sure you're an ace at that normally, but right now you could pass out and hurt yourself."

She studied him for a long moment. "There's a motel in Lake Avalon that advertises the fact that James Dean slept there. I can't remember the name of it."

Yeah, right. "I thought I passed the test."

"My sister's names and ages are in my personnel file."

"So if I'm the bad guy, why aren't I killing you?"

"Maybe Flinn wants me alive. Maybe I was shot by accident."

"Wants you for what?"

She backed away, into the bedroom, one hand holding on to the door. "When I'm done changing, I want you gone."

He stepped forward, prepared to protest, but she closed the door in his face. The lock engaged before he could react. "Do you think that's a good idea?" he called. "What if you need help?"

No answer.

Mac sighed. "It's the Royal Palm Inn, by the way. The motel where James Dean slept. And you're nuts if you think I'm going back out in this weather, especially with the waterfall where the road used to be."

No answer.

Either she was ignoring him, or she'd already passed out.

CHAPTER **SEVEN**

Sam made it to the bed before her knees buckled. She sank down on the edge, her head spinning and her shoulder throbbing. Uncontrollable chills made every tight muscle ache.

She couldn't stay here, not with a man she didn't trust. She had no idea what Flinn was up to, or even where he'd been when Zoe had knocked on her door. Mac Hunter could be a clever operative sent to keep her off-balance, to make her feel safe until Flinn arrived. An unlikely scenario, but she hadn't become one of N3's top operatives by taking chances.

It was possible that Mac Hunter really was a friend of her sisters. He knew the Royal Palm Inn, after all. And he certainly behaved nonthreatening enough, despite the strength in the lean lines of his body. When he'd turned his back on her, she'd noticed the ripple of muscles beneath his T-shirt, signs of regular, hard workouts. And those arresting greenish brown eyes, so intense when they studied her, seemed to peer right into her soul.

Stop, she thought. Striking eye color and a hunky build had nothing to do with a man's objectives. He might act harmless, but he wasn't, especially when she could barely keep herself on her feet. Bottom line: If he was an operative, she was screwed. If he was a civilian, *he* was screwed. Flinn would have him killed in an instant if he thought N3 had been compromised. For Mac Hunter's sake, as much as for her own, one of them had to get the hell out of this cabin.

Easing the quilt off her shoulder, she craned her neck to see the blood-soaked bandage so neatly taped to it. He'd clearly done nothing to pack the wound to keep her from losing more blood. Sloppy field triage . . . and more evidence that he wasn't a highly trained covert operative.

Determined, and annoyed with herself for wasting precious time, she dropped the quilt. Gritting her teeth against any involuntary groaning, she pushed herself to her feet. Simple plan: Get dressed and get out. Where she'd go then, she had no idea.

She picked up the black T-shirt and shook it out, noting it smelled of the fabric softener she'd expected when she'd first entered the cabin. A wave of memories washed over her: pillow fights with her sisters and getting whapped full in the face with the scent she associated most with home. Her throat started to ache with the effort of holding the emotion back. Home. It had been so very long. And Charlie and Alex . . . she hadn't laughed in years, not like she had with them.

Come on, Sam. Keep it together. You've got to keep it together.

But exhaustion and blood loss had weakened her defenses. And grief . . . God, Zoe.

"You okay in there?"

She spun toward the door and regretted the fast motion as the room whirled. Had he been standing at the door, listening?

She braced against the side of the bed. "I'm fine," she said, surprised at the dry croak, then repeated it in a firmer voice. "I'm fine."

She listened for footsteps to indicate he'd walked away but heard only silence. She imagined him on the other side of the door, unruly dark hair falling over his forehead and the shadow of beard darkening his jaw. "Trust me," he'd said. The key words. Samantha Trudeau always seemed to trust the wrong people. Not anymore, even when the man in question exuded honorable energy as intensely as sex appeal.

She worked the sleeve of the T-shirt up her injured arm then poked her head through the neck and slid her other arm through the remaining sleeve. As she pulled the hem down over her breasts, she released a shaky breath. The simple effort had drained her, leaving her limbs leaden, but at least she felt less vulnerable.

Next, she dragged her sodden jeans off the table by the bed as cold perspiration gathered along her top lip and at her hairline. She couldn't stop shivering and wanted nothing more than to sink onto the bed and curl into a ball.

You can do this, Sam. You're *trained* to suck it up and get the job done.

And the job right now was to get dressed and get out.

She gritted her teeth to keep them from chattering, and stood up.

Mac dumped her damp bag onto the sofa, telling himself he had every right to go through her things. He had to protect himself, and she wasn't providing the answers he needed. Besides, he'd already seen her naked. Looking through her purse wasn't nearly as intimate—or interesting.

The usual contents of a woman's bag scattered across the worn upholstery. Brush, compact, lipstick, keys, a travel-sized packet of Kleenex, sunglasses, tampons, small bottle of Tylenol. One last shake, and a gun bounced onto the cushion, black and ominous.

His heart hiccupped.

The girl had a gun.

Not girl. Woman. Who'd obviously participated in some kind of combat, considering her scars . . . and the fact that she'd been shot.

He remembered the fake ID identifying her as Claire Hogan, research assistant for a biomedical facility where a key scientist had vanished. There'd been speculation in the Lake Avalon newsroom that a right-wing zealot had probably kidnapped the guy to keep him from conducting research with embryos. News of the disappearance had died down after a series of tornadoes had ripped through the Midwest. Media preferred disaster news with shocking photos over a missing scientist, but that didn't mean the feds had stopped looking.

So maybe Samantha Trudeau was law enforcement, sent to Biomedical Research Corp. undercover to investigate.

Sure, that made sense. FBI, probably.

That didn't stop him from thinking it'd be a good idea to hide the gun. Last thing he wanted to do tonight was find himself staring down its barrel because he refused to hit the road like she'd ordered.

Then he heard a soft *thump* in the other room, as though a body had hit the floor.

"Shit," he muttered and jogged over to the bedroom door. "You okay?" he called. "Samantha?"

He tried the knob just to be sure, and, yep, it was locked.

He pounded a fist against the wood. "Samantha? Hello? Sam?"

No answer.

Great. Just great.

He ran into the kitchen and jerked open one drawer after another until he found a screwdriver and a hammer. Back at the door, he tapped the flat edge of the screwdriver between the door and its frame next to the knob and hoped like hell something as simple as this would work on the low-tech lock.

The lock popped, and the door swung open. Mac didn't have time to feel triumph, because she was indeed on the floor, on her back with one hand resting on her stomach and the other flung out next to her, her head rolled to the side and hair obscuring her face. He knelt beside her and put his fingers to the base of her throat. The strong thump of her pulse calmed his own racing heart.

"Good, that's good. You're not thinking about expiring on me anytime soon. So let's get you back into bed, okay?"

He gathered her into his arms and settled her on the sheets. He started to draw the quilt over her still form when he noticed the darkening patch on the shoulder of the black T-shirt. "Damn, I told you you were bleeding again."

He sat on the edge of the bed and, grasping the hem of the shirt, drew it up so he could see the red-soaked bandage. His heart double-timed at a sight he couldn't possibly ignore. One full breast, a perfect, pale handful tipped with a perfect circle of pink. Right next to it, its perfect twin. Perfection everywhere.

Her nipples pebbled as if aware they were being watched.

He suddenly didn't need crackling flames in the fireplace to get warm.

Swallowing hard, he closed his eyes. "Don't be a dork, dork. Finish what you started before she bleeds to death."

He retrieved the first-aid supplies from the other room, then quickly stripped away the bloody shirt. He replaced the bandage with a bulkier wad of gauze and did the same to the exit wound, beyond relieved when he could cover all that smooth, enticing skin with a clean T-shirt and a pair of his boxers.

In the living room, he fought the urge to sink down onto the sofa and breathe out a long sigh. Instead, he had to find a decent hiding place for a gun. Then he had to figure out what to do about the rapidly growing chill in the cabin.

About three hundred feet from the tiny, dark cabin that protected the key to his dreams from the ice-cold rain, Flinn Ford huddled with Deke and Tom, who carried enough firepower to stage a small coup.

"We'll move in at first light," Flinn said. "I want radio silence, and I want everyone behind me. I'm the only one who approaches her."

"And the male?" Deke asked.

"Take him into custody. I need to know who he is, what she's told him. No chatter in front of him, and blindfold him before you put him in the SUV. Got it?"

The other two men gave curt nods.

"Last thing: Don't underestimate her. She's unpredictable. She's smart. And she's fast. If she makes a run for it, shoot to maim, not to kill. I need her alive, at least temporarily."

Two stony faces showed no emotion, and Flinn had to clench his jaw against a bitter scowl. Heartless bastards didn't know what it meant to care about a woman. And how much it ripped you in two when you had to hurt her.

CHAPTER **EIGHT**

He snuggled up to her naked back, burying his nose in silky, rain-washed hair as he looped his arm around her waist and gently drew her back against his front. Keeping warm had never been so . . . enticing.

"What are you doing?" she murmured into her pillow.

He smiled at the sleep-roughened edges of her voice. "Warming you up."

She breathed out a noncommittal "Hmm."

He liked her half-asleep. With her soft and acquiescent, he could fool himself into believing this was a casual Sunday morning, blues a low throb on the stereo while they cuddled after a night of lovemaking. It was perfectly natural to slide his hand over the curve of her hip. He smiled at her intake of breath as his fingers grazed the smooth skin of her firm abdomen. Any second now, she'd snap at him to knock it off. And he would. With some effort. Because that was the kind of guy he was. A gentleman to the core.

For now, he lazily explored, walking his fingertips over the lower rungs of the ladder of her ribs, seeking and finding the hairline scar he'd noted earlier. From a knife wound, he figured.

She shifted under his hand, restless, and he stilled, waiting for her to settle before continuing his gentle exploration of sweet, satin skin.

Her palm slid over the back of his hand, and he paused again. But instead of stopping him, she guided his hand higher under the T-shirt, until he felt the ticklish stab of nipple against his palm. Holy mother of God. She was *encouraging* him.

He closed his eyes as he cupped her breast for the first time, fascinated by the soft, warm weight in his hand. When his thumb dragged over her nipple, teasing it into a firmer erection, she shifted her head back against his shoulder and moaned low in her throat. She wiggled a little, brushing her butt up against him in erotic invitation. She turned her head slightly, bringing her lips within inches of his, her breath cool against his cheek. "Is that what I think it is?"

Something was off here. *Seriously* off. This was *not* the same woman he'd had to pick up off the floor. Not that he was complaining. Oh, *hell*, no.

She shifted in his arms so that she faced him, showing no signs of discomfort, and one finger bumped over his top lip and trailed tantalizingly along his bottom lip. "It'd be a shame to let it go to waste."

Before he could respond, she pressed soft, warm lips to his and kissed him. Gentle at first, tentative, but growing in depth and aggression until her tongue swept into his mouth. Every cell of his body focused on her mouth devouring his. She kissed like she looked—intense and deadly and . . . and . . . *why* was he still thinking?

When she pulled slightly away, coming up for air, he brushed the hair back from her face with one hand. He loved the way it felt between his fingers. Silky. Everything about her was like that. Satiny and smooth yet with an underlying layer of muscle and danger. She could fuck him or snap him in two in a heartbeat—

She straddled him in one efficient move, leaning over him for another slow but thorough, openmouthed kiss that left him gasping and harder than he'd ever been. Chriiiiiiiiist.

He put his hands on her arms to slow her down. "Careful," he croaked. "Your shoulder."

"It's all better, thanks to you," she murmured against his lips as she circled his wrists with strong, slim fingers and flattened them to the bed, her midnight hair falling forward. The ends swayed over his face in soft, feathery caresses. "Be still," she ordered, her storm-blue eyes dark with intent. "Don't move."

He obeyed because he couldn't believe how incredible this was . . . how . . . unlikely . . .

Working his shirt up to his neck, she began kissing her way

across his chest. Her tongue wrapped around his left nipple, and he arched his head back into the pillow. Oh, God, oh, God.

He had to touch her, *had* to, but the minute his palms skimmed over her arms, she stopped and pierced him with narrowed eyes. "I told you to be still."

God, that *voice*. Every time she spoke, a chill of excitement thrilled through him. He imagined her reading a book on tape, something sultry and erotic . . . any man listening would end up helplessly and painfully aroused.

As though she'd read his mind, she repositioned herself and curled cool fingers around his cock. She began a firm, masterful stroke that had the air gusting out of him. Holy . . . holy . . .

And then, just when he thought he'd embarrass himself and explode into her hand, she took his rigid cock into her mouth. Her magical tongue swirled and massaged and licked like she'd never get enough, a low, approving hum in the back of her throat. He wrapped his hand in her hair to help guide her and closed his eyes. Wow, just . . . wow . . .

Sam started awake, panting and disoriented, her heart thundering in her ears. Dream, she thought. Just a dream. Except the throbbing ache between her legs was all too real . . . as was the man cuddled up to her back, his erection pressed firmly against the fabric covering her hip.

She rolled away from him before thinking, and gasped as pain ripped through her shoulder.

In the next instant, he loomed over her, wide awake. "What is it? What's wrong?"

Instinct kicked in, and she thrust upward with the heel of her hand, catching him under the chin and snapping his head back.

He tumbled backward off the bed, hit the floor with a crash and a grunt and lay still for a silent second before sitting up and shaking his head to clear it. "Fuck! What'd you do that for?"

Sam stared at him, disoriented, as her eyes adjusted to the dark. She could have sworn he'd been going down on her . . . except she hadn't been herself—

Oh. Of course. It really had been a dream—a very *erotic*

one—but it hadn't been hers. Her empathy had tapped into *his* dream.

It had been so long since she'd slept in such close proximity with another person that she'd forgotten that particular aspect of her psychic ability. Sometimes flashing on what was going on in someone else's head was a curse . . . though, *this* dream she'd been enjoying. *A lot.*

Her cheeks began to burn as she realized she was disappointed that he wasn't as naked as he'd been in the dream. Had he dreamed those rock-hard abs for himself or did they ripple under the cotton of his white T-shirt in reality, too? And did those faded jeans camouflage the same impressive—

"Look," Mac said as he scrubbed his hands over his face. "I know I didn't get the hell out of Dodge like you told me to, but you were unconscious, and I didn't want to leave you like that. And . . . and you were cold. *Really* cold. Shivering, in fact. I didn't know how else to get you warm . . . so I . . . so I . . . well, hell."

"You got into bed with me." She fought to suppress a smile. He really was kind of cute when flustered. And *hot* when aroused. He was also far too much of a good Samaritan. Didn't he know it never paid to worry more about someone other than yourself?

"Right," he said with a sigh. "But it was all perfectly innocent. You're dressed. I'm dressed. It was just about getting warm. I guess I . . . I guess I got a little *too* warm. Kind of tough to control certain things when I'm asleep."

"It's okay. I get it."

A trickle of blood on his chin caught her eye. Gritting her teeth against the ache in her shoulder, she got off the bed, grateful for the T-shirt and boxers he'd put her in, and knelt in front of him. "Are you okay? It looks like I might have done some damage."

Bracing herself to suppress the empathic flash, she gently angled his chin to inspect a small cut on the right side of his jaw. She must have nicked him with a fingernail. But then the texture of his razor stubble grazing against her fingertips distracted her. It was nice. As was his jaw, angular and strong.

The realization that she found him far more appealing than any man she'd met in a long, long time made her quickly draw her hand back.

He blinked at the abrupt move, and she wondered if the brief expression that rippled over his features was disappointment . . . and why did it matter? His presence here was trouble, period.

"Who are you?" he asked. "Some kind of secret agent?"

She forced out a hollow laugh. "Yeah, right. Isn't there a first-aid kit around here? I should clean this for you."

"Um, yeah. In the kitchen. But it's not necessary. I've done worse shaving."

"You don't want it getting infected. The kit's in the kitchen?"

He put his hand on her arm to stop her, and she flinched, unprepared for the unexpected contact. As she absorbed the empathic hit of the blow to his chin, dizziness eddied through her head. Her legs folded as easily as a new colt's.

"Whoa!" Mac caught her good arm to help ease her back to the floor.

She kept her head down, waiting for the vertigo of bouncing from his consciousness back into her own to pass. Her defenses were in such disarray that leveling her system took longer than usual.

"Maybe you should wait here," he said. "I'll get the kit."

"Just give me a minute." She pushed his supporting hand away, embarrassed by how weak she must seem in front of such a strong man. Not that she should care, but still. She was used to having perfect control of her ability, calling on it when she wanted it, not getting caught off-guard.

"How about we compromise and go together?" Mac got to his feet and extended a hand.

She braced herself before accepting his help up, relieved that when their hands touched, nothing from inside his head flooded into hers.

In the kitchen, where early morning light seeped through the red-and-white-checked curtains above the sink, Mac quickened his pace to get to the first-aid kit before she did. He probably seemed way too eager, but he'd stashed her gun inside, assuming he'd be the only one making use of the kit. He didn't want her flipping up the lid and thinking he'd tried to pull a fast one on her. Even though he had.

He'd just stuffed the gun into the waistband of his jeans and jerked the tail of his T-shirt over it when she said, "Did you hear that?"

He paused in the act of drawing a chair out from the table and turned toward her and the door. The anxiety in her voice alarmed him as much as the idea that someone could actually be in the cabin with them. "I didn't hear anything."

Then he saw a shift in the shadows. Samantha saw it, too, because she started so violently that she wobbled. Mac stepped up behind her and steadied her with his hands at her waist just as a tall, wiry man with a shiny bald head materialized out of the darkness of the hall.

Under Mac's hands, Samantha stiffened, then took another step back and bumped solidly against his chest. He kept his hands where they were, noting the tremors that began to ripple through her. This wasn't the cavalry.

"Flinn." Her voice was no louder than a rough whisper.

Ah, shit, Mac thought. Wasn't Flinn the guy she was running from?

The bald guy smiled, showing very white, very straight teeth. Mac guessed his age as middle fifties, though the man obviously didn't want to look his age, judging by his too-tan complexion.

"Samantha," he said, slow and low, almost an affectionate purr with an underlying menace. Then his dark eyes rested on Mac, flat and cold. "Hello."

Mac managed what felt like a sick smile. "Hello." Harmless schmo, he thought, that's me. All I'm doing here is keeping the storm trooper on her feet.

Under Mac's hands, a coiled tension replaced Samantha's shakes, as though she'd mind-over-mattered her fear. Her strength was impressive.

The other man's Colgate smile didn't waver as he flicked his dark eyes up and down her body. "Are you all right?"

"Watson clipped me when he took out Zoe." The peeved

woman who'd demanded her clothes earlier was back in charge. "Did he botch the shot or was only wounding me part of the plan?"

The bald head tilted slightly in question. "Plan?"

"You've never mastered playing dumb, Flinn."

"And you've never been dumb, Samantha. So let's say you come home. It'll be easier on everyone that way."

"It was never going to be easy the minute you had Zoe killed."

"Zoe went rogue."

"Bullshit!"

Mac felt the rage vibrate through her lithe body. If she'd had her gun, he was certain Flinn of the shiny head and shinier smile would be bleeding out at their feet. He had to fight the urge to ease the weapon out of his waistband and hand it over.

Flinn raised his hands in a calming gesture. "What exactly did Zoe tell you?"

"I'm not playing this game with you. And I'm not going anywhere with you, either. Not alive. Not anymore."

Flinn sighed. "I'm sorry to hear that."

Mac almost choked as two hulking soldiers stepped out of the shadows behind Flinn. They aimed what looked like rocket launchers at him and Samantha.

She didn't flinch at the sight of the big guns, but she did lean back a bit, as though seeking more support from Mac's body. "So you're going to kill me, too, then?" she asked.

Mac winced at the idea of another bullet tearing through her flesh, and he calculated the odds of how quickly he could put himself between her and the rocket launchers. Not good. And why would he, anyway?

"I'm not going to hurt you, Samantha," Flinn said. "I just want you to come home so we can talk. Or we could talk here."

"I'd rather not."

"Because of your friend?"

"He's not my friend. He's just some guy who can't follow a map and ended up at the wrong cabin."

Mac straightened his shoulders. He happened to kick ass when it came to reading maps.

"He seems protective," Flinn said, his scrutiny of Mac shrewd as he conducted a pre-death autopsy with only his sharp gaze.

Samantha heaved a dramatic sigh. "Fine, I'll come with you. But he stays here."

Mac was already mentally shaking his head. No way was he letting her go with this guy. "I don't like that idea," he said in a low voice near her ear.

"Shut up," she hissed over her shoulder.

A small smile twisted Flinn's lips. "He seems like more than a friend."

"He's no one. Let's go before I change my mind."

"It's not that easy. If you've compromised us—"

"I haven't. You know me, Flinn."

"And you know me, yet a minute ago you accused me of having Zoe killed."

"I misspoke. I . . . I've lost a lot of blood."

As if to prove it, she leaned more heavily against Mac, though he worried that wasn't part of the act. Or perhaps she was trying to tell him something?

"Let's do this easy, Samantha," Flinn said, cool-as-you-please. "No need for drama. Deke and Tom here are going to pat you both down. Then we'll take a drive back to the District and get that shoulder taken care of. After that, we'll sit down and have a nice, calm talk. Does that sound agreeable?"

Mac's stomach twisted with dread. Agreeable, my ass. At some point during all that nice, calm bullshit, they'd both end up with bullets in the head. That's why Samantha had said he was no one. She was trying to protect him. Well, he wasn't some sissy man who needed protection, damn it.

Tightening his hands at her waist, he pressed up against her until the gun in his waistband dug into her back. That's a gun in my pocket, baby, though I am also very happy to see you.

Flinn arched a questioning brow. "Samantha?"

"Actually," Mac said, stepping abruptly around her and turning his back on Dr. Evil to face her. "You know, great as this has been and all, I'm going to just . . . you know . . . take off now."

She stared up at him in shock, her steel-blue eyes screaming *what the hell are you doing*? But when he eased the tail of his T-shirt up with one hand, his movements as minimal as possible, her attention shifted down.

"Call me sometime, okay?" he added. "After the sugar daddy here gets over himself."

A rocket launcher poked into his back, and his gaze locked on hers. She really did have arrestingly beautiful eyes. For a commando.

"You're insane," she said through her teeth, but she grabbed the gun from his waistband, shoved him sideways with surprising strength and fired twice in quick succession.

Mac watched from the floor in stunned fascination as both Deke and Tom toppled, tidy bullet holes in the center of their foreheads.

She hesitated when it came to the smarmy Flinn, however. "What did you do to me?" Her voice shook as much as her hand, her finger flexing on the trigger, but her expression was cold and hard.

"I saved you," Flinn said. "When you most needed someone on your side, I was there for you. N3 is your family, Samantha. And family doesn't point guns at each other."

Mac stifled his snort of disbelief. Guess that rule didn't extend to the thugs.

"Did you do to me what you did to Zoe?" Samantha asked.

Flinn's smug smile twitched but didn't falter. "What did Zoe tell you?"

She firmed her grip on the gun, her face twisting into a mask of tightly controlled pain and anger. "You mean before you had her *killed*?"

Flinn finally had the sense to raise his hands in supplication. "Let's stay calm, Samantha. Don't do anything you'll regret. We can talk this through, and everything will be okay."

"It's too late for that." She jerked the gun toward the chair Mac had pulled out from the table. "Sit."

Flinn didn't move.

She pulled the trigger.

Mac scuttled back, instinctively covering his head with one arm. Holy shit!

Silence followed, and when he dared to look, he saw a very unhappy Flinn. No bullet hole marked his forehead, which was more than Mac had expected.

He glanced at Samantha, noted the lethal determination firming her jaw, and got that she hadn't missed by accident. Her formerly trembling hand couldn't have been steadier now.

Mac swallowed, glad he wasn't Flinn. And impressed, not to mention a bit freaked out, by how comfortably she held that gun. Like it was a part of her.

"Sit," she repeated.

Flinn, hands still raised, did as he was told, a weird smile curving his lips.

Samantha flicked barely a glance at Mac. "Tie him up."

He didn't bother asking with what. He scrambled to his feet and started going through kitchen drawers until he found twine. Samantha's hands may have been deadly steady, but his had to be registering 6.0 on the Richter scale. She'd killed two men without flinching. Granted, they'd pointed huge guns at them, but still . . .

On his knees behind Flinn's chair, he wrapped the twine around the man's wrists several times, oddly indifferent when the bastard squirmed and complained, "Too tight."

"Bummer," Mac mumbled and wrapped it tighter, surprised, and a bit ashamed, at his own malicious satisfaction when the guy gave a pained grunt. That's what you get for messing with my girl. The thought made him go still for a moment. My girl? Where had that come from? Jesus, one erotic dream and—

"His legs, too," she said. "And his weapon . . . it's in a holster under his left arm . . . get it and his cell phone and get rid of them."

"He's got a gun?" Mac figured he should be embarrassed at the way his voice squeaked at the end. But, Jesus, the guy had a gun and hadn't even bothered to draw it? That took some pretty big balls to think he didn't need a weapon to take on this woman. Or perhaps Dr. Evil was delusional.

A few minutes later, Mac sat back on his heels and admired his handiwork. "Not bad for a guy who can't follow a map."

When he got no response, he looked around and saw that Samantha had silently slipped away.

"She's going to get you killed," Flinn said.

"And what were you going to do? Serve me brunch?" Mac got up and walked around the chair so he could pat down the left side of the man's jacket until he felt the gun. He had to fumble to release the snap securing it in place. Sheesh, the douche bag hadn't even prepared in advance for the possibility of pulling his weapon. Mac finally managed to remove the gun from its holster. He carefully placed it in the sink, well out of its owner's reach, then began going through the pockets of the fuming, red-faced man in search of his phone.

"We can make a deal," Flinn said. "Anything you want."

"A million dollars."

Flinn was so smooth he didn't even roll his eyes. "That could be arranged."

Mac snorted as he pulled the phone from the guy's inner jacket pocket. "Right. I'd have a tough time spending it while I'm dead. Amazon.com doesn't ship to the afterlife."

"I give you my word that no harm would come to you."

Mac bent so that he was eye to eye with the soulless bastard. "Yeah? You ever give that word to Samantha?"

Cold, dead eyes stared back at him. "You have no idea what you're doing. Whatever she's told you, it's a lie."

"Watch it. Your pants are on fire." Mac dropped the phone on the floor and stomped it into pieces.

"You're a foolish man," Flinn said.

"Better foolish than tied to a chair in the middle of nowhere." He moved to the drawer that held dish towels and used one to gag Dr. Evil.

Then he tried not to shudder as he glanced at the dead men on the floor near the door. Two precise shots. She hadn't even hesitated.

God, he hoped he hadn't chosen the wrong side.

CHAPTER **NINE**

In the bedroom, Sam set aside her SIG and used one hand to shake out her damp jeans, her other arm pressed against her side to limit the jostling that sent sharp, head-spinning pain through her shoulder.

How had Flinn found her so quickly? She knew that no one had followed her out of DC. She'd even ditched her car and work cell phone to prevent GPS from pinpointing her location. She'd never mentioned this cabin to anyone she worked with. Even if she had, they couldn't have found it easily because its ownership was linked to the Lake Avalon newspaper rather than the Trudeau family.

Yet Flinn had found her within a day. He had to have some way. God, had he tracked her by her personal cell phone? How could he even know she had it? She'd been so careful, almost OCD about it. She'd obviously underestimated him, underestimated his paranoia, his lack of trust. And if he knew about that secret phone, that most likely meant he'd been keeping much closer tabs on her than she'd ever thought, and—no, wait. Ah, crap. Of *course*.

The transmitter.

It had been so many years since the implantation . . . Still, she should have remembered. Would have, probably, if she hadn't been so upset about Zoe. Not to mention bleeding and running for her life.

How the hell was she supposed to get the damn thing out by herself?

Little white spots began to jiggle in front of her eyes, and she sat on the edge of the bed. She was so screwed.

"You need some help?"

She jerked her head up and immediately had to suppress the surge of nausea. She was worse than screwed. And she'd managed to get this guy, this *nice*, *good* guy, screwed as well.

"I'm—"

"Fine. Yeah, I know. So what's the plan?"

She narrowed her eyes. "Plan?"

"Yeah. I figure we're hitting the road in the next, oh, thirty seconds or so?"

"We?"

He cocked his head. "You're not strong enough to get out of here on your own, and there's no way in hell I'm giving you the keys to my car. Even if I did, you wouldn't be able to drive it over the bumpy terrain out of here without passing out and hitting a tree. Like it or not, you need me."

"I don't *need* anyone." She pushed to her feet, the wet jeans grasped in one hand, intending to get dressed and get out. She'd figure out what to do about the transmitter later.

It took her only a few seconds to realize that getting dressed one-handed didn't work, especially when the clothing was wet denim. She sank back onto the bed. Defeat loomed like a huge black shroud above her head, threatening to drop down and suffocate her.

Mac pivoted and walked out of the bedroom, and she raised her head to watch him go. Good. Common sense had finally kicked in. If he was smart, he'd be in his car and out of there within a matter of minutes.

But then he came back, a pair of black drawstring pants in one hand. "You'll swim in these, but they're dry, and the waist is adjustable."

Without waiting for a response, he eased the jeans away from her and dropped them on the floor. "You'll need to stand up."

She reluctantly did as he said, and he stepped behind her, reaching his arms around her so he could position the pants at her front. All she had to do was step into them, but indecision paralyzed her. He needed to go. He needed to leave her here and go *now*.

But then she'd have no means of escape.

Behind her, Mac silently waited.

She sifted through her options. She could knock him cold and take his car. Which would leave him here with Flinn, who would kill him to keep him quiet. Bad idea. *Really* bad idea.

She could hike out while Mac drove in the opposite direction, putting as much distance between them as possible. Assuming she could walk more than a few hundred yards before the last of her strength deserted her.

Only one option remained: She could kill Flinn.

But no, God, she couldn't. He was a federal agent. And she didn't know what was going on. What if Zoe had jumped to the wrong conclusions?

Besides, could she even kill a bound, unarmed man, especially one she'd known for fourteen years—and, God help her, had felt affection for? Shooting Deke and Tom had been different. They'd have shot her dead after one gesture from their boss. Flinn, however, was tied to a chair.

Closing her eyes, she bit her bottom lip. She had no choice. She *did* need Mac. At least to get off the mountain. Once they reached civilization, she'd have him drop her at the first gas station or convenience store and send him on his way. With any luck at all, Flinn would never be able to identify him.

Resolved, she grasped Mac's arm with her good hand to steady herself. She realized too late that she hadn't braced for the skin-on-skin contact, and the empathic flash of his disbelief when she'd shot Deke and Tom raced through her. His horror reminded her of the first time she'd seen someone die violently. She remembered the pain on her father's face, heard again the burble of his choked breathing as he'd bled to death in her arms. Two people had died before her eyes that day, one at her own hands.

"Hey." Mac's gentle nudge drew her out of the memory before it could drag her down. He joggled the drawstring pants, as though to say, Come on already.

Using his muscled arms for support, she stepped into the pants and helped him draw them up her legs, then watched as he deftly drew the drawstring snug and tied it. He had big hands, she noted. Tender hands. Chaste, too, because he'd done nothing more than secure the pants, not even brushing his fingers against her skin.

"See?" he said, his voice low near her ear. "I can be useful."

She shivered at the feel of his breath on her neck and his strong, warm arms around her, fought the urge to drop her head back against his shoulder and let his strength support her. But, no, she couldn't do that. He was already compromised, maybe too much for her to save him.

He was right, though. He could be useful.

"I need you to do something else for me," she said.

He released her and took the few steps so that they faced each other. "Name it."

She looked up into his hazel green eyes and wondered how he could be so giving when she'd dragged him into a situation that could very well get him killed. Was he for real?

He arched one dark brow, and she realized he was waiting for her request. "I need you to go to the kitchen and get the smallest, sharpest knife you can find."

Deep trenches appeared in his forehead. "What for?"

"There's a transmitter imbedded under the skin between my shoulder blades."

The forehead creases smoothed as the blood drained from his face. "A what?"

"It's broadcasting my location to my employer. That's how Flinn found me so easily."

"You're telling me you're *LoJacked*?"

"I need you to remove it."

He raised his hands and backed away. "No way am I cutting into you."

"You have to. I can't reach it myself."

"Then let's just . . . let's find an ER and have a doctor do it."

"There isn't time. When I leave here, it needs to be gone or he'll follow. It has to come out *now*."

"Forget it. I'm not doing it."

He'd taken two steps toward the bedroom door before she grabbed his arm, her grip strong and desperate. "I'm dead if you don't do this. Do you get that?"

He scrubbed his hands through his hair as he paced away. "Fuck. *Fuck*."

"Please," she said softly.

He faced her, looking sick and torn, and she waited, keeping her gaze locked with his. She wasn't above mustering a few tears if that's what it took.

Shaking his head, he released a defeated sigh. "Fine. I'll get the knife."

Mac sat on the side of the bed, bent over a stretched-out, stomach-down Samantha Trudeau, the tip of the knife poised—and jittering—above a tiny scar at the base of her right shoulder blade. That's where she said the transmitter had been injected beneath her skin fourteen years ago.

A *transmitter*. What kind of barbarians did this woman work for?

She had her head turned away from him, both arms wrapped around a pillow, her version, he supposed, of a bullet clasped between her teeth.

"So who is he? That guy in the other room . . . Dr. Evil."

"Don't talk. Just do it."

"You want me to do this with a steady hand or not? Because at the moment it's like I've got Parkinson's. I have a feeling that the more I shake, the more it's going to hurt."

"He's my boss," she said, voice muffled in the pillow.

"I got the impression you don't trust him."

"We don't have all day."

"I'm getting there, okay? Just give me a minute." He focused on willing his palsied hand to take a chill pill.

She turned her head to look up at him, her long, raven hair shifting against the pale skin of her neck. "You can do this."

He snorted. "After all this time, you don't know me at all. I'm not the guy people count on in a pinch."

"You are now."

Wincing, he dug in with the knife. She stiffened then buried her hiss in the pillow.

"I'm sorry," he murmured. "I'm sorry, I'm sorry, I'm sorry."

Blood welled around the tip of the blade, and he felt her skin under his bracing hand go clammy. "Almost there." She didn't need to know he had no idea what he was doing. "Just hang on."

Where the hell was it? He didn't even know what he was looking for.

"What does this transmitter look like? Will I know it—"

He broke off when what looked like a tiny piece of translucent cartilage oozed out on a well of blood. He pinched it between two fingers and held it up. Had to be it. It was too perfectly round and smooth to be anything but something that didn't belong.

"Got it," he said on a relieved sigh.

Samantha didn't respond, and he could tell from how lax her body had become that she'd passed out. He smoothed his palm over the satin skin of her middle back to soothe her, marveling at the shift in his gut. He was *such* an idiot.

Then he got to work cleaning and redressing the bullet wounds and the new cut. The bleeding appeared to have stopped, finally, and the bullet wounds didn't look like they were getting infected. Small favors.

He'd just gotten her turned over and into one of his dark blue flannel shirts when her gray blue eyes fluttered open.

"Hey." He snagged the tiny transmitter he'd set on the bedside table. "Lookee what I found."

A weak, shuddery breath passed over her lips before she met his gaze. Her eyes slid briefly out of focus. "That's not it."

His stomach plunged to his knees. "What?"

"Kidding."

"You're *teasing* me? Seriously?"

She grasped his arm with a grimace. "Help me up."

Fearing she'd start bleeding again if she exerted herself too much, he assisted her into a sitting position. He sat beside her while she rested, his hand braced at her lower back to help keep her upright.

"I need to question him," she said.

"I don't imagine he's going to be all that cooperative—" He broke off at her sideways glance. Of course. She had a gun.

And a kitchen full of knives. And warrior training. She had ways of making him talk.

"Let's get you buttoned up first."

She braced her right hand on his shoulder and said nothing as he fumbled with the fasteners on the flannel shirt. He'd never buttoned a shirt that he wasn't wearing, and the angle was all wrong, not like when he'd stood behind her and secured the drawstring of her pants. It didn't help that just scant inches from the tips of his fingers were a pair of the most perfect breasts he'd ever seen. His heart thundered in his ears, and he was overly conscious of the soft, cool feel of her breath against his hands as she watched his progress. The closer his fingers got to her breasts, the tighter she gripped his shoulder. Interesting.

He needed to talk to distract himself from the intimacy of the moment. "I don't suppose you're going to tell me what's going on here."

"I can't."

"If you did, you'd have to kill me?"

"Something like that."

"That guy out there . . . he *is* the bad guy, right?"

She raised her head and met his eyes straight on. "Yes."

"And his friends? They would have used their rocket launchers to kill us?"

"They're not rocket launchers. They're SIG SG 550 assault rifles."

"I know that . . . I mean, I know they aren't rocket launchers. My point is that they're just as scary as rocket launchers."

"Depending on how they're set to fire, they can tear you into just as many pieces."

"Thank you for that graphic image. So answer the question."

"They would have killed you."

"And what about you?"

"Flinn has other plans for me." Her gaze flicked away. "Otherwise, they would have blown us away without hesitation."

Mac's stomach did a queasy dance. He hated her world

already, and he'd just been introduced. "When you're done questioning him, are you going to kill him?"

Her lips tightened, and she deliberately refused to meet his eyes. "Go outside and get into your car. I'll be out in ten minutes."

CHAPTER **TEN**

A m I part of the same science experiment as Zoe?"
Flinn looked back at her, unimpressed by the gun she pressed to the middle of his forehead. His skin still bore faint depressions from the dish towel Mac had used to tightly gag him, making him look as though he'd just awakened from having his face pressed into a wrinkly pillowcase.

"Who took you in when you hit rock bottom?" he asked. "You were going to prison. Who gave you a home? Fed you? Trained you?"

"You *La Femme Nikita*'d me for your own gain. You've used me for fourteen years. *Experimented* on me."

"We've had a mutually beneficial relationship, Samantha."

She had to fight the urge to put a bullet between his eyes. For years, she'd let him do whatever he wanted to her, in the name of making N3 the best team possible. Drug research. Psychic evaluations. Endurance tests. All for the greater good of N3 and its mission to protect the United States from the threats of do-badders the world over. For a long time, she felt she'd had no choice but to submit. Be a good soldier or go to prison. That was the deal, and she lived with it. But now a friend was dead. And it appeared her boss, a man she'd trusted despite his arrogance and flaws, had crossed the line with his scientific research.

She firmed her grip on the SIG. "Zoe said she was pregnant and that there was no way it was a natural conception. How did that happen? And why? What's the plan?"

"Zoe's confused, Samantha. You know her. She's always been a drama queen."

"Stop talking about her like you don't know she's dead and tell me why you impregnated her."

"I can't talk with a gun—"

"Have I been impregnated, too?"

"Samantha—"

She pressed harder with the SIG. "Answer. The. Question."

"And then what? You're going to kill me? The man who saved you when you were a troubled teenager? The man who gave you your life back? A very *good* life, by the way. Have you ever wanted anything that I didn't give you?"

"I wanted to see my family." She hated the break in her voice, the sign of weakness. But, then, her family had *always* been her weakness. And Flinn had shrewdly used that against her from the start.

"You know that wasn't possible. Contact with you would have put them in danger. You willingly gave them up when I offered you the opportunity to use your ability working for N3. We're the good guys, remember?"

"I was eighteen. I didn't know what I was doing, what I was giving up. And besides, you said I would spend the rest of my life in prison if I didn't agree to join you."

"Yes, because you killed a man. In cold blood."

"It was an accident!" She was helpless to stop the renewed flood of guilt and horror at what she'd done. Accident or not, the man had died at her hand.

"A jury wouldn't have seen it that way," Flinn said.

She shook her head, struggling to keep on track. "You're trying to distract me with old history. Am I pregnant or not?"

"I can't tell you what you want to know, Samantha, not like this. I don't trust you to spare my life once you have what you want. So let's make a deal: We leave here together. We return to N3 headquarters, where you can get the medical attention you need. I'll answer your questions then. I promise."

She blinked back tears of frustration. He wasn't going to tell her anything, and even if he did she couldn't trust he'd tell the truth. The only way she would get a definitive answer was to find a drugstore and get her own damn test. If it was positive, then she'd go from there. But where? Oh, God, what would she do if . . .

Keep it together, Sam, she thought. Don't lose it now.

"Samantha, please be reasonable."

She adjusted her hold on the SIG. She wanted him to know he wouldn't win. Not this time. "When I walk out that door, you won't be able to track me anymore. The transmitter has been removed."

A look of pure concern blanched his features. "That was a very bad idea, Samantha. Don't you remember what I told you would happen if it was ever tampered with?"

Her heart thumped. What? Oh, crap. Crap, crap, crap. "You're bluffing."

"Think about it. I told you that the transmitters all have fail-safes in the event an operative is kidnapped and the captors remove it. You must rememb r that."

What the hell was he talking about? He *had* to be trying to manipulate her.

"Listen to me very carefully," he went on urgently. "You have to untie me. We need to get you back to N3 before the fail-safe kicks in."

"No! There is no fail-safe. I would remember that."

His gaze bore into her, his concern, even if it was fake, intense. "Within ninety minutes of the removal of the transmitter, a powerful drug will be released into your bloodstream that will wipe your memory clean. It's designed to prevent our agents from being tortured for information. You can't share information that you no longer have."

"You're lying." Oh, God, he had to be lying. He had to be.

"I'm not lying." He jerked at his bonds, his face reddening. "Damn it, Samantha, I'm not lying!"

She backed out of the kitchen and ran to the front door. His frantic voice rang in her ears as she stumbled onto the porch. "Samantha! *Samantha!*"

She saw Mac straighten in the driver's seat of the SUV, his expression both apprehensive and questioning. Shutting down her doubts, she got into the passenger's seat and sat back on a hiss of a pain. "Let's go."

"Are you okay?" he asked.

She glanced sideways at him, struck by his concern. He had no idea what she'd dragged him into, no idea that the only way out would be oblivion. "No. I'm not okay."

CHAPTER **ELEVEN**

For the next five minutes, Mac focused on maneuvering around the debris in the road and checking the rearview mirror every three seconds for more bad guys. So far, no one followed.

As the truck rolled to a stop at the washed-out section of road, he considered the water streaming by. It lacked the violent, frothy rush of the night before, but he still didn't feel confident driving through it, four-wheel drive or not.

"Back up and build up some speed."

He glanced sideways at Samantha. She was unnaturally pale again, as though she'd lost more blood. The circles under her eyes made them appear a darker blue, the exhaustion in them undeniable.

No. I'm not okay.

She'd said nothing beyond that except an order to drive, that ugly gun of hers still gripped in her right hand. At least she didn't point it at him.

"We need momentum," she said, impatient. "If you can't do it, get out and I will."

Saying nothing, he threw the truck into reverse and watched the mirror. His leg muscles twitched to gas it, just to show her she hadn't allied herself with a pussy. Instead, he said, "Brace yourself. It's going to be bumpy."

She switched the gun to her left hand and rested it on her thigh, then placed her right against the dash and clenched her jaw.

He switched into drive and pressed the gas pedal to the floor. The truck bounced over the mud and rocks, brown water geysering into twin arcs on either side. The violent jolts would have tossed him from his seat if the seat belt hadn't locked him in place.

When they'd made it to the other side of the washed-out road, he glanced at his passenger. Whitened fingertips dug into the dash, her teeth gritted so tight he swore he could hear them grinding. He didn't ask if she was okay this time. He already knew her answer: Drive.

The going got easier then. The road debris lightened to wet leaves, mud and the occasional tree limb, though none were big enough to block the way.

To be honest, he wasn't in the mood to talk. He'd just watched a woman kill two goons, and she'd done it with about as much emotion as a palmetto bug. For all he knew, she'd killed Dr. Evil before she'd stumbled out of the cabin. Maybe she'd kill *him* once he took her where she wanted to go. As vacations went, this one was not going to make the Letterman top ten for good ones.

Eventually, she released her grip on the dash and eased back in her seat on a shaky sigh. The fact that she'd let the sound escape at all surprised him. Maybe she wasn't as tough as she seemed.

"I need your help," she said softly.

More surprise. "You need *my* help. I'm the guy you said was no one back there."

"I was trying to make it clear that you don't mean anything to me."

"Gee, thanks."

She rubbed at her temples as if she had the kind of headache that gripped your head in sharp dragon talons. "Just . . . let me focus for a minute."

He watched the road and wondered why her explanation hurt his feelings. He couldn't possibly mean anything to her after only one day. Except he was pretty sure his role as getaway driver was saving her life right about now, not to mention digging himself deeper into a potentially criminal hole he might not be able to haul himself out of.

"What's the closest town?" she asked. "Mid-sized or bigger."

He glanced over, noting that she kept blinking as though

repeatedly losing focus. Was the blood loss getting to her? "I'm not that familiar with the area, but the last decent-sized town I saw on the way here was Front Royal."

"Good. Let's go there. Find a motel, something off the main roads that takes cash, something family-run. No chains that have computer systems. Make up a name. We're married, and I'm not feeling well. You just want a place for me to rest. Does this SUV have GPS?"

"No. Why?"

"Good, that's good. We don't have to ditch it."

"Ditch it?"

"Park in the back of the motel, out of sight of the road, or even a few blocks away if you can. Then just wait until I come out of it."

"Come out of what?" Aw, hell, that bald bastard had done something to her. Mac knew he never should have left her alone with him.

"I need you to just listen. I don't have much time."

"Time? What does that mean? Is there a deadline I'm not aware of?"

"Please, just listen. You don't have to remember what I tell you. All you have to remember is . . ." She trailed off, in a hurry but also trying to pick her words carefully. "After . . . afterward, you have to touch me."

He gaped at her. Was she delirious? But, no, her skin didn't bear the flushed signs of fever. She did look desperate, though. And scared. And that scared *him*. This woman, who wore the scars from blades and bullets, who shot down two bad guys without blinking—at least, he was still hoping they were bad guys—wasn't supposed to look *scared*. "What the hell are you talking about?"

"Watch the road."

The tires on her side hit the rumble strip on the shoulder, and he jerked the wheel to swerve back into the lane. "Shit," he muttered.

"I'm empathic," she said. "It's a psychic ability that allows me to tap into your past experiences. It's triggered by skin-on-skin contact."

"Okaaaay." Great, she was nuts. Dr. Evil was probably the loony police, and Mac had helped the whackjob escape. Damn it, he never did manage to get the important things right in his life. He stole a quick glance at the gun resting on the seat between them, noted her fingers were loosely wrapped around the butt. Making a grab for it would probably rank a ten on the stupid-o-meter.

Instead of responding, she switched gun hands again, then reached over and gripped his bare wrist with chilled fingers. He flinched as much at the unexpected contact as the sharp hiss of air that she sucked through her teeth. He glanced over to see she'd clamped her eyes shut and pressed her lips together. Concentration or pain? Maybe both. He had no idea what she was doing, but he didn't try to shake her loose, certain he would jar her injured shoulder if he did. As absurd as it was, the last thing he wanted to do was hurt her.

Then, as quickly as she'd grabbed him, she let go and sagged back with a moan, her head falling back against the seat. "God."

He stole a quick glance at the road, doing his damnedest to keep the SUV in its lane, then shifted his attention back to her. She'd gone so pale her skin looked waxy. His heart beat hard and fast against his ribs, concern alternating with the urge to park the truck, get out and walk away. No, make that: *Run* away.

"What just happened?" he asked.

A wince creased her forehead. "Some asshole beaned you in the head with, what, a pipe of some kind? An aluminum baseball bat?"

His foot lifted off the gas, alarm an electric current zipping up his spine. "What?"

"Keep driving."

He obeyed automatically. How the *hell* could she possibly know what Skip Alteen had done to him?

"When I touched you just now, I relived the moment when an intruder crept up behind you and cracked you in the skull with a blunt object. You were contemplating a bottle of liquor at the time. Absolut vodka. And thinking about what a loser you are."

"Jesus." He couldn't think beyond that. *"Jesus."*

"It's called empathy." She sighed, sounding more spent than a combat-weary soldier. "A jacked-up kind of empathy," she added under her breath.

"How could you—"

"I don't have time to explain. You just have to trust me."

"*Trust* you? You're kidding, right?"

"I have to tell you some things. *Now.* Please don't interrupt me with questions. After I'm done, after I . . . forget . . . you have to touch me."

"After you forget *what*?" It was like they spoke two different languages, and neither had even a basic grasp of the other's.

"The transponder you removed from my shoulder released a drug into my system. It's going to wipe out my memory. Flinn said ninety minutes, but it's probably more like fifteen. I have to tell you what I need to know, and after the drug takes effect, you're going to put your hand on me, skin-on-skin, so I can retrieve the information from you in an empathic flash."

"Are you sure the drug hasn't already taken effect? Or maybe you've lost too much blood. Because you're sounding, well, crazy. And not the simple kind. I'm talking bat-shit crazy."

"You don't need to understand. You just need to *listen*. In one hour, maybe two, we can go our separate ways. That's all I need from you. Two hours. Just give me that then go away."

Their eyes met. He could see in the dark depths of hers that she truly believed the fairy tale she'd fed him. Yet the prospect of this nightmare ending in as little as an hour . . . well, he couldn't deny the high quotient of temptation on that. They'd be in the DC metro area by then, too. He could easily take her to a hospital and turn her over to the professionals who wear white and keep a handy supply of sedatives and straitjackets.

He checked on the gun. Her fingers had tightened on the grip, and he had no doubt that if he refused, she wouldn't hesitate to use that weapon to get what she wanted. He really, *really* had no desire to end up with a gun pointed at his head, especially by a woman who looked inches from losing it.

"Fine," he said.

CHAPTER **TWELVE**

She didn't like the way he watched her, like a cat planning his next pounce.

Sam let her body melt farther into the seat when he agreed. Easier than she'd thought, yet she'd noticed the speculation in his greenish brown eyes before he'd acquiesced. He probably had his own plan—a stupid plan that would get them both killed. But, damn it, she had no choice now but to go with it and hope for the best. Time was ticking away.

Based on the nausea building steam in her stomach, she suspected Flinn had indeed told her the truth about the fail-safe. The drug might be responsible for the piercing headache, too, but her reluctant sidekick's painful past probably had caused it. Figures she'd end up with a guy who'd gotten violently whacked over the head and not a klutz who'd simply slammed his finger in a car door.

Regardless, she needed to get her thoughts in order so she could tell Mac what she needed to know in a way that would make sense to her after she lost her memory. It was a long shot, but it was all she had.

"You were right," she said. "I'm an intelligence operative. The man we left tied up at the cabin is Flinn Ford. He's my boss at N3."

"N3?"

"National Neural Network. It's a secret division of the FBI. The agents have psychic abilities."

He cast a dubious glance at her. "A secret division of the FBI with psychic operatives? How gullible do you think I am? I'm the epitome of the grizzled old newspaper reporter. Without the grizzled and old parts."

She blinked as she studied him. Grizzled? Not in the least. Handsome, yes. And those dimples . . . my God, they were adorable. She shook her head, then grabbed at the car door to steady herself against dizziness. She had to stay on topic.

"Flinn impregnated a fellow N3 operative named Zoe Harris. I think he's trying to create some kind of super psychic spy by combining the DNA of two N3 empaths."

The car's front end dipped forward slightly as he took his foot off the accelerator. "Holy shit."

"Don't slow down. Keep. Driving."

"Okay, okay. Just chill."

"I'll chill as long as you don't slow down."

He cranked his speed back up to a non-attention-getting 65 mph. "How did you hook up with these people?"

"That's not important."

"Look, maybe I could just take you to Lake Avalon. Charlie and Alex can help you—"

"No!" She bit her lip as a stab of longing pierced her chest. She hadn't seen her sisters in so long. Hadn't heard their laughter, shared in their joys. Alex was in love, Mac had said. Sam couldn't even imagine her baby sister being old enough for a serious romantic relationship. Last time she'd seen her, Alex had been a precocious thirteen-year-old, totally enamored of every stray animal she could find.

And, crap, she'd let her mind wander again. Losing focus like this had to be the drug working its way through her system. And it was happening much faster than the ninety minutes Flinn had told her.

"Charlie and Alex can't help me," she said, in control again.

"But we removed the transmitter, so Ford can't follow you, right? Why not just leave it all behind and go home? Your family would love to see you again. They'd find a way to help."

She rested her head against the car seat and closed her eyes. So tired. So . . . so tired. "I have to find out what he planned with Zoe. She has a sister. She'd want me to . . ." She trailed off, losing the thread. Zoe has a sister . . . why was that important again?

"If Zoe were any kind of friend to you, then she'd want you

to be safe. With people who love you. And I know law-enforcement types who can help."

That snapped her straight. "No law enforcement. No police. No FBI. No CIA."

"How about DEA? Secret Service? U.S. Postal Inspectors?"

"This isn't a joke."

He gave a sheepish shrug. "Sorry. Humor . . . that's how I deal with stress. And you have to admit, this is . . . stressful." Then he muttered, "Understatement-of-the-year alert."

She massaged the ache in her forehead with the tips of cold fingers. She couldn't think straight, her thoughts growing sluggish and scattered, disconnected, as though a kind of numbness deadened the firing of her synapses. It was happening too fast. She had so much more to tell Mac. "I need to contact . . . Sledge." She used his nickname deliberately. The less Mac knew about other N3 operatives, the better. "He can help."

"Sledge? As in hammer?"

She couldn't think of his number, though. Couldn't even bring forth the first three digits of a number she knew as well as her own. Luckily, she had a backup: "His number's in my phone." She glanced around the interior of the SUV. "Where's my bag?"

"It's back at the cabin."

Crap. *Crap.* Everything she needed to survive was in that bag. Her personal cell phone. Contact numbers. Money. "We have to go back."

Mac snorted. "I don't think so."

"Turn around."

"We're not going back."

"We *have* to. My bag—"

"Is probably now in the custody of the guy who's after you. Remember him? Bald? Smarmy?"

"Yes, of course. Flinn." As she said it, she realized he hadn't meant that as an actual question. She couldn't keep up.

"Why is he after you, anyway? Isn't that information you're going to need, you know, later?"

"He wants to . . ." She trailed off, not sure suddenly. Think,

think. "He wants to stop me from telling his superiors what he's doing." Yes, that sounded right. Didn't it?

"So if this N3 is part of the FBI, wouldn't his superiors be at FBI headquarters? We can go there right now. It's not that far from here, in downtown Washington."

She tried to think of Flinn's boss, but either the drug had destroyed the memories or she'd never known. Is that even how the drug worked? Slowly nibbling away at her mind? Or would it happen all at once? She'd blink and everything would be gone. She'd be blank. *Focus.* "I don't know who his superiors are."

"Then how do you know you work for the FBI?"

She didn't. At least, not now. Surely she wouldn't have blindly followed Flinn without question. Would she? No, wait, she'd had no choice. He'd blackmailed her—

"Samantha?"

"Sam."

"Sorry?"

"Don't call me Samantha. That's what Flinn calls me. But I'm Sam. I've always been Sam."

"Okay."

The colors blurring by outside the SUV window were so pretty. Reds and golds and yellows. She'd liked fall ever since the first time she'd witnessed the colorful change in season while on vacation with her family in the Shenandoahs. Winter? Not so much.

She blinked her eyes open—when had they closed?—and tried to get oriented. She was supposed to be doing something important. Studying for a test. No . . . weapons training. That was it. She had to learn how to handle a gun. "Keep it pointed down range," a male voice told her. "Okay, sight down the barrel. That's it." She imagined the target before her bore the face of the man who'd stolen her life. "Release the safety with your thumb."

"You doing all right over there?"

A different male voice, this one concerned, pulled her back into the present, into an SUV driving down a twisty, wet road at the height of fall. Her senses took a long, lazy spin as the truck followed a curve. Oh, right, an N3 drug was eating away at her memory. And there was something important she had to tell this man. What was his name? Mac something. Mac . . . *something*. And she needed to tell him . . . damn. Tell him *what*?

Oh, right.

"It's already started. I don't know how long I'll be out, but wait it out. Don't take me to the hospital. Don't use your credit cards or cell phone. Don't panic. Just . . . wait."

His eyes, fixed on the road, narrowed, and she thought that was kind of funny, really. He didn't believe a word she said, yet worry radiated off him in waves. He must be a pretty nice guy to be so kind and caring about someone like her.

Focus, she thought. Stay on topic. Think.

"When I'm conscious again, touch me. Understand?"

He didn't respond.

"Understand?"

"Yeah." His lips barely moved.

"Promise me you'll do what I said." A decent guy like him had to be a stickler for promises.

A muscle at his temple flexed, but he said nothing. No nod, either.

"Promise."

He swallowed but still didn't look at her. "Fine."

She let her shoulders relax. She had no choice but to trust him. And, oddly, she *did* trust him. He exuded honorable intentions. And strength. And dimples. And muscles . . .

Her eyes slipped closed, and she fought the pull of sleep . . . why was she fighting it again? If she was so tired, why didn't she just sleep? She didn't have anything else to do while someone else did the driving.

"Sam? Hey, Sam."

His voice followed her down into a deep, dark hole.

CHAPTER **THIRTEEN**

Flinn Ford bit out every swear word he could think of as Marco Ricci, his least-favorite among N3's goon squad, sliced through the cords biting into his wrists. "Fucking goddamn son of a bitch. What took you so long?"

"I left DC as soon as I lost contact with Deke and Tom, sir. Got here as fast as I could."

"Yes, yes, I know. Just . . . Samantha's transmitter has been removed. I know she got rid of her work cell phone, but please tell me we're tracking the GPS on her personal cell."

"Negative, sir. She doesn't have it with her."

Flinn scowled at the imposing Italian man. Dressed all in black like Deke and Tom, he was muscular and tall, a permanent frown etched into his features. Flinn wanted to take his head off for reasons that had nothing to do with the fact that an injured Samantha and an unarmed civilian had gotten the drop on him and two of his weapons-laden men.

"At least tell me someone got the tags on that Jeep."

"Yes, sir. Deke called it in before . . ."

As Marco trailed off, Flinn glanced at Deke's unmoving body on the floor, eyes open and staring. Next to him, Tom sprawled in a similar pose, just as dead. Regret nudged him. He'd liked Deke and Tom. Good soldiers. Competent and committed to the cause. Samantha had taken them out without hesitation. Irrefutable proof that he wouldn't be able to reason with her.

He stood, rubbing his sore wrists, and walked to the small refrigerator. Inside, he found a can of Coca-Cola and popped it open. The two hours he'd spent tied to a chair, cursing

Samantha and that bastard she'd hooked up with, had left him thirsty. "I'm not going to lose her, Marco."

"Yes, sir. I've traced the tags to the Avis rental agency at Dulles Airport, sir. The guy's name is Mackenzie Hunter of Lake Avalon, Florida."

"What's his relationship to Samantha?"

"I don't know, sir."

"Wait, did you say Lake Avalon?"

"Yes, sir."

"That's Samantha's hometown. And Hunter's from there, too? Yet she insisted she didn't know him. I suspected she was trying to protect him." How long had Samantha and this man been in touch? What had she told him about N3?

"Sir?"

Flinn tamped down the black anger. "What else do we know about Hunter?"

"As requested, Natalie is compiling a more detailed report, but it will take some time, sir."

Sir. The overabundance of respect irked him. He didn't even know when Tom and Deke had stopped *sir*-ing him to death, but it had been a relief. Now all he had was Marco, the muscle he liked the least.

He rubbed a hand over the smooth skin of his head. "Let's put a tap on the phones of Samantha's family members in Lake Avalon. Parents and two sisters. If she tries to contact them, we can trace the call from that end. Does the Jeep have GPS?"

"No, sir."

"Fuck!" Flinn fought the urge to crush the can of Coke in his fist.

Marco's dark expression didn't change. "Sir?"

"The transmitter's been tampered with, Marco. She's out there right now with no memory of who she is. *What* she is."

"Yes, sir. Isn't that the way the fail-safe is supposed to work, sir?"

Flinn gulped down some more Coke. That was indeed how the fail-safe drug worked. For a couple of days, anyway. And then it wore off. He'd never told his operatives that part. What good would the fail-safe do if under interrogation an operative told his or her captors that all they had to do was wait out the drug's effects, that within a few days, they could begin the interrogations and torture all over again and get what they wanted?

The drug was specifically designed to suppress only episodic memory—the what, when and where of personality. The operative retained the instincts and skills of a trained government agent. The goal was to block the operative's access to sensitive information for at least three days, giving N3 enough time to mount a rescue. Unlike intelligence officers in other agencies, his operatives were not easily expendable. They had abilities that no amount of training could instill in even the most ambitious agent. And there were far too few of them. At least, there were *now*. He would change that very soon. First, he had to retrieve Samantha. Once he had her back, forcing her to cooperate would be the easy part.

"Sir?"

Flinn glanced at Marco, who maintained parade rest, legs set wide, hands behind his back. Awaiting his orders instead of thinking for himself. Flinn detested people who didn't think for themselves. Samantha did and, while that was a problem now, it had been the reason she was one of his most competent operatives.

"We've lost three men, Marco." He clenched his teeth at the renewed surge of anger at Samantha for costing the team so dearly, and at such a critical time. "We need more muscle."

"Yes, sir."

"I have to return to the District for a meeting, but I need you to stay here and clean up this mess. I'll check in with Natalie and have her line up some new men in the area. You can pick them up on your way back."

"Yes, sir."

"And I need a new cell phone. That bastard Hunter destroyed mine."

CHAPTER **FOURTEEN**

Carrying two white plastic grocery bags from the drugstore a block away, Mac stepped into the dimly lit motel room and shut and locked the door on a weary sigh.

He could see from there that Samantha . . . *Sam* hadn't budged under the covers of the double bed in the center of the tiny room—the best he could do with half of the hundred bucks he'd had in his pocket. A Motel 6 clone, minus five, in Front Royal, Virginia.

He'd spent the better part of three hours ignoring the relentless chant in his head: Idiot, idiot, idiot.

As soon as she'd lapsed into unconsciousness, he should have taken her to the nearest hospital, promises be damned. Without the sister connection to Charlie and Alex, he might have. Or maybe not. He had no idea anymore. Just as he had no idea how the hell she'd known about his altercation with Skip Alteen's pipe wrench.

Charlie must have mentioned the psycho's rampage in Lake Avalon when she'd told Sam about Alex's shooting. Both incidents had happened at the same time, so that made sense. Except for the part about Sam not having any clue who Mac was, so why would Charlie tell her anything about him?

And there was the small detail about the bottle of Absolut he'd had cradled in his hands when Alteen knocked him senseless. No one knew about that. Not even Charlie.

God. Absolut. What he wouldn't give now for a shot, or three, to take the edge off.

Just as well. Drunken man on the run with an amnesiac spy with psychic gifts sounded too much like a lame pitch for Hollywood.

He started to pace, and three steps into it, he realized he should have picked up some food while he'd been at the drugstore. Sam might be hungry when she woke up. Were there restaurants nearby? He'd been so focused on her state of unconsciousness that he hadn't paid any attention to the motel's location, beyond the drugstore in the next block.

He could go to the front desk and ask for directions to the nearest fast-food place. That wouldn't undermine the "my wife is ill and needs a place to rest" story he'd fed the teenager at the desk. Of course, the sixteenish girl in heavy black eye makeup had handed over a room key without once making eye contact or putting down the cell phone glued to the side of her head. He doubted she gave a crap about his "wife's" need to rest.

He went to the bedside table and opened the drawer, hoping for a phone book. Nothing.

Okay, this was silly. Sam was unconscious. She didn't need food right this minute.

What he really needed to do was talk.

He checked his watch. Almost eight. Maybe Charlie was home from work by now.

He dug the new prepaid cell phone out of one of the plastic bags and went to work on the packaging. Maybe Charlie could give him some advice on how to deal with her sister.

By the time he got the phone out of its hard-plastic shell, he was ready to hurl it across the room. The entire time, Sam didn't stir. A little mumbling in her sleep might have calmed him. Assuming she didn't mumble about killing people.

He sat in the creaky, worn-out chair in the corner and started thumbing the numbers for Charlie.

"Hello?" Charlie sounded breathless and hesitant.

"It's Mac."

"Oh, hey. I didn't recognize your number. What's up?"

"I'm . . ." He trailed off, gaze fixed on the steady rise and fall of Sam's chest.

"Mac?"

Your sister's a psychic spy, and there's this slimy asshole out to get her and now she has no idea who she is or that the slimy asshole wants her dead . . . or something. What the hell should I do?

Yeah, he could say that. Easy. And then the loony police would be after *him*.

"Mac? Are you there? Is everything at the cabin all right?"

"Everything's great. I, uh, just wanted to say thanks again for persuading me to come up here."

"Are you sure you're okay? You sound strange."

"You just haven't heard my relaxed voice in a while."

She laughed. "Okay."

"I . . ." He needed a segue, a way to initiate a conversation about Sam without sounding like a lunatic. "I was looking at the photo on the fireplace. The one of you and Alex and Sam."

"Sure, I know the one."

He heard rustling in the background—maybe sheets—and whispered words that included "Mac" and "right back," and a low rumbling voice in response. She must have been in bed with Noah. And she'd sounded so breathless because he'd interrupted something sweaty and naked . . . at eight o'clock at night. Jesus, they were rabbits. "Is this a bad time? I can—"

"No, it's okay. What's on your mind?"

"I just . . ." He jammed a hand through his hair, frustrated with himself for not thinking this through. Typical of Mac Hunter, really. Talk first and regret later. And Charlie, bless her soul, had tolerated just about every fuck-up from him he could muster. From dumping her to score a promotion at work to making a complete ass of himself after he'd realized his mistake. Lucky for her, Noah Lassiter had swept in to pick up the pieces. Lucky bastard.

His gaze strayed again to Sam, and his heart did a restless tango against his ribs. More than anything, he wanted to protect this woman who'd hijacked his life. Was that weird?

Charlie's voice cut into his thoughts. "Mac?"

"You, uh, your sister . . . Sam . . . she took off shortly after the picture was taken, right?"

"Yes. As soon as she turned eighteen."

"Do you know why she left?"

A long pause, as if Charlie were trying to figure out where

he was going with this. "She and Mom had a fight. That wasn't all that unusual, because, you know, Mom has her issues."

He grimaced as he remembered Charlie telling him about her mother's "issues," which included an extremely short temper with middle-child Charlie. "So do you know what she . . . Sam, I mean, did after she left Lake Avalon?"

"No idea."

"You don't know what she does for . . . a living." She kills people, he thought. That's what she does. Is that a *living*?

"This is bizarre, Mac. You called to drill me about Sam?"

"I'm curious, that's all. You know me. Reporter to the bone."

"Gee, can't relate," Charlie said with a laugh that didn't sound all that amused. "Honestly, I don't know what she does. I don't even know where she lives."

"You talk to her every now and then, though, right?"

"I have a cell phone number for her, but I don't think it works anymore." She paused when her voice cracked. "Used to be, if I left her a message, she'd call back within a couple of days, but I haven't heard back from her in weeks."

"Have you tried to find her?"

"Noah and I are trying now, actually. Alex and I have a couple of things we want to talk to her about, but no joy. I figure she'll either show up again someday or we'll eventually find out she's . . ." She trailed off, emotion thickening her voice again.

"Find out what?"

"That she's . . . dead."

His heart gave an ominous thump. "Dead? Why would you think *that*?"

"Just a feeling." Charlie sounded stronger now, maybe even resigned. "Sam was a daredevil when we were kids. She loved motorcycles, fast boats and bad boys. It didn't take a double-dog dare to get her to throw caution to the wind. I don't imagine she ever grew out of that, considering how she ran away from home and never looked back."

His gaze shifted to the unconscious woman on the bed. He sensed that Sam *had* looked back. And she'd done it with regret, based on her reaction when she'd realized he was friends with her sisters. She'd gotten a longing look in her eyes, and she'd seemed genuinely concerned about Alex.

"What's this about, Mac?" Charlie asked. "Why are you so interested in Sam?"

"I, uh, well . . ." He trailed off, on the hunt for the right words. And then he decided to just tell the truth. He was a terrible liar anyway. And he was *way* out of his element here. "Look, I arrived at the cabin, and Sam was there."

"What? Are you kidding? She's with you now? That's great!" Charlie's excitement seemed to vibrate the phone in his hand. "Can you put her on so I can talk to her?"

"The thing is . . . she's—" He cast a glance at Sam. He couldn't tell Charlie that her sister was a spy. That was Sam's story to tell. But he also couldn't leave Charlie in the dark. She had a right to know that her sister needed help. "There was an . . . incident at the cabin. Some bad people are after her."

"Bad people?"

"She's on the run, Charlie. She's involved . . . in something."

"Tell me where you are. Noah and I will come—"

"I don't think we can stay in one spot for too long."

"God, Mac, what the hell? Is Sam there with you? Can I talk to her?"

"She's sleeping." He winced, but it had seemed better than saying, She lost consciousness after being drugged out of her memory.

A long beat went by in which Mac knew Charlie debated how to respond. "Is she okay?"

"I'm not sure."

"You need to tell me where you are. Noah—"

"We can't stay here. We need to keep moving."

"Mac, please. If Sam needs help—"

"I'm helping her. I'm—"

"Noah can get law enforcement involved. And so can—"

"No! No law enforcement. Seriously. I know this is crazy, but I'm not sure who to trust right now."

"You can trust me and Noah."

"I know that. Of course, I know that. I meant about getting

law enforcement involved. I don't think that's a good idea. I . . . Jesus, I'm sorry. I shouldn't have said anything. Now you're going to be all freaked out—"

"Don't worry about that. Just tell me what you're going to do."

He had no idea. But he also knew how much Sam meant to Charlie and Alex. "I'm going to keep her safe. I promise."

"That's not what I meant."

"I know it's not. But I need you to know that, okay? You can count on me for this." *Like you couldn't count on me when we were together.*

"Mac, please. Just tell me where—"

"I'll bring her home. I'm going to bring your sister home."

Charlie made a choking sound, as though trying to hold back a sob. He heard another sound in the background, the low thrum of Noah's voice asking, "What's wrong?"

Sam sighed then, and Mac glanced over at the bed in time to see her eyelids flutter. "I have to go," he said into the phone. "I'll call you again as soon as I can."

He cut off the call and powered down the phone before Charlie could respond.

CHAPTER **FIFTEEN**

Flinn Ford slipped out of the conference room and snatched his new, vibrating cell phone from the interior pocket of his jacket. The name of his favorite N3 research analyst on the caller ID display heartened him. "Talk to me, Nat."

"We've got a fix on Hunter, sir. He's in Front Royal, Virginia."

Flinn's insides fluttered with relief. He'd reluctantly returned to DC for the time-wasting meeting he'd just ducked out of, but Marco was still well west of the District, hopefully not far at all from Front Royal. He'd be able to locate—and sit on—Samantha and Hunter in no time.

"How'd you find Hunter so fast?"

"He called Samantha's sister in Lake Avalon. Used a pre-paid cell phone. Probably thought he was being sneaky. Dumb-ass." A brief pause, then, "Sir."

Flinn grinned at Natalie's disgust, as well as her belated respect. He'd always been fond of her. Too bad she had no psychic abilities. "Do you have coordinates? Marco's out that way."

"He's on his way to Strasburg to meet with one of the new hires you requested."

Flinn's grin grew. "Very efficient, Nat. I'm impressed."

"I aim to please."

"And you hit the target every time. How close is he to Strasburg?"

"He left the cabin about fifteen minutes ago," she said.

"Divert him to Front Royal to detain Samantha and Hunter. I'll meet him there." He'd have to decide then what to do with them.

"And the new hire?"

"Send someone else to pick him up."

"Should I arrange some backup for Marco, sir? Sloan's in Alexandria waiting for the handoff in Old Town. Should go down any minute, and then he could hit the road—"

"I don't want Sloan anywhere near this thing," he said sharply. Then he softened his tone before he went on, to let her know he wasn't angry with *her*. He just didn't trust Sloan Decker these days. "Samantha's well out of commission by now, and Hunter's a civilian. He doesn't even know how to handle a weapon."

"Yes, sir."

"And Nat . . . let's keep all of this between you and me. There's no reason to get Assistant Director Leigh or anyone else involved. Do we understand each other?"

"Of course, sir. You know you can count on me for whatever you need."

He examined the reddened stripe around his left wrist where the twine had cut into his flesh. He thought of his cell phone, smashed to bits under Hunter's heel.

He had a score to settle with that man.

CHAPTER **SIXTEEN**

Sam stirred again under the covers, and Mac went still in the chair across from the bed. She was regaining consciousness, and this was the part of the plan he had no clue how to handle. She'd told him to touch her as soon as she woke. But how would she make sense of something so unbelievable? *He* couldn't make sense of it, and he *had* his memory.

Her head moved, and he watched her eyes open more fully. She blinked slowly, trying to get oriented, and her brow soon furrowed.

Confusion had set in.

He edged out of the chair and approached the bed. When he stood beside it, he waited for her eyes to track and focus on him, then he smiled and sat on the edge, careful to keep his distance from any possible skin-on-skin contact, as well as trying to appear as nonthreatening as possible.

"Hey," he said softly. "How're you feeling?"

Her eyes narrowed, lost focus. "Where . . . who . . ."

He gave her flannel-covered arm a gentle squeeze. The deep blue of the shirt she wore—his shirt—made her eyes a darker shade of blue. "It's okay. You're safe. Just relax."

She glanced around, trying to recognize the room. "Where . . ."

He'd really hoped she'd exaggerated the extent of her memory loss. But, no, she'd told the truth. "We're in a motel in Front Royal, Virginia," he told her. Slow and gentle. No reason to get agitated. "Your name is Samantha Trudeau. I'm Mac Hunter."

"Who . . ."

"We're friends, Sam."

She tried to push herself up but stopped with a ragged

moan, her hand going to her shoulder as her features blanched whiter still. "What—"

Mac grasped her uninjured shoulder to stop her from trying to sit up farther. "Just be still for a minute, okay?"

"What's wrong with my shoulder? Did I have an accident?"

"Yes. It's going to be fine, but you need to baby it for a while." When she appeared reluctant to ease back down, he grabbed the extra pillow, helped her to sit up then stashed it behind her back.

She watched him the entire time, forehead creased, eyes still slightly out of focus. The need to sleep obviously pulled at her, but she fought it. "I know you?"

"Yes. We're friends."

"I don't remember . . ." She rolled her head on the pillow to stare up at the ceiling. "Why don't I remember?"

He sank back onto the edge of the bed. This was the part where he was supposed to touch her so she could "flash" on his memories using her "empathy." He couldn't force himself to do it. The fear in her dark blue eyes already tore at him. He couldn't scare her more, regardless of how competent she'd been when he'd seen her in action. That was then. This Sam Trudeau had no memory. This Sam Trudeau was vulnerable and lost.

He decided to lie, just until she had her bearings, until he'd had a chance to figure out what to do. "You had a bad reaction to a drug."

"I did? What kind of drug?"

"Painkiller. For your shoulder. The doctor said it would take a few days, but you'll be fine."

Her gaze flitted around the room, as though she tried to reconcile medical care with this grungy motel setting.

"We're on vacation," he said. "Hiking in the Shenandoahs. Do you remember the Shenandoahs?"

"I . . . don't know. Hiking? I don't remember hiking. I don't remember . . . you."

"You hurt your shoulder, and we checked in here to give you some time to feel better. That's when you reacted badly to the pain medicine."

"Oh."

"The doctor said the adverse reaction will affect your memory. It's temporary." Amazing how effortless it was to lie.

She frowned. "I've never heard of . . ."

"That's probably because of the memory thing. The best thing you can do is just relax and let me do all the work, okay?"

She let her head fall back against the pillow. "Dizzy."

He knew how that went. After his encounter with Skip Alteen's pipe wrench, he'd ridden the Sit 'N Spin for weeks. "It'll pass." He hoped. "Do you need anything? Bathroom?"

"No."

That surprised him, but then, she hadn't eaten or drunk anything since he'd found her in the cabin. She might have been dehydrated even then. "How about something to eat? It'd take me just a few minutes to make a run."

"Not hungry."

"You need to eat and drink something. It's been a long time."

"Later," she murmured, already drifting off.

"I'm going to go get some food, okay? Just rest. Don't try to get up while I'm gone. I don't want you to fall if you get dizzy." He paused, but she didn't respond. "Okay, Sam?"

She nodded without opening her eyes.

"I'll be gone only a few minutes."

The steady rise and fall of her chest indicated she'd already fallen back to sleep.

After tucking the covers securely around her—and resisting the silly urge to lean down and kiss her forehead—Mac grabbed the room key and headed out the door.

As soon as she heard the door click shut, she opened her eyes and shoved aside the covers. She took a moment to gather her strength before using her good arm to push herself into a sitting position. Colored stars burst before her eyes, and she breathed through the pain and the spinning.

God, she felt bad. Weak and dizzy and confused.

He'd said his name was Mac Hunter. He'd called her Sam Trudeau. The names meant nothing to her. Nothing meant anything. This motel room. The hiking accident. Especially the buzz of white noise inside her skull.

All she knew for sure: Mac Hunter was a liar. He'd avoided her gaze when he'd told her about hiking. Classic mistake. Funny how she knew that with such certainty yet couldn't remember her own name. Or his name. Or how she got here. Or where "here" was.

Sitting on the edge of the bed, she hunched her shoulder against the deep throbbing ache and wiped the back of her hand over the dampness of her forehead.

Everything hurt, like she had a terrible flu. Maybe she did.

Or maybe she'd been tortured for months then dumped here with a good-looking man with kind eyes and dimples who assured her she was safe and insisted on feeding her, a scenario designed to gain her trust.

The alarm she felt at the thought—and what must have happened to her to cause such suspicion despite her memory loss—persuaded her to stop wasting time and *move*.

As she swayed to her feet, her stomach shifted and clenched, and she had to grab on to the headboard for balance. Okay, so moving fast wasn't an option.

The soft pants she wore hung from her hips. Not hers, she realized. Same for the flannel shirt that drooped off one shoulder, revealing the bandage underneath.

These weren't her clothes. Where were *her* clothes?

She scanned the room for luggage or duffels. Saw nothing except two white plastic grocery bags on the table in the corner.

Another horrible thought struck her: Maybe these *were* her clothes, and they no longer fit because she'd been a prisoner for so long that she'd lost a significant amount of weight. But, no, that didn't make sense. The clothing was so clean that the scent of fabric softener clung to it.

When she trusted her legs, she checked out the grocery bags and found bandages, hydrogen peroxide and a bottle of Advil in one. No prescriptions. That didn't seem right. Shouldn't there be antibiotics for her shoulder?

The decimated packaging for a prepaid cell phone filled

the other bag, the phone gone. Not that she would have known who to call, except maybe 911.

Next stop: the bathroom.

Her wobbly legs got her there upright. When she turned on the light, she squinted against the brightness, raising a hand against the stabbing glare. Her head ached, a steady, throbbing bass line of pain behind her eyes.

Hangover? Not from alcohol, she thought. Well, possibly. But more likely from drugs, which fit with what Mac had told her. But she still didn't believe him. Something was off here . . . more off than just her memory loss.

At the vanity, she braced her hands on the sink and studied her reflection, hoping for a spark of recognition.

Long, curling black hair. Eyes that were more slate than blue, underscored by the dark circles of fatigue . . . or sickness. Straight, narrow nose. A subtle cleft in her chin. Pale skin. She didn't look healthy. Too thin, too drawn, exhaustion etched into the lines in her forehead.

Worse: She didn't know those lines.

Or the rest of her face.

Her legs started to shake, threatening to buckle, but she stayed in front of the mirror, determined to gain control over her body. She didn't have much time before Mac returned.

Getting the shirt unbuttoned required dexterity her fingers were reluctant to deliver, but she kept at it until she could ease the fabric over and off her bandaged shoulder. Then, shivering in the chill bathroom, she went to work on the haphazard surgical tape. Her breath whistled through her teeth as she pulled the gauze away to reveal massive bruising around a puckered, viciously red hole in her flesh.

She realized then that the back of her shoulder sported a similar bandage.

Her vision abruptly tunneled, and she backed away from the vanity until she bumped into the wall. She sank to the floor and dropped her spinning head into her hands.

She'd been shot.

CHAPTER **SEVENTEEN**

Shouldn't I wait for backup, sir?"

If Flinn and Marco had been in the same place, Flinn might have knocked the stupid shit upside the head. Instead, Marco was outside a motel in Front Royal, Virginia, while Flinn tried to speed west on Interstate 66, only to be slowed to a maddening crawl by road construction.

He never would have consented to let Marco go in alone to secure Samantha, but the dumb Italian had reported that Hunter had exited the motel room. That left Samantha alone and vulnerable—and much easier to secure without the unpredictable civilian around to fuck it up.

Flinn slammed on the brakes, stopping inches from rear-ending the dipshit in the BMW in front of him. How he hated Virginia drivers.

"With all due respect, sir, I think it would be safer to—"

"You're not being paid to think," Flinn ground out between his teeth. "If you're afraid to do your job, you don't belong with N3. I'd be happy to start the paperwork for your transfer."

"That won't be necessary, sir." No frustration or animosity crept into Marco's tone or expression. The perfect soldier.

Flinn still planned to get the lunkhead kicked out of N3 as soon as the drama with Samantha was resolved. He didn't understand what Andrea Leigh saw in the man. But he'd tolerated Marco from the beginning because he had to carefully pick his battles with the assistant director. No sense in burning capital over a useless subordinate.

"Samantha might react on instinct. Do *not* underestimate her."

"Yes, sir."

"Do exactly as I say. Understand?"

"Yes."

"Let's do this before Hunter returns."

The door in the other room opened, and Sam raised her head, blinking against the bright bathroom light. Her head felt muzzy and unclear. She must have fallen asleep or passed out for a few minutes.

She assumed Mac was returning with food. For a moment, she wondered whether he was the one who'd shot her. He'd obviously lied about the hiking accident. But if he *had* shot her, why would he take care of her afterward?

Unless he wanted something from her and hadn't gotten it.

Pain flared in her shoulder as she pushed to her feet. Somehow, she had to get away from him. Somehow, she had to find someone who knew her, who could help her remember. How she would do that, she had no idea.

She had the flannel shirt back on and two buttons fastened, her hands shaking less now that she had somewhat of a plan, when the bathroom door opened. She whirled, expecting Mac Hunter, and prepared to deck him for walking in on her without at least knocking.

Instead, a thickly muscled man with a black crewcut and a gun pointed at her stepped slowly across the threshold.

She backed away until the backs of her knees bumped against the edge of the bathtub. She barely managed to maintain her balance.

The man had dark, cold eyes and an expressionless face. "Come with me, and no one will get hurt, Samantha."

Her name on his lips startled her more than the gun in his hand. "You know me."

He didn't respond, a coiled tension in his muscles. He was a snake preparing to strike. Where Mac had made her feel safe, even as he'd lied to her, this man oozed danger.

She would have backed away even farther, but she was trapped. She braced, ready to fight if necessary. But, first, she wanted answers. "Who are you?"

* * *

Mac ran the three blocks to the Jeep, his breath sending clouds of steam into the chilly fall air. When he'd returned to the motel room seconds ago, letting himself in quietly so as not to disturb Sam, he'd been shocked to discover she wasn't alone. A man who had to be another of Flinn Ford's henchmen had her cornered in the bathroom. Mac had dropped the bags of fast food and started running the three blocks to the SUV.

There, he fumbled the keys out of his pocket and unlocked the passenger-side door. His clumsy fingers mismanaged the latch on the glove box, but he finally got it open and shoved a hand inside to retrieve Sam's gun. He wished now he'd stashed it somewhere in the motel room after he'd liberated it from her lax fingers in the car earlier. He could have had it aimed at that thick-necked dickwad right now.

Racing back to the motel, Mac didn't think about anything but getting to Sam, helping Sam, hoping to God he wasn't too late. At Room 109, he eased the door open and stepped inside. Outside the bathroom doorway, he swung the gun up to point at the head of a man who looked big enough and bad enough to break Mac in two with a flick of one thick wrist. Dr. Evil must get his goons from Muscles 'R Us.

"Time for you to go," Mac said.

Mr. Muscle glanced over his shoulder, startled.

At the same moment, Sam shifted, lightning fast, and before Mac could blink, she had the henchman bent forward over the vanity, his right arm twisted up and behind his back. She kept viciously twisting that arm until his fingers relinquished their grip on his weapon. The gun hit the tile floor, and she used her foot to expertly sweep it out the door and onto the carpet in the other room, well out of Marco's reach.

Mac let his breath out in a relieved—and impressed— huff. Hot damn, the woman could *move*.

Mr. Muscle jerked against her grip, but she held fast, pissed and surprisingly strong. "Who are you?"

"Marco Ricci. Flinn sent me to pick you up."

"Who is that?"

"Flinn Ford. He's our boss."

Mac watched her face in the mirror. Uncertainty creased her forehead, maybe because not only didn't she recognize the name—she couldn't—but she also must have noticed that Marco hadn't appeared the least bit confused or surprised by her questions. He *knew* she had no memory.

Marco must have glimpsed the uncertainty, too, must have taken it as a sign of weakness, because he jerked back, hard, sending Sam careening back against the wall opposite the vanity. A pained grunt exploded from her, and her knees buckled. He turned and grabbed her and pushed her into Mac.

Mac caught her with one arm, the momentum knocking him back a step. He fought to keep his balance without letting her fall, knowing even as he did it that he'd taken his eyes off the biggest threat. He had only the impression of that threat lunging at them.

"Shoot him!" Sam shouted.

Mac pulled the trigger.

Marco reeled back. The edge of the bathtub smacked into the backs of his knees, and he toppled backward, landing on his ass in the tub.

Mac might have laughed at how ridiculous the bulky man looked with his huge legs draped over the edge of the tub. But he was too busy thinking, holy shit, he'd just *shot* the man. And that man was *pissed* as he clamped a hand over the blood oozing from his upper left arm and growled several "fucks" in a row, each one growing in intensity.

"Mac."

Mac hesitated to look behind him at Sam. He didn't even know how she'd gotten there. He'd lost track of her in the chaos—the chaos he'd caused when he'd made the mistake of looking away from Marco. He wouldn't make that mistake again.

"Mac," she said again, her calm voice a sharp contrast to Marco's violent stream of expletives. "I've got him."

He finally glanced at her. She stood a few feet behind him, about where Marco's gun had stopped its glide onto the carpet. She held that gun in one steady hand, sighted on the man bleeding in the tub. She might have sounded calm, but her face—dead pale and sheened with a film of perspiration—looked murderous. Her left arm hung limp at her side.

"Are you okay?" Mac asked. Stupid question. Of course she wasn't. Her injured shoulder had just been slammed against the wall. It was a miracle she was still standing.

And then he noticed her finger flexing on the trigger. "Don't."

She froze but didn't shift her eyes from Marco.

Much as Mac wanted to kick the living shit out of the man for hurting her, he wasn't going to let her add a third to today's body count. "We need to get out of here," he said. "The cops'll be here any minute."

She didn't waver, and neither did the gun in her hand, gripped so tightly her knuckles turned white.

"Do not trust this man, Samantha," Marco said. "He doesn't know who you are."

She flicked a questioning glance at Mac.

"He's trying to manipulate you," Mac said.

"He doesn't know *what* you are, Samantha," Marco said.

Her indecision appeared to grow, worry lines creasing her forehead.

Mac knew he needed to gain her trust. If he proved he wasn't a threat to her, maybe she'd believe he really wasn't. Relaxing his stance, he tucked her gun at his lower back.

Alarm widened her eyes. "You didn't put the safety on."

"Shit." He fumbled the gun back out and peered at it. He had no flipping idea where the safety was.

"Behind the trigger," she said.

He spotted the tiny button and pushed it. "Got it. Thanks."

He gave a sheepish shrug as he restashed the gun at his lower back. "Guess it's kind of obvious that I'm not much of a bad guy if I don't even know how to work the safety."

When the tension in her shoulders relaxed some, he knew he'd said the exact right thing. "So . . . we should probably tie him up, right? So he can't follow us. We can use the cord from the window blinds." Been there, done that.

She nodded. "Get it."

While Mac attacked the blinds, Marco worked on Sam. "You're making a mistake, Samantha."

"Shut up." Her voice was low and lethal.

You tell him, Sam.

"There was an accident," Marco said, softer now, apparently shifting gears. "You were injured. That's why you don't remember."

She said nothing.

"Your name is Samantha West," Marco said. "You're a covert operative for the FBI."

She let out a choked, disbelieving laugh. "Right."

"Flinn Ford recruited you as a teenager. You've been working with him, with us, for several years. He's concerned about you."

"Is that why he sent a goon with a gun after me?"

"The weapon was to protect you."

Mac walked up with the cord dangling from his fingers. "So that's what you were doing when you pointed it at her. You were *protecting* her."

Marco's narrowed black eyes cut to him. "You don't know what you're dealing with. She's unpredictable in this condition."

"Yeah, well, she might not have her memory, but I have mine." Mac turned his attention to Sam, fine with it when she chose to keep her focus on Marco. "This Ford guy and his thugs tracked you down. They tried to kill us."

If possible, she went even paler. Mac didn't have to be psychic to know that she was confused about who to believe. "You are Sam *Trudeau*," he went on. "Your family lives in Lake Avalon, Florida. You have two sisters who love you and desperately miss you."

"You made a choice a long time ago, Agent West," Marco said. "Your family doesn't know what you've become. They wouldn't understand. They'd only—"

Mac took a step toward Marco, almost overwhelmed by the urge to punch or kick or otherwise strike the man. "You don't know squat about her family, so shut the hell up."

He reined in his temper and tried again to reason with Sam. "Look, just think about what's happened here. Why would I, a man who doesn't know where to find the safety on a gun, charge in here to save you from this guy who looks like some kind of mercenary? Isn't it obvious who's on your side?"

She hesitated for two more seconds, then thrust the gun at Mac, handle first. "Cover him. I'll tie him."

Mac exchanged the gun for the cord, relieved. Sam Trudeau was a smart woman.

"Get up," she said to Marco.

The other man awkwardly maneuvered his massive body out of the tub, swearing profusely. When he managed to get to his feet, he clamped a bloody hand around his upper arm, a muscle throbbing at his temple. "Flinn won't let you go. He'll hunt you down."

"Shut up," Mac snapped. "Do what she tells you to do and maybe you'll walk away from this."

Marco rolled his eyes. "Fucking amateur."

Silent, Sam steered him into the larger room, then dragged the chair away from the small desk. "Sit."

Marco obeyed, and she knelt behind the chair, all focus and concentration. The big man started swearing all over again when she angled his injured arm back to tie his hands, but her stony expression didn't change.

She's so cold, Mac thought. Even now, so vulnerable without her memory. He couldn't blame her. No way would he be all smiles and snarky comments in her situation. And then he realized Marco was watching him, a slight smile curling the corner of his mouth. Years of reporting experience had made Mac an ace at reading body language.

This guy had a plan.

"Be careful, Sam."

She didn't acknowledge Mac's repeated warning as she finished securing Marco's left ankle to the chair leg then moved behind him to double-check his wrists. She couldn't get her thoughts straight, couldn't focus on the facts. If this Flinn Ford really was her boss, shouldn't she trust—

Marco suddenly clamped cold fingers around her own, and she tumbled out of reality and into something else . . .

Pain rips through my arm, and the gunshot's echoes are deafening. He shot me. That prick shot *me! Fuck, it burns—and then I'm on my ass in the tub, fireworks shooting out of the top of my head—*

"Sam!"

She shot to her feet and fought the dizzying blackout wave, steadying herself with a hand on the back of the chair. When she focused on Mac, she saw that his face was whiter than before, eyes wide and questioning and so very blue.

She put a hand over the sleeve of the flannel shirt and winced at the answering acid-burn of pain. What the hell happened? Had Mac shot her by mistake? But, no, he wasn't babbling apologies. She'd seen how he'd reacted after he'd shot Marco. He'd been white-faced and freaked. This man didn't take shooting someone, even accidentally, in stride. Besides, her sleeve sported no bullet hole. Yet, she felt the unmistakable trickle of blood making its way down her arm.

"Sam, are you okay? Are you with me?"

Mac again. Demanding and panicked.

She would have nodded, but a surge of pain behind her eyes stopped her.

Mac moved toward her. Wrapping his fingers around her wrist, he gently turned her hand palm down.

Instead of the pain she'd expected, fear flashed through her, along with an image of herself cornered in the bathroom by Marco. No, not *her* fear. That was Mac's point of view, Mac's fear . . . how was that even possible? How could she know so intimately what *he* had felt and seen then?

"You're bleeding."

She heard the horror in his voice, had just a glimpse of the streams of blood flowing over the back of her hand, before the room slipped again, into another memory that wasn't hers.

"I'm an intelligence operative. The man we left tied up at the cabin is Flinn Ford. He's my boss at N3."

I knew it. I knew she was a spy. "N3?"

"National Neural Network. It's a secret division of the FBI. The agents have psychic abilities."

"A secret division of the FBI with psychic operatives?" Okay, not a spy. She's nuts. Crackers. Totally whack. And she actually thinks she can fool me. *"How gullible do you think I am? I'm the epitome of the grizzled old newspaper reporter. Without the grizzled and old parts."*

"Flinn impregnated a fellow N3 operative named Zoe Harris. I think he's trying to create some kind of super psychic spy by combining the DNA of two N3 empaths."

CHAPTER **EIGHTEEN**

Mac knelt at Sam's side on the floor, alarmed at how quickly her eyes had rolled back before she'd dropped. He'd never seen anyone pass out before, and it was heart-stopping.

After another glance at Marco to make sure he was indeed secured, Mac turned his full attention on Sam. He checked for the pulse at her throat, relieved to find it strong and even.

What was he supposed to do now? Carry her out of here? Go on the run with a woman who didn't remember she was a spy? A *psychic* spy. A *trigger-happy* psychic spy.

Jesus. This was more bizarre than any episode of *The Twilight Zone*.

Her eyes fluttered open, and she instantly winced.

He shifted to block the light streaming through the window from hitting her in the face, inordinately relieved to have her back. "You okay?"

She blinked several times, apparently having a tough time focusing.

Mac set aside the gun, though he kept it well within reach, and went to work rolling up the sleeve of her shirt. The sleeve that had no bullet hole in it, yet she bled as if she'd been shot.

She didn't protest but pressed the heel of her free hand to the center of her forehead with a low moan.

The muscles in his chest clenched. "Headache?"

She gave a barely perceptible nod.

"Did you hit it when you fell?"

"I don't think so."

He checked her arm. Blood smeared over her pale skin, and he grimaced at the mess—and metallic scent—while his stomach did several flips. The whole time, she lay still, her breath hitching every few seconds.

He hated that he could do nothing for her pain and did his best to be gentle as he sought the source of blood. It didn't take him long to find the small, round puncture. He shifted himself, rather than her arm, and found the matching wound on the backside of her arm. It was uglier and messier than its twin.

He sat back on his heels. How the hell did a bullet pass through her arm without also passing through her sleeve?

"We have to go."

She was right. Why the cops weren't already pounding down the door, he had no idea. Probably budget cuts. Or maybe the sound of gunshots wasn't unusual in this part of town.

First things first: He had to stop the bleeding.

Pushing to his feet, he headed for the bathroom, where he grabbed a hand towel. Back at Sam's side, he wrapped the towel around her arm and tucked the ends down between the fabric and the uninjured part of her arm. It wasn't perfect, but it would do until he had time to tend to it properly.

She grasped his arm, her grip strong despite the clamminess of her skin. "Help me up."

He steadied her as she swayed to her feet. She looked sick, like she might keel over any second. "Are you—"

"I'm fine. Let's go."

CHAPTER **NINETEEN**

Are you sure taking the Suburban was a good idea?" Mac asked.

"Yes." Sam's fingers nimbly accessed the navigation menu. "If he escapes his bonds, he'll still be stuck without transportation."

That made sense. Assuming the guy didn't just commandeer someone else's ride. But that would take time, Mac reasoned. So, regardless of what Marco managed to do, they still had a head start.

He relaxed a fraction. That was when his hands, clamped tight around the steering wheel, started shaking. Reaction had set in.

In the course of an hour, he'd pointed a gun at one man's head and shot another. The unfamiliar acrid, burned scent of his shirt—the smell of gunpowder—turned his stomach. He'd *shot* a man. Not dead. But he still wanted to pull over and throw up. At least he'd hit the guy in the arm instead of the head or chest.

Determined not to think about it, he glanced at the navi screen. He was impressed that even though Sam didn't know who she was, she still knew how to work the menus.

"Where are we going?" he asked.

"We're heading south on Commerce. Pick up Highway 55 east."

"Toward Washington? Shouldn't we keep to the country?"

"I need to find a place to hole up until dark," she said.

"We."

"What?"

"*We* need to find a place to hole up until dark."

She didn't nod or correct herself, and Mac got that she was already making plans to ditch him. "About sixty miles from here," she said, "there's a Metro station."

He nodded. "The DC subway. Perfect. And then what?"

"You drop me off and go home."

"Easier said than done. I don't live around here, and my plane ticket home isn't good until next week."

"Then you'll figure something out. It's not my problem."

He glanced sideways at her. "Thing is, you're kind of my problem."

"They won't go after you. They want me."

"Do you even know who 'they' are?"

"It doesn't matter. They're not after you."

Instead of continuing to argue with her, he pulled into a new neighborhood that had dirt for lawns and a freshly paved road. Most of the homes lining the street were still being built, and he could practically smell the new wood, vinyl siding and fresh paint.

She tensed in her seat, sitting up straighter. "Where are you going?"

"I'm finding a place to park so I can clean up your arm."

"I don't think—"

"The Suburban has tinted windows. No one can see in."

"We need to keep moving."

"We left Super Mario back there without any transpo. And he doesn't know which way we went. We can take ten minutes to prevent you from getting a nasty infection."

Her eyebrow ticked up, and he glanced away, surprised at how he already knew what that slight change in her expression meant: *What the hell are you talking about?* Even more surprised at the clench in his gut that could mean only one thing: He was starting to care about her. Not just her safety or getting her home in one piece. He was starting to really *care*. A flush started creeping up his neck.

"Super Mario?" she asked.

"Just trying to deal," he said, more or less under his breath.

Spotting a two-story home with stone accents, a two-car garage and a FOR SALE sign in the yard, he steered the SUV into the pristine concrete driveway and killed the engine. "There. We're just here to check out the real estate."

He snagged the bag of medical supplies from where he'd dropped them on the floorboard. As he fished out the bandages, surgical tape and hydrogen peroxide, he tried not to think about how he was about to treat this woman for yet another bullet wound—one that he had no idea how she'd received.

She sat still and quiet, head resting against the seatback, while he turned in the driver's seat and began to unwind the towel he'd wrapped around her arm. The metallic scent of blood filled the truck and, swallowing against the surge of bile in his throat, he folded the towel so that a clean, blood-free portion was visible. He drenched that part with hydrogen peroxide.

"This is going to sting," he said.

"I can handle it."

Of course she could.

"How's the headache?" he asked.

"Still there."

"The same or worse?"

"It's starting to let up."

He could tell by the pinched look around her eyes that she was lying. Her headache was massive. Not that there was anything he could do about it.

He went to work on what he *could* do—cleaning up her injured arm. Three swipes into it, he realized his mind was about to be blown.

Her skin under the blood was unmarked. Not a bullet wound in sight.

What the fuck? He'd *seen* it. Hadn't he? Or had he seen what he'd expected to see? But, no, there'd been no mistaking the double wounds. And, besides, there was *blood*.

As if alerted by his stillness, she rolled her head toward him. "What?"

"Uh . . . you tell me."

Frowning, she angled her head to peer down at her clean upper arm. "Oh."

"Oh? That's all you've got?"

Her forehead creased, and she rubbed at it. "Memory's gone, remember?"

"But you get that this isn't normal, right?"

"And up until now, everything that's happened has been normal?"

"Okay, you've got me there. But you did have a bullet wound right here, didn't you? I didn't imagine it."

"It felt like a bullet wound."

"And you're an expert. Considering." He cocked his head. "Maybe I should check your shoulder."

A roll of said shoulder put three vertical creases above the bridge of her nose. "That's still there. I can feel it."

"Does that make sense to you?"

"None of this makes sense." She leaned back in the seat with a weary sigh. "I'm a spy." She said it with a hint of exhausted wonder.

"A *psychic* spy. And, yet, you don't seem all that concerned."

"It sounds too ridiculous."

He laughed softly. At least he wasn't the only one who found everything that was happening unbelievable. "So . . . why hole up until after dark?"

"It's easier to swipe a car at an auto-repair shop. Many leave the keys in the cars for customers who are picking them up after office hours."

"Funny how you know all these tricks, and your way around Washington, despite having no memory."

"Yeah, funny. I'm going to sleep off this headache now."

He watched her eyes slip closed and couldn't suppress the urge to reach out and lightly sweep some stray hair behind her ear. Her skin felt warm and smooth under his fingertips. "I'll be here when you wake up."

He didn't realize until he was backing out of the driveway that he'd just touched her, skin-on-skin, repeatedly, and nothing had happened, no psychic trip into his head as she'd promised.

"Not so empathic after all, are you?" he murmured.

Unbidden, her earlier statement echoed in his head: *I'm a spy.*

His stomach did that free-fall thing where it felt as though he'd taken a running leap off a very tall cliff. She must have taken a hike through his head and hadn't realized it.

Otherwise, how could she know she was a spy?

CHAPTER **TWENTY**

As Flinn sliced through the cords binding Marco's wrists, he winced at the pungent odor of blood—and ground his teeth together to suppress his anger. He should have been taking Samantha into custody right now, not freeing this dimwit. Yet, he couldn't very well chew the man out. It wasn't that long ago when Marco had had to cut through Flinn's bonds after Samantha and Hunter got the drop on him.

Freed, Marco got to his feet and gave the chair a violent kick. It crashed into the radiator, then landed on its side.

Flinn smirked. So the he-man wasn't so stoic after all. "Feel better?"

"No, sir."

"I'm shocked Hunter was able to even hit you."

"It was a lucky shot, sir. Still going to rip him apart next time I see him. Sir."

Flinn flashed his most approving smile. Maybe the guy wasn't all that bad. "Permission to proceed granted."

Marco gave a grim nod. "Thank you, sir."

Flinn's phone vibrated in his inside jacket pocket. He fished it out and checked the display, pleased to see his favorite research assistant was calling. He flipped the phone open. "Natalie, tell me what you've got on this Mac Hunter."

He listened to the brisk shuffle of papers in the background. "He moved to Lake Avalon, Florida, almost three years ago from Philadelphia. Both parents deceased. One remaining family member: younger sister, Jennifer, freshman at Florida State. Hunter has been her legal guardian for the past dozen years. He's a journalist at the *Lake Avalon Gazette*."

The red flag he'd expected started an insistent wave. A media type finding out about N3 would be bad. Very bad.

"He seems like an all-around good guy, sir," Natalie said, a wistful tone in her voice, as though she wanted to date him.

"We can't have a journalist knowing anything about N3."

"Surely Sam would know better than to—"

"She has no control over what she does or doesn't tell him right now. He already knows too much." He paused, rubbing his palm over the top of his head. "You said Philadelphia? Any remaining family ties there?"

"None that I've found, sir."

"Friends?"

"I've run his cell phone and landline numbers, checked his e-mail. He appears to have no close contacts in Philadelphia. He exchanges calls and e-mails most often with his co-workers in Lake Avalon. Sam's sisters are among his closest contacts."

"Is she mentioned in any of his e-mails?"

"Not that I saw, sir."

"Maybe in a way that could be code?"

"I'd have to study the e-mails. What exactly would I be looking for?"

"I want to know whether Samantha knew Hunter would be at the cabin and vice versa."

"For what purp—" She stopped. "You think Sam was planning to go rogue like Zoe did?"

"Just take a second look for me."

"Of course, sir. Right—"

A beep overlapped the last word, and Flinn checked the caller ID. Andrea Leigh. Shit. "I have to go. Andrea's calling. You're sure you've kept this all under the radar?"

"Most definitely, sir. I haven't breathed a word to anyone, and I've been using my personal laptop."

"Excellent work, Natalie. I'm going to reward you when this is all over."

"Thank you, sir." Her pleased flush all but bled over the airwaves.

Flinn switched over to the assistant director's call. "Hello, Andrea. How may I help you?"

"I've been waiting for you to update me on Agent West."

"I'm sorry I haven't gotten back to you sooner. I'm in pursuit."

"Perhaps this has become a bigger problem. Do I need to alert the director?"

"Not yet. We need to tread lightly. A civilian is involved." He kept the journalist part to himself. No reason to alarm the boss just yet.

"Fine. But keep me informed. I don't like playing catch-up."

"Will do." He kept his annoyance at her commanding tone firmly in check.

A click answered him, and he lowered the phone, his thumb on the "end call" button. He had to concentrate to keep from clenching his jaw so hard his teeth hurt.

Bitch wouldn't be so high and mighty once he had all the power and she had nothing.

CHAPTER **TWENTY-ONE**

"Sam? Hey, Sam. Want to wake up for a minute?"

She had to fight to open her eyes and keep them that way. Where was she? Who was she? "What?"

"We're changing cars."

She focused on the face in front of her—handsome, with greenish brown eyes and dimples that deepened as he gave her a reassuring smile. Mac Hunter. He was unhooking her seat belt.

She looked around, trying to get oriented.

She'd been so deeply asleep that she had no idea where they were or what time it was or what they were doing in a crowded parking lot.

"Where are we?" she asked.

"We're switching cars."

She looked around again. "This isn't—"

"Don't worry, I've got it covered. All you have to do is get into the new car." He got out and walked around to her side.

Too sluggish to argue—all she wanted to do was sleep—she obediently exited when he opened her door. With his hand light at her elbow, his fingers barely making contact with the fabric of the flannel shirt, he steered her into a silver sedan. Within seconds, it seemed, he had her belted in and was spreading his leather jacket over her.

"Go back to sleep," Mac murmured. "Everything's fine."

She snuggled into the comforting scent of leather and Mac and shut her eyes, letting the world around her dissolve into something else . . .

The electrical current arced through her body, hard and fast, turning muscles rigid and bowing her back off the mattress. She fought the restraints at her wrists and ankles, just barely managing to suppress a moan as her vision whited out and a buzz grew in her ears. She was dimly aware of two men standing on either side of her, one in a white doctor's coat—Dr. Toby Ames—and the other in a standard dark suit reminiscent of the kind Fox Mulder wore on The X-Files. *Flinn Ford. Her boss.*

And while she couldn't focus in on them, or see their expressions, she sensed their intense interest. She was their science experiment. N3 operative Samantha West—new life, new name—a butterfly pinned to corkboard.

In the distance, she heard one of them say, "Now."

Cool fingers brushed over her forearm almost reverently, and everything around her instantly shifted into another time, another life that wasn't her own.

Hooray! Daddy's home from work early!

I jump up from my Legos—wait till Daddy sees the helicopter I made!—and run for the stairs. I'm careful on the steps, just like Mommy always says, one hand on the railing as I force myself to walk. But it's hard. Daddy never gets home from work early. Mommy says that's because he works too hard.

At the bottom of the stairs, I can see him in the kitchen. He's still wearing his coat, the long, black one that makes him look like a spy from one of those old movies he and Mommy like to watch. "Daddy!"

He doesn't hear me, because he's suddenly shouting at Mommy. I stop in the hallway and lean against the wall to watch and listen. Daddy's pacing and yelling. I don't like it when he yells. It scares me. He's been yelling a lot lately. And moping. At least, that's what Mommy calls it when I'm Mr. Cranky Pants.

"It wasn't enough that the bastard ran the company into the ground, but now he's taking me down with him!"

Mommy sets aside her dish towel and moves toward him,

her hand raised to touch his arm. "Slow down, honey. What-ever's happened now, we'll work it out. We've been okay so far."

He smacks her hand away.

I take a step back, my tummy starting to gurgle, the way it does when I'm upset. I should go back upstairs, but I stay by the wall. Mommy might need me.

"You're not getting it!" Daddy shouts into her face. "Not only have we lost everything—my job, my pension, our life savings, the house—but now he's putting the blame on me. It's my word against his, and he's set everything up so it looks like I'm the one who had access to the offshore accounts and looted the company. Do you know what that means? It means prison, Jackie. Prison for me, welfare and food stamps for you and Flinnie."

He stops and braces his hands on the counter. I think he's crying. That scares me more than the yelling. Daddies aren't supposed to cry.

"It's over," he says in a sad voice. "It's all over."

He reaches inside his coat and takes something out as he turns back toward Mommy.

Mommy makes that face she made that one time I was run-ning down the stairs toward her and tripped. It was kind of funny afterward, but now it's not. Now it's scary.

Mommy takes a step toward Daddy, reaching out with her hands, and he says, "I love you, Jackie."

Then there's a loud noise, like one of those booms that fire-works make when they explode in the sky. And Mommy falls backward against the cupboards. Something's on the front of her flowery blue shirt. Something that looks like cherry syrup.

She falls to the floor. "Mommy!"

I'm running toward her, yelling her name. She doesn't look right. She looks sick, like she's going to throw up any second.

"Mommy!"

She sees me and starts shaking her head. "No, Flinnie, no. Go to . . . your . . . room."

I fall to my knees beside her. She pushes me away with a cherry syrup–covered hand. "Go to your . . . room. Now."

I look up at Daddy, confused. Why isn't he helping Mommy? She needs help!

Daddy stands over me. He looks mad and sorry at the same time. Sort of like that time he came home from work and Mommy made him spank me because I'd been bad.

"Flinnie," he says. "I love you."

He holds out the thing he held out to Mommy. It looks like a—

GUN!

"No!" Mommy screams and grabs at my shoulders, pushing me down, shoving me to the floor as she rolls over on top of me.

That noise bangs again, and Mommy flinches against me. A burning pain stabs into my side, and I start to cry.

Another bang, followed by a heavy thump. Out of the corner of my eye, I see Daddy on the floor beside me and Mommy. He's not moving.

"Mommy?"

She's not moving, either. Her weight on my back is so heavy I can't budge. I realize her nose is pressed against my cheek, and I strain to turn my head so I can see her face.

"Mommy?"

Her eyes are open and staring.

I think she's dead.

Oh, no, oh, no.

I start screaming. "Mommy! Mommy!"

She fell out of the memory that wasn't hers, back onto the bed in Dr. Ames' lab. Back to the scene of the science experiment and the aftermath of an electrical current. Her side burned as though scorched by a fireball, and she shifted restlessly, clenching her fists against the pain and restraints, against her reality. Oh, God, she hated her life.

"Samantha?" A hand gripped her shoulder, gave her a slight shake. "Samantha, can you hear me?"

She knew that voice, knew it belonged to the man whose childhood memory had just blown her world apart. Flinnie.

She squeezed her eyes more tightly closed, not ready to open them, not ready to acknowledge what she'd seen, what he'd experienced as a child. His unrelenting, cold focus made sense to her now. He'd pursued law enforcement as a career to seek justice, to take down crooks like the one who'd destroyed his family.

"Come now, Samantha," Flinn said, patient as always. "We need you to open your eyes and talk to us."

"What the hell—is that blood?" Dr. Ames sounded alarmed.

Hands lifted her top from where it lay against her belly. The cotton material clung for a moment, wet and sticky. "Holy mother of God," Dr. Ames murmured.

Flinn's hand on her shoulder tightened. "What is it? What's wrong?"

"She's got a wound here, a deep furrow, like she was grazed by a bullet. How the hell did that happen? Was she injured when you brought her in?"

"No. She was fine. Besides, you would have noticed when you hooked up the electrodes."

"Where exactly did she go in your head?"

"I tried to direct her to a time I fell out of a tree as a kid."

"Was someone shooting at you at the time?"

"No," Flinn snapped. "I was a child." *He paused a moment, then breathed a low* "Fuck" *in dazed realization.*

"What?" Dr. Ames asked as he pressed a soft pad to the pain in her side.

She flinched at the pressure, releasing a protesting whimper. She yearned to push them both away so she could turn onto her side, curl around the pain and sink into a deep, dreamless sleep. She wouldn't even care if she never woke up. All she wanted was sleep.

"She carried the aftermath of the memory into her own reality," Flinn said.

"What?" Dr. Ames sounded annoyed.

"The electrical shock . . . we expected it would enhance her psychic ability, but this is far beyond anything I ever *imagined. Not only did she relive a moment in my history, but she physically bears the scars."*

"You're telling me she's exhibiting a wound that you received in the past?" The doctor's incredulity couldn't have been more apparent. "That's . . . unbelievable." The pad pressed to her side lifted. "The bleeding is slowing."

"Have you seen anything like it with the others?" Flinn's voice faded as he paced away.

"No, never. It's . . . remarkable." Paper shuffled, as though the doctor flipped through a medical chart. "Agent West's potential is staggering. When do you plan to send her into the field?"

"She's only nineteen," Flinn said, sounding defensive. "She still needs months of training, maybe more. And you'll need time to figure out a way to suppress this . . . psychosomatic reaction. We can't have her bearing other people's injuries while on assignment."

"That will require more testing."

"Fine, whatever you need to do."

Sam forced her eyes open at that. More tests? No way in hell. She'd die first. The bright light overhead stabbed into her eyes, but she couldn't lift her hand to shield them. She curled her hands into fists and jerked against the restraints.

"Ah, here she is," Dr. Ames said.

She turned her head toward the voice and squinted at N3's doctor of psychic spying. He had red hair, pink skin that looked fresh-scrubbed and a thick layer of freckles that disappeared into his hairline. A grown-up Opie with all his hair.

He shined a penlight into one eye and then the other, sending twin spears of pain into her brain. "How do you feel, Agent West?"

She tried to moisten her lips, but her mouth was impossibly dry.

"Agent West?" he repeated. "Can you tell me how you feel?"

"Headache," she murmured.

He made a note in her chart. "Tell me what you saw."

She shifted her gaze to Flinn and had to swallow against

the choking sensation that rose with the memory of his terror. Her *memory* now. His childhood tragedy was forever imbedded in her mind.

She strained against the leather cuffs at her wrists, wanting to scream, to just lose it and shriek until her voice gave out. She was tired, exhausted from being their guinea pig for whatever they cooked up—drugs, electrical shocks, sleep deprivation—to test the extent of her psychic ability. She couldn't take any more.

She implored Flinn with her eyes. "I want to go home. Please."

"You have to focus, Agent West," Dr. Ames said. "I need you to answer my questions."

She kept her gaze locked on Flinn's face. He was the one who'd brought her here. Maybe he could take her back. "Let me go to prison. I'll do my time. I just want to see my family."

Dr. Ames' blue eyes narrowed as they skewered Flinn. "Did you not explain to her that she can't have contact of any kind with her family?"

"What?" She tried to push herself up into a sitting position, dizzy and frustrated by her inability to move freely. "No, let me go. Please." God, she felt sick. Sick and tired and alone . . . so alone.

"Your past life is over, Samantha," Flinn said. "You're a federal agent now. Anonymity is key. That's the trade-off you made when you agreed to my proposition."

"I don't understand. You never said—"

"Every detail was spelled out in the contract you signed."

"I didn't have enough time to read the—"

"It doesn't matter now, Samantha. You signed it. You're legally bound by the federal government of the United States to adhere to the contract. That means no contact whatsoever with your family or friends from your past life. Samantha Trudeau no longer exists."

Sam opened her eyes to the dark of night, the *swish-thump* of windshield wipers and the hum of tires on wet pavement. For a moment, she kept still, assessing the situation before giving away her consciousness. Her shoulder throbbed, and a thick, aching fuzziness filled her head. The dream—or perhaps a flashback, considering its vivid reality—was already evaporating like cold water on hot asphalt, wisping into the air before she could grasp all of its meaning.

She remembered another dizzying rush of information, the one that had flooded her mind back in that dingy motel room. Much of it rushed through her again, a cacophony of memories that made no sense. Many of them, along with the flashback just now, terrified her.

"I'm an intelligence agent. The man we left tied up at the cabin is Flinn Ford. He's my boss at N3."

"N3?"

"National Neural Network. It's a secret division of the FBI. The agents have psychic abilities."

She shut her eyes and willed the panic to subside. She was a spy. A *psychic* spy. With no memory. And a man named Flinn Ford, her boss, wanted her dead.

Why? And . . . *really*? Psychic? Psychotic sounded easier to accept.

"Flinn impregnated a fellow N3 operative named Zoe Harris. I think he's trying to create some kind of super psychic spy by combining the DNA of two N3 empaths."

She searched her memory for Zoe Harris and came up empty. She couldn't even feel grief that the woman had been killed. She remembered telling Mac that Zoe had a sister and that Zoe would have wanted her to do . . . something. She didn't know what. Warn her, most likely. Her memory of that flood of information yielded no name for Zoe's sister.

Damn it.

She'd obviously tried to tell Mac as much as she could about her situation, to try to orient herself after she lost her memory, to give herself enough information to go on. The attempt had failed. The images came through so fragmented, so overwhelming, mixed with liberal doses of Mac's disbelief and anxiety, that very little of the mess made sense to her. Who was this Sledge? How could he help her? And if her boss at the FBI wanted her dead, did that make her a good guy or a bad guy?

She had no idea where to begin.

She searched her memory, as fragile and insubstantial as cotton candy, and got nowhere. When her temples began to pulse with pain, she gave up the effort and decided to focus on the present.

She knew this much: She was in a car. A new one, judging by the new-car smell.

A man sat next to her. A man with a clean scent that reminded her of the fresh rain that streamed in rivulets down the passenger-side window. She was warm and toasty, under the spread of a leather jacket that carried the same scent as the man in the driver's seat.

Security.

Perhaps a false sense of it.

With no memory, how would she know if she was safe?

She thought of another face, a face that she somehow knew belonged to the leather jacket. Warm, greenish brown eyes, at once concerned and quizzical. Dimples that deepened along with a self-deprecating smile. A light stubble of dark beard that shadowed a strong jaw. A rich voice that resonated with both humor and resolve. Broad shoulders and muscular arms that promised to catch her when things spiraled out of control.

Mac Hunter.

A name and face that promised safety despite the lies he'd told her the first time she'd awakened to him. Interesting that his presence next to her in the car somehow reassured her, yet she knew next to nothing about him. And she sure wasn't going to find out anything by playing possum.

She shifted straighter in her seat and brushed the hair out of her eyes. "Where are we?"

"Oh, hey," Mac said, glancing sideways at her and grinning. "You slept a long time."

His smile, both eager and relieved, warmed her. She could do this. "How long?"

"Six hours."

Had they been driving the entire time? "Where are we?"

"Middle of South Carolina. I've been keeping to the back roads to avoid the interstate."

Good idea, she thought, and wondered whether he'd made that choice on his own or because she'd told him to do that before she'd lost her memory.

Then something else about the car registered. It wasn't the Suburban she remembered from before. "This is a different car."

"I switched while you were out. Made a stop at a restaurant that has valet parking and swiped a set of keys when the valet's podium was unmanned. Smooth, huh?"

And much more likely to have the cops on their tails sooner rather than later, especially once Flinn tracked the Suburban's GPS to its location. Damn it, why hadn't Mac followed her instructions to take a car from an auto-repair shop after closing time?

"Disconnected the battery on the Suburban," he said. "Figured that would disable the GPS, buy us a little more time."

Oh. Okay. She couldn't deny the good thinking there.

"Switched the plates, too. This is a silver Camry. There's about a billion of them on the road. So far, so good, I think, considering no one's bothered us for six hours."

Satisfied, and impressed, she let her muscles relax some, feeling as though she could melt into the comfortable seat and drift off for another six hours. God, she hurt. Everything ached. Her head, her shoulder. A spot between her shoulder blades itched, and a roll of her shoulders pulled at the tape of a smaller bandage there. What was that from?

"You must be starving," Mac said. "How about we stop at the next diner and get some food? I could use some time to stretch my legs."

She gave him a distracted nod, though food didn't make the top five of her priorities at the moment. "Where are we going?"

"Lake Avalon, Florida."

"Home," she said at the same time she thought it. An automatic response?

"You remember that Lake Avalon is home?" Mac asked, surprised. "That's a good sign."

Her stomach twisted with uneasiness, and she frowned. Shouldn't the thought of home evoke a warm and fuzzy sensation? Yet her instincts started screaming at her as urgently as a storm-warning siren. She'd just had a flashback in which Flinn Ford told her she could have no contact whatsoever with her family or friends.

Samantha Trudeau no longer exists.

"We can't go to Lake Avalon," she said. "It's not safe."

"We've been on the road for hours, Sam, and no one's looked at us twice. I think we're in the clear."

"He'll go to Lake Avalon and wait for me there."

"So we won't go anywhere in Lake Avalon that he expects us to go."

"But—"

"Look, we can't avoid this guy on our own. I'm not a government agent, and you don't have your memory. We need help, Sam."

She rubbed at the center of her forehead. Think. She had to *think*. A name came to her from her frantic words to Mac before she'd lost her memory. "What about Sledge?"

Mac glanced askance at her, one eyebrow sharply arched. "You remember?"

"No, but I . . . yes. Maybe. I'm not sure. It's all a jumble in my head. Not a whole lot of it makes sense right now."

Mac was silent a long moment before he responded. "Before you lost your memory, you told me you have a psychic ability. You said you can touch me and . . . and tap into my memories or my past or something. You said it all so fast, I can't remember it all. You said it worked through skin-on-skin contact."

She nodded. "I remember that from what I saw earlier. It was a kind of . . . flashback or something. It was like I was you, and you were listening to me tell you . . ." She trailed off, as though sorting through the memory again. "It was overwhelming."

"Is that why you passed out? Because that scared the bejesus out of me."

"Probably. The memory rushed into my head too fast. It was like my brain couldn't keep up." She paused, remembering his reaction in the flashback. "You thought I was nuts."

"I wouldn't go using the past tense on that just yet."

"But I do have this ability. I did tap into your memory. That's how I remembered the name Sledge."

"You didn't tell me who that is. You just said the name. Does it mean anything to you?"

"No, but I obviously thought he could help since I told you about him."

"So how do we reach him?" Mac asked.

"I don't know."

"That's probably not even his real name. How many people do you know named Sledge?"

"At least one."

His lips curved into an amused smile. "Doesn't help."

"I just don't think Lake Avalon is the place to go."

"That's where your family is. And they're very well connected when it comes to law enforcement. Both your sisters are involved with cops."

"No. Flinn will use them against me." She knew this with certainty, even as the thought of home created a sharp clutch of longing in the center of her chest.

"He can do that whether we go there or not," Mac said. "In fact, he's probably already making plans."

She shot him an alarmed glance.

He gave a helpless shrug. "Just saying. It seems like his style."

"I think it'd be best if you dropped me off somewhere and took a vacation in Montana or Canada."

"No. No way. You need me, Sam. I'm not leaving you."

"Why? What . . ." She shook her head, at a loss. "Why are you doing this? I mean nothing to you."

It took him several seconds to respond. Finally, he said, "I promised your sister."

"You—What?" Her pulse began to throb in her ears.

"While you were out of it, I called Charlie. I promised her I'd get you home in one piece."

"You . . . you *called* Charlie? From the motel?"

"No, no, of course not. And not from my cell, either. I bought a prepaid phone at the drugstore. One of those untraceable kinds."

"They're *not* untraceable. Yes, your name and information aren't associated with a specific phone, but the calls can still be traced from the other end."

The car slowed as he lifted his foot off the gas. "What? No. No, they're not traceable. I'm sure of it."

"I'm a spy. Don't you think I know how this stuff works?"

"Well, there is the memory thing."

"I didn't forget this."

"I just thought—"

"You thought wrong. Your name isn't connected to the phone. But your location *is*. All Flinn had to do was keep tabs on my sisters' lines in case I called them for help then have the call traced from their end to my location."

"Shit. That's how the son of a bitch found us in Front Royal."

She glanced out the side window, too tired to sustain her irritation at his inability to follow simple directions. She probably hadn't given him enough information in the first place. She'd most likely said: Don't use *your* cell phone. And he hadn't.

"I'm sorry," he said. "I—Jesus, I'm sorry."

She closed her eyes. Why did she feel as though she'd just kicked a puppy? A really cute and cuddly one. One that smelled . . . heavenly. Like leather and fresh rain and . . . hunky man. She couldn't squelch her urge to ease his anxiety. "We survived."

"That asshole got his hands on you. If I hadn't been an idiot . . ."

"There's no point in beating yourself up about it. Let's focus on finding a place to stop. We can figure out our next move while we get something to eat."

His shoulders sagged in the dim light of the car. "Okay. Sure. That sounds like a plan I can live with."

She realized a moment later what she'd just done: She'd

responded in a way that implied that they were indeed in this together. "We *can figure out* our *next move*." When had she made the transition from "What am *I* going to do" to "What are *we* going to do"?

And was she handing a good man a death sentence?

CHAPTER **TWENTY-TWO**

The Garden City Diner in Orangeburg, South Carolina, was a brown-brick, A-frame building with a bright red roof made of Spanish tiles. Inside, a forest of tropical flowers, potted palms and ferns surrounded red vinyl booths and a long counter with cushioned metal stools.

The diner smelled of French fries and rich coffee, and Mac's stomach growled in anticipation of some low-country comfort food.

"I hope they have mac and cheese," he said as he slid across the bench seat in a corner booth. "The baked kind with crunchy stuff on top like Paula Deen makes. And don't even bother to rib me about a guy named Mac wanting some mac and cheese."

When Sam didn't respond or sit, he glanced up. She stood beside the table, anxiety etching lines in her forehead.

"What?" he asked.

"Switch places with me."

"Why?"

"I need to see . . . everything."

Instead of arguing with her spy instincts, he switched to the opposing seat and watched her gracefully slide in across from him. With her back to the wall, she quickly scanned their surroundings, evidently searching for possible threats among the other customers ordering up or devouring late-night snacks. It was a hell of a way to live.

The waitress, a middle-aged black woman in tight faded jeans and a pink T-shirt that displayed the words *"life is good"* on her ample breasts, ambled over. "Howdy, folks. Welcome to the Garden City. I'm Roz. Coffee?"

Mac smiled at her. "Please. Fully leaded."

"Water, please," Sam said.

While the waitress splashed steaming coffee into Mac's cup, Sam continued stalking the other patrons with her eyes. The glimpse Mac had gotten as they'd walked in had revealed a couple of trucker-looking guys chowing down at the counter, an elderly couple quietly arguing as they shared a piece of coconut cream pie and a pair of leather-clad biker dudes tearing through matching mounds of fried catfish and hush puppies. Almost all of them paid more attention to the TV in the corner, tuned to a reality show he didn't recognize, than to their respective companions.

"What do you see?" Mac asked.

Sam blinked before focusing on him with guarded eyes. "What? Nothing."

"What are you looking for then?"

"I don't know. I guess I'd know it if I saw it." She scanned the diner again, this time finding something she sought. As she slid out of the booth, she said, "I'm going to the ladies' room. If the waitress returns, I'll have a salad. Whatever they have."

He wondered whether he should follow. What if she slipped out the back door and took off on her own? Of course, if she did, there wasn't much he could do about it. If he tried to stop her, he had no doubt she could put him down with one karate chop. Or tae kwon do chop. If tae kwon do had such moves. He had no idea. And what did it matter?

Jesus, he was so wiped he could barely function.

When Roz returned with Sam's water, Mac said, "I can go ahead and order for us."

Roz took out her pad and pen. "Ready when you are, hon." Her drawl was low and gravelly.

"I'll have the shrimp and grits with side orders of hush puppies and mac and cheese. My friend will have the double bacon cheeseburger with everything, French fries, onion rings and the biggest chocolate shake you can make."

Roz smirked. "I heard her say she wants a salad."

Mac leaned toward her and lowered his voice to a conspiratorial level. "But she *needs* a cheeseburger. Don't you think she's too skinny?"

"Honey, every white woman on God's green earth would kill for that girl's body."

"Well, I happen to like a little junk in the trunk."

Roz threw her head back and laughed, sending her breasts into a vibrating jig. Her dark brown eyes twinkled. "Then we'll get your sweetie fattened up in no time."

She continued to chuckle as she made her way back to the kitchen with a relaxed sway of her rounded hips.

Sam returned from the restroom, her appearance a sharp contrast to Roz's healthy glow. Her skin stretched taut over her cheekbones, dark circles highlighting the pallor of her complexion. She'd pulled her dark hair into a tidy ponytail, which emphasized the sharpness of her collarbones and the honed angles of her jawline. She appeared so much more thin now, as though the drug that had stripped her of her memories had also stripped her of needed pounds.

Her sharp eyes scrutinized the other patrons again while her fingers began to pick apart the paper napkin holding her flatware.

"You can relax," Mac said after a full minute. "No one knows where we are."

Her steel blue eyes shifted to meet his, and he saw that her senses were jacked up as if she'd downed a double shot of sugar-laden espresso from Starbucks. Jesus, he thought, from sleep drunk to wired in the space of half an hour.

"How do we know each other?" she asked.

The question, blunt and out of nowhere, made him sit back. He had to resist the urge to squirm under her unflinching gaze. She must be one hell of an interrogator in her spy life.

"And don't lie this time," she added.

He picked up his coffee and took a slow sip, the whole time cognizant of her hyperalertness to his every move. Such riveted attention from such a strikingly beautiful woman unnerved him. He imagined she could undress him with just her shrewd gaze. And, for an unguarded moment, he wished she would. He wouldn't complain for one nanosecond about getting into bed naked with this woman . . . or getting up against a wall or on the floor or . . .

"Please stop trying to figure out how to answer and just tell me the truth."

He couldn't suppress a small smile. Wasn't thinking about the answer. Was thinking about sex. Hot, naked, sweaty sex with a spy.

He shifted to allow more room in the tightening crotch of his jeans. What the hell was *that* about? He wasn't some randy teenager drooling over his first *Sports Illustrated* swimsuit edition. No, Sam Trudeau was *way* hotter than any over-tanned, over-siliconed babe in a bikini.

Before he could summon the brainpower to respond, Roz returned with several plates of food.

Sam frowned at the burger and fries but said nothing. Her eyes widened as Roz set the chocolate shake in front of her. It was served in a Big Gulp–sized frosted glass with whipped cream and a cherry on top.

"Y'all need anything else for now?" Roz asked, her smile wide and sweet.

Mac waited for Sam to protest and insist on a piddly salad. Instead, she muttered, "Everything's fine. Thank you."

Roz shot Mac an exaggerated wink before waddling away.

Sam thumped her foot against Mac's shin under the table, and he yelped. "Ow, hey! What'd you do that for?"

"Don't flirt with her."

He grinned, enjoying the fire in her eyes. "Why? Jealous?"

"No, you idiot. She'll remember you."

He opened his mouth to tell her that was the most ridiculous thing he'd ever heard but then said nothing. Maybe she was right. She was the one with the spy skills, after all.

Sam nudged the shake toward him. "This must be yours."

He slid it back toward her. "Nope. Drink up. Eat up. You need fuel. You haven't eaten all day."

She glared down at the huge burger dripping with cheese, strips of bacon drooping over the sides under the crowning bun. "You heard me say I wanted a salad, right?"

"Heard you loud and clear." He dug into his shrimp and

grits and tried not to roll his eyes at how amazing they tasted. Creamy, salty goodness.

She picked up a French fry and sat back to nibble at it, leaving the burger untouched.

"You've got to be kidding me." He snagged a crispy onion ring off her plate. "Aren't you about to gnaw off a paw?"

"I'm used to going without when I'm on a mission."

"How do you know that? Do you remember starving on a specific mission?"

Her frown deepened, bringing out the three vertical lines above the bridge of her nose, but she said nothing.

Mac sampled a fry next. As it crunched between his teeth, he gave in. "If you really want a salad, I'll go ask Roz to bring you one." The last thing he wanted was to deprive the woman of at least *some* calories.

"You've already done enough to make certain she'll never forget us."

He shrugged as he drew the heaping bowl of baked mac and cheese closer to his plate. "I can't help it. I'm unforgettable."

She winced at that. The exact opposite reaction from the indulgent smile he'd been angling for. Damn, he hadn't meant to needle her about her amnesia. Time to change the subject. He could at least give her *something* she wanted. Answers.

"You asked how we know each other. I work with your sisters. Charlie and Alex. At the *Lake Avalon Gazette*. Does any of that ring a bell?"

The way she gazed back at him, unblinking, gave him her answer. Not one tiny ding.

"Your dad owns the paper. Or owned it, actually. Billionaire came in last year and bought him out of the newspaper. Relaunched the *Gazette* with a beefed-up staff and reduced space for advertising as a sort of test to see if the community would buy a newspaper not beholden to advertisers. So far, it's working." He paused when she reached for an onion ring. That looked promising. "Your dad's living for golf these days, and appears to love it."

"What do Charlie and Alex do at the paper?" Her features

softened as she asked, as though she somehow remembered shared affection with them.

"Charlie's a reporter. Damn good one, too. Alex is a photographer. Also kicks ass. They're the ones who talked me into going to your family's cabin for some R&R. That's actually where you and I met."

"So . . . no hiking accident." Her lips quirked at the memory of his lame cover story.

"I was trying to keep you from freaking out. You have to admit that the stuff you told me before you lost your memory was pretty unbelievable."

"But you believe it now, don't you?"

"I believe you're in trouble and that you need my help."

She nodded, as though she could accept his answer even if she didn't like it. "So what about my mother? You mentioned my dad and my sisters but nothing about my mom. Is she dead?"

"No," he said quickly. "Not at all." But he hesitated, unsure what to say. He barely knew Elise Trudeau. What he did know was that Charlie didn't talk about her mother. Alex didn't, either. He'd thought that was because they worked with their dad at the family paper, and so did Mac, so it was natural that their relationships would include their dad but not their mother. He suspected, though, that the issue went far deeper than that.

"Well?" Sam prodded.

"She's active in the community. Fund-raising, charity events, ladies who lunch, stuff like that."

Sam's expression turned shrewd. "You don't like her."

"I don't know her."

"What you do know, you don't like."

"I sense that she and Charlie don't have the best relationship. I suppose I feel protective."

"What about Alex? Does she get along with our mother?"

Mac thought about that for a moment. "I really don't know. Charlie never mentioned any issues between Alex and their mother."

"So you're . . . close to Charlie."

The way she said it, and the dawning understanding on her face, had him setting down his fork and scrambling to explain. "Whoa, wait. Don't go there. It's not like that."

"Yes, it is. I can tell by the way you say her name."

"Like hell you can tell."

"Your lips quirk. And your eyes . . . darken. Are you in love with her?"

"No."

She didn't respond. She just watched him, head slightly cocked.

"No," he said more firmly. Then, as she continued to pierce him with an I'm-taking-apart-your-soul-and-looking-inside stare, he sighed and pushed away his plate. "Yeah, fine. I was. But it was a year ago, and I'm over it. Besides, she's got the man of her dreams now, so even if I did have a thing for her, it's a moot point."

"Why do you feel so guilty about it? I'd understand regret or disappointment or even anger. But why guilt?"

A cold shaft of alarm caught him off guard. "What are you doing? Reading my mind? Because that's really uncool."

Her eyebrows arched in surprise. "No, of course not. I can't—"

"You're a psychic spy. Of course you can."

"I'm not that kind of psychic. I can sense your emotions. And I can read your face, your expressions."

"You're a human lie detector."

"I'm a trained government spy."

They both sat back when Roz approached with the coffee-pot to top off Mac's cup. "You folks about ready for dessert? We've got some delicious pecan pie, and the banana pudding's to die—" Noticing Sam's nearly untouched food, she cast a worried glance at Mac. "Might should I bring her a salad after all?"

"No," Sam said, and used both hands to pick up the huge sandwich. "I just haven't had a chance to dig in yet because we've been talking." She flashed an all-teeth smile and obediently took a large bite of burger.

Mac watched as she chewed, swallowed and went in for

another big bite. Maybe it was weird, but the flexing of her jaw muscles, the way her throat worked as she swallowed, were just about the sexiest things he'd ever seen.

"It's really good," Sam told the waitress, her mouth adorably full.

Also sexy, Mac thought.

"All righty then." Roz threw a little wave over her shoulder as she walked away. "You folks enjoy."

Mac couldn't stop himself from grinning. "Oh, she's going to remember you, whether you want her to or not."

She ignored his amusement and continued to eat.

He decided that even if she consumed only half the cheeseburger, he'd consider that a major win. Already, color was returning to her pale cheeks. He had to work to suppress a satisfied smile when she adjusted the straw in the chocolate shake then sucked her cheeks hollow getting her first taste of the thick ice cream. Jesus, was he horny or what? Because *that* was *definitely* the sexiest thing he'd ever seen.

To get a grip, he spent some quality time stirring his fork through his bowl of mac and cheese. What the hell was wrong with him? Yeah, okay, he was tired. Tired and whipped and freaked out. And of course the spy was distracting. How could she not be? She wasn't like anyone he'd ever met, let alone any *woman* he'd ever met. In fact, he couldn't remember a time when he'd ever wondered idly how a particular woman would look in black leather. He imagined hip-hugging leather pants and a laced-up bustier that pushed the goods together and up, just waiting for a—

The thought stalled when he realized Sam had stopped eating, her attention riveted on the TV in the corner.

Mac twisted in the booth to take a look. The reality show had ended, yielding to an eleven o'clock newscast. At the moment, a publicity shot of a silver-haired, craggy-faced man with bushy eyebrows flashed on the screen.

"Who is that?" Sam asked.

Mac faced her. She'd abandoned her burger and shake, and he weighed the idea of trading information for every extra bite she took. He decided against it when her gaze, cold and intense, met his. Earlier, he'd considered her every gesture sexy as hell. This look, however, was just plain lethal.

"That's Arthur Baldwin," he said. "Ponzi scheme extraordinaire. Why?"

"I know him."

CHAPTER **TWENTY-THREE**

I really think this is a bad idea," Mac said as he followed Sam back to the stolen Camry. The woman could book when focused on a mission. "We don't know how you know him. What if he's got Flinn Ford on speed dial?"

"This man can tell me more about who I am. He can help."

"You don't know that. I mean, this guy isn't your stereo-typical Southern gentleman. He's kind of a rat bastard, if you ask me."

She paused in the process of opening the passenger-side door. "Why?" she asked over the top of the car. "What do you know about him?"

"While he was governor of South Carolina, he engineered a pyramid scheme that cost thousands of people their life savings. It blew up on him when the stock market tanked. He pinned the collapsed scam on his two sons, who were partners in his invest-ment firm and supposedly running it while he was in office. They're sitting in prison now while he's drinking pina coladas on Kiawah Island." He paused. "Does any of this sound familiar?"

She shook her head without speaking, then opened the car door and got in. Mac did the same but didn't put the key in the ignition right away.

"I think we should continue on to Lake Avalon," he said.

"Isn't Kiawah Island near Charleston? How far is that?"

"A couple of hours, but—"

"Then we should check it out. I need more answers, Mac. Just knowing I'm an empathic spy for the FBI isn't enough."

His brain stalled. She'd called him "Mac." She hadn't called him by name since he'd met her. He wasn't sure why that seemed significant, but it did.

"What?" she asked, impatience lacing the word.

He blinked, realizing he'd stared for too long. "I guess I'm just thinking that chasing after this guy seems a bit impulsive. I mean, if you want information about who you are, we should go to the source. Someone several levels above Flinn Ford at the FBI, for instance."

"That'd be an excellent plan if my instincts weren't telling me not to trust anyone at the FBI or any other feds. I need to gather as much information as I can before I approach any type of law enforcement. Which means I need answers from people who know me—and possibly know Flinn. Arthur Baldwin knows me. I'm sure of it. At the very least, maybe he can tell me something that gives me a direction. Right now, I'm just a fish flopping around on the bank with no idea how to get back into the water."

Unconvinced, Mac jammed the key into the ignition, but instead of twisting it to start the car, he sat back. "Your sisters know you, too," he said quietly. "Maybe you should focus on figuring out more about who you are from them."

When she didn't respond, he added, "If this Arthur Baldwin guy is the kind of people you hang out with in your spy life, then maybe . . ." He trailed off with a shrug, reluctant to be too blunt.

"Maybe what?"

"Maybe you're better off not knowing the gritty details about who you are."

Sam turned her head to look out the windshield, the muscles in her jaw clenched against the unwanted surge of panic at Mac's words. Suddenly, she *didn't* want to know more about who she was. She had a feeling she wouldn't like it, judging by the personality of the man pursuing them. What if she were just as calculated and—

"Look," Mac said, cutting into the thought. "I didn't say that to hurt you."

She glanced at him, careful to keep her expression neutral, determined to not let him see that his words *had* hurt her.

What he thought of her didn't matter, she reminded herself. Surviving mattered. Somehow, she knew that that's all that ever mattered. "You didn't hurt me. You can't if you don't know me, right? We aren't friends."

He winced as though she'd struck a nerve. "I don't know about that. I mean, we did just share some French fries and onion rings."

Leave it to this man to boil the meaning of friendship down to the absolute minimum. "Is that all it takes in your world to be friends?"

"I shot that huge Italian guy to keep him from hurting you. That counts for something, doesn't it?"

She actually wished she could buy into his perception. A friend in such a hostile world would be nice. Leaning her head back, she sighed. "Maybe."

God, she was tired. And while she'd enjoyed the few bites of cheeseburger she'd managed, the food now sat in her stomach with the weight of a bowling ball.

As Mac steered the car onto the road beside the diner, Sam checked the name of the highway and direction: 301, east. Good. That was toward Charleston.

"Why don't you try to get some more sleep?" Mac said. "You're still exhausted."

He reached over and patted the back of her hand. She didn't hear what he said next, because the interior of the car shifted away.

"Jenn, look, I'm sorry, but this is how it's got to be. You can't handle it here anymore. You're getting into trouble every time I turn around."

"Philadelphia is our home, Mac. It always has been."

"Not anymore. Not without Mom and Dad—"

"It's all we have left of them!"

"Jenn, damn it, we're going to lose everything." I don't know how to make her understand. *"I can't afford to support us both and pay the mortgage and the taxes on the house. I just don't make enough at the paper, even with the substitute teaching."*

Mom and Dad mortgaged our childhood home to the hilt.

It'll never be worth what's owed on the loan. It's called under water, and I'm most definitely drowning.

"What about getting a job at the *Inquirer* instead of that tiny little weekly?"

That small and trembling voice kills me. "They're not hiring reporters right now. We need to move somewhere less expensive." *And less likely to turn my kid sister into a juvenile delinquent.*

"Mac, come on. I don't want to go. My friends are here—"

"So are mine. But my friends aren't drinking and driving during a school day while I blissfully hop into the passenger seat and don't wear my seat belt."

She rolls her eyes, so over this. "Nothing happened."

"Because that cop pulled you guys over. You were lucky nothing happened. We've already learned that bad luck is genetic in our family."

She crosses her arms and plops onto the sofa, a recalcitrant child rather than a sophomore in high school. "You can't make me go."

I sit next to her, exhausted by the past year. Mom's car wreck was horrible enough. And Dad's dive to the bottom of a liquor bottle still pisses me off to no end. Fucking . . . weak . . . coward. They both left me in charge of getting a teenage girl through adolescence when I can barely summon the give-a-shit to get out of bed in the morning.

"I'm sorry." *Maybe she'll give me a break. Just this once.* "I don't see another way. If we stay here . . . I just don't see how we'll ever get ahead. You might not be able to go to college."

"I don't have to go. I'll get a job so I can help with the—"

"I don't want you to do that. You're too young."

She rolls her eyes again, in the way only a teen girl can without physically saying, I hate your fucking moronic face.

But she's gearing up to relent, and relief tugs at the corners of my mouth. The smile wants to turn bitter. I'm supposed to be on the investigative-reporting staff at The New York Times *by now. Guess that's off the table.*

"You'll like it in Lake Avalon." *I bump her shoulder with mine.* "It's warm in the winter."

She all but pouts. "Scorching in the summer."

"Beaches."

"Hurricanes."

"Sunshine almost every day of the year."

"Massive bugs that'll steal your lunch money." Her lips twitch. She's trying not to smile.

My shoulders relax. I'm going to win this one. Halle-freaking-lujah. "No state income tax."

She groans. "Like that matters to me."

"It will if it means more trips to Starbucks."

"Yeah, like some podunk town in Florida has Starbucks."

"Actually, Lake Avalon has a really great coffeehouse. The Java Bean. You don't need a line of home equity to buy a latte there, either. And the chocolate chip cookies are awesome."

She leans her head on my shoulder and releases a soft sigh. "Do they have scones? I like scones."

"Sam? Sam!"

She blinked open her eyes to Mac's frantic expression, confused by the damp, cold breeze on her face. It took her a long moment to realize he wasn't in the driver's seat anymore, that the car was parked haphazardly on the side of the two-lane highway. He'd gotten out of the car and opened her door so he could lean in to try to rouse her. Her cheeks vibrated with the vague impressions of his insistent taps.

"You with me?" he asked, peering into her eyes, his gaze dark but intense under the Toyota's dome light.

Nodding, she pressed back against the passenger seat to put distance between them. His body gave off heat like a furnace, but instead of wanting to shrink away from it, she yearned to get as close to him as she could. Instinct, or something—self-preservation?—kept her back.

"You okay?" He shifted back to a squatting position outside her door.

The scent of damp decay wafted in from outside, carried on the nighttime sounds of tree frogs, crickets and the distant swish of tires on puddled asphalt. The moon peeked through clouds, high and bright in the sky.

Her head felt heavy and achy, her vision smudged around

the edges. Disorientation stuck to the inside of her brain like wadded plastic wrap, and she had to focus to smooth out the wrinkles. She was on the road, on the run, with Mac Hunter. They were on their way to Charleston to meet Arthur Baldwin, a man who might be able to tell her more about her identity.

"Sam?"

She closed her eyes tight, willing away the throb in her temples. "How long was I gone?"

"A couple of minutes. I was getting ready to call 911. What the hell happened? One second we were talking about you taking a nap, and the next, you were catatonic."

She had no idea what to say. She'd gone into his past, relived the moments with his sister as though they'd happened to her. Now, with a clear head and no catastrophe to deal with at the moment, she fully comprehended her psychic ability.

It's called empathy.

And she'd tapped into a very tough conversation Mac had had with his little sister.

The muscles in her chest constricted as it hit her that he'd lost both of his parents far too soon, and tragically. He'd sacrificed his own hopes and dreams to do what was best for a loved one. How amazing was that?

"Hey."

The soft word turned her head back toward him, and even in the darkness, she could see the depth of his concern. Or maybe it just emanated off him in empathic waves. "I'm okay," she said.

"Maybe we should see a doctor."

"I feel fine."

"I'd feel better if—"

"I was in your head."

He jerked back an inch. "What? You were what?"

"You touched me, didn't you? Right before I blanked out?"

"I don't remember . . . no, wait. Yeah, I did. I touched your hand, and just like that you were gone."

"That's how I told you it works when I was telling you everything I could before I lost my memory. I said it was skin-on-skin contact."

He rose to his feet with a crack of knees. "Your psychic ability, you mean."

She had to duck her head to see him clearly and was struck by the way his dark hair gleamed in the moonlight, though his eyes remained shadowed.

When he took a step away from the car, shoving his hands into the pockets of his jeans, she unbuckled her seat belt and got out to stand beside him. "Don't you want to know what I saw?"

"Was it something bad?"

She smiled then, the expression feeling unnatural on her lips. "It was something sweet. Really quite sweet. You and your sister . . . Jenn?"

He nodded. "Jennifer. She's a freshman at Florida State."

"You were trying to talk her into moving from Philadelphia to Lake Avalon."

"That wasn't sweet," he said with a snort. "That was hell."

When he started to turn away, she stopped him with a hand on his sleeve. "You gave up so much for her."

"Not really. I mean—"

"*The New York Times*?"

He edged back a pace. "Oh. Wow, that's—you're creeping me out right now. You got all that from a simple touch?"

"That's what I did—*do* for the FBI. Imagine how handy it must be to find out what a terrorist knows simply by touch."

Mac whistled. "No waterboarding necessary." He cocked his head. "But I touched you right after we left our buddy Marco back at the motel. You were pretty out of it, like you couldn't stay awake, but I touched you more than once and nothing happened. At least, you didn't respond as if anything happened."

"Maybe it's erratic. Or maybe the memory drug has messed with my system in other ways."

"You had a pretty bad headache at the time. Maybe that interfered with your ability?"

"Maybe."

They fell quiet, and Sam felt again his frustration and sadness from the flashback. Yet his fierce love for his sister—and determination to protect her—had taken precedence. Sam ached for the man who'd sacrificed so much to do what he considered the right thing.

"I'm sorry you had to give up your dream," she said.

His shoulders lifted and dropped with a shrug. "No big. Lake Avalon's a nice place to live. If you factor out the pipe wrench–wielding psychopaths, that is."

The edges of her vision darkened as that memory from his past washed over her again. Weird how she seemed to have more memories about his past than her own. A pulsing ache began in her temples, and she pressed her fingers to both sides and tried to massage it away.

"Another headache?" Mac asked.

She nodded.

"Maybe you're getting psychic hangovers."

Oh, if it could be that easy. "That sounds so benign."

"A nap helped then." He gestured toward her open car door. "You can sleep while I drive. Once we get to the Charleston area, we'll need to find a place for the night. Unless you want to kick down the Ponzi dipshit's door in the middle of the night."

She laughed at that. And, just as smiling had felt so odd, it struck her that her body seemed unaccustomed to laughing as well. She hoped that was because of the amnesia, and not because her real life was that sad.

CHAPTER TWENTY-FOUR

"You need to find her," Dr. Toby Ames said. "Time is running out."

Flinn noted that the doctor's tone carried an unusual tinge of anxiety. This was the same man who barely batted an eyelash when a researcher destroyed some recently harvested, and irreplaceable, fetal cells. That had been before the latest developments, though—before the project ended up in the ICU in critical condition.

"I'm doing everything I can, Toby," Flinn said into his cell phone. "Relax." Which was kind of ironic advice, considering the doctor's call had interrupted his evening of pacing a path into the living room carpet. The latest update on Samantha's whereabouts—only an hour ago—had been the same: still missing.

"The more time that goes by, the more difficult it will be to—"

"I know," Flinn said. "I'm as eager as you are to get this thing done."

"You don't seem to appreciate the delicacy of what I have to do. The procedure is—"

"Christ on a cracker, take a breath." Flinn did the same. It wasn't like his partner to freak out, and the last thing he wanted to do was irk the man. Without Toby and his ability to use the specialized knowledge they'd obtained from the researcher in San Francisco, Flinn's hopes for success would take a hit. And that would displease his partners.

"I'm just worried, Flinn. We've lost Zoe, and since Andrea sent Mikayla to Afghanistan, we've lost access to her—"

"I promise you I'll let you know as soon as I have Samantha

in my custody. And I *will* find her. Mikayla, too. That will just take a little more time."

Toby let out a long breath. "Where do you think Sam's going?"

Flinn pressed his lips together tight. "The worst possible place. Home."

"But you've drilled it into her head for years that it's not safe."

"She doesn't remember that."

"Then perhaps we should both get to Florida. We'll be in position to move quickly once she's intercepted."

Flinn nodded. A good idea. "I'll have Natalie arrange your flight."

"What about you?"

"I'd prefer to remain flexible."

"What should I tell Andrea if she asks?"

"Tell her you're taking vacation." For such a brilliant scientist, the man could be dim sometimes. "And don't worry, Toby. Things have a way of working themselves out."

Toby grunted. "The eternal optimist. It never seems to occur to you what will happen to us if we get caught."

Flinn grinned into the phone. "Because we won't get caught, Dr. Ames. We're on a mission from God."

He was still smiling when he cut off the call.

CHAPTER **TWENTY-FIVE**

Sam sat straight up in bed, heart hammering. What was that?

"It's just thunder."

She turned her head toward the soft voice, blinking against muzziness and almost total darkness. "Where are we?"

"Motel outside Charleston. Remember?"

She had a vague memory of falling into bed as soon as she and Mac had entered the tiny room. He'd roused her to clean her bullet wounds and change the bandages, and she must have fallen asleep the moment he'd finished.

"Everything's okay, Sam. Go back to sleep."

Accepting the soothing explanation, she shifted into a more comfortable position under the warm weight of blankets and drifted back to sleep, into an unfamiliar world . . .

The bubbles popping in her champagne misted her skin as she sipped from the fluted glass. The music, soft and lilting, complemented the elegant décor. Shiny gold curtains draped to the floor in place of walls, and the flames of dozens of white candles flickered as murmuring partygoers moved by them.

The political fund-raiser had drawn guests with myriad backgrounds: from rich socialites obsessed with being seen to businessmen hoping to secure favors by openly supporting the candidate.

She spotted her target near a fountain of melted chocolate, a fat red strawberry grasped between his stubby fingers. As he bit into the fruit, his snake-like eyes darted around the room. Despite his pear shape, he wore a surprisingly well-

tailored suit. His scalp gleamed with perspiration through his thinning blond hair.

She could relate to his nerves. This was her first test. She couldn't afford to screw it up.

She focused on breathing slow and deep to control the thrum of anxiety in her ears.

And decided to get it over with.

Pasting on a flirtatious smile, she walked over to the mark . . . no, that was her father's . . . Ben's word. Flinn preferred "target," saying it had a mission-centric connotation. A matter of semantics, in her opinion. Either way, someone was going to get screwed.

"Is that as good as it looks?" she purred as she reached for a plump strawberry.

The fumes from his aftershave—a blast of something too antiseptic to be sexy—nearly choked her, but she managed to maintain eye contact as she sank her teeth into the juicy berry and hummed her appreciation.

His gaze fixed on her mouth, pupils dilating. "Hello."

She discarded the stem into a napkin and helped herself to another strawberry. "I'm Samantha. My friends call me Stormy."

He started to grin, revealing a mouthful of crooked teeth. "My friends call me Jake."

Jake the Snake, to be exact, she thought. So cliché for a scumbag. She held out her hand. Here goes. "Nice to meet you, Jake."

His cold, clammy hand closed around hers.

Oh, yeah, there it is, there it is. Ah, yes, yes, yes.

The pleasure builds, builds, and I shift my grip on her wrists so I can ready the knife. She starts screaming again, fighting, trying to wrench her wrists free from where I've pinned them above her head. That's it, that's it. I love it when they fight.

"Beg." I lean down and breathe it into her ear, emphasizing the command with a violent thrust.

She whimpers, turns her head away. "Please."

"Louder." Another brutal thrust, sending pleasure singing to the top of my head. Almost there. The knife handle fits my palm like it was made for me.

"Please!"

I smile into her terrified eyes. "Your wish is my command."

I slash the blade across her throat.

Blood spurts at the exact right moment.

She dies with me inside her, and I howl with the power of it.

"Just give her a minute. I'm sure she's fine."

"What the hell happened?" Jake the Snake's voice carried an unmistakable "I didn't do anything to her, I swear!" tone.

She opened her eyes to Flinn's tanned face above her. She recognized the displeasure that narrowed his dark gaze. "Ah, there you are, Samantha." His tone was polite, concerned. "You gave us somewhat of a scare. Can you sit up?"

As he helped her into a sitting position, she glanced around, mortified to discover she was on the parquet floor of the ballroom, a small, curious crowd forming a loose circle around her. No wonder Flinn was irked. She hadn't remained inconspicuous as instructed.

The fabric of her black dress clung to her right thigh, and she glanced down at the cold, wet spot, wondering what it was. Then she spotted the shattered remains of her champagne glass not far from where she sat.

"Here, have some water." Flinn pressed a cool on-the-rocks glass into her hand.

She sipped obediently, wishing she could make her hand stop shaking so much. But the horror of what she'd experienced in Jake the Snake's head washed through her, and she had to fight to keep her dinner down.

"She's all right," Flinn said, addressing the crowd in his infinitely charming way. "Just give us a little space, if you don't mind."

The onlookers took their time wandering away, including Jake, who cast a disappointed glance over his shoulder.

She took several fast sips of the ice water to combat the rising bile in her throat.

"Let's get you up," Flinn said.

She handed him the glass and let him help her, grabbing hold of his solidly muscled arm to maintain her balance when a queasy spinning swirled through her senses.

"Dizzy?"

"Yes."

He set aside her water glass then escorted her toward the door, his arm tight around her waist. "Your body hasn't adjusted fully to the drug cocktail."

"I don't like the way it makes me feel. I'm not in control."

"We're working on the pharmacology. We'll have to get Dr. Ames to dial this particular incarnation down a notch. We can't have you passing out before you've completed your mission, though I'm certain that with time and practice, you'll be able to better manage your reactions. I have a feeling you forgot your training as soon as you made contact."

She had. How could she not? How could she possibly remember training when that *was going on in her head?*

Outside the ballroom of the ornate hotel, Flinn led her to the elevator, smiling and nodding at the curious women in glittering diamonds and concerned men in impeccable tuxes.

Alone in the elevator, they faced the mirrored doors. Her tight black dress covered both her arms yet barely reached mid-thigh, and her hair was swept up in a curly 'do that made her look a decade older than twenty. Despite dramatic eye makeup and artfully painted red lips, she looked pale and sick.

Trapped.

"What did you see?"

Flinn's question startled her, and she shuddered as Jake's memory was unleashed inside her head all over again.

"Samantha?"

"He's a monster."

"Yes, of course. But what kind? I need specifics if I'm going to get us what we need."

"It was too much. I felt . . . everything."

"That's the intent. The drugs are doing exactly what they're supposed to."

"I don't like it." She started to shake at the remembered pleasure Jake had experienced as he'd slit that poor woman's throat. Pulses of it lingered between her legs, and revulsion whited out her vision.

Flinn's hand tightened on her arm. *"Get yourself together, Samantha."* Impatience edged his tone. *"Do I have to remind you what's at stake here?"*

Despair dug brutal talons into her heart. He didn't have to remind her of the deal she'd made.

He said nothing more as the elevator opened on their floor. He led her down the hall and used a key card to let them into a large suite of rooms. As he shut and locked the door behind them, he said, *"Take off your dress."*

Her blood froze in her veins. *"What?"*

He chuckled at her reaction, genuinely amused. *"I want to check your patch. Remember that Dr. Ames said the material is experimental. I need to make sure it's still properly secured so that you're getting an adequate, and steady, dosage."*

"Oh. Right."

She shivered as she pulled the dress over her head while he sat in an ornate wingback chair in the corner and watched her. His gaze wasn't predatory, but she couldn't ignore the spark of interest she glimpsed. The fact that he hadn't yet tried to force her into a sexual relationship surprised her. But she supposed there was still time.

She kicked off her heels before approaching him, preferring to be as non-sexy as possible for his scrutiny.

"Ready?" he asked.

She braced herself and focused on breathing, just as Dr. Ames had instructed. Breathe. Focus. Breathe. Focus.

When Flinn's hand smoothed over her hip, it was cool and dry, how she imagined a snakeskin would feel. Nothing from his past burrowed its way into her head, thank God. Maybe she could do this after all. She simply hadn't been prepared for the horror of Jake's mind.

"Ah, yes, very good work." Flinn's warm breath feathered over the skin of her lower back as he leaned in close, as though inspecting a tiny tattoo. "It blends perfectly with your skin tone."

"Do I have to wear it all the time?"

"It's essential to enhance your psychic abilities. Without it, you would be cast into your target's memories without the ability to focus on your objective."

"It's just . . . it itches."

"You'll get used to it. It's preferable to prison, is it not?"

Goose bumps spread over her body. Sometimes she thought prison would definitely have been better. At least there would have been a point where she'd have completed her sentence.

Ford sat back with a dismissive wave of his hand. "Get dressed, and we'll talk about what you saw."

She rubbed her arms. "I'd like to take a shower first." She felt dirty, violated. Interesting, considering she was the one who'd infiltrated Jake's mind without his knowledge.

"Make it a quick one."

She walked into the bathroom, shut the door and fell to her knees in front of the commode.

CHAPTER **TWENTY-SIX**

Mac jerked awake, heart pounding and eyes blinking to adjust to the darkness of the motel room, the vague impression of a loud noise ringing in his ears. What the hell? Had someone walked by the door of the motel room and coughed loudly?

He checked the red glow of the alarm clock. Four A.M. They'd checked in to a Charleston motel—a nicer one than in Front Royal—and sacked out only an hour ago.

Sitting up, he flicked on the lamp between the two double beds and squinted at the resulting bright light. The realization that Sam's bed was empty cleared his disorientation in less than a second.

Then he heard the noise again. It didn't come from out in the hall. Sam was in the bathroom, vomiting.

"Shit." He tossed aside the covers and got up to drag on his jeans. He left them unbuttoned, more worried now about the silence from the bathroom than the fact that he hadn't finished putting his pants on.

Outside the bathroom door, he lightly knocked. "Sam?"

"I'm okay." The toilet flushed, followed by water splashing against porcelain.

"Do you need anything? I can get some ice or ginger ale or something."

Instead of answering, she opened the door.

He stepped back in surprise and took in her white bra and bikini briefs. If it hadn't been for the pallor of her face and the stark whiteness of the bandage at her shoulder, his brain would have gone right to sex, do not pass go, do not collect two hundred dollars, do not stop until the world ends in bright, explosive color.

It took him a moment to grasp that she stood just as frozen as he did. Her gaze had fastened on his chest, and as he watched, fascinated, her eyes slowly dropped over his abdomen and down to the unbuttoned fly of his jeans. A pleasant pink began to flush her cheeks.

Well, hello. Either partial nudity embarrassed her, or she'd just gotten the same electric charge seeing him half-naked as he'd gotten seeing her.

But then he wanted to knock himself upside the head for being such a dolt that he was more focused on sensual curves and lust than helping the poor woman sit down after tossing her cookies.

When he stepped back, her eyes widened, as though she realized she'd been staring.

Join the crowd, baby.

"Sure you don't want some ginger ale? The machine's just down the hall."

She shook her head, chafing her arms as though chilled.

Mac snagged the shirt she'd left at the foot of her bed and helped her into it, careful to avoid jostling her sore arm. Damn, how sexy was it that his flannel shirt smelled like her? Like caramelized sugar and something exotic that he couldn't identify. Not cinnamon. Maybe nutmeg or allspice?

Ah, shit, she was trembling. He really needed to focus.

"Here, sit on the bed." He led her over, and as she did as he bade, he pulled the thick, dark beige blanket off his bed and settled it snugly around her shoulders, careful to not make contact with any skin. "How's that? Better?"

She nodded, burrowing her chin down against her chest. She looked as small and vulnerable as a little kid wrapped in a blankie.

"Talk to me, Sam. What happened? Did you remember something?"

Her teeth chattered. "I had a . . ."

"A bad dream?" He sat across from her on his bed, so

intent on her pained expression that he bumped his knees against hers. "Oops, sorry."

"S'okay." She went on shuddering.

"How about some coffee to warm you up?"

"It'll pass in a minute."

"How do you know?"

She furrowed her brows. "I guess I don't. Sure, make some coffee."

Eager to do something, anything, to help, he pushed off the bed and got to work tearing into the prepackaged coffee filter and tucking it into the basket of the coffeemaker. When his hands jittered, he shook them out, telling himself to chill. She was fine. No harm, no foul. It was just . . . Jesus, she was sick. Wounded. Stricken by amnesia. Traumatized by other people's memories. Hunted by a ruthless madman.

The woman couldn't catch a break.

He filled the glass carafe with water from the bathroom then dumped the contents into the maker. "Should take just a few minutes."

He turned to face her, starting to plunge his hands into the front pockets of his jeans only to discover they were still unbuttoned and barely hanging on at his hips. "Oh, damn." He fumbled with the buttons, flashing her a sheepish smile. "Sorry about that."

Her lips quirked, and she glanced away.

That tiny smile did more to lift his spirits than a 50-yard-line seat at a Super Bowl pitting the Dolphins against the Eagles. "So . . . do you want to talk about it? The bad dream, I mean."

"Not really."

"Maybe it'll help."

"Help what?"

"I don't know. Help . . . something. It obviously freaked you out enough to make you hurl."

One eyebrow ticked up. "Hurl?"

"Barf. Puke. Blow burrito chunks."

She winced at the graphics. "Yeah, I got what you meant.

I just hadn't heard it put like that in a while." Her forehead creased, and she added, "I don't think."

"I think you should talk to me about the dream. What if there's something in it that doesn't make sense to you but does to me? I'm a newshound, you know. I know the odds are a long shot, but you never know." He stopped, feeling like an idiot for all the words he'd managed to cram into his argument. It was just . . . she made him nervous.

She seemed to think it over for a long moment. When she spoke, her voice was low. "I don't think it was a dream. I think it was a flashback."

Oh, wow. There's something new. "What makes you think that?"

"It was . . . so real."

His heart started to thump harder as he got up to pour the finished coffee into a foam cup for her. "Creamer or sugar?"

"Black is fine."

He turned to hand her the warm cup and watched her cradle it in her hands as though savoring the heat it gave off.

"If it was a flashback," he asked, "then does that mean your memory is coming back?"

"Possibly."

"That's great."

She simply nodded without saying anything. Decidedly unenthusiastic.

"It's not great?" he asked.

She shrugged her right shoulder.

A chilled finger of realization trailed up his spine. The flashback had made her violently sick to her stomach, so it couldn't have been a happy one. "Oh."

He lowered himself back to the bed across from her. A long minute of silence went by in which he noticed she had yet to sample the coffee. "You're not drinking."

"I don't think my stomach can take it."

"I thought you wanted . . ."

She shrugged that one shoulder again. "You seemed to need something to do."

"Wow. Am I a lame bastard or what?"

"You're not lame at all. You're very . . . sweet."

He smirked at her. "Sweet. Just what every guy wants to hear."

Every time a woman had told him he was sweet, she'd dumped him soon after. Not that he thought he would ever get romantically involved with this particular woman. But still. Who could blame him? Sam Trudeau was the most beautiful, most perfectly made woman he'd ever met. She also made him feel . . . things he hadn't felt in a very long time. Protective and curious and energized . . . and way too warm. He couldn't help but think of seduction and sex when he was near her. And, hell, he wanted to pound that Flinn Ford fucker into the ground. Such violent urges were so not like him.

"I was at a party."

His attention turned outward as she burrowed deeper into the blanket. He didn't say anything, just waited for her to go on.

"It was a test. My assignment was to find a particular man at the party and . . . and . . . mine his memories." Her eyebrows drew tightly together. "I don't remember that specifically from the flashback. The terminology, I mean. But I recall Flinn saying something about that, about mining memories."

"Maybe that's what you do for the FBI? Use your empathy to mine bad guys' memories to find out what crimes they've committed?"

"Maybe."

"So, what happened?"

She didn't respond right away, as though gathering herself. "I saw a man kill a woman while he was raping her."

Mac felt as though she'd thrown a brick at his chest full force. "Holy God."

"It was . . . awful. I felt . . . everything. He was enjoying it, and I felt it. The blood . . . was . . . it was everywhere. Oh, God." Her voice broke, and she covered her mouth with one shaking hand.

Mac moved fast to rescue the teetering cup of coffee from

her other hand. After setting it aside, he sat beside her on the bed and gathered her to him, wrapping both arms securely around her. The quivering of her body just about did him in. "Hey, hey, it's okay, it's okay. That guy is probably in prison now, right? If he was your assignment, then you must have helped put him away."

"I don't think I can do this, Mac. I'm not strong enough."

"Yes, you can. I'm here to help you. You don't have to do it alone."

She let go of the handful of blanket she'd been clutching to her chest and dug her fingers into his bare arm. Instantly, she stiffened, and her breath caught.

He stilled, realizing she must have flashed on what he was feeling and thinking. He hoped whatever she glimpsed didn't include an image of her naked and under him.

She relaxed in slow degrees. "I don't know which side I'm on," she said softly. "What if I'm on the wrong side?"

The muscles in his chest clutched painfully. "I highly doubt you're the bad guy, Sam."

"How can you be sure?"

"You're forgetting that I know your sisters. Charlie and Alex are the best people I've ever met. They're good, *really good*, people. And you're made of the same stuff." He rubbed her back through the blanket in slow, soothing circles.

She rested her head on his shoulder. "I'm so tired."

"I know you are. Just sleep, okay? I'll be right here the whole time."

"Promise?"

"Yeah, I promise."

It took only a few moments for Sam to fully relax in Mac's arms, but when she did, she dropped into a deep sleep, only to find herself furiously packing . . .

"I'm coming with you."

Sam hesitated as she reached for the pile of underwear in

the dresser drawer. She'd feared this from her younger sister.
"No, Charlie, you're not. I'm sorry."

"If you're worried about me carrying my own weight, you
don't have to. You know I can keep up."

Sam turned to face her, unable to stop the flinch at the
sight of the fading bruises on her sister's pale face. Their
mother had done that to her. Sam could still feel the heavy
thuds against her own flesh and bones as she'd absorbed her
younger sister's memory into herself. The rage surged all
over again, and Sam had to turn away to focus on controlling
it. She could—and would—prevent that from happening to
Charlie again. She just needed time.

"Sam, come on. Please?"

"Who'll look after Alex?"

"Dad," Charlie said. Quick, as though she'd anticipated
the question.

Sam snorted as she tossed the underwear into her duffel.
"Like he looked after you last week?" It still irked her that
their mother had suffered no consequences for hitting her
middle child. She would, though. Soon. The thought of how
Sam would make her pay raised the fine hairs on her arms.

Realizing Charlie hadn't responded, Sam tossed a quick
glance her way to see her picking at an imaginary piece of
lint on the hem of her T-shirt.

"Alex doesn't do stuff that pisses Mom off," Charlie said.
As if what their mother had done was somehow her own fault.

Biting her lip, Sam turned back to packing. "Then you
shouldn't, either."

"Don't you want to know what's up with the photo album?
Why doesn't she want us to see it?"

Because she has a secret. *But Sam didn't say that. Or men-*
tion that she knew what that secret was—and that it would
mean the end for their mother's ironfisted reign as the queen
bitch of the house. Both her sisters would find out soon,
though. "You need to respect her privacy, Charlie. She'll
share when she's ready." When I make her.

"It's not like I was snooping. I found it by accident. I
needed to borrow—"

"It's okay. You don't have to explain it to me."

Charlie flopped onto the bed next to Sam's half-packed bag. *"Where are you going to go?"*

Northern Illinois. Her mother had fled from there. From a small town called Sycamore. Sounded lousy with trees. And cold compared with the heat and humidity of Florida. *"I don't know yet."*

"You should have a plan. That's what Dad always says."

Dad. Thinking of him nearly crumpled her resolve. Not her dad. Not technically, anyway. A trip into her mother's head had told her as much, and given her the name of the man who was her biological father. Ben Dillon. She planned to meet him very soon. *"I'll make a plan on the way."*

"What about culinary school? You're all set to go in Tampa and everything. Being a chef is your dream."

"There are cooking schools in . . . everywhere. I'll figure it out."

"Nana's going to be mad." The words seemed to strain Charlie's already-low voice.

"I'll explain before I go." Sam had a feeling that out of everyone, their grandmother would understand the most.

"Won't matter. She's still going to be mad."

Sam gave her sister a smile that she knew looked far more sad than Charlie needed. *"You, too?"*

The tears finally overflowed as Charlie nodded.

The guilt surrounded Sam's heart like a fist and squeezed. Stoic, stubborn Charlie had never been a crier, and now the tears spilled freely.

Sam went to her sister and hugged her, clamping her eyes closed against her own emotion. *"I'll be back. I swear I will. And then everything will be better."*

Charlie clung to Sam, sniffling and swallowing, refusing to let her go the first time Sam tried to draw back. *"Promise you won't forget about us?"*

"I promise."

CHAPTER **TWENTY-SEVEN**

Flinn rolled over and fumbled for his ringing cell phone on the bedside table. After a caller ID check, he flipped it open. "Give me the news, Natalie. I'd like to start the day in a good mood."

"We've located the Suburban in the parking lot of a strip mall in the Fair Oaks area of Fairfax County. Car battery was removed, which disabled the GPS."

"Clever." He sat up, rubbing one hand over the razor stubble roughening his jaw.

"Restaurant with valet parking reported a stolen 2009 Toyota Camry yesterday. Silver. No GPS or LoJack."

"Damn it." And like that, any hope of a good mood fled. Flinn rubbed at yesterday's knot still parked at the nape of his neck.

"I know. Can't get a much more generic car than that," Natalie said. "Plates have most likely been switched, too."

"Finding that car will be next to impossible. Samantha would know to stick to back roads."

"Even without her memory?"

"The drug in her system temporarily affects only episodic memory."

"I have no idea what that means, sir."

Flinn reminded himself that curiosity was one of the things he liked best about this research analyst who eagerly broke the rules to assist him. Hero worship at its best. He planned to reward her well. "Episodic memory is what makes you who you are. Procedural and semantic memory is your knowledge of the world around you and how things work. Samantha no longer knows who she is or what she's done in the past, but she still knows how to handle herself as an N3 operative. Her episodic memory will eventually begin to return."

"That's amazing."

"Yes, it is."

"Dr. Ames developed that, didn't he? He's a genius."

Flinn's flush of well-being went cold. He didn't like sharing adoration, especially when the man he had to share it with was in the process of losing his cool and possibly jeopardizing everything Flinn had worked for. "Speaking of Dr. Ames, please arrange a flight for him to either Tampa or Fort Myers, whichever's cheapest. As soon as possible."

"Yes, sir." She sounded hesitant, probably because his tone had gone cold and professional. Served her right.

"Use my personal American Express. Send the itinerary to Dr. Ames' personal e-mail. And don't mention the trip to anyone or in any work e-mails. Got it? As far as any of us are concerned, Dr. Ames is going on vacation."

"Of course, sir. I wouldn't—"

He snapped the phone closed. He was so fucking tired of promising young women disappointing him.

CHAPTER **TWENTY-EIGHT**

Sam woke, tension suffusing every muscle as she assessed the threat level. Someone was holding her. Someone who snored softly near her ear. Someone with strong arms, a solid chest and a clean, soapy scent. Someone who made her feel safe in a hostile world.

Mac Hunter.

As the name came to her, she unclenched her muscles, savoring his heat against her and the even in-out of his breathing.

She couldn't imagine what she would do without him. While her memories swirled and eddied like dangerous riptides, Mac had become her life jacket, helping to keep her head above the tide of chaotic information.

Amazing that he'd stuck by her. Maybe he wouldn't have if he hadn't promised Charlie that he'd get her home in one piece, but she had a feeling that he would. He'd given up his dreams to provide his own sister with a stable home. This was a man who'd risk his life for a stranger.

She hoped to God that she was worth it.

He adjusted position then, burying his nose against her T-shirt-covered collarbone, pressing himself more closely against her, as though seeking body heat . . . or more intimate contact. A soft humming sound in his throat sent a shiver through her, and she wondered if he was dreaming.

She thought of the brief flash she'd gotten of his thoughts earlier, when he'd comforted her. Simple contact—she'd clung to his arm—and all his sympathy, concern and horror had flooded through her in a rushing wave. She wondered whether she could control that wave, or direct it. Her flashback with

Flinn had suggested she could. And she was in the perfect position to experiment now.

Holding her breath, she shifted so that Mac's nose brushed the side of her neck, focusing all her attention and energy in his direction.

The motel room blurred . . .

She moans deep in her throat, wrapping her arms around my waist, and arches under me. My breath catches as I realize that in the dark she's managed to wriggle herself into a position where all I have to do is shift maybe an inch and I'll be inside her. Doesn't help that her breath, fast and uneven, is hot near my ear.

"What are you waiting for?" she whispers. Low and sexy. Jesus. "Come in."

I close my eyes and swallow hard. If I sink into her now, I'll be coming in less than a minute.

"Don't worry about it," she murmurs, scraping my back lightly with her nails. "I'm ready."

A guy can't argue with that. I thrust, and she rises, and we fit together perfectly on a simultaneous gasp. Oh, hell, yeah.

Her head drops to the pillow, and I lower my lips to her exposed throat, where I move only my mouth as I kiss her neck, her jaw, the underside of her chin. She smells of popcorn balls and nutmeg, her skin as smooth and silky as satin. I want to live in this moment forever.

But she has other plans. Other plans that thrill the fuck out of me as much as prolonging our time like this. She grasps my hips and pushes at the same time that she presses herself down into the mattress. Oh, God, I'm sliding out of her. The dragging sensation explodes the pleasure, and I can't stop nature from taking over. I begin to thrust, fast and mindless at first, then forcing myself to go slow. Not yet, not yet.

She moans again, restless against me as I deliberately take my time kissing her, telling her with my tongue and my lips that I'll always be there for her. Always.

Her hips move faster, urging me on, trying to quicken the pace again.

"Wait," I gasp. "Wait."

"Now," she whispers, low and throaty. "Please."

I have no choice. I bury my face against her neck and take her, plunging into her again and again, biting into my bottom lip to keep from coming too soon even as the urgency builds, builds, builds.

She gasps and arches, and I raise my head to watch, fascinated by the way the muscles in her long neck stretch taut and her lips part in a silent, gasping "oh" as the orgasm rolls through her.

I say her name, once: "Sam."

Surprise dropped her out of the moment, and she landed back in her own head, breathless and way too warm.

Sam.

He was having a sex dream about *her.*

Behind her, Mac's body telegraphed his enjoyment of the dream, and she had to resist the urge to wriggle backward a little closer, to seek assuagement for the throb between her thighs. Having been in his head in those moments, she hadn't reached climax, though she'd watched herself come, through his eyes. Or rather, her dream self. God, that was weird.

And frustrating as hell.

Biting into her lip, she held still and berated herself. This was inappropriate on so many levels. She never should have tried to get into his head. What an absolute invasion of his privacy.

Yet . . . she couldn't deny that what she'd seen—felt— warmed her through and through.

He was dreaming about her. *Her.*

She started to smile. Then frowned. What the hell was wrong with her? Had she suddenly regressed to the maturity level of a teenager? Didn't she have bigger things to worry about? Closing her eyes and with a small shake of her head, she shoved the thoughts away. Forget it, Sam, she thought. Just forget it.

She drifted for a few more minutes, letting herself enjoy the feel of Mac's breath against her neck, shivering a little at the ticklish sensation. She thought of the earlier times she'd accessed his memories, the resulting headaches. Yet, this time she felt fine. Was that because she'd prepared herself for the flash? Or maybe since it was her first empathic experience of the day, her brain didn't feel overtaxed. She'd also deliberately sought the flash, so maybe her intentions had an impact, too.

And *what* an impact. She shuddered at the remembered passion he'd felt with her in his erotic dream. And then she wondered how long it had been since she'd snuggled with a man. Or something hotter and sweatier.

Her brain stuttered at that thought. Was she married? Engaged? Otherwise involved?

She checked her left hand. No tan line where a ring used to be.

That didn't necessarily mean anything.

And if she were attached, then cuddling in bed with Mac Hunter—and eavesdropping on his naughty dreams—was inappropriate.

After gently extricating herself, smiling in spite of it all as Mac grumbled in his sleep and rolled onto his back, Sam tucked the blanket back around him, careful to steer clear of his still-obvious, um, excitement jutting against the bedclothes. But, God, it was impressive.

Face—and the rest of her—heating all over again, she headed for the bathroom. She'd get cleaned up and ready to go before waking him. Hopefully by then, he wouldn't be quite so . . . aroused. She hated the thought of having to wake him up in that state. The last thing she wanted to do was embarrass him.

In the bathroom, her brain firmly in the moment, she confronted her reflection with a wince. Pale. Dark circles. Unruly dark hair. She needed a shower, but the bandages covering opposing sides of her shoulder made the idea a no-go. Mac had changed them, and checked her healing wounds, before they'd gone to bed, but that's about all they'd had energy for.

Using her good hand, she awkwardly washed her hair in the sink and wrapped a towel around her head. Already, she felt better.

In front of the mirror, she angled her body to try to get a look at the third bandage that rode the valley between her shoulder blades. Mac had told her that's where the transponder had resided. When he'd dug it out of her flesh, it had triggered a chemical reaction of some kind that had wiped out her memories. The idea of a drug that powerful floored her as surely as the fact that she had a psychic ability.

She was about to get dressed when she remembered the moment in her flashback when Flinn Ford had inspected "the patch." She turned again and studied her right flank, the area where Flinn had focused his attention.

Right there, high on her hip, was a square inch of thin fabric the same tone and texture as her skin. If she hadn't known to look, she wouldn't have noticed. While she'd complained of itching in her flashback, that wasn't the case now.

It took her several minutes with the edge of her fingernail to pry up an edge. Then she ripped it off, fast like a Band-Aid, and flinched at the resulting sting.

Scrutiny of the scrap of fabric told her nothing. It had no logo, no words of any kind. Looked as innocuous as a piece of tape. Yet she knew from her flashback—and Flinn's attention to it—that it was far from innocuous.

It's essential to enhance your psychic abilities. Without it, you would be cast into your target's memories without the ability to focus on your objective.

A knock on the door startled her.

"Sam? You okay?"

"Be out in a minute," she called, unable to prevent a small smile at Mac's hovering ways. He made her feel so protected.

She was also relieved that now she didn't have to worry about waking him up while his body did an inspiring imitation of a tent pole.

"Are you absolutely sure about this?"

Sam glanced over at him in the driver's seat. "Yes."

Mac sensed she'd managed to sound more confident than she felt. He couldn't blame her. He was nervous as hell, and it wasn't his past they were going to confront. Assuming the former governor of South Carolina could answer her questions and didn't meet them in the driveway with a shotgun. And that thought *didn't* come from any bigoted feelings toward Southerners. Mac just feared that a guy like Arthur Baldwin, the kind of man who had screwed over dozens of friends and family members for money then let his own kids take the fall . . . well, that sounded like a nasty, dangerous guy to him.

He cruised to a stop at a traffic light on the way to Kiawah Island. The morning sun glinted off the bumper of the antique car in front of them, and the scents of saltwater and ocean air wafted in through the open windows. While the temperature wasn't particularly high—around fifty so far this morning—it wasn't the cold and damp of fall, as it had been in northern Virginia.

Mac took a moment to think about how different things would be now if he had escaped somewhere other than the Shenandoahs. He'd probably be bored off his ass by now and fighting the urge to head home. Instead, he'd awakened this morning dreaming about Sam and . . . well, painfully aroused. Heat crept up his neck, and he kept his eyes straight ahead, hoping like hell that Sam didn't choose this moment to look over at him again.

Thank God she had already been out of bed and in the bathroom. He only prayed he hadn't sprouted wood while spooning her. What if that's why she'd gotten out of bed to begin with? How embarrassing would that be?

Then again, he was a *guy*. And he'd been holding a very warm, very pliant female in his arms, a female he seemed to find ever more appealing the more time they spent together. A female who kept soldiering on no matter how many times the universe smacked her flat.

"It's green."

Her voice snapped him out of his thoughts, and he gassed it a bit too vehemently. "Any of this terrain look familiar?" he asked.

"It looks like . . . Florida."

He wondered whether she'd started to say "home," in which case he would have agreed with her. This area of South Carolina and Lake Avalon had much in common. Both had squat, disorderly palm trees, towering palms and pines as well as meticulously maintained landscaping and the small signs popular in beach communities that had ordinances designed to keep the area looking tidy. Golf appeared to be just as big of a deal here, too, judging by the signs pointing the way to the Kiawah Island Golf Resort.

"Let's find a diner that looks relatively busy," Sam said.

"Good idea. I'm starved." The bagel and coffee he'd scarfed at the hotel's continental breakfast less than an hour ago had already worn off. And Sam had to be even hungrier, because she'd eaten only a few bites from a bowl of Cheerios. He really didn't like how wan she looked, either.

"Not for food," she said. "We need to talk to some locals to see if we can get some specifics about where Baldwin lives."

"Oh." Damn. He was so lusting for some down-home biscuits and gravy. "I already have his address."

"You do? How?"

"Google."

"You're kidding. That easy?"

He shrugged it off, though the admiring gleam in her blue eyes pleased him. "I used the PC in the hotel's business center while you were in the bathroom after breakfast." He cast a searching glance at her, remembering how pale and shaky she'd looked when she'd joined him. "Were you sick again?"

She waved a dismissive hand. "It's just stress."

"Maybe we should stop at a diner anyway, or go through a drive-thru, so you can get something in your stomach."

"It's fine. I'm used to it."

"It's not healthy to be used to starving, Sam. We should at least try some oatmeal or something."

"We?" Instead of looking annoyed, though, she smiled at him.

"What?" he asked, blushing at the erotic image that popped into his head. Sam, naked and under him, smiling up at him as he thrust slowly and relentlessly into her heat. Jesus, but she was sexy as hell when she smiled. And when had she started smiling at him anyway?

"You don't have to take care of me," she said.

"Really? Because you've been doing a lot of getting shot, zoning out and throwing up. And there's the whole losing-your-memory thing."

"I'm incredibly high-maintenance. How do you put up with me?"

He grinned, his heart doing a subtle flip when she flushed slightly just before looking away. Okay, this was weird. And promising. Highly promising. Which was silly, really. Straight-laced everyman Mac Hunter getting lucky with a gorgeous government spy? Please. Stuff like that happened only in movies.

"Oh, hey," she said, sitting straighter in her seat and pointing at the golden arches sign of McDonald's. "How about an Egg McMuffin with sausage?"

"Says the woman who wanted a salad last night."

"Yeah, I know. But an Egg McMuffin sounds good. And hash browns."

He steered into the parking lot. "So you remember Egg McMuffins," he said lightly.

"I know what they are and how they taste. I don't specifically remember the last time I had one, though. Isn't that bizarre?"

"Since your memory loss was drug-induced, it probably has something to do with blocking certain . . . I don't know what you'd call them—"

"Neural receptors." She didn't appear to have to think about it.

"Okay. That's obviously familiar."

She nodded as she pressed the tips of her fingers against her temples.

"Headache?"

"It just started pounding."

"That seems to happen every time you try to tap into specific memories."

"Like a deterrent? God."

"Drive-thru or go inside?"

"Let's do drive-thru so we don't waste a bunch of time."

"It's like you're reading my mind," he said.

When the phone rang in the other room, Flinn slammed down his razor and went to answer it. He needed to hear something good, damn it, or he was going to go ballistic on the next person who irritated him. "Flinn Ford."

"I've got good news, sir," Natalie said. "I obtained the police report that the owner of the stolen Camry filed."

"And?"

"He reported that there's a cell phone in the car, in the storage cubby between the front seats. It has GPS."

"It's on?"

"I already tried to get a lock on it and yes, it's on."

Flinn rubbed a hand over his still-damp jaw and began to pace, excited energy sparking along his nerve endings. "Tell me you know where they are."

"Charleston, sir. It's kind of odd, actually. They're headed toward the coast. We assumed they were going to Lake Avalon, but—"

"Do you have men on them?"

"Not yet, sir. It would take several hours to get anyone to the area, so I wanted to check with you before—"

"I'll take care of it." He clicked off the call as he strode into his office. After waking his laptop out of sleep mode, he Googled "bail bonds" in Charleston, South Carolina. He visited a couple of Web sites until he landed on one for AAA Bail Bonds that displayed the photo of a huge, muscled man wearing a cheap suit and a friendly smile. The tagline read: "I Handle State and Federal Bonds. No Job Too Big or Too Small. MasterCard and Visa Accepted."

Flinn dialed the number.

A young woman who sounded as if her world had ended that morning answered on the third ring. "Triple A Bail Bonds."

"I want to hire a bounty hunter to track down a couple of fugitives."

"Hold, please."

Flinn waited, tapping his fingers on his desk.

"Lloyd Gould. How can I help you?"

"There are two fugitives in your area who are worth a large amount of cash if you retrieve them for me."

"Do you have access to the Internet? You can fill out a form on our Web site and—"

"I'd like to avoid the formalities. How does ten thousand dollars sound?"

A pause, and then, "What's the location of these two fugitives?"

Mac clutched the McMuffin in one hand while he steered with the other. Next to him, Sam tore into her breakfast as though she hadn't had a decent meal in months.

"Mmm, this is so good," she said.

"Guess you're not feeling sick anymore."

She stopped chewing and cocked her head as if to think about it. "Guess not."

"Maybe you were sick because your stomach was empty."

"Or maybe I'm—"

He glanced sideways at her, curious as to why she'd broken off so abruptly. She was looking straight through the windshield, her blank stare a sharp contrast to the amused tone of her voice just before she'd stopped talking.

"What?" he asked.

She didn't react. Didn't chew. Didn't swallow. Didn't blink.

"Sam?" She looked catatonic again. Damn! He hated this empathy shit.

Before he could begin the process of pulling the car over, she turned her head to blink at him. "I'm sorry, what?"

Relief let him breathe again. "Where did you go just now? Were you having one of those empathic moments?"

"No. I wasn't even touching you."

"I know, but you zoned out like you do when you . . . you know."

"Oh. No. It was nothing. Just . . . thinking."

"About what?"

She looked down at her half-eaten McMuffin as though considering wrapping up the rest and tossing it. The pink that had hued her cheeks while they chatted faded away, leaving her complexion pale again.

"Sam?" he prodded.

"I wasn't thinking about anything."

He knew a lie when he heard one. At least from her. But he also knew when to let it go. She didn't want to share, and he wasn't the kind of guy to try to force her to. As if he'd get anywhere if he did.

Silence filled the car as he drove and they finished their breakfast sandwiches. By the time they'd crumpled up their wrappers and stuffed them back into the bag, Mac was steering the Camry onto the street where former South Carolina governor Arthur Baldwin resided. Typical of island roads, gravel shoulders flanked the narrow street, the rough asphalt humming under the Toyota's tires. Massive beach homes sat high above the ground on stilts on both sides of the road, towering above the luxury cars parked underneath. Most of the homes looked new, or at least sported a fresh coat of pastel paint in pink, blue or yellow.

"I think it's at the end of the street," Mac said.

As he parked at the end of the driveway, he took in the white-shuttered, blue gray beach house somewhat camouflaged by surrounding palm and magnolia trees. It wasn't as big as its neighbors, meaning it didn't look like something a millionaire would live in, but who knew what kind of extravagance resided inside?

Mac shut off the car and glanced at Sam. "Ready?"

She nodded but made no move to open her door.

"Sam?"

"Maybe it's stupid, but I hope that whatever we learn in there doesn't change . . ." She shook her head with a soft laugh.

"Change what?"

"Nothing. It's foolish to think there's anything even to change."

"You mean, between us?" he asked, surprised. And hopeful. "It's been two days."

His point exactly. "Well, I am your only friend right now. It's like you're Jason Bourne and I'm . . . I guess I'd be the . . . well, the resourceful girlfriend who gets killed at the beginning of the second movie. Hmm, not sure I care for that comparison on a couple of levels."

He glanced at her, expecting an exasperated but slightly amused expression. Instead, her brows had drawn together in a way that looked suspiciously like hurt.

He rushed to amend his point. "I mean, I'm your only friend that you *know* of. Because of the amnesia. Of course you have other friends. I was just—"

"It's okay. You're probably more right than either of us knows anyway. Not that it matters. So, shall we?"

Before he could respond, she pushed open her door and stepped out into the ocean breeze.

CHAPTER **TWENTY-NINE**

As Sam strode up the walk, the fresh and salty ocean breeze in her face, she pushed stray hair out of her eyes and studied the front of Arthur Baldwin's home. Nothing about it sparked recognition, but all that could mean was that she'd had contact with him somewhere other than here.

Her stomach did an ominous dance, and she pressed her hand to her abdomen, willing her nerves to calm. Had to be nerves, right? Couldn't be . . . anything else. Couldn't be. And she refused to even think it anyway. Nothing she could do about anything until she got her memory back or figured out why her boss wanted her dead . . . whichever came first.

At the door, with Mac reassuringly beside her, she knocked and waited.

The door opened after about thirty seconds, and Arthur Baldwin stood there in frozen shock. "What are you doing here?" His raspy voice, as though he'd smoked a carton a day for the past forty years, carried not one tiny welcoming note.

His longish white hair was brushed back from his face, a contrast to the golden brown of his skin. In red plaid shorts and a yellow polo shirt, he appeared to be on his way to the golf course. The man had to be well into his seventies, but he had a healthy glow about him that most likely came from a privileged life of eating well and regular exercise.

"May we come in and talk to you?" Mac asked.

Sam jolted at the sound of his voice. She'd been so focused on trying to recognize Arthur Baldwin beyond the picture she'd seen on the newscast last night that she'd forgotten to say anything.

Baldwin shifted electric blue eyes to Mac. "Who the hell are you?"

Mac held out his hand. "Mac Hunter, sir."

Baldwin seemed to shake his hand automatically before Mac continued his pitch. "Sorry to bother you on such a beautiful morning, but my friend and I would like to ask you a few questions."

Sam marveled at his professionalism—and the absolute conviction in his tone that Baldwin would invite them in with a hale and hearty hello. Perhaps they could sip mint juleps on the back porch.

Then, amazingly, Baldwin stepped back and gestured them inside. His eagle gaze remained on Sam the entire time, and she imagined that if looks could kill, she'd be well on her way to the embalming table. Her stomach clutched at the thought that however she knew this man, it wasn't pleasant.

Once Baldwin shut the front door, he turned to face them. "If your boss sent you here to shake me down for more money, go ahead and try. I already told him I've got nothing left."

"Money?" Sam repeated. Not what she was expecting.

Baldwin's face twisted into a mask of such hatred that she took a step back.

And then he lunged at her, his hands going for her throat.

Mac cleanly cut Baldwin off from his assault and shoved him against the far wall with a thump, where he pinned the man with a forearm across his throat.

"Easy!" Sam shouted, grabbing onto Mac's arm.

He backed off as fast as he'd attacked, leaving behind a wad of wrinkles where he'd grabbed Baldwin's shirt, and cast a chagrined glance at her. "Sorry."

Baldwin straightened away from the wall and smoothed a hand over the front of his polo. To Sam, he said, "It doesn't matter what your muscle does to me. I've got nothing."

Mac snorted. "You think *I'm* the muscle? You obviously haven't seen this woman in action."

Baldwin kept his hard eyes on Sam. "Apparently you don't know her as well as you think you do."

Sam took a steadying breath. Her stomach was staging a revolt against the Egg McMuffin, and she feared a coup if she didn't sit down soon. "Look, can we sit and talk?"

"I've already told you. There's no more money. Don't you people watch the news? I'm as broke as you can get."

"This beach house is pretty nice, Artie," Mac commented.

Baldwin's eyes narrowed to slits. "I owe more than it's worth, so the bank is letting me stay here and pay rent."

"Yet, if you're able to pay rent, you must have income from somewhere," Mac said.

Sam put her hand on his upper arm to subtly warn him to back off. Such hostility—and violence, judging by how quickly he'd intercepted Baldwin—from a normally mild-mannered man surprised her. "We're not here for money," she softly reminded Mac.

"Right." He rolled his shoulders as if to loosen tightness. "Guess I can't control my journalistic instinct to try to flush out a lying politician."

Sam did her best to give Baldwin a nonthreatening smile, trying not to notice the way his eyes widened, as though her smile unnerved him far more than it reassured him.

"I just want to ask you some questions," she said. "I promise I'm not here for any other purpose or on anyone else's behalf."

Doubt lifted Baldwin's bushy white brows. "Forgive me if I find that difficult to believe."

"Ten minutes," Sam said. "Please."

Baldwin's shoulders stiffened further as he turned to walk into the house. "As if I have a choice," he muttered.

Sam followed him, and Mac fell into step beside her. "So . . . any bells ringing yet?"

She shook her head.

"He obviously knows you. I think you scare the bejesus out of him."

"I noticed."

"You're one badass mo-fo, aren't you?"

The fact that he gave her an impressed smile just made her stomach twist further. "You think I should be proud of the fact that this man is frightened of me?"

"It's not like he's a minister running the local food bank. He's a douche bag who ripped off the people closest to him and let his kids go down for it. Yeah, you should be proud that your presence makes him quake in his old-man shoes. Maybe if we're lucky, you could make a fast move toward him and see if he pees himself."

She stopped walking and faced him, anger flushing warmth into her face. "This isn't a joke."

Mac raised his hands, palms out. "I know. I'm just . . . damn it, that guy's a dick. Sorry if I think he deserves to squirm." He gave her an intense, soul-searching once-over. "Wait a minute. You're bugged that you're the one making him squirm. Were you hoping that you're one of those nice spies who rescues kittens from trees? I'm ninety-nine percent sure you're not."

Now she was the one wanting to squirm. Instead of responding, she turned her back on him and followed Baldwin into a sitting room at the back of the house that looked out over a private beach. Sliding glass doors were closed against the chill outside, but the sound of the rush and retreat of the ocean waves bled through the glass. Other than a black microfiber recliner with a well-worn seat, the furniture was white wicker with solid blue cushions. A large flat-panel television hung on the wall adjacent to the glass doors, tuned to a news channel starring a ranting political commentator.

Baldwin said nothing as he settled himself into the recliner, picked up the TV remote and muted the sound. His demeanor screamed defeat.

Sam sat on a wicker chair and clasped her hands in her lap. She didn't want to feel sorry for this man, but she did. Maybe because she feared—no, she was *certain*—that she'd played a significant role in his despondency.

She cleared the tightness from her throat. "Mr. Baldwin, could you tell me how we know each other?"

He stared blankly at her. "Excuse me?"

"You made a reference earlier to my boss. You meant Flinn Ford, right?"

He turned a suspicious gaze on Mac. "What is this?"

"Just answer the questions, Artie, and everything will be fine," Mac said.

Baldwin pressed his lips together. "Flinn Ford is the man who blackmailed me, yes."

Blackmail. Terrific. She swallowed and shifted to try to alleviate the tension in her back. "What role did I play in that?"

Baldwin pushed out of the chair, his features twisting in rage. "What the hell is going on here? Is this some kind of joke? Are you people here to fuck with me? I told you! I've got nothing! And even if I did have anything, the deal is off. You people broke your end of the bargain. I'm ruined now. My life is *over*!" Spittle flew from his mouth, and his face turned heart-attack red. "I did everything I was supposed to do. *Everything*. I played by your fucking rules. I gave you millions of dollars. Fucking *millions*. And my brother still went to prison and when the market collapsed and I lost everything and the rumors began to fly, you did nothing to help me. I have nothing now. I *am* nothing. Because of *you*."

"Mr. Baldwin, please calm down." Sam rose, fearing he would send himself into cardiac arrest. She grasped one of his flailing arms, fingers digging into his shirt as she braced to angle his arm behind his back to control him. He yelped.

In her peripheral vision, Sam saw Mac jump to his feet. "Stay there!" she ordered.

The distraction was all Baldwin needed. He yanked away from her, whipped around and backhanded her.

The floor dropped out from under her.

Mac leapt forward and grabbed the older man's wrist before he could deliver another blow. The first had been so lightning fast, Mac hadn't seen it coming any more than Sam had. One instant the man had been gesturing wildly, and the next, he'd taken a swipe at Sam that had sent her reeling. Now, she slid in slow motion down the wall, limbs boneless, eyes fixed and far, far away.

Shit, shit, shit. Mac had to all but wrestle the struggling Baldwin back into his recliner. "Stay put," Mac growled when the older man started back up.

Baldwin ignored the order, and Mac had to push him back

with a none-too-gentle hand to the chest. He would have preferred to punch the living daylights out of the bastard. "Move and I'll knock you flat. I'm not kidding."

"What's the matter with her?" Baldwin asked, the fury in his gaze morphing into worry. Not for Sam, though. The pathetic old geezer feared what would happen to him if he'd harmed her. "I lost control of myself for a moment. I didn't mean to strike her."

"Yeah, like you didn't mean to attack her when we first got here, either, right?"

"I'm a crazy old man. You people took everything from me. I've got a right to be angry."

"Whatever. Just stay put. You can go back to watching your TV in about two minutes."

Mac turned his back on Baldwin and knelt next to Sam. He had no idea how to snap her out of her fugue state. He tried her name first, uncertain whether touching her would make the situation worse. "Sam?"

And just like that, she blinked.

Relief sagged his shoulders. That was easy. "You're back."

Her eyes tracked to him in such a sluggish way that the muscles in his chest retightened. If possible, she looked whiter than she had all morning. "You okay?"

She gave a distracted nod as she pushed to her feet, ignoring his offer of a hand up, and turned toward Baldwin, who sat still and tense in his chair. She gazed at him for a long moment, her breathing heavy but steady. "Your brother Jake. Where is he?"

Mac didn't move, not liking the coiled tension in her muscles, the controlled rage in the way she breathed. "Who's Jake?"

Baldwin's eyes narrowed to slits of ice, and his hands tightened on the arms of the recliner until his knuckles lost color. "Fuck you, bitch. Fuck both of you!"

Sam lunged at him, pinning him in his chair with a strong hand at his throat. The muscles in her forearm flexed as she squeezed.

Mac took an alarmed step forward. "Hey—"

"Stay back!"

Mac stopped.

Baldwin's face started to turn purple, and his eyes bulged, a strangled cough escaping his lips.

"Where. Is. *Jake*." Sam's voice had gone low and deadly.

Baldwin gagged, sputtered. His lips moved in a soundless "Fuck . . . you."

"Sam, you're killing him." Mac tried to speak in a reasonable tone.

He didn't think she'd heard him. Or perhaps she ignored him. "Sam," he said more firmly.

A beat later, as though it took a few seconds for his warning to reach her brain, she loosened her grip.

Baldwin heaved in a raspy breath.

Sam kept her hand at his throat, her other hand braced on the arm of his chair. "Tell me where he is or I'll crush your trachea. You'll be breathing through a tube for the rest of your miserable life."

Jesus. Mac's head spun a little at the threat. If he'd been at the other end of it, he would have pissed himself. And this was a woman he'd earlier thought had to have the most adorable smile on the planet.

"My brother is dead," Baldwin rasped. "You killed him."

Sam backed off so fast that she stumbled into Mac. He caught her with his hands at her waist and steadied her. She shoved him away, though not violently, and pushed by him.

Mac started to follow her but turned instead at the sudden ruckus behind him.

Baldwin was charging after Sam, and Mac blocked him like a defensive linebacker. "Oh no, you don't."

As Mac shuffled the older man back to his chair, Baldwin started screaming after Sam's retreating back. "You killed him, you fucking bitch! You killed my brother!"

Mac wrestled him down and practically had to sit on him to get him to stay. When the old man's energy finally ran out, he sagged against the cushions, tears streaming down his face. "That bitch and her boss cost me everything."

When Mac was reasonably sure the man was done fighting,

he straightened up. "Did she set up the Ponzi scheme that ruined your friends and family?"

"It was because of her I did it. She and that bastard Flinn Ford didn't give me a choice. And then, they betrayed me."

Mac didn't know what to say to that. And he was more worried about what Sam was doing outside. What if she took off without him? But, no, he had the keys to the Camry. Still, he decided that what happened to her was more of a concern to him than this broken con artist of a politician.

"Have a nice day, asshole," Mac said, and left.

Mac found Sam sitting on the top step of Baldwin's porch, arms wrapped tightly around her middle, her stare vacant. The sight made his heart jump with dread.

He trailed a light hand over her shoulder. "Ready to go?"

She rose without answering, and they walked together to the car and got in.

He said nothing as he started the car and backed out of the driveway. He could tell from her utter stillness that she wasn't ready to share what she'd seen in Baldwin's head when she'd touched him. Or what Baldwin had been screaming about. *You killed him, you fucking bitch! You killed my brother!*

The silence took them to Highway 17. Mac estimated they could be in Lake Avalon sometime the next day, depending on stop-and-go traffic and the winding, indirect back roads with varying speed limits. Taking the interstates would have been so much faster, but he didn't dare. Too many police, and who knew how deep Ford's connections went.

"His brother was a serial rapist, the one I told you about from my flashback."

The dead quality to her voice startled him. Not that he could do anything about it. Except listen. "You saw that when you touched him?"

"When I met his brother Jake at a fund-raiser, I . . . mined his memories to get information Flinn Ford could use against Arthur to blackmail him."

"Blackmail him for what?"

"Money. Some kind of research. I targeted Arthur, too. Sorted through his memories to find out if he knew about his brother's vice. He did." She pressed the tips of her fingers to the center of her forehead. "God."

"Head hurting again?" Wasn't it obvious? Jesus, he felt inadequate.

She nodded without looking at him or letting up with the pressure of her fingers. "I can't imagine how I did this all the time as part of my job without wanting to blow my own head off."

"Maybe you took something for the pain."

She didn't respond, just sat with her eyes closed and head down, barely breathing.

"Did you find out from Baldwin what kind of research Ford was doing?" Mac asked. Maybe distracting her would help. Or maybe it would make the pain worse. Damn it, he hated not knowing what to do for her.

"I don't think Baldwin knew. He set up the pyramid scheme to keep money flowing to Flinn. In return, Flinn kept his secret that Baldwin knew about his brother's crimes but hid that from law enforcement while he was governor. When the pyramid scheme collapsed and the spotlight landed on the Baldwins, rumors began to fly that Arthur knew what Jake had done. Flinn didn't do anything to try to shield Arthur. He let him go down in flames. In fact, Arthur suspects that Flinn's the one who tipped off the press to his knowledge of Jake's crimes."

"Jesus," Mac said. Tangled webs indeed.

"Arthur thought I came today to finish him off because the flow of funds had stopped."

"But according to the news reports, the scam collapsed months ago."

"He was scared. Logic doesn't play a part when you're that scared."

"Well, he knows now that you weren't sent to kill him."

She was silent for a long moment, and Mac kept quiet, figuring she'd keep talking if she felt like it.

"He said I killed his brother. It didn't occur to me that killing people is part of my job for N3."

Mac looked back at the road and thanked God she had to be touching him to know that he was remembering when she'd shot down the two goons with guns. Self-defense all the way, but still, he feared she might have more deaths to feel guilty about.

"To be fair," he said, "Jake Baldwin was a serial rapist. He deserved whatever he got."

She shifted her head as though something had occurred to her, or the headache had increased exponentially.

"What?" Mac prodded. "Is the pain getting worse?"

"No. I just . . . it's a weird coincidence that I had that flashback about Jake while we were on our way to confront Arthur."

"Maybe it's not a coincidence. Maybe when you saw the picture of Arthur Baldwin on the news, it triggered something in your mind that led you to that particular flashback. Have you had others?"

"I remembered the day I left Lake Avalon. I was talking to Charlie while I packed." She smiled slightly. "We talked about me going to culinary school."

"Really? Interesting." He imagined her chopping vegetables with a huge chef's knife, all sweet and innocent, a cloud of flour dusting the tip of her nose. Then, just like that, she flicked the knife into the throat of a bad guy bearing down on her.

No way should that image have been any degree of hot, but damned if he didn't have to shift in his seat to allow more room in his jeans.

He shoved the image from his head. "Did that flashback happen after I told you I'd talked to Charlie on the phone?"

"It was after . . ." She angled her head, trying to connect the dots, or perhaps hesitating to tell him that she'd already figured out the shape the dots formed.

"After what?"

"It was after you promised to be there for me while I slept."

"Oh." A rush of warmth swept up his neck as he remembered holding her and how right it had felt.

"After that, I dreamed of a similar promise I made to Charlie," she said.

"Your subconscious knows Charlie's important to you."

"If she's that important to me, then why haven't I seen her or Alex in more than a decade?" She looked out the window as she spoke, but he didn't have to see her face to know she was fighting tears. He could hear them in the thickening of her voice.

"I'm just taking a stab in the dark here," he said. "I have no idea how the brain works. But doesn't it make at least a little bit of sense that while you're adrift without your memory, your mind would try to find something to anchor itself to?"

She gave that idea some thought. "I suppose that makes sense."

"Wouldn't that mean, then, that your memory isn't completely gone? It's trying to come back."

When she didn't respond, he glanced over at her. She was staring straight ahead.

"That's a good thing," he said. "Right?"

No answer. Not even a blink.

"Sam? You do want your memory back, don't you?"

"Depends on how many people I've killed."

CHAPTER **THIRTY**

Sam roused from a light sleep as the rhythm of the car's movement changed. She opened her eyes to see that Mac was pulling into a gas station that looked so ramshackle and deserted she was surprised it was even open. The sign, faded from hours in the Southern sun and countless rain showers, identified the station simply as Eddy's.

He shut off the car. "Need anything? Bathroom break? Snacks? Maybe some water?"

She squinted at the sagging roof and gray, weather-beaten wood that formed the sides of the shack. The parking lot itself was nothing but a layer of gravel. "I'm thinking the bathroom here might be condemned."

He rubbed the back of his neck. "You're probably right, but we're kind of desperate for gas. Maybe there's a Stop N Rob up the road that has a decent bathroom."

"Stop N Rob?"

He chuckled. "Newspaper-speak for those convenience stores that always get robbed late at night."

"Ah."

He got out of the car and, heeding the PAY BEFORE YOU PUMP sign taped to the fuel dispenser, strode into the shack. The hingeless door banged shut behind him.

Sam pushed open her door, stepping out into fresh air that carried just a hint of gasoline fumes, and stretched muscles that had gotten stiff from the hours in the passenger seat.

Cars whizzed by on the two-lane highway that stretched past the gas station, and a strong breeze swayed through the palm trees and pines that lined both sides of the road. Clouds promising a thunderstorm crowded the sky overhead.

Mac returned and started pumping gas while she pressed both hands to her lower back to stretch.

"Looks like rain," he said as he perused the ominous clouds.

Sam almost smiled, struck by how normal everything seemed in that moment. A man and a woman on a road trip. No worries here.

A black Ford F-150 pickup turned into the station, crunching gravel beneath its tires. The passenger, sporting a military-short crew cut and eyes that looked too small for his massive bald head, checked her out as the truck rolled by. Tension didn't tighten her already taut muscles until the driver leaned forward and stared past his friend at her. He had shaggy brown hair and an honest-to-God handlebar mustache.

Apprehension ran up her spine like red flags on a pole. She might have had no memory, but she knew trouble when she spotted it.

While the truck parked in a spot in front of the run-down building, Sam casually walked over to the driver's side of the Camry, where Mac kept watch on the dollar total on the pump.

"Almost done?" she asked.

"Just about."

"Might want to wrap it up." She cut her eyes toward the men in the truck as both got out and slammed their doors, not appearing to be in any real hurry.

"What?" Mac mouthed.

She reached past him and put the hose back in its cradle then opened the back door of the car. "Get in."

He stared at her. "For real?"

She nudged his shoulder, and he ducked into the backseat while she opened the driver's door and slid behind the wheel. The keys weren't in the ignition. Crap. "Keys?"

Out of the corner of her eye, she saw the two men striding toward them, their pace picking up. Crap. *Crap.*

The key ring appeared beside her head, and she snatched it from Mac's fingers, grateful he hadn't argued or asked questions. "Buckle up," she ordered and started the car.

She saw the two men draw guns at the same moment that

she shifted into drive and floored the accelerator, sending gravel flying. She swerved the car onto the highway, grateful that the coast was clear, and caught a glimpse in the rearview of the two guys clambering back into their truck.

"Who the hell is that?" Mac asked from the backseat.

"Hired guns."

"How did they find us?"

"Don't know. Hang on."

She whipped the car into a hard right turn, sending them careening onto a side street that was more narrow than the highway and had no line down the middle. The black Ford followed on smoking tires.

"Get your head down," Sam said.

"What about *your* head?" Mac shot back.

"Is your seat belt fastened?"

"Fuck."

She raised her chin so she could watch him in the rearview as he fumbled to get the safety belt hooked while the car jumped and jittered over the uneven road. Every bump sent a pulse of pain through her healing shoulder, but she ignored the discomfort and focused on what she had to do.

"Hang on!"

She jammed on the brakes and jerked the steering wheel to the left, sending the car into a screeching one-eighty that ended with the Camry facing the direction they'd just traveled, heading straight into a game of chicken with the Ford.

The driver of the pickup stood on his brakes and turned, skidding to a stop lengthways across the street and creating a roadblock with the truck.

"Oh, shit," Mac said.

"No problem," Sam murmured, and shoved the gas pedal to the floor.

The front end of the Camry slammed into the left front tire of the truck, and an air bag exploded in her face.

Mac spat blood out of his mouth—he'd bitten his tongue—and raised his head to get his bearings. Air bags had deployed inside the Camry. One of the side-curtain air bags in the back had smacked him square in the left side of the head, sending a thick cloud of stinging gas and dust into the air.

The silence seemed deafening after the roar of the engine, screech of tires and crunch of metal. Nothing in the car moved, and his heart skipped several beats. He released his safety belt then scrambled forward to grab onto the back of the driver's seat. "Sam? Sam!"

She shifted in the seat, shoving at the air bag that had blasted out of the steering wheel.

"You okay?" he asked.

She didn't respond as she put the car in park, restarted it— Mac couldn't believe it actually fired up—and shifted into reverse, her actions clumsy as the deployed air bag got in her way. She braced her right hand on the headrest of the passenger seat, her forehead creased in either concentration or pain, and floored the gas.

"You're blocking my view," she told him. Not a hint of anxiety in her tone.

He scooted across the seat to the other side, out of her line of sight, and watched the pissed-off guys as they tumbled out of their pickup and kicked at the front left tire that the impact had all but folded under the truck.

Meanwhile, Sam threw the Camry back into drive and gassed it onto the grassy shoulder and around the crippled Ford. Mac looked back to see the two men arguing with each other instead of grabbing their weapons and trying to shoot at the Camry. Hired guns, indeed. Thugs in Ford's immediate chain of command wouldn't have given up so easily.

At the main highway, Sam pulled into traffic as if the front end of the Toyota weren't crunched.

"We need a new car," she said casually, as if she'd said nothing more important than, "I could use a cigarette."

Mac barked out a laugh. "Ya think?"

He wedged his way between the bucket seats to claim the passenger seat and looked around at the destruction inside the car. No glass had broken, but the air bags had made a huge mess. "Nice driving," he said, rolling his left shoulder, already sore from where his body had jerked against the safety harness. "You learn that in spy school?"

"Apparently."

"How'd they find us?"

"The car must be LoJacked."

"Can't be. It took them way too long to track us."

After several miles of silence, Sam pulled into the parking lot of a shopping center and drove around to the back. A trailer sat at a loading dock, but there was no activity around it. She parked the Camry and shut it off. Without a moment of just sitting there to breathe, she got out and went to the trunk.

Mac followed, sparing a glance at the front, which was surprisingly intact, though noticeably crunched. "What're you doing?" he asked as he joined Sam at the back.

"Trying to figure out how they tracked us." She popped the trunk and checked out the contents: a navy blue gym bag, an ice scraper, a pair of black winter gloves and a small plastic bin with a lid that held maps and a first-aid kit.

"Nothing suspicious," Mac said.

Sam reached for the gym bag, zipped it open and dumped it upside down. Out tumbled running shoes, a wrinkled T-shirt and shorts, socks, a hand towel and the smell of dried sweat.

"What are you looking for?"

She didn't respond as she stalked to the passenger side of the Camry, opened the door and flicked open the glove box. Inside nestled more maps, a small flashlight, a couple of insurance cards, the vehicle's registration and the car's manual. She leaned across the seat and lifted the lid on the center console, groping inside with one hand, eyes narrowed with purpose.

Mac had to bite back annoyance at her lack of communication. "I could help you look if you'd tell me—"

Her expression changed to one of triumphant, and she withdrew her hand from the storage compartment.

Mac stared in disbelief at the silver Motorola cell phone resting in her palm. He reached for it. "Does it have GPS?"

"All cell phones have GPS. The important question is, is it on?"

He flipped it open, then winced as the display lit up in welcome. "Well, shit."

"I lost them."

Flinn got up and shut the door of his office. No one was within earshot, but he didn't want to take any chances. "How could you lose them? I told you exactly where to find them." Flinn had to fight to loosen his grip on his cell phone before he snapped it at the hinges.

"Bitch disabled my truck. Where do I send the bill for the repairs?"

Flinn's rage boiled over. "I'm not paying to fix your fucking truck, you fucking moron! You didn't get the job done!"

"You didn't tell me the bitch knew how to drive like goddamn Vin Diesel."

"I told you not to underestimate her. Did you hear me say 'woman' and decide you could take her without any effort?"

"Look, dude, it didn't work out. Not my fault. Now, are we going to settle this like adults or do I need to get angry?"

Flinn snorted into the phone. "You have no idea who you're dealing with, *dude*. I'll have your licenses pulled by the end of the day. Enjoy your unemployment."

Flinn slammed his phone closed and fired it at the nearest wall.

CHAPTER **THIRTY-ONE**

Sam's eyes grew heavy as she watched the thick, green foliage of Georgia fly by in a 55-miles-per-hour blur.

It hadn't taken them long to swipe another car. They'd parked at a gas station and waited for a trusting soul to leave his keys in the ignition and his car running while he ducked inside for a doughnut, coffee, cigarettes or something else he would dearly regret. As soon as Mac and Sam reached the next town, they visited a busy mall parking lot, where they traded that car, an older-model white Chevy Cobalt, for a dark blue Honda Accord. Sam hot-wired the Honda while Mac searched it for any wayward cell phones, then switched license plates on both the Cobalt and the Accord.

Now, they were back on the road, Mac behind the wheel. The even, quiet roar of the tires, interrupted in regular intervals by subtle, horizontal seams in the pavement, insisted on lulling Sam to sleep. She fought it as long as she could, only to slip into a past her conscious brain didn't remember . . .

The tiny gray room, everything about it cold and metallic, seemed to close in on her on all sides. A large mirror occupied the upper half of the unpainted concrete wall she faced. She imagined police detectives lined up on the window side, watching her, discussing her.

"That's Samantha Trudeau. Killed the man who killed her daddy."

The scent of blood turned her stomach, and she swallowed convulsively, refusing to glance down and acknowledge the spatter on her hands and arms, across the front of her white

T-shirt. Every cell in her whole body seemed to twist with fear, weighed down by guilt.

The door to the chilly room opened, and in walked one of the officers who'd arrested her. He didn't look much older than her nineteen years. Crew-cut blond hair, crisp navy uniform, freckles and some lingering acne. Despite their shared youth, his deep brown eyes looked old, as though they had seen too much in too little time. A year ago she couldn't have related in any way. She could now.

"Detective Don Stewart, Miss Trudeau. We met earlier." He pulled out the folding chair across the scarred, metal table from her. "I'm going to take your official statement. Let's start from the beginning."

"I want to make a phone call." She needed her father. Her real *father*.

"Not until I've gotten your statement."

"Then, can I have a lawyer?"

"You haven't been arrested. Really, Miss Trudeau, you're making this more difficult than it has to be. Just tell me what happened. Start at the beginning."

"I already told you. Robert Radnor killed my father."

"Clearly, you don't understand what I'm asking you. I want to know what happened *after* you arrived at Mr. Radnor's office with a loaded gun."

She pressed her lips together, fighting for a composure long gone. "The sequence of events began when he killed my father."

"Miss Trudeau—"

A harsh knock cut him off, and a tall, thin man in a dark suit entered the interrogation room.

"I'm in the middle of taking a statement," Detective Stewart snapped.

"Not anymore," the other man said, smiling gently at her. "I'll take it from here."

Stewart got to his feet. "Who the hell are you?"

Still smiling, the man in the suit retrieved a badge from his belt and flashed it at the officer. "FBI Special Agent Flinn Ford. I'd like a word with Miss Trudeau."

"I don't think—"

"Your lieutenant will explain, Detective."

As Stewart stormed out, Sam warily watched as the FBI agent walked around the side of the table toward her. He had light brown hair thinning at the crown and eyes so dark they looked black. She guessed his age at late thirties to early forties. The way he assessed her, as though inspecting a car for sale, sent a chill through her. If he tried to kick her tires, she'd kick back.

Instead, he extended a hand. "It's an honor to meet you, Miss Trudeau."

She didn't take his hand. Who knew what kind of horrors lurked in the mind of an FBI agent?

His smile broadened into amusement. "No touching, eh?"

Part of her wanted Detective Stewart back. Reading him was easy. This man was slick, smug, the kind who'd call himself a straight shooter but would shoot crooked at every opportunity.

"Has a medical professional examined your injuries?"

She lifted a hand to run light fingers over the swelled flesh around her eye. The memory of Radnor's fist smashing into bone burst in her head like a dying light bulb. "It's fine."

"That's not what I asked."

"I've been to the ER."

He pulled out a chair but didn't sit. "You're in some trouble, Samantha. I can call you Samantha, can't I?"

"I want to call my dad in Lake Avalon, Florida. His name is Reed Trudeau."

"Perhaps you'd like to hear what I have to say first."

"I'd rather talk to my dad."

"I have a way out of this trouble you're in, Samantha. Would you like to hear it?"

She would, very much. But she also knew better than to trust this man. She didn't trust anyone, not anymore. Except her sisters. And the man she'd called "Dad" her whole life. She was such a fool. She'd wanted answers from the side of the family she'd never met. Her self-centered, closemouthed mother hadn't provided answers, so she'd sought them on her own. She'd been desperate to find the man who'd helped give her life, the man who'd helped give her the ability to experience other people's crappy, soul-sucking memories. She'd just wanted answers.

She refocused on the FBI agent, realizing he waited for her response. What had he said? He had a way out for her. She didn't believe him.

He angled his head. "You understand what I mean, don't you? I have a way for you to avoid spending the rest of your life in prison."

Her heart jittered. "I haven't been convicted of anything. I haven't even been arrested."

His smile didn't waver, all white teeth. "Let's go over the facts, shall we? You confronted Mr. Radnor, a well-respected lawyer in this Wisconsin town of sixty thousand people, in his office with a loaded gun."

"He killed my biological father, Ben Dillon."

"And the good folks of Janesville have never heard of him."

She waited, unsure of his point.

"People here liked Mr. Radnor," he said. "He did good work for many of them."

"He was an asshole."

One corner of Flinn Ford's mouth ticked up. "A well-liked asshole whom the good people of Janesville respected. And who are you to those same people?"

"I'm the biological daughter of the man Mr. Radnor killed."

"You're the young woman who helped her father try to blackmail Mr. Radnor. You're a liar, Samantha. A con artist. And a killer."

She had no response to that, so she just stared at him as blankly as she could while black spots splattered her vision. A killer. Oh, God, she was a killer.

He finally sat down with a creak of metal. He was so big that the chair looked like something out of Barbie's Jailhouse. "The FBI was watching Mr. Dillon. Why do you think the federal government would be interested in a common grifter?"

"He crossed state lines."

His smile blossomed into a full-blown grin. "You're smart. Excellent. Ben Dillon first came to the FBI's attention when he took his con-artist ways from Illinois into Wisconsin. And then we noticed something about him. Something special."

She couldn't stop her shoulders from stiffening.

"His cons had an extra element to them," he went on. "The common grifter cons people who are gullible, stupid, softhearted or any combination of those traits. Mr. Dillon, however, targeted intelligent, wealthy men in positions of power. That takes something extra." He paused for dramatic effect. "It takes psychic ability."

Her stomach knotted tight. "That's ridiculous."

"Mr. Dillon would have told you that that response would have been more convincing if you hadn't said it so quickly." He folded his pale, manicured hands on the table. "It won't do any good to deny it, Samantha. I already know all about Mr. Dillon's psychic gift. I also know that you share it."

"No, I don't." She struggled to control the shakes.

"You used that empathic gift on Mr. Radnor yesterday afternoon at the sidewalk café."

"It wasn't to—"

"You're on FBI surveillance tape, Samantha. You and Mr. Dillon. You bumped into Mr. Radnor and used that contact to learn of his fondness for underage girls, which you and Mr. Dillon used to trick him into propositioning you so your father could take incriminating photographs that he could then use for blackmail."

Oh, God, that was a completely different scenario than the one Ben had laid out for her. And yet it made perfect sense.

"Mr. Dillon was wanted for many crimes," the agent said. "Did you know that?"

Her face grew warm. "No."

She wasn't surprised. Not now. Yesterday's events put in stark relief the differences between her biological father and her father in Lake Avalon. The man who'd raised her in Florida loved her without condition, in spite of the many rebellious *reasons she'd given him to scowl and rant. Ben Dillon of Chicago gave her what she couldn't get in Florida: answers. He assured her that her psychic ability was a gift, not a curse. And then he turned around and tricked her into using her gift for financial gain.*

Her stomach flipped all over again at the wrongness of it all. He'd told her Robert Radnor was the worst kind of man, that they were going to stop him from victimizing girls and young women. The glimpse she'd gotten inside Radnor's mind had shown her that Ben was right. She'd gone along with his plot to expose the predator, excited to use her gift to do good things. Ben never once mentioned the word black-mail.

"He should have protected you, Samantha," Agent Ford said. "He should have done everything in his power to take care of you, his long-lost daughter. But he used you, didn't he? He used you and your ability to try to cheat a good man out of his money."

She swallowed hard. "Mr. Radnor was not a good man."

He leaned forward and dropped his voice to a level meant for secrets. "I can get you out of here, Samantha. I can offer you a new life. A place to call home."

"I already have a home." And she wanted to go back. So bad. She missed Charlie's sarcasm and Alex's innocence. Missed Dad's warm bear hugs and deep, reassuring voice. His strong sense of right and wrong. He wouldn't have liked Ben Dillon. Not at all.

"What was the gun for, Samantha?" The FBI agent's voice, deep and sharp, cut into her thoughts.

"I wanted to scare him." She answered without thinking.

"The gun was loaded, and you knew it."

"Yes, but—"

"You pointed it at him and shot him. Point-blank."

"That's—"

"You shot him, Samantha. Isn't that right?"

"Yes, but—"

"You shot and killed Mr. Radnor. With your father's gun."

"It wasn't—"

"You've already said yes, Samantha. You've already confessed."

Those words smacked her in the forehead. Confessed? She hadn't confessed. No way. Had she?

"I asked you if you shot him, and you said, 'Yes.' That's a confession." He nodded toward the security camera in the corner. *"It's on tape."*

The blood drained out of her head, and white sparkles twinkled at the edges of her vision.

Flinn Ford wasn't done. "I said I would help you, remember, Samantha? You have choices. You can stay here and face a judge and jury that will without a doubt sentence you to life in prison for the murder you just confessed to, or you can come work for me at the FBI."

CHAPTER **THIRTY-TWO**

Sam woke to sun streaming in through the windshield. Narrowing her eyes against the glare, she raised a hand and peered around. Mac wasn't in the driver's seat. The car sat in a parking area that faced an open, grassy lot. A Little League game appeared to be under way on a baseball diamond in the far corner of the fenced-in area.

The Accord's windows were down, a light breeze blowing in while it shuffled the fronds of towering palm trees. She twisted in the seat to take stock of her surroundings and saw the parking lot belonged to a two-story, off-white Mediterranean-style building with large, arched windows.

The sound of a car horn bleated in the distance, and the excited shrieks of kids drew her gaze back to the ball game. Moms and dads watched the kids from the sidelines. One female spectator idly rolled a baby stroller back and forth while she cooed at the fussing baby inside.

Sam couldn't imagine that kind of existence. Even though she'd forgotten 99 percent of her past, she knew instinctively that her life had nothing whatsoever to do with baby strollers and walks in the park.

Make that: She'd forgotten *98* percent of her past. She'd just remembered the part where Flinn Ford shrewdly hooked his talons into her and never planned to let go. And she'd been a naïve little idiot, too scared and too out of her league to know how to defend herself. Maybe she'd been that naïve little idiot her whole life.

Suddenly needing more air than what made it through the windows, she shoved open the car door and got out. She walked to a nearby bench and sat down, wondering where Mac was and why he'd left her alone and asleep. Someone so easily could have compromised her position. God, civilians could be so—

"Sam!"

She jerked her head up, startled at the sound of her name, then relieved to see Mac jogging toward her, a white plastic bag dangling from one hand. At first, she was struck by how incredibly good he looked. All that lean muscle filling out well-worn jeans and a black T-shirt, his dark hair disheveled in the breeze, his jaw shadowed with a rapidly darkening beard. His eyes were so warm, so kind—

Then she remembered their situation, and irritation quickly chased away her appreciation of his good looks. She rose to meet him. "Where were you?"

"Running a couple of errands. Didn't you see my note?"

A note? For the love of Pete, were they in high school? "I didn't see a note."

"I left it on the dashboard for you." He glanced back at the Accord, shielding his eyes against the sun. "Damn, the breeze must have blown it onto the floorboard. Sorry about that."

He flashed his innocent, puppy-dog smile, an expression that sharply contrasted his ferocity when he'd slammed Arthur Baldwin up against the wall that morning.

"Where are we?" she asked.

"Jacksonville, Florida. Oh, and I picked up some dinner." He hoisted the bag. "Hope you like Mexican." He took a quick glance around. "Maybe we can find a picnic table. Don't know about you, but I'm sick of the car." He spotted a table under a large jacaranda tree and gestured. "Over there okay?"

She nodded as she fell into step beside him. The breeze blew hair back from her face, and she could swear she smelled the salty scent of ocean water in the air.

He flashed her a sideways grin as he settled the plastic bag on the picnic table and started fishing through it. "I got us some chips and guacamole, too. The woman at the library— she's the one who recommended the place—said the guac there is the best on the planet. Which might not be the most reliable endorsement, because the place is called Burrito Planet."

Her dream about Flinn eased to the back of her mind. For now, she decided, she would share in Mac's enthusiasm for the simple things in life, like guacamole and talking to strangers. "Do you strike up a conversation with everyone you meet?"

"Occupational hazard. It's amazing what strangers will tell you when you show some interest." He set two bottles of water on the table, then lined up four wrapped burritos, each the length of a paperback novel and as thick as his muscled forearm.

"We've got ground beef, chicken, grilled veggies and Barbacoa, which is shredded beef. What'll you have?"

She couldn't help but smile at how much the man loved his food. "Which do you want?"

"I'm a gentleman, which means you get to pick first. Or, you could try them all. You probably don't remember what you like."

"I'll start with the chicken."

"The Burrito Planet guy said that's their best one." He handed it over. "I'm opting for the ground beef. He said that one's spicy enough to take the varnish off your chest." He grinned. "I think English might be his third or fourth language."

She laughed as she cracked open her bottle of water and took a long drink. It was so odd to have such an innocuous conversation, yet it felt so right. She just hoped that her unsettled stomach could handle what she was about to put in it.

Across from her, Mac chomped into his burrito and *mmm*'d deep in his throat, a low, sexy sound that had her body growling in response.

"What were you doing at the library?" she asked quickly before her head could road-trip down a path she wasn't prepared to explore.

"I sent Charlie an e-mail."

She stopped unwrapping her burrito. "You what?"

"Relax. We're in Jacksonville, and we're coming up on rush

hour. Even if Ford's people track us, we'll be long gone by the time they get anywhere near the area."

She didn't relax, too tense from the anxiety of being on the run, not to mention the disconcerting flashbacks. The uncertainty of everything was getting to her. She hated constantly looking over her shoulder, not knowing who to trust or when Flinn and his muscle might bear down on them again. Most of all, she hated that being with her, helping her, put Mac in the line of fire. She wished he'd never gotten dragged into her mess. Yet, if he hadn't, she knew exactly where she'd be right now: dead. And what if he ended up dead because of her?

"Sam, come on, I mean it. You need to relax. I was careful, I swear."

"What did you say?" She tried to sound casual despite the fear that his good intentions had once again given away their location—or at least where they planned to be.

"I asked Charlie to bring Alex and their respective boy toys to meet us at a hotel in St. Pete."

She smirked at his use of "boy toys." She wouldn't mind making *him* her boy toy . . . and, God, where had *that* come from? She picked up her burrito and hoped she didn't look as flustered as she felt. "St. Pete?"

"St. Petersburg. Just south of Tampa, about a hundred miles or so north of Lake Avalon."

"Right. I remember that now."

"I told her to leave their cell phones and any navigation systems at home and make sure they're not followed. I also suggested they borrow someone else's car. Their boyfriends both have law enforcement backgrounds, so they'll know how to get that done."

"Flinn will be monitoring their e-mail accounts."

"I figured as much, so I didn't mention St. Pete or the name of the hotel."

"Then how will Charlie know where to meet us?"

"I asked her to meet us at 'that place that we went that time.' When we were dating, we took a weekend away from Lake Avalon only once. She'll know what I mean."

She couldn't stop the dubious arch of her brow. "How can you be sure?"

"We both love that movie *Broadcast News* from the late eighties. We didn't understand it when it first came out, of course, because we were only, like, eight or so. But Charlie has the DVD, and we've watched it over and over, laughing our asses off because what it says about the sad state of the news business is still true, twentysomething years later."

Sam smiled in spite of her anxiety. Sometimes the man talked in circles. Funny that that trait in anyone else would have driven her up the wall. But in Mac, she found it was . . . adorable.

"So, right, back to Charlie and the hotel. There's a line in the movie, where Albert Brooks calls Holly Hunter and says, 'Meet me at that place that we went that time.' Or something like that. They're such good friends that she immediately knows what he means. Charlie will get it, too."

Sam wasn't sure what to make of his assertion of his and Charlie's closeness. Jealousy seemed inappropriate, especially considering the unspoken rules between sisters: Thou shalt not date your sister's ex-boyfriends. At the same time, she wondered what Charlie had been thinking when she'd let this man go. She couldn't imagine a kinder, sweeter . . . hotter guy. And while she didn't remember Charlie in all her 3-D personality and foibles, she did have the sense that her sister was no dummy.

"Sam?"

She blinked. "I'm sorry. What?"

He reached across the table to cover her hand with his. "It'll be okay. Trust me."

She braced for the shock of memory, but other than a lightning flash of dizziness, nothing happened. Unless she counted the surge of warmth from his palm, the zing of adrenaline that pumped her heart faster, the urge to roll her hand under his and slide her fingers between his . . .

Mac jerked his hand back. "Oh, damn. Sorry. Are you—"

"Nothing happened."

"Really? That's great. Isn't it?"

"From the standpoint of getting a headache, it is. From the standpoint of getting to relive something horrible that happened to you, it *really* is." She gave him a smile that trembled some. She was such a wuss for a government spy. She hoped she wasn't this weak on the job.

"Kind of weird, though, isn't it?" He peered at her so intensely she started to flush. "You got nothing?"

"Maybe my system is settling down. It's been so out of whack . . . I really don't know how it works. It might be inconsistent. I might need to concentrate to make it happen. Or maybe because I've already tapped into your memories more than once, my ability's acclimated to that."

"That'd be handy. Even if that's not the case, you've already tapped into the absolute worst thing to happen to me physically: the guy with the pipe wrench." He straightened across from her, a wide smile sending his dimples into sharp relief. "Oh, hey. I got something for you at the library."

He pulled a folded piece of white paper from his back pocket and handed it to her with a flourish, as if presenting her with a diamond ring on a silver platter.

Curious, and smiling at his anticipation—he could do such topsy-turvy things to her insides—she unfolded the paper. It was a printout from a newspaper archive.

"I found it at the Web site of *The State*. That's the newspaper in Columbia, South Carolina."

The headline from the article made her suck in her breath: "Former Governor's Serial Killer Brother Slain in Prison." The news story stated that Jake Baldwin, brother of Arthur Baldwin, had been found dead in his cell by prison guards. His cellmate had strangled him over a pack of cigarettes.

"You didn't kill him," Mac said. "When Artie said you killed his brother, he must have meant metaphorically. You most likely helped send him to prison, which then led to his death."

She couldn't bring herself to smile with relief. Because while she was relieved she hadn't killed Jake Baldwin in cold blood, as she'd feared, she knew something Mac didn't: According to her flashback with Flinn Ford, she'd killed another man—Robert Radnor. For revenge.

No matter which way she rolled the dice, they kept coming up killer.

CHAPTER **THIRTY-THREE**

Hunter has made contact with Charlie Trudeau in Lake Avalon."

At Natalie's excited voice, Flinn let loose a smile so wide his cheeks pushed his sunglasses up. "That's excellent."

"It's written in a rough code, but they're meeting somewhere that they've been together before. Hunter warned her to dump her cell and GPS and use a friend's car."

"Samantha's on the ball even without her memory." Not that he was surprised. A woman like her, with smarts, beauty and balls, came along rarely. Add her psychic abilities, and she was the perfect spy. Too bad all that talent had to be wasted.

Natalie's voice broke into his musings. "Our closest field office is in Tampa. Should I contact them to arrange a tail on the sister?"

"Yes. Good work, Nat. Good work. Tell them it's a need-to-know investigation and that they're not to do anything but surveillance."

"Yes, sir. Anything else?"

"Please contact Marco. Have him on a flight to Fort Myers within the next two hours."

"What if Sam's not meeting her sister in Florida?"

"She must be. Hunter told the sister to borrow a friend's car, so wherever they're meeting is within driving distance of Lake Avalon."

"Oh. That makes sense."

"Keep me posted, Nat."

He clicked off the call, sat back in the driver's seat of his Audi and tapped his fingers on the steering wheel. The DC traffic hadn't moved the entire time he'd talked to his research analyst. Either road construction or an accident ahead. Not that he cared now. The important things were moving again. Soon, he'd have Samantha back.

And if, God forbid, he *didn't* have Samantha back, he'd at least have her sister to use against her.

CHAPTER **THIRTY-FOUR**

The closer they got to Tampa and St. Petersburg, the faster Mac's heart thumped with dread. Though he hadn't mentioned Sam in the e-mail, Charlie was smart enough to know the reason behind all the cloak-and-dagger business, especially since he'd told her three days ago that he was with Sam and that bad people were after her. And once Sam had her sisters and their cop boyfriends to help and protect her, where would that leave him? He'd be the guy with no law enforcement skills. No gun. No fancy bodyguard training. No ability to punch a bad guy into next month. It was unlikely that Sam would need someone to make a joke when the going got violent. Which meant she wouldn't need him anymore.

He glanced at her sleeping in the passenger seat, her face still and peaceful, turned toward him. Funny that this was the first time she'd napped facing him rather than the window. Probably meant nothing. Maybe he was an idiot to hope it meant something. But still.

Sighing, he decided to focus on getting her to safety. He'd worry about what might happen next when the time arrived. If only the tight knot in his gut would loosen. If only his chest muscles didn't cramp when he thought about leaving her with her sisters and walking away.

He'd be kidding himself if he thought a badass government spy would stick with a guy like him. If Sam hadn't desperately needed help, no way in hell would she have tolerated him as long as she had. He realized he should start accepting now that his time with her was reaching its end. And, hell, maybe he should celebrate the fact that bad guys would no longer be trying to put him out of his misery.

"Why are you frowning?"

He turned his head to find her beautiful blue eyes sleepy but open and fixed on him. He shrugged. "No reason."

"While I can't see inside your head at the moment, I can still sense your emotions. You're worried."

He laughed softly. "Well, yeah, I'm worried. Guys in black hats are after us."

He glanced at her to see confusion cinch her brows together. "Black hats?"

"Good guys wear white hats. Bad guys wear black."

"Oh. I don't think I've seen Flinn Ford in a hat."

"You probably just don't remember. Amnesia and all."

"Good point. But, for the record, I think he'd look goofy."

Mac laughed. "Goofy" was not a word he'd expected to pass Sam's very full, very kissable lips. "Especially if it's one of those really tall, stovepipe hats."

"Abe Lincoln on steroids."

"With none of the honorable intentions."

As they laughed together, she shifted so that she lay more on her back than her side and looked around. Not much to see in the dark. "How close are we to St. Pete?"

"About an hour and a half or so."

"Will they be waiting for us?"

"I told Charlie we wouldn't be in until tomorrow. I figured if I told her we're arriving tonight, she'd be waiting for us and you wouldn't get a chance to settle in and prepare yourself mentally."

"That wasn't necessary."

"You haven't seen Charlie and Alex in a long time. They're both going to be pretty damn aggressive with the questions, especially Charlie. She's one of those gung-ho, won't-take-no-comment-for-an-answer reporters."

"You know her so well."

He shrugged. "We're good friends, despite the . . . you know."

"Why did you break up?"

He cocked his head to one side to relieve the tension in his neck. So odd to be talking about Charlie with her sister. Especially *this* conversation. "I was an idiot."

"So you regret it."

"Well, yeah. Don't you regret it when you're an idiot?"

Her answering laugh was strained.

"Sorry. I keep forgetting you don't remember." He chuckled. "That's pretty funny."

"We're getting punchy."

"I think I bypassed punchy about three days ago."

"Have we known each other three days already?"

"Seems like three years." He paused. Did he just say that? "I mean—"

"It does seem like years. I don't blame you for being sick of it all."

"I'm not sick of *you*, though. Just to be clear."

Her teeth flashed white in the dim light of the car. "I'm not sick of you, either."

That sounded like maybe she liked him. Jesus, how old was he anyway?

Her sigh pulled him back out of his head. "I just wish things could be different," she said.

"I don't know. We're doing okay so far. I mean, we're alive."

She released a choked laugh. "Sure, there's that."

"For the record, the only thing I'd want to be different is Flinn Ford trying to kill us. Otherwise, best vacation ever."

She turned her head to stare at the darkness outside.

Mac let the silence drag on for a few minutes. Maybe she needed some time in her own head. But then the need to tell her about Charlie got to him. He wanted her to understand what happened between them, wanted to make it clear that he and Charlie were okay and that there'd be no weirdness if he and Sam . . . whatever.

"I was offered a promotion at work."

Sam looked at him. "I'm sorry?"

"Charlie and I had just started dating when I was offered a promotion that would have made me her boss. The newspaper has a strict no-fraternization rule, so I had to choose between the relationship and the job."

"Oh."

"Before you think, 'What a complete dick,' let me explain."

"I wasn't thinking that."

"You should have been."

"Okay, I'll think it now."

He laughed under his breath. "Terrific. So I have this kid sister—"

"Jenn."

"Right. Jenn. When the job opening came up, it was at the same time that I was trying to figure out how I was going to help her pay for college. Do you know what small-town reporters make? Well, maybe you do, what with your dad's history owning the *Lake Avalon Gazette*. But it's not much. The promotion made a big difference in pay for me."

"It sounds very responsible."

"That's what Charlie said. Of course, when she said it, her voice was dripping with sarcasm."

"That's Charlie."

He looked at her sharply. "It is?"

Sam didn't get why he seemed so shocked until it hit her. She pushed up straighter in her seat.

"Your memory is coming back."

She thought about it for a long moment, hoping to conjure up a face and a voice to go with the name Charlie. She managed both, but the images and sounds came from the flashback she'd had about leaving Lake Avalon, not anything solid from actual memories.

"Don't try so hard," Mac said. "Maybe it's better if it just comes to you instead of trying to force it."

"You're probably right." She blew out a breath that whispered through the stray hair on her forehead. "So you dumped my sister for your job. Did she kick your ass?"

"Nope."

"Maybe I should do it for her."

He grinned at the feral thrill that coursed through him at the idea of Sam wrestling him to the ground and having her way with him.

"You're supposed to quake in fear, dumbass, not look forward to it," she said with a lazy drawl.

He tried his best to lose the grin but couldn't. "Sorry. You're just so incredibly hot when you get tough."

She held his gaze until he had to look back at the road, but he saw her eyes glitter and wondered if her cheeks had pinkened in the dark. He could definitely feel a flush slinking up his neck. This was most definitely flirting.

Sam said, "How inappropriate would Charlie think a statement like that is? Considering."

He gave it some thought. "I don't think she'd care. She moved on very quickly, and she seems happier with Noah than she ever was with me. He pretty much swept her off her feet, and I don't think he's put her down yet."

"Hmm."

He didn't know what to make of her noncommittal response. Had she been merely making conversation or was she trying to figure out where he stood with Charlie because . . .

The thought trailed off as he realized how deeply he was kidding himself. Tough-chick psychic spy for the FBI Sam Trudeau falling for *him*? A guy who didn't know the difference between a Glock and a SIG. A guy who knew so little about cell phones that he'd led the bad guys right to Sam the first time he'd made a call.

Not likely.

CHAPTER **THIRTY-FIVE**

Flinn checked the caller ID on his cell before answering. Relieved that Natalie caught him before he boarded his flight to Fort Myers, he flipped the phone open. "What's going on, Natalie?"

"I just heard from the Tampa field office, sir. The agent assigned to keep an eye on Charlie Trudeau has reported that he's lost her."

Flinn turned his back on the other fliers at National's Gate C38. "*Lost* her? How?"

"The gentleman accompanying her has defensive driving experience, sir."

"Well, goddammit, how the fuck did he outdrive the fucking FBI?" Catching the startled look of a young mother with a toddler, he stalked far enough away that he could talk without being overheard.

"I don't know, sir," Natalie was saying, a tremor in her voice. "All I know is that the agent chose not to endanger civilians by attempting pursuit."

"Who else was in the car? Besides Charlie and the man doing the driving?"

"No one, sir. Just the two of them."

"So the other sister might still be in Lake Avalon."

"Shall I put in another request with the Tampa office?"

"Yes. And then I want you to check Hunter's credit records for places he and Charlie might have stayed together. You said he indicated in his e-mail that he wanted to meet somewhere they'd gone together in the past."

"Yes, sir. Uh . . . I assume you want me to do that under the radar, sir?"

"Yes. I'm scheduled to land in Fort Myers in about two hours. I'll get into Lake Avalon an hour or so after that and call you then."

"I hope I'll have good news for you, sir. Fly safe."

He snapped the phone closed and clamped it in his fist until his knuckles started to ache. He should have mobilized the troops and gotten to Lake Avalon sooner. If only he'd known for sure that Samantha would go there.

He just hadn't expected her to jeopardize her beloved family.

CHAPTER **THIRTY-SIX**

Sam yawned as Mac scrolled through the channels on the Accord's stereo. He stopped on a station playing soothing piano music.

Nice, she thought, and closed her eyes, falling quickly into that twilight moment between consciousness and sleep . . .

She stalked past the receptionist's desk, swatting away the grasping hands of the bastard's top-heavy, redheaded secretary, and shoved open his fancy office door. The slimy lawyer swiveled toward her, away from the massive window behind his desk that displayed an incongruously sunny day. Not the kind of day a nineteen-year-old girl should lose her just-found biological father, even if he hadn't been the perfect man she'd hoped. Everything she'd gone through to find him . . . and it was for nothing. Nothing.

"You killed him." Her voice was shrill, hysterical. "You killed my father."

The receptionist grabbed at her sleeve all over again, and Sam shook her off, shooting a don't-fuck-with-me glare into the other woman's alarmed features. "Back off!"

Robert Radnor rose to his feet with a creak of expensive leather. He appeared no more perturbed than if the prosecution had just yelled "Objection!" during an airtight case. "It's all right, Heather. Could you close the door on your way out?"

Heather hightailed it out of there fast as Sam advanced on Radnor, the slam of the office door a vague echo in her roaring ears.

"How many people did you buy off to avoid charges?" she asked through her teeth. She hoped the microphone she'd taped under her shirt would pick up more than the wild

pounding of her heart. The cops wouldn't do their jobs, so she would do it for them. And she had protection this time. The small gun her father had given her last month rested cold and hard against her lower back, where she'd tucked it in the waistband of her jeans. Just in case he wasn't afraid.

"I didn't have to buy off anybody," he said, grinning in all his straight-white-teeth, spray-tanned, expensive-suited glory. "I'm a well-known, well-respected lawyer in this town, and you and your daddy are obviously trailer trash out to get rich quick by blackmailing upstanding folks. Law enforcement around here knows the score."

She clenched her fists. "I saw it happen. I saw you kill him."

"And you think the cops give a good goddamn what some two-bit whore has to say? Your daddy came at me with a knife. I defended myself."

"There was no knife!"

He gave an expansive shrug. "Cops investigated and cleared me. What can you do?"

"It was only money to you. You didn't have to kill him."

"Your daddy fucked with the wrong man, little lady. It's not my fault he had a soft skull."

She lunged at him, intent on making him hurt for what he'd done. And as he laughed, he caught her wrists to stop her from slapping him, and she flew right into his head.

"You went too far with my girl."

I almost laugh at the red-faced sorry excuse for a pimp. Went too far? Didn't go far enough. I'm keeping my calm, though. This asshole has no idea that he and his whore are trying to blackmail the wrong guy.

"She made an offer then refused to carry through with it. I was just trying to keep the little whore honest." *I cut my gaze toward the tramp in question. She's huddling in the corner. Pathetic and traumatized. Eye already sporting a shiner. I should have hit her harder, the bitch. And copped more than a feel afterward.*

Mr. Pimp Blackmailer takes a step toward me, tries to intimidate me into backing away. But I stay put, the messed bed at my back. The room smells like bleach and cigarettes. And my hard-on has wilted. I glance at her again and wish to God she'd gotten that lush mouth on my dick before this ass-hole busted in. Jeeee-sus, she was hotter than a firecracker ten minutes ago. Right before she started her I-changed-my-mind shit.

He points a shaking finger at my nose. "I've got pictures of what you just tried to do to my little girl. You want to keep them out of the newspapers and your wife's mailbox, you'll fork over ten grand. Get it?"

He turns his back on me—moron—to try to comfort the whimpering whore in the corner. Looks to me like he showed up late for his role.

"You okay, Sammie?"

"You've been drinking," she says. Accusing. Voice cracking.

"I know. I'm sorry. It won't happen again."

"He hit me. And tried to—tried to—"

"Don't worry, Sammie. Everything will be fine."

"You said we were going to expose him as the predator he is, not blackmail him."

"We can do more with money. You'll see."

"I want to go home. Back to Lake Avalon."

"We'll talk later, okay? Let's get out of here. Mr. Radnor has a lot to think about."

I've thought about it. I'm not paying this prick jack shit. He's going down.

I grab the creaky old wooden desk chair and crack it over his head.

She lets loose a shocked squeak of despair as he crumples on top of her. "Dad!"

While she starts to scream and push at his unmoving body, I walk out without looking back. Maybe the headache from the chair will make the con artist think twice before he puts his kid on the line for a shakedown again.

*   *   *

When she snapped out of the past, gasping, Radnor's hand was under her shirt, cupping her breast with a smooth, hot hand. He'd backed her against the wall while she'd been gone and now canted his pelvis so he could rub his growing erection against her hip.

"Don't!" She shoved at his chest, whipping her head to the side to avoid his questing lips. "Help! Somebody help!"

He laughed. "No one's going to save you this time, Sammie. It's just you and me finishing what we started."

Fury that he used her father's nickname for her burned through the center of her chest, and she wriggled her hands between them to push against his chest. "Get off me."

"You know you want it. That's why you came back. You were just as frustrated as I was that Daddy interrupted us."

He leaned against her resistance, his greater weight pinning her, and bracketed her throat with a strong hand, cutting off her air. "Daddy's not here to interrupt this time. Don't worry, Sammie, I'll make it worth your time."

He released her throat and kissed her, lips grinding against her already bruised mouth, teeth cracking against hers. As she struggled for air, his hands grasped her hips, jerked her against him, and his breathing went fast and shallow. "Oh, yeah, keep wiggling like that. That's exactly the way I like it."

She tried to reach the gun digging into her back, but he had her plastered so tight against the wall she couldn't maneuver her fingers around the grip. His teeth sank into the flesh where her neck and shoulder met. She gasped and struggled harder. He responded by using one hand to fumble at the fastener on her jeans.

The shift in how he held her let her heave her hips forward. The move put space between her back and the wall but also bumped her body more intimately against him.

He laughed low, his breath hot against her throat. "Oh, yeah, you're getting into it now, aren't you? Christ, you're unfuckingbelievably hot. Keep moving just . . . like . . . that."

Her fingers grasped the cold grip of the gun just as he

*shoved his hand down, into the front of her jeans. She cried
out, a sob catching hard in her throat.*

*The gun popped free of her waistband, and she managed
to angle it toward him with one hand at her side, the position
awkward. He pressed harder against her, leaning his weight
in to secure her while he undid his pants.*

She cocked the gun.

He stilled at the clicking sound, pulled back. "What—Shit!"

He let go of her to make a grab for the gun.

She pulled the trigger.

Sam woke to the slowing motion of the car as it banked into a
turn and bumped over a few potholes. She kept her eyes closed
and breathing even, the sound of the gunshot echoing in her
ears while her heart hammered against her ribs. It took her
several moments to breathe through the fear, to remind herself that she was safe, with Mac, and Robert Radnor couldn't
hurt her anymore. Or anyone.

And now she knew that Flinn Ford had trapped her.

Yes, she'd killed Radnor. But she hadn't *planned* to kill
him. She'd *planned* to get his confession on tape and see justice done. She'd brought the gun for protection. A foolish,
grief-stricken girl who'd stopped thinking clearly the moment
her world imploded right on top of her. Flinn had taken advantage of her confusion and fear.

But, thank God, *oh, thank God*, she wasn't the cold-
blooded killer Flinn had led her to believe. At least, not that
time. Who knew what she'd done since?

I want to go home.

She still wanted to go home. The thought of it both excited
and terrified her. What if her family couldn't handle what she'd
become? What if *she* couldn't handle what she'd become?

"Sam? Hey, Sam."

She opened her eyes to the artificial light of parking lot
lamps and blinked several times, surprised to realize the car
had stopped.

"Over here."

Even in the dim light with his features in shadow, she felt the warmth of well-being at knowing it was Mac who sat next to her. "Hi."

"You okay? You were sleeping pretty deeply the past hour."

"Did I snore?"

"Can't you see my ears bleeding from all the noise? Sheesh."

Smiling wider—he had such a knack for lightening the weight of her dread—she pushed away the lingering effects of the latest flashback and looked around. "Are we there?"

"Yep, we're in St. Pete. I thought we'd grab some dinner before checking in at the hotel since Charlie and Alex aren't due until morning. I'm starving. What about you?"

She nodded. "I could eat."

"Are you okay with seafood?"

"Hello, grew up in Florida."

"Hey, I grew up in Philly, and cheesesteaks aren't on my list of favorites."

As they walked across the parking lot, the breeze blowing off the gulf was cool and salty. Being out of the car, breathing in fresh air, felt great. And as they walked side by side to the restaurant door, she smiled some at the foolish hope that Mac would take her hand. When he didn't, she admonished herself for the disappointment. Knowing him, he kept his hand to himself to avoid sending her careening through his memories.

She reached out and caught his fingers with hers, bracing herself mentally for whatever might telegraph itself from his past. Nothing did, and she let her shoulders relax, smiling at the pleased look Mac cast her way as he snugged her hand more firmly into the heat of his.

Her curiosity about his thoughts got the best of her, and she tried a quick trip into what he was thinking. Just for a second.

Nothing.

Odd, she thought. When she'd slipped into his head when they were snuggled up together, she'd barely had to think about it. If she couldn't control it at will, how could she rely on it to do the job of a government spy? Was there a trick to her ability, a way to trigger it other than simply by touch? Or maybe her handlers had used drugs in some way to enhance her ability. She thought of the patch she'd pulled off her hip. Maybe that was its purpose.

Mac opened the restaurant door for her, and she preceded him inside. The décor was standard for a seafood joint: Fake fish, netting and life rings draped the dark wood paneling, and a lobster tank occupied a section of the entryway.

All was fine until the faint fishy smell reached her nose. Nausea immediately followed, and she turned toward Mac. "I'm sorry, but this isn't going to work for me."

He didn't question her—she probably looked as green as she felt—just grabbed her hand and pulled her back outside. The fresh air helped push back the nausea as he led her back to the car. Once she was settled in the passenger seat, and Mac was behind the wheel again, he asked, "What was that about? It didn't smell that bad."

"I don't know. Guess my stomach is just sensitive." She wondered whether removing the mysterious patch had screwed up her body's chemistry.

"Sam?"

"Uh . . . I don't know."

"Is there something you're not telling me?"

Busted. How did he do that? Wasn't she supposed to be the one with psychic abilities? She cast him a small, chagrined smile. "I might have removed one of those patches, like what smokers wear when they're trying to quit."

"So you're a smoker?"

"I don't think so. I had a flashback of Flinn Ford checking it. I highly doubt he'd be that interested if it were a nicotine patch."

"So it was for something else. Jesus, Sam, why didn't you tell me? If something had happened to you, I wouldn't have known what to do."

"To be fair, I've just told you, and you still won't know what to do if something happens."

"Well, yes, that's true. But I could have at least alerted ER staff to the existence of the patch if . . . well, shit. What else could it have been for? Birth control maybe?"

She hadn't thought about that. And it would make sense during a mission in which taking a daily pill would be inconvenient. Of course, that assumed she was sexually active enough to require constant birth control. Was that possible? Did she have a lover she didn't even remember? And here she sat, falling for Mac Hunter . . . no, wait . . . really? She was *falling* for Mac?

"Sam?"

She glanced at him, startled by the intensity of his stare. "I'm sorry. What?"

"Could the patch have been for birth control?"

"Maybe."

"Have you felt different since you took it off?"

She debated lying then wondered why she should. She trusted Mac with her life. "My empathy seems to be behaving differently."

"How so?"

"It's less . . . immediate."

"What does that mean?"

"Before, I could get right into another person's head and know what they were thinking then and there. Now, I don't think I can."

Without a word, he grasped her hand, folding it between both of his, and watched her face.

Her stomach tensed at the warmth of his large hands engulfing hers, the depth of emotion in his eyes as he peered at her. Her pulse kicked up a notch. She liked his face. His angular jaw and a day's growth of beard—even the sharpness of his concern—did nothing to temper the kindness evident in his features. She sensed that he was unlike any man she'd ever known.

"Anything?"

She laughed under her breath. She'd been so distracted by her reactions to him that she'd missed anything that her empathy might have picked up. She focused now, and her heart rate started to skitter, because while she didn't land in his head, she felt the heat rise between their hands. When his thumb shifted over the inside of her wrist in a light caress, she drew in a fast, surprised breath.

He suddenly let her go and smoothed both of his palms over the thighs of his jeans as though he didn't know what to do with them now. His chuckle sounded strained. "If you'd been in my head right now, we'd both be blushing furiously. So I think it's safe to assume that you can't log in at will."

"Log in?" she asked, lips quirking.

"Well, that's kind of how it works, right? When you make contact, it's like you're logging in to someone else's memories."

"I suppose so. I hadn't thought of it that way."

"You must know how to search, too, since you used the ability in your spy life."

"Like on the Web?"

"Sure. I mean, what good is being psychic to earn a living if you can't direct your gift in a way that gets you the information you want?"

She thought of her biological father and how he'd used her ability to get information so he could try to blackmail Robert Radnor. Flinn Ford had used her the same way. Did she actually do *anything* with her ability that was for the benefit of decent people?

"Sam?"

She met Mac's eyes in the light from the parking lot lamps. "I'm sorry. What?"

"What's the matter?"

He could read her so well, in the dark and without one ounce of psychic ability. After only a few days. It made her heart ache to realize that as soon as everything returned to the status quo—*if* it did—she would lose him. No way would a man as kind and decent as Mac Hunter want a life with a woman like her, a spy who helped blackmail people.

He reached out and tucked stray hair behind her ear with exceedingly gentle fingers. "Talk to me, Sam."

She closed her eyes, savoring his tender touch for as long as she'd have it.

"Could you be pregnant?" he asked gently.

And like that, her reverie crashed and burned. Not that it was an out-there question. Her brain had been doing a fine job of shying away from the thought ever since she'd tapped into his memory of her descent into amnesia.

Flinn impregnated a fellow N3 operative . . .

It certainly wasn't out of the realm of possibility that he'd used her in the same way. Right this minute, she could be serving as the vessel for Flinn Ford's science experiment.

"I know it's not my place—"

"I'm not feeling sick anymore," she cut in, deciding to declare the discussion over without saying so. She just didn't have the fortitude right now to go there. "Can we find some dinner? Something not seafood."

Mac paused a moment, obviously not satisfied with her response. But he must have come to the conclusion that feeding her was more important than talking, because he started the car. "How about Italian?"

Her stomach growled. "Mmm. As long as garlic bread is involved."

He chuckled. "I wouldn't have pegged you for a garlic bread kind of woman."

"Why not?"

"A spy with garlic breath just doesn't sound effective. What would you do if you had to hide behind a curtain? The bad guys would know you were there in a heartbeat."

"That's why I always carry breath mints." She much preferred this light banter to worrying. And they'd slipped into it so easily.

"Now, see, that wouldn't work either. Bad guys can smell minty breath, too."

She shrugged. "Maybe the bad guys I target have no sense of smell."

"Interesting idea." Then he pointed off to the left toward a brightly lit strip mall in yellow stucco. "There's an Italian place right over there. Pizza Planet. Like Burrito Planet. It's a theme." He flashed her a grin. "How appropriate, seeing as how you've rocked my world."

She laughed, and her heart did a dance that felt both unfamiliar and exactly right.

CHAPTER **THIRTY-SEVEN**

The hotel was just as Mac remembered it: comfortable and welcoming. The palm trees, ferns and floral-patterned cushions adorning the wicker furniture dotting the lobby crooned, "Relax, you're on vacation. Put your feet up. Read a book."

As he waited at the check-in counter, he watched Sam wander over to the open-air back of the lobby and stop to look out at the beach. Lights from the hotel illuminated only the first few feet of surf about six yards from where she stood. Tables and chairs dotted the sand between the hotel and the waves, some occupied by hotel guests sipping drinks.

He watched the night breeze stir through her dark hair, watched her wrap her arms around her middle, as though hugging herself. She looked too tense in such a relaxing environment. At least, Mac mused, she'd eaten a decent dinner— salad, lasagna and garlic bread, followed by a brownie sundae, which they'd shared. As they'd eaten and had a light conversation, he'd seen healthy color bloom in her cheeks for the first time.

If she had any chance of relaxing, he decided, this hotel should do it.

He recalled being there with Charlie, the gentle gulf breezes stirring the curtains in the hotel room against the soundtrack of waves advancing and retreating. He'd thought at the time it was perfect, because he was there with the woman he loved. But he knew now that what he'd felt for Charlie had not been love. Deep affection, yes. He'd enjoyed being with her, enjoyed talking with her, enjoyed laughing with her.

But when he'd looked at her, he hadn't had that feeling in

his gut that felt like hanging at the very top curve of a roller coaster just before the big plunge, followed by the exhilarating sense of flying, the wind in his hair and the anticipation of the stomach-flipping loop-de-loops. He felt that way with Sam, and he was only just getting to know her. He imagined that weightless, I-can-take-on-the-world-and-win feeling would get even more intense the longer he knew her.

"Your key cards, Mr. Walker."

Mac turned to the clerk, a thirtysomething young woman with short brown hair and glasses that sported rectangular black frames, and accepted the small envelope. "Thanks."

"The penthouse suite is on the eighth floor. I'll have the bellman bring up your bags."

Penthouse suite? Hallelujah. "No need. We're good."

"The concierge took care of the special requests you stipulated when you made the reservation, too. You'll find everything you asked for in your suite."

"Excellent."

"If you need anything at all, please don't hesitate to call the concierge."

"Will do."

With one last thank-you smile at the clerk, he walked over to Sam and stood beside her for a minute. She didn't say anything, didn't even seem aware of his presence.

He took the time to breathe in the salty air, hoping the rhythm of the waves would soothe some of his tension. Soon, Sam would be reunited with her sisters. She wouldn't need him anymore. What if she, or Charlie and Alex, asked him to leave? After all, he'd have no more ties to any of them, no reason to hang around and get in the way.

After a few more moments, he decided he'd deal with what happened next when it happened.

He gently bumped Sam's arm with his.

She drew in a breath and looked at him. He'd obviously jolted her out of some deep thoughts. Not for the first time, he wished he had a psychic ability to help him figure out what she was thinking and feeling.

"Ready?" he asked.

She nodded and fell in step beside him.

In the elevator, she said, "The name you used to check in—Simon Walker—is that . . ."

"Yep. Billionaire investor a la Warren Buffett. He rescued the *Lake Avalon Gazette* last year. I suggested Charlie check with him about borrowing his credit card."

"And he'd be okay with that? Isn't he your boss at the paper?"

"Yes, but he's also a seriously good guy. Once Charlie explained that there was an emergency, I'm sure he was willing to do more than was necessary."

"That probably wasn't a good idea to get him involved."

"We needed credit, Sam. We couldn't very well check in under our own names, or even fake names, or pay cash. Simon isn't related to any of us, so it's unlikely Ford can track us through him."

When she continued to look stressed, he sighed. "I know this isn't your usual high-tech-spy way of doing things, but it seemed like a good way to fly under the radar."

"No, that's not it. You did fine. I didn't mean to look critical. It's just that, based on the situation with Arthur Baldwin, Flinn could be extremely well connected with wealthy people like Simon Walker."

"We can trust Simon. I'd stake my life on it."

The suite of two bedrooms, a sitting room and a small kitchen impressed Mac. The furnishings, in black wood and red fabrics, looked like something out of an interior design magazine. As he wandered into the first bedroom to check it out, he whistled with appreciation at the sixty-inch plasma TV adorning the wall across from the king-sized bed. Another, smaller bedroom was similarly appointed.

Sam met him in the sitting room, which held another large television, a sofa in red microfiber, two club chairs in black leather and a glass coffee table piled high with shopping bags of varying sizes and colors.

"Your boss didn't spare any expense, did he?" Sam said as she sank onto the overstuffed sofa.

"That's the way Simon Walker rolls. Without him, the Trudeau family newspaper would have joined the ranks of all the other newspapers shutting down the past few years. He's taken a special interest in Charlie." At her arched brow, he quickly added, "In a grandfatherly kind of way. He loves the newspaper business as much as she does, so they have common ground. He wouldn't dream of doing anything that would jeopardize her or anyone close to her. So you don't have to worry, okay? Simon's one of the good guys."

She smiled slightly. "Okay."

He sat next to her and nodded at the bags that bore names such as Dillard's, Gap, CVS and Best Buy. "Looks like he sent us some stuff."

He tore into the Gap bag first. "If there's a clean pair of jeans in here, you're going to want to cover your ears, because I'm going to let out a big ol' whoop."

Sam laughed softly as she pushed to her feet and walked through the kitchen into the bigger bedroom, where the balcony doors had been opened to let in fresh air.

Mac let her go without comment, ignoring the sinking in his gut. She was already putting distance between them, preparing for the moment when she'd tell him to get lost.

He focused on the moment and pulled out not one pair of new jeans but six pairs—two in his size and four in varying women's sizes.

"Oh, hell, yeah," he said under his breath.

The bag also contained several pairs of men's and women's cargo shorts, T-shirts and light jackets. The Dillard's bags held undergarments, pj's and socks. The CVS bag yielded various toiletries, and the Best Buy bag contained an inexpensive notebook computer and, wonder of wonders, six prepaid cell phones. Flinn Ford wouldn't be able to trace a call from one prepaid phone to another.

Mac was grateful that the even number of phones—one for each of Sam's sisters and their significant others as well as ones for Mac and Sam—hopefully meant no one planned to make him hit the road anytime soon. Except maybe Sam.

When Sam didn't return to the sitting room, he joined her on the large balcony. She stood with her hands resting lightly on the railing as she stared up at the stars, brilliant points of light against the inky black of the sky.

"Charlie and I were here at Christmas," he said. "Of course, our room was about a quarter the size of this one, if that. They did luminaria on the beach, so most of the lights were off. The sky was so clear we could see all the stars you don't normally see because of the city lights. It really does look like the pictures. You know the ones where the stars look like a dust pattern sweeping across the sky? Captiva does luminaria at Christmas, too. I haven't gone over to check it out, though. I think I'll do that this year."

He smiled as he thought about it. He hadn't felt the urge to do anything like that in ages, perhaps since he and Jenn had moved to Lake Avalon. Funny what having bad guys threaten your life could do for your appreciation of it.

Sam still said nothing, and she'd curled her fingers tight around the railing.

"You okay?" he asked.

"I'm nervous."

"It's been a long time since you've seen your sisters."

"What if they hate me?"

"I've known Charlie and Alex a long time. They're not haters."

"I made promises I didn't keep."

"We all make promises we can't keep, Sam. It's part of life. And even if that's true, I'd bet my life that you meant to keep every promise you made, but circumstances got in the way."

She cast him a sad smile. "You're a good man to assume the best. I suspect I don't deserve it."

"I suspect you do."

Sighing, she looked back out at the darkness. "I don't know what I'd have done without you this week."

Great, here it comes, he thought. The big brush-off. As much as he wanted to grab her to him and never let her go, he instead gave a vague shrug. He wasn't a grabber. And he cer-

tainly wasn't the kind of man to impose his presence on someone who didn't want it. "I did what anyone would have done in
my position."

"I don't think that's true." She turned toward him, eyes
glimmering in the light bleeding onto the balcony from the
room. "Thank you." She brushed a kiss over his cheek. "For
everything."

Surprise arced through him at the contact of her lips
against his skin. It wasn't nearly enough. When she started to
step by him, he caught her with his hands at her waist and
drew her back. He saw her eyes widen just before he tugged
her forward and slanted his lips over hers. Her mouth was soft
under his, unresponsive. This is so stupid, he thought. How
could you be such an idiot?

But before he could pull back and fall all over himself
apologizing for being a jerk, her lips moved, then parted on a
small, shaky moan. She started kissing him back, one hand
sliding up his arm to the back of his neck, where her fingers
sifted through the hair curling against his nape. She tasted
like garlic and tomato sauce and the future.

His brain went blank when her tongue glanced off his, and
all the blood in his body seemed to rush to one place and he
went instantly, painfully hard. Oh, Jesus, kissing her made the
top of his head feel like blowing off.

Yet, as much as he wanted to start easing her clothes off
and touching her everywhere possible, kissing her soft skin
and making her tremble for him, he forced himself to back
off and breathe. He didn't release her, though. He held her
close against him, swaying some in the night air, the ebb and
flow of waves and the soft murmur of voices far below a backdrop to the moment.

As he held her, smoothing his hands over her back in
soothing caresses, he focused on trying to get her to relax
against him. It took several minutes before he actually felt the
tension begin to leave her body. *Finally.*

"I wish things could stay just like this," she whispered.

"This *is* pretty nice." Being naked would have been even
better. Exactly the right thing to think, dumbass, when you're

trying to control yourself. And then he imagined her palm-sized breast cupped in his hand, his thumb sweeping back and forth over a bare nipple. Shit, shit, shit. So not helping.

Her warm hands bracketed the sides of his face, and their eyes met. He saw invitation in hers and didn't have to be asked twice. When he kissed her this time, he backed her against the glass door and trapped her there with one hand braced against the glass and the other cupping the back of her head. His thigh nudged between hers, and he felt her intake of breath as his thumb stroked the delicate skin under her ear.

He kissed her for a long time, nipping at her bottom lip, tangling his tongue with hers, their bodies pressed close together but all attention focused on what they could do to each other's mouths and tongues.

Heaven, Mac thought. Absolute fucking heaven.

And he didn't want it to end, didn't want to walk away from this . . . ever.

He drew back from the kiss reluctantly, watching her face, her eyes, for a clue to the next move. She looked deliciously dazed, slate eyes dark and heavy, mouth already swollen from their kisses.

He ached to carry her to bed and make love to her all night. Ached to thrust inside her, into all that scorching, wet, Sam heat. But he forced himself to hold back. It had to be her move. Maybe it was too soon for her, at a too-vulnerable time. The last thing he wanted to do was take advantage. Not to mention the fact that she still had a bullet wound in her shoulder.

He hated his gentleman genes with a fiery passion right now.

In the next moment, she leaned in, taking his mouth with hers, and he reveled again in the soft warm play of her lips, the gentle sweep of her tongue against his. Catching his hand in her silken hair, he cupped the back of her head, pressing her closer, taking her deeper, his breath sucking in as her right hand slipped under his shirt and up, up, warm palm caressing his nipple so firmly that his eyes tried to roll back. Good sign. *Excellent* sign. But still . . .

He broke off the kiss with a mighty effort, his body screaming at him to stop thinking and go with the moment. It took all of his will to ignore the growing urgency. "Shouldn't we take it easy? Your shoulder—"

"Is fine. Don't make me beg."

He grinned. "No begging, huh? That's too bad. I like begging."

"There's still time. Just please tell me you have protection."

"A smart man never leaves home without it," he said, patting his back pocket, where he kept his wallet, a condom tucked inside.

Smiling, she captured his mouth again, the stroke of her tongue against his just about setting him off like a rocket. He shifted to walk her back into the closest bedroom. They paused at the foot of the bed, still kissing, breath coming faster now, ragged and urgent. Mac's fingers undid the buttons of her shirt, sure and quick, eager, until he could nudge the flannel off her shoulders with both hands. She dropped her arms straight, letting the shirt pillow around their feet. He hated seeing the white bandage at her shoulder, the stark reminder that she was injured, that this might cause her pain. Her strong fingers on his jaw demanded that he shift his gaze from her shoulder to her eyes.

"It's fine," she said, voice low and raspy, sexy as all fucking hell. "*I'm* fine."

He had to focus on breathing as she undid her bra and let it drop, then he watched, fascinated at the darker tone of his own skin against the vanilla of hers as he smoothed a hand down between full, palm-sized breasts tipped with rosy nipples. When he cupped one, his thumb stroking the nipple into pointed awareness, she dropped her head back on a shaky moan.

Need spiked at the sight of her arched neck, his cock so hard and ready that it neared painful. But he was determined to take his time, to show her how much he cared, that this wasn't just about sex.

Trailing kisses over her temple, her cheek, her eyelids, he caressed her breasts, kissed his way down to the hollow of her throat, where he played his tongue against her skin, tasting salt and soap and Sam. At the same time, her hands went to work on the fly of his jeans, and his heart kicked into a more frantic gear, an insistent, surging pulse in his groin.

When he urged her down onto the bed and braced himself above her, every cell in his body rejoiced as she slid her hands down his hips, taking his jeans with them. The material of his boxers hung up on his jutting cock, and he held his breath as her hands freed him from the confines of his underwear. He was almost self-conscious at how huge and hard he was, clear evidence of how badly he wanted her, but then she wrapped her fingers around his heat and squeezed, and his elbows threatened to buckle.

She'd stroked him twice, sliding her palm over the head of his cock, gathering some of the moisture at the tip for easier gliding, when he tensed, his balls already drawing up for the countdown, and put a hand over hers. "Stop," he choked out.

A satisfied smile curved her full lips, a sexy, lung-sucking heat in her dark blue eyes, and he felt himself start to fall head over heels, a breathless dive of rushing air and hot, stroking rays of sun against his skin.

He helped her wriggle out of her drawstring pants and panties, revealing miles of creamy skin, firm muscle and soft angles, all for him. She bent one leg, parting her legs for him, and his grin grew at the explicit invitation. Yet he ignored it, focusing instead on sucking her right nipple into his mouth, his thumb and forefinger tending to the other, plucking and squeezing and kneading while his tongue and teeth did similar tricks, until she arched into his mouth, hooking one calf around his thigh and pressing her flat belly against his cock.

That part of him jerked at the contact, weeping for some attention, but he denied that for now, having to grit his teeth, instead easing back from her so he could trail his fingers down her ribs, caressing and tickling, paying close attention to the gasps and hitches in her breathing. He had to force himself to go slow, when all he wanted to do was plunge and take and fuck. At the juncture of her thighs, he stilled his fingers, smiling at the cessation of her breath, the air thickening with anticipation.

"Please," she whispered, her mouth against his shoulder.

Ah, Sam begging. Who knew it would be so sweet . . . and *hot*?

He teased her first, with just the tips of his fingers, kissing her at the same time, his tongue stroking and exploring as his fingers inched toward her wetness then retreated. With his palm cupping her hip, he felt the tiny jerks in her muscles as she fought the urge to press against him.

"I want you, Mac. I want you now," she breathed against his mouth, nails of one hand digging into the skin of his upper arm enough to leave marks as her other hand groped for his cock, gripping and stroking and trying to angle him for penetration.

He chuckled at her desperation, swallowed at the heaven of her hand on him, the almost overwhelming urge to let go. *Easy, boy. Not yet.* "Just hold on. I'm not done playing yet."

She set her teeth against the join of his neck and shoulder and groaned. "I'm so going to kill you when this is over."

He released a choked laugh. "Trust me. You're killing me now."

Then, clamping down on the need, the want, the holy-shit-I'm-going-to-fucking-die-if-I-don't-get-inside-her-soon, he shifted on the bed, easing his torso down between her legs, and laved his tongue into her belly button, loving the quivers in her muscles, the faint, musky scent of woman on the verge. Smoothing his hands over her inner thighs, he massaged and kneaded until the muscles relaxed, until her hands tangled in his hair, and she let her legs fall open wider. He could smell her desire now, heady and so intoxicating that he had to take a moment to think cold thoughts to keep from losing it. The North Pole . . . Alaska . . . Iceland . . . Antarctica . . .

She jerked and gasped at the first touch of his tongue, fingers tugging at his hair, and he smiled. This was going to be so much fun. Holding her steady with one arm snugged around her thigh, he played her with his mouth and fingers, sweeping into her with the flat of his tongue, sliding one finger, then two, inside her heat at the same time. Within minutes, she cried out and bucked, muscles bunching and shuddering, thighs trying to clamp around his head to stop him, or perhaps slow him down. He held her open and continued the onslaught, lapping at her heat, the flood of her desire, focusing on drawing out the contractions of her body around his fingers, the building tension in the muscles of her thighs, the sobbing sounds of her breath.

She peaked again, a hard, shuddering, body-rigid orgasm, before he gentled his strokes, easing her down until she could breathe and her thighs began to relax some. As he kissed his way over her stomach, pausing to play awhile with pebble-hard nipples, drawing a few more breathy hitches out of her, he couldn't stop himself from grinning like an idiot.

"You okay?" he murmured when he finally made it back to her lips and kissed her, a deep, drugging melding of lips and tongue and teeth.

"Mmm," she replied, too sated to do more than hum.

Her fingers trickled through the soft hair at his nape, and he closed his eyes as she rubbed the sensitive spot right behind his ear. He thought she might drift off to sleep now and wondered what he would do if she did. Well, that was easy: He'd go to bed with an aching hard-on or take care of it all by his lonesome, which wouldn't be nearly as satisfying, but if he had to—

She shifted, pushing him onto his back and straddling his thighs, rising above him with wild, sweat-damp hair and sex-glazed eyes. She caught her bottom lip between her teeth as she wrapped long fingers around his cock and pumped him, somehow knowing just what he liked, the pressure, the glide and slide and thrill . . . but not too much, not too firm to send him careening over the edge. He loved the way her dusky gaze took him in, roaming his features, her soft lips curving as though she approved of everything she saw. So . . . fucking . . . sexy.

She leaned down and nibbled at his chin, the corner of his mouth, then murmured against his lips, "I want you inside me."

He didn't have to be told twice.

With a growl, he rolled her under him, muscles jumpy and jittery. After snagging his jeans from beside the bed, he fumbled out his wallet and then the condom. He had to hold his breath while he rolled it on. But then he was guiding himself to her, clenching his teeth until his jaw ached, come on, hold on, hold on, and then he was inside her an inch, and the breath hissed through his teeth as, laughing, she arched her hips to take him in another inch, and then another, and then she wiggled just a little, hooked her ankles around his calves and angled just right and daaaaaaaaaaamn, he was all the way in, completely surrounded by the sweetest, hottest, sexiest woman ever.

Breathing through his nose, he ground out a shaky request, "Hold still."

She obliged—mostly—only her hands continuing their exploration of the muscles in his back, then down over his butt where she gripped hard and whimpered a little, trying to pull him deeper, her breath uneven in his ear, her hips straining under him.

He rested his forehead against her cheek and gathered the tatters of his control. Women were so damn lucky. They could come all night without needing time to recover. Or maybe he was just so far gone for this woman that he'd never be able to control himself for as long as he wanted to. Closing his eyes, he pulled air in through his teeth as he eased almost completely out of her wet heat and then sank back in, again and again, urged on by the way her head arched back into the pillow and her throat worked on a ragged swallow.

Her long, low moan stole his ability to think. He thrust harder and faster, gathering her close against him, pumping his hips, feeling the pause just before she peaked, loving the anticipation in the tense lines and curves of her body. When all that wet heat contracted around his cock, light exploded behind his eyes. For long seconds, he heard nothing but the roar in his ears, felt nothing but the intensity of a shattering climax and the rush of heat rising, gushing, spilling out of him.

"Ah, God, Sam," he groaned. "Sam."

Even when the orgasm eased off, leaving him only semierect, he kept thrusting, helpless to stop the shudders coursing through him, helpless to back off the ultrasensitive sensations of being this close to Sam, of being inside Sam. He didn't want it to end, he never wanted it to end.

And then, unexpectedly, her body convulsed in his arms again, her mouth open against his shoulder in an intense, silent cry, her breath heaving against his sweat-slicked skin. She gasped out something, her own name, he thought at first—obviously he'd misheard—and then she was clinging to him, her face buried against his neck, her body limp and struggling for air.

Smiling, giddy even, he shifted so he could kiss her. One of her hands gripped tight around his forearm as he cradled her head in both palms and lazily kissed her, stroking into her mouth with his tongue, tender and loving. The remaining tension trembled out of her muscles, and she went even more lax against him.

He thought he might love her.

And she was going to get rid of him the first chance she got.

He closed his eyes as he eased back and settled her snugly against his side, their breathing synchronized but calming. She continued to stroke her palm over his pecs, until she curled her fingers into his chest hair and tugged slightly.

"You won't leave, will you? When my sisters get here?"

He almost laughed out loud with relief.

"I mean, you're all I know right now," she went on. "I feel . . . safe with you."

He pulled her to him for a tight hug. "I'm not going anywhere."

CHAPTER **THIRTY-EIGHT**

Flinn Ford was so wired by the time he checked in at the Royal Palm Inn in Lake Avalon that the sign declaring JAMES DEAN SLEPT HERE just above another that read UNDER NEW MANAGEMENT didn't impress him in the least. Neither did the lobby with its totally Florida décor, from the wicker furniture with cushions bearing large pink-and-blue flower designs to the large green plants that turned the lobby into a virtual forest. He could practically feel the freshly generated oxygen filling his lungs.

Letting the bellboy deliver his bag to his room without him, he headed into the nearly empty bar adjoining the lobby and took a stool under a thatched overhang that brought to mind a tiki hut.

"What can I get you?" the female bartender asked. She had a gracious smile that showed impossibly white teeth against the backdrop of a lightly tanned, unlined face.

"Whiskey and Seven. Make it adult sized."

Her teeth practically glowed in the dark as she slapped a rocks glass on the bar and filled it with whiskey and 7Up. "Any snacks tonight?"

"What's good?"

"Jalapeno poppers'll kick your butt."

He chuckled at that. Her prettiness lifted his spirits. "How did you know my butt needed kicking?"

She threw her head back and laughed, cleavage jiggling enough to be enticing without being vulgar.

"Bring me an order," Flinn said.

As she walked away, he flipped out his cell phone and called Natalie. "What've you got for me?" he asked as soon as she answered.

"I found charges on Hunter's credit card to the Hotel Sand-piper in St. Petersburg last December. No joy on placing him and Sam there now, though. They can't check in without a credit card, so I'm still searching for a connection."

Flinn knocked a knuckle on the shiny surface of the bar. "Keep looking. It's all we've got. Get an agent over there to scope out the guests, too. Send them pictures of Hunter, Saman-tha and her sisters."

"Will do, sir."

"Any luck locating the other sister? Alex?"

"I'm afraid not, sir. An agent from Tampa has checked her home, the home of her boyfriend, her parents' home and her workplace. There's no sign of her."

"So she's in hiding."

"Or she's left the area," Natalie said.

"If she has, it's to meet with Samantha. We need to find her. Keep the Tampa agent on it."

"Yes, sir."

"Someone's going to screw up eventually." He paused as the bartender returned with a plate of steaming poppers. He flashed her a thank-you smile and waited for her to move away before he continued talking to Natalie. "In the meantime, I need Marco and Dr. Ames to establish a small medical facil-ity in Lake Avalon."

"Sir?"

"Have them secure an abandoned building on a less-traveled road. Something small, a former urgent care or pet clinic would be ideal. After the hurricane and flooding last year, that shouldn't be too difficult. Equip it with power generators, lights, running water, etc. Are you writing this down?"

"Yes, sir."

"Consult with Dr. Ames for a list of required medical equipment and supplies. Tell him to keep it to items that can be obtained at regular retail establishments. Everything he needs for the procedure. As soon as the location is secured, they need to hire some people to help get it ready."

"Is there a time frame, sir?"

"It needs to be ready by tomorrow afternoon latest."

"That's quite a—"

"Get day laborers in there to get it done. Whatever it takes."

"Okay."

"I'll check in with you in the morning."

He snapped the phone shut on her next question, picked up a jalapeno popper and sank his teeth into it. Hot, salty cheese oozed onto his tongue, followed by the heat of spice. He savored the textures and the flood of flavors.

Taking Samantha apart after everything she'd put him through was going to provide even more pleasure.

CHAPTER **THIRTY-NINE**

It was two in the morning when Sam braced her hands on the vanity in the bathroom. Pain pounded in her head, an insistent throb in her temples that pulsed like something had burrowed into her skull and now tried to claw its way out. Her entire body felt rubbery and fluid, as though lovemaking with Mac had unlocked her muscles.

Or something else.

The tile walls blurred and shifted, and suddenly she was in the past, fingers locked firmly around her mother's slim wrist.

"He's not my father. Dad's not my real father." The realization sliced sharp and deep.

Her mother looked both horrified and terrified. "Of course he is, Samantha. How could you think—"

"I saw it. Just now, in your head. When I touched you, you were thinking I don't look anything like Dad, how could anyone not realize I'm not his?"

"Saman—"

"Who's Ben Dillon? Is he my real father? Where is he?"

Her mother tried to jerk away, but Sam held fast and firm, determined to get answers. "Tell me, Mom. Tell me about him or I'll tell Dad the truth." She gave her mother a chance, but she didn't take it, so Sam used her final bit of ammo. "Tell me, Eliza."

Her mother's thin lips thinned further at the name, her actual name. "Northern Illinois. Outside Chicago."

"Where, specifically?"

"Sycamore. He doesn't want you. He never wanted you. I wanted you, Samantha. I did what was best for you. You have to believe me. He's not a good man."

Sam jerked back into the present and slid down to the ceramic tile floor of the hotel bathroom on a soft moan, her back against the vanity, her aching head cradled in her hands. Another memory took her over . . .

The front door, dark wood with three, small, diamond-shaped windows in a vertical line, swung open. He wasn't what she expected based on her mother's disgusted attitude toward the man. No beer gut, rotting teeth and suffocating body odor. He was handsome, with thick, chestnut hair and eyes the same dark blue as hers. Lean but not skinny, wearing faded blue jeans and an untucked green polo shirt. Just a normal guy.

"Ben Dillon?"

"Sure thing. Who's asking?"

"I'm your daughter."

His grin revealed white teeth. "Yeah? Which one?"

Her expectations took a header off a cliff. "I . . . I . . ."

"I'm just joshing you, kid." He cocked his head. "What's your name?"

"Samantha Trudeau."

"Doesn't ring a bell."

"My mother is Elise."

He leaned against the door's frame, shoving one hand into a back pocket. "Don't know anyone named Elise."

"Eliza?"

He straightened away from the door and took a step back. "Holy fuck. I thought she ran off and had an abortion. At least, that's what I hoped—" He stopped, and his face flushed. "I mean, shit, you're my kid?"

"I have some questions."

"I'm sorry, hon, but I don't have your answers. I was nothing more than the sperm donor. Your mom didn't take care of business like she should have. That's not my problem. I've got nothing, so . . . sorry to disappoint you."

Heat began to creep into Sam's chilled cheeks. "She loved you." She knew, because she'd experienced her mother's anguish when this man ditched her.

"Not my fault she believed every word I said. I was a teen-

ager, for Christ's sake. All I cared about was getting my rocks off."

Sam tried her damnedest not to let her disappointment show. "I still have questions. Of a genetic nature."

"You sick or something?"

"I'm . . . I . . . I think I'm psychic."

It took several moments for his shock to subside. Then, while a small smile twitched at the corners of his mouth, he stepped back and gestured her inside. "Please come in."

Sam fell out of the memory to find herself on the cold bathroom floor, curled into a tight, shivering ball. Tears ran freely from her eyes, and her head felt as though a dam had burst, letting everything behind it spill out in an unrelenting wave . . .

"You tipped off the local police in Columbia, South Carolina, didn't you?" The heat in Flinn's cheeks indicated his blood pressure had spiked.

Sam stood on the other side of his large, gunmetal desk, hands behind her back, her expression serene. Like the good soldier he trained her to be. "Tipped them off about what?"

His chair squeaked as he pushed himself to his feet and braced his hands on his black leather desk blotter. "Arthur Baldwin called. He said his brother has been taken in for questioning in a serial-killer case down there."

"That's unfortunate."

"You're the only one who could have told them who to look at, Samantha."

She didn't wither under his glare. She was done cowering, done denying that she had at least a little bit of power here, even if it wasn't enough to get what she wanted most: to go home. "Perhaps he left behind witnesses when he raped and killed that last helpless woman," she said.

"Witnesses who didn't bother to come forward until now, right after I've got that bastard Arthur right where I need him?"

"You still know he knew about his brother's illegal activities. Isn't the threat of that getting out enough to keep him in line?"

"It will have to be, but it wasn't part of the original deal. He's pissed, and that jeopardizes the entire project."

"Maybe you could try getting research funds the legal way."

"You know I can't do that, Samantha. The American people don't understand what I'm trying to do here. They couldn't accept it any more than they could accept the idea that aliens exist."

"I don't understand it, either. Perhaps you could explain this 'project' to me. Maybe I can help."

"In due time."

Frustrated with his refusal to confide in her goaded her to take a verbal swipe at him. "Are you ever going to admit that Arthur Baldwin is the businessman who drove your father to kill your mother and commit suicide?"

Flinn sank back into his chair. "How can you possibly know that?"

"You taught me to mine memories, remember? Do you think you're immune? My question is, why didn't you kill Arthur Baldwin a long time ago?"

He recovered his composure and gave her a bitter smile. "Revenge is sweetest when you can draw out the suffering. I've waited a long time for this. I won't tolerate your interference, Samantha. You go behind my back again, and I'll punish you. Do you understand?"

She braced against the fear that tried to weasel its way into her newfound bravado. He wouldn't hurt her. He needed her. "I understand."

Back on the bathroom floor, Sam couldn't stifle a soft whimper as memories gushed into her mind like a waterfall pounding rock . . .

Sloan Decker slipped up beside her in jeans that hugged muscled thighs, a black cowboy hat and a denim Western shirt with pearly snaps. He saluted her with the drink in his hand, bestowing a charming, for-the-pretty-lady grin on her. "We're aborting the mission."

She smiled back, feigning flirty and flattered. "Why? All I need is a little more—"

"Flinn thinks you've been compromised."

"I just talked to Adler on the phone. He sounded fine."

"The intel is iffy, but Flinn doesn't want to take the chance. We'll have to use what you've got."

She suppressed her eye-roll. "I can handle this."

"Preaching to the choir, Sam. Meet me out back in two."

She sighed.

"Sam."

The set of his chiseled jaw gave off "just do it" signals.

"Fine," she said. "Two minutes."

A minute and a half later, Sam left her still-full Tanqueray and tonic on the polished surface of the bar and slipped off the wooden stool. As the beat of country music thrummed in her chest, she wound her way through the bodies crowded around the pool tables toward the back. How had Adler made her? She was certain that all he saw when he looked at her was sex on spike heels. All she saw when she looked at him: a slimy security specialist bankrolling a terrorist attack to boost business.

"Stormy, girl, where are you off to?" Vince Adler's voice boomed behind her.

She turned a full-wattage smile on the over-tanned man, whose slicked-back black hair gleamed despite the muted lighting. "There you are. I was about to give up on you."

"Got hung up in traffic. You weren't leaving, were you?"

"I was in search of the ladies. Any clues?"

"I'll walk you there." His hand settled at the small of her back, subtle pressure steering her.

"Thank you." She shifted to grasp his fingers, giving them a small squeeze as his intentions filtered into her mind. Get her outside and into the Caddy. Jimmy will take it from there.

Jimmy, his nephew, who had a knack for helping Adler get what he wanted. Bastards, both of them. And proof that Flinn's intel was on the money.

In front of the ladies' room, she said, "Thanks for the escort."

Instead of letting her go, his grip shifted to her elbow and turned rough. He said nothing as he propelled her toward the exit.

"Vince?"

"Shut up."

He shoved the door open, and cold air rushed in to greet them. Sam saw the black Cadillac Escalade—but no Jimmy—at the same moment that Sloan stepped out of the shadows and placed the barrel of his SIG nine mil against the nape of Adler's neck.

"Let the lady go," Sloan said, deep and low and menacing.

A grim smile curved Adler's lips. "My men have you surrounded. You're outnumbered three to one."

Sloan snorted. "That was true about three minutes ago." He jutted his chin at Sam and tossed her a pair of plastic zip cuffs. "Want to do the honors, Stormy?"

She pushed a red-faced Adler against the brick wall and zipped the restraints on him. "You took out six guys in three minutes?" she asked Sloan, as incredulous as she was impressed.

He grinned at her, all teeth and male ego. "There's a reason my code name is Hammer."

CHAPTER **FORTY**

Mac rolled onto his side, reaching for Sam in the dark, already smiling as naughty thoughts tumbled through his head. He'd start with her nipples, he thought. Fingers first, then tongue and perhaps a little teeth. Her nipples were extra sensitive, and he could make her arch right off the bed when he played them just right.

But Sam wasn't in bed with him anymore, and the sheets where he hadn't been lying felt cool to the touch.

He sat up and reached for the lamp on the bedside table. He heard a noise at the same moment that the light chased the darkness from the hotel room. In the bathroom. Not vomiting, thank God. Something else, though. Something he didn't immediately recognize, and when he did, his skin flashed cold.

"Shit." Shoving aside the bedclothes, he hopped out of bed, grabbed his boxers and stepped into them as he half-walked, half-stumbled to the bathroom door. "Sam?"

Nothing but silence on the other side of the door.

"Sam? You okay in there?"

He heard her sniff, followed by what sounded suspiciously like a hiccup.

He knocked a knuckle against the door. "Sam?"

When she still didn't respond, and his heart started jumping all over the place, he said, "I'm coming in, okay?"

He turned the knob and pushed the door open a couple of inches. He froze when he saw her. She was on the floor, her back against the side of the tub and her face buried in a towel. Her hair hung around her face and hands in damp strands. She shook so much her shoulders quaked.

"Jesus, Sam," he murmured, opening the door fully and going in to drop to one knee beside her. "What's wrong?"

She shook her head, face still buried in the towel. She was crying. No, not just crying. Sobbing.

He reached for her without thought, and his alarm grew as his palm brushed over her back and he felt the cold, wet material of the pajama top plastered against her back.

"You're soaked to the skin. What the hell happened? Did you have a nightmare?" As he asked, it hit him: flashback. A really bad one this time.

"Oh, baby," he said softly, and pressed a kiss to the crown of her head. "Let's get you into some dry clothes, okay?"

She raised her head finally, her swallow audible. Tears and grief had left her eyes red and puffy. "I'm fine. I can change myself."

His chest muscles squeezed at the ragged hoarseness of her voice. "I know you can. But you don't have to. I'll help you."

"You've done enough."

He stilled at her flat tone. This was not the same woman he'd made love with repeatedly throughout the night. "Talk to me, Sam. What's going on?"

He thought she wasn't going to answer, but then her eyes latched onto his for about half a second before skipping away. "I remember everything."

His stomach did a slow roll. "Shouldn't that be something to celebrate?"

She pushed to her feet and brushed by him to go to the sink, where she splashed water on her face then blotted it dry. Then she headed into the bedroom, dragging the sodden top over her head along the way.

"What are you doing?" he asked.

"I have to go."

"Go? Go where?"

"Away from here." She fished a top and jeans out of the Dillard's bag and started tugging off the tags. "My instincts were screaming at me not to come here, but I agreed to it anyway. I should have listened."

He followed her around the room as she dressed. "Maybe

you should take a breath and think this through. You're safe here."

"But you're not." She stopped in midstep and covered her face with both hands. "Oh, God."

He put a hand at her hip to steady her. "What, Sam?"

"Charlie and Alex."

"They'll be here soon."

"It's not safe for them. They . . . you . . . *all of you* can't be anywhere near me."

He grasped her shoulders and turned her fully toward him. "You need to calm down."

"I don't have time—"

"Take time. Please."

She pressed her shaking hands against his bare chest, palms flat, and looked into his eyes. Her gaze lost focus, and a light shudder coursed through her. A moment later, she was back, eyes overflowing as she quietly shattered before his eyes.

"We made a mistake," she said. "*I* made a mistake. I never should have let this happen when I had no memory."

He released her and stepped back, dread buzzing to the top of his head. "Is there someone else?"

Tears streamed unchecked down her cheeks. "No."

"That Sledge guy you wanted to call when we first got into this. Is he—"

"No. He's a friend. That's all. There's never been anyone else, Mac. Only you. But I can't do this. I can't be here at all."

He had the impression that she never allowed herself to cry like this, especially in front of another person. "You need to talk to me, Sam. Tell me what you're thinking."

She swiped at her running nose. "Flinn will use Charlie and Alex to flush me out."

Surprise that she'd actually told him threw him off, but he recovered quickly. "We've taken precautions. No one can possibly know they're coming here."

"And what about after we leave? I can't protect them forever, Mac." Her voice broke on his name. "I have to go."

The anger rolled over him in a wave, eroding his usual, easygoing control. "So, what, you're just going to take off on your sisters again and not look back for another fourteen years?"

She winced and looked away, closing her eyes for a brief moment before sniffing and meeting his gaze, stronger now, resolved. "You know it's not what I want."

He turned away, unable to look at her without wanting to shout at her to stop being a damn spy and be the woman she'd been the past three days. "I think it is what you want. Going back to Lake Avalon would be hard. Making things right with Charlie and Alex would be hard. And you're all about the easy way, aren't you?"

"You don't understand."

He whirled toward her. "No, *you* don't understand! I've been friends with Charlie and Alex for a long time. You broke their hearts when you ran away, Sam. And now I've brought you back to them, and you're going to walk away before you even see them again? What the hell?"

"This isn't about Charlie and Alex," she said softly.

"Like hell it's not."

"I didn't want to come back here. I told you—"

"Oh, so it's my fault your sisters are going to lose you all over again. That's bullshit, and you know it. You're the one in control here. You're the one who gets to make the decisions, and your decision is to run. That's *easy* for you."

She advanced on him fast, and the next thing he knew, she'd shoved him up against the wall. "It's not easy. It was *never* easy."

He grasped her wrists and turned fast, twisting her around so that her back was against the wall, the maneuver far more gentle than she'd done with him. When she struggled against his grip, he leaned into her, front to front, subduing her with his superior weight. She might have been a trained fighter, might have been able to take him apart limb by limb when in fighting form, but at the moment she was shaky and drained, and he easily pinned her.

"You can't muscle your way out of this one, Sam."

She tried to yank away, but he held fast. "You can't just pack up and walk out of here like the past three days didn't happen. You have people who care about you, who want to help you."

"You don't know anything—"

"You think I don't know what it's like to find yourself at rock bottom? Believe me, sister, I've been there. I was there a week ago, stressed out of my mind and in danger of heading straight for the bottom of a bottle. Your sisters snapped me out of that. Now I'm returning the favor."

She turned her head aside, closing her eyes tightly, as if she could shut him out by pure will. He jerked her forward by the wrists and waited until she looked at him again. He didn't have to wait as long as he'd expected.

"All I'm asking," he said, "is that you think about what you're doing. You're not yourself."

"I haven't been myself for the past three days."

"I don't think that's true. You've been more yourself the past three days than you've been in fourteen years."

"There's no way out of this, Mac. Don't you think I would have tried a long time ago?"

"It's time you made the choice to trust someone to help you."

"I can't."

"You have to."

"Flinn will kill you. He'll kill Charlie and Alex. My parents. He'll take everyone I love away from me. You don't know him like I do. He's . . . evil."

"And what's to stop him from using any one of us, or all of us, to flush you out after you leave?"

"I'll make sure that doesn't happen."

"How?"

"I don't know yet, but I will. You'll have to trust me."

"Sam." He said her name softly, and for the first time in his life, words failed him.

So he kissed her.

It took her several seconds to respond, but her arms finally went around his neck, and she kissed him like she was dying. She tasted of salt and grief and desperation, and he gave her everything he had to show her they could get through this. Together.

* * *

When Mac carried her to bed, she let him. When he gently laid her out and undressed her with intimate care, she let him. When he murmured and sighed and kissed her eyes and brows and temples, caressed her aching breasts with reverent hands, she let him. She lost herself in him, lost the thread of why she had to leave this man, lost the fear and doubt and pain. Love rolled in to fill the empty places left behind, love and warmth and security.

When he slipped into her, hot and hard and oh so sweet, she arched to meet his thrust, her eyes open and fixed on his, his name on her lips.

"Mac."

He smiled as he moved, slow and easy, taking his time building the pleasure, never looking away from her gaze as he stroked into her. He made love to her with tender ferocity, telling her with his body and his eyes that if she left him, she'd die. Again. Sam Trudeau died fourteen years ago. Mac Hunter had resurrected her in three days.

A tear slipped back into her hair, and he stopped it with his lips. His breathing grew ragged in time with hers, and he kissed her more urgently as the pleasure grew, kissed her with lips and tongue and teeth, demanding that she accept what he was showing her, giving her. His heart. His soul.

"I'm falling in love with you," he murmured against the side of her neck, against the throb under her skin.

Her heart soared with those words, followed by her body, the climax detonating inside her like a supernova, flashes of light and heat and release arching her head back on a serrated moan. He followed a moment later, a harsh groan escaping his lips as his body vibrated against hers. When he buried his face in her neck, his breath fast and uneven against her skin, she opened herself to his release. It rolled through her on a second wave, just as intense and blinding as the first. Her muscles stretched taut, and her name echoed in her—his— mind.

Sam. Oh God, Sam.

The depth of his emotion and love shook her, shocked her.

She didn't deserve this. She didn't deserve him.

And yet she clung to him, reluctant to let go.

He started to withdraw, but she put her arms around him to hold him in place, savoring the connection, the minute twitches of his softening cock nestled inside her. He responded with a soft kiss at the corner of her mouth, a nuzzle of his nose against her cheek.

"We're going to be okay, Sam," he whispered.

She closed her eyes as he settled beside her and gathered her into his arms.

"We're going to be okay."

She wished she could believe that.

CHAPTER **FORTY-ONE**

Sam eased out of bed, careful to not jostle Mac even the slightest bit. When he stirred and murmured in his sleep, she leaned over and pressed a tender kiss to his forehead.

"I'm falling in love with you, too," she whispered as she trailed gentle fingers down his temple and over the sandpaper texture of the light beard covering his jaw.

Then she grabbed her clothes and went into the bathroom, where she cleaned up before quickly pulling them on. When she looked in the mirror, she paused, surprised by the flush in her cheeks, the dazed expression in her eyes. She looked like a woman who'd been thoroughly loved, thoroughly satisfied. And yet was thoroughly confused.

She ran a hand down the front of her body, over her abdomen. As if in answer, her stomach lurched and churned.

She braced a hand on the vanity as her knees trembled. What was she doing? She didn't have the strength to take on Flinn by herself. She needed help.

But how could anyone else help without endangering themselves? Flinn would do anything to get her back, not because he wanted *her* or couldn't live without *her* or valued her work as a spy, but because of the life she carried.

She closed her eyes, fighting against the nausea, fighting the sense of violation. If she were indeed pregnant—and she believed she was—she knew when Flinn had done it. She'd known when it happened but hadn't had enough information to pull the threads together. Now she did.

She'd awakened the morning after, out of it and woozy. Flinn sat in the chair beside her bed, waiting for her to wake up. He laughed at her, saying she'd drunk too much the night before. She obviously couldn't hold her liquor.

He'd brought her home after dinner and put her to bed. Stayed with her in case she woke in the middle of the night and needed something. The kind, caring boss and friend. He'd even made her scrambled eggs and bacon for breakfast, chattering away about innocuous news events and other topics she couldn't follow because her head hurt too much.

Thing was, she couldn't imagine she actually drank that much. She certainly couldn't remember anything beyond a glass of wine with dinner. And even that she'd only sipped because she never knew how alcohol might interact with the drugs that bolstered her empathy.

She knew now, for a fact, that Flinn had drugged her that night.

The thought had crossed her mind then, but she'd shaken it off. It briefly occurred to her again later, when Zoe had insisted he'd impregnated her against her will. But why *would* he drug them? They both already did everything he told them to, with a few tiny exceptions in Sam's case.

Over the years, he'd made it clear in multiple subtle ways that he owned her, that he could use her for whatever purpose he wanted. To prove it, he and his scientist partner in crime, Dr. Toby Ames, had devised all sorts of tests to learn how to enhance and expand and take full advantage of her gift. Because of her, N3 knew how to get the most from its psychic operatives. Because of her, N3 knew that an agent pumped full of this drug and that drug could precisely mine the memories of anyone he or she touched.

On top of all of that, Flinn had roofied her.

And now she was pregnant.

She wondered how he managed that part. He hadn't raped her. She would have noticed the signs afterward. And that would have been an inexact science timing-wise.

Instead, after he drugged her, he must have called Dr. Ames, and that equally sick bastard, the one who'd pumped just about every drug imaginable into her veins—just to see what would happen to her empathy—had shown up with doctor bag in hand and pumped her full of something else.

She wondered whose sperm they used. Had to be that of another psychic operative if they were indeed trying to create empathic spies. She couldn't imagine any of her fellow spies being a willing donor, though, so they'd probably drugged the donor, too.

After all that, though, the thing she had the most trouble believing was that Flinn would have the patience to wait for a child to grow into the super spy he wanted. He'd have to wait at least two decades. By then, Flinn would be pushing seventy.

That didn't make sense.

She curled her fingers against her belly, closing her eyes. The answer lay beneath her palm. A tiny life created inside her against her will.

And somehow, some way, the thought of that tiny life flushed warmth into her veins.

She'd never considered being a mother. She'd thought life had forced her down a road that precluded having a family. She'd pushed thoughts of never loving a child who needed, *wanted* only her far from her mind, refusing to let herself even think about it.

Now, against all odds, she was going to be a mother.

And whatever Flinn Ford's plans, she wouldn't let him take that away from her.

CHAPTER **FORTY-TWO**

After pulling on a royal blue cotton top and jeans, she liberated one of the prepaid cell phones from its bag, gathered up the notebook computer that Mac had already used to check, but not send, e-mail and returned to the bathroom.

Sloan Decker's cell phone number came to her as if she used it every day. Before she'd lost her memory, she practically had.

His deep voice answered after the first ring. "Decker."

"It's Sam."

"Holy Christ. Where the hell are you? You just vanished. And after what happened with Zoe—"

"I need to see you. Just us."

"That can be arranged."

"Your line isn't secure. I'll get you the information in the usual way."

"Got it."

She cut off the call, then opened the notebook computer where it sat on the vanity. Opening a Web browser, she went to the Google home page and accessed the Gmail account she and Sloan used for secure communication. They changed the account name and password every six months, and neither of them ever accessed it from their home or work computers or cell phones. She typed in the password then started a new e-mail message. When she was done giving him the information he'd need to find her, she saved the e-mail as a draft then signed off.

In Washington, DC, Sloan would be on his way to the library to check the drafts folder for the message she'd left him. No one could trace it because it had never been sent over the network. Now all she had to do was find a place to hide for the next several hours, until it was time to meet Sloan.

She savored one last look at Mac, who lay on his back, snoring, one hand flung over his eyes. She memorized every handsome detail, her throat closing and her eyes burning, before she slipped out the door and into the hall. As she shut the door gently behind her, she closed her eyes and took a moment to breathe, to calm her frantic heart.

She didn't want to do this.

She had to.

And not just for herself. She had to do it for Zoe. Zoe had a sister out there who had no idea what had happened to her. And there might be other N3 operatives who were pregnant with a Flinn Ford science project. She couldn't just walk away and let—

"Sam?"

A flinch tensed already tense muscles, and she opened her eyes to see her sister striding toward her. Her lungs seized, preventing her from taking a breath.

Charlie.

Tears flooded her eyes, and she blinked them away. She needed Soldier Sam now, not Sister Sam. But, God, it was *Charlie.*

Charlie paused before her, her intriguing eyes—light brown irises encircled in dark brown—bright with excitement and something else. A growing wariness.

"Going somewhere?" Charlie asked, cocking her head.

She looked slim and healthy in a pink tank top and navy shorts that had white stripes running up the outer thighs. Her long, reddish-brown hair was captured in a loose ponytail, as though she'd rolled out of bed only minutes ago and headed right to Sam and Mac's suite.

Sam swallowed hard. Charlie had a right to that wariness. Sam was about to fulfill her worst expectations.

"I have to go."

Charlie's eyes narrowed, the excitement dimming to disappointment. She made no move, just stood there, watching Sam with a guarded expression and that knowing tilt of her head. "Didn't you just get here?"

"I'm sorry, Charlie. I truly am."

"Go where?"

"It doesn't matter."

"It matters to me."

"I shouldn't be here. It isn't safe for you."

"Then why did you come? Why did Mac ask Alex and me to meet you?"

Sam's heart thudded in her chest, and she let her gaze dart past Charlie's shoulder. Was Alex here, too? Just down the hall, still sleeping or perhaps brushing her teeth in preparation for their reunion? Just a glimpse of her sweet kid sister would mean the world.

"Alex isn't here," Charlie said.

Sam didn't have to be empathic to hear the tension in her sister's voice. "Is something wrong?"

"She's—" Charlie broke off and swallowed. "She's having some trouble."

Alarm stiffened Sam's shoulders. "What kind of trouble?"

Charlie's eyes narrowed. "I thought you had to get going."

"If Alex needs help—"

Charlie's incredulous laugh cut her off. "You're ready to run to her rescue *now*? After fourteen years of being the absent big sister?"

Sam took a step back, which brought her up against the hotel room door. This wasn't how she'd pictured this. But how foolish had she been to think a reunion would be all hugs and exclamations of "I've missed you so much"?

"I'm sorry," Sam said. "I am. I wish I could explain—"

The door at her back opened so fast, she stumbled back a step before she caught herself. She turned to face Mac, expecting recriminations and disappointment, but he just broke into a broad smile when he spotted her sister. "Hey, Chuck."

Charlie rolled her eyes. "You know I hate it when you call me that."

His grin grew as he enfolded her in his arms for a heartfelt hug. "Why do you think I do it?" He met Sam's eyes as he rubbed a hand over Charlie's back. "How you doing, Charlie? You okay?"

She nodded as she pulled back from him. "I'm great. You?" She studied him, approval growing with each second. "You look good, Mac. Really good."

He nodded. "Got my mojo back." He cast a glance at Sam, his eyes dark and guarded. Hurt. "Had some help."

Sam had no doubt he knew she'd snuck out on him, intending to leave without a word. She considered piping up with an "I was heading out to get coffee," but Mac deserved better from her. He deserved better *than* her. He and Charlie both did.

"So," Mac said. "Why don't we get out of the hall?"

Charlie shot Sam a questioning look, as if daring her to take off now.

Sam stepped back into the hotel room ahead of them, conscious of the glances Mac and Charlie exchanged, carrying on a conversation with nothing but their eyes. She suppressed the surge of jealousy. She had no right to feel so possessive of a man she planned to leave.

In the small sitting room, which contained the red sofa and two club chairs that formed three sides of a square, Mac gestured vaguely. "You two can get comfortable, and I'll make us some coffee."

Sam hesitated. She needed to *go*. Yet, it would take hours for Sloan to catch a flight to Florida. She'd planned to hole up somewhere and wait. Did it make a difference where she hunkered down for the next several hours?

She met Charlie's cool gaze, and her heart sank. She'd blown this on so many levels.

"Actually, Mac," Charlie drawled, "Sam was just on her way out."

He paused in the door to the kitchenette and sighed. "Look, I know this is weird, but—"

"You know what's weird?" Charlie cut in. "The cell phone I get in the mail every few years with speed dial to her voice mail. Every once in a blue moon—meaning hardly ever—she returns my messages or calls to check in, like she's some kind of . . . I don't know . . . mob witness or something. That's what's weird."

Sam's knees began to do their impression of Silly Putty.

Sitting down would have helped, but she didn't dare risk moving. She should have left when she had the chance, should have taken the easy way and been done with it.

"You sounded happy on the phone," Mac said to Charlie. "When I told you I was with Sam, you said you'd been looking for her."

"I *was* happy," Charlie said. "I've been looking forward to seeing her again for days now, barely able to contain myself. And then I get here and catch her trying to slink away all over again, and it made me mad. I mean, what the hell, Sam?"

Sam couldn't control her wince. And she had no idea what to say. Charlie was right about everything. She had no defense.

"Tell her, Sam."

She flinched as much at the rasp in Mac's voice as at his words.

Before she could gather her nerves enough to speak, though, a knock sounded at the door.

"That's probably Noah," Charlie said. "He was still sleeping when I slipped out." She flashed a narrow-eyed glance at Sam. "I left him a note after I charmed the guy at the front desk out of your room number."

Charlie went to the door and opened it to a large, muscular man with dirty-blond hair and an impressive five o'clock shadow. He wore khaki cargo shorts, a white T-shirt and an expression that looked like thunder.

As soon as Charlie kissed him, though, his facial muscles relaxed. She murmured something that only he could hear, something that sounded like "Good morning," before she turned back toward Sam and gestured. "Noah, this is my sister Sam." To Sam, she said, "Noah Lassiter."

Sam hesitated to take the hand he held out, and just as she decided to suck it up and go with it, his dark eyes flickered with something—recognition, understanding, compassion—and he lowered his hand with a small smile and a never-mind nod.

"It's good to meet you, Sam," he said.

She tried to smile but failed. She should have run earlier. Maybe it wasn't too late.

Mac said, "I was going to make some coffee, Noah. Give Sam and Charlie some time to talk."

Noah took the hint and ambled after Mac into the kitchenette. "I hope you've got the good stuff. The crap in our room is for wimps."

Then Sam and Charlie were alone. Charlie went to the sofa and sat down, gesturing for Sam to take a club chair. Sam did as requested even while her head screamed at her to lunge for the door and flee. No good could come of a conversation filled with the lies she had no choice but to tell.

"So," Charlie said. "Tell me what?"

CHAPTER **FORTY-THREE**

Mac stood at the railing with his coffee, looking out at the glittery morning and letting the sound of the waves and the cool, salty breeze eat away at his anxiety. The tension that knotted his shoulders had yet to let up, apparently settled in for the long haul. Not surprising, considering he'd awakened to an empty hotel room and the realization that Sam had left him. If she hadn't encountered Charlie in the hall, she would have been long gone by now. God knew where. He never would have seen her again. Never would have known what happened to her, whether she lived happily ever after or whether Flinn Ford had her throat slit in a dark alley.

The door behind him slid open then closed, and Noah settled onto a low-slung deck chair made of weathered teak. "Now, *this* is good coffee."

Mac glanced over his shoulder to see the other man enjoying a healthy gulp. "Simon Walker has good taste."

Noah nodded. "Indeed."

Mac faced the water again, wishing he could have the balcony to himself to wallow in how absolutely crappy he felt. That's what happens when the woman you declare your love to walks out without a proper, or even improper, good-bye.

"Is Sam CIA?"

Mac turned back toward Noah, surprised. "You think she's a spy?"

"She's got a vibe."

"There's a spy vibe?"

"I know law enforcement. She's not that. She doesn't stand stiff and straight like a soldier, so she's not military. I don't get a mercenary vibe off her. So what's left? Black ops? Spooks?"

"FBI," Mac said with an impressed nod. "A secret division called N3."

"National . . ."

"National Neural Network." Mac expected Noah to snort in disbelief, but when he didn't, Mac braced back against the railing and watched the other man carefully. "It's a unit of psychic spies."

Noah whistled through his teeth, yet arched no eyebrow and released no you're-fucking-kidding-me bark of laughter.

Mac cocked his head. "Sam thinks her handler, or boss, is trying to create super spies by combining the DNA of empaths already working for the feds."

"How?"

"I don't know. She just got her memory back, and we haven't had a chance to get back to that conversation."

"Wait. Her memory?"

"These N3 people have access to some high-tech tools that the private sector has no clue about. James Bond–type stuff. When we first met, she had me dig a transponder out of her back. Messing with the tracker triggered a chemical reaction of some kind that wiped out her memory."

"Christ."

"Yeah, it's been fun."

Mac settled onto a deck chair that matched Noah's and sighed, exhausted and . . . hurt. Jesus, he was a putz to think a woman like Sam would ever stay with a guy like him.

"I've got some connections I can tap into," Noah said, "to see what's what."

"Sam's leery of the feds. She doesn't know who to trust."

"I know how to keep it under wraps. It might take awhile to work through the channels, but we'll figure it out."

Mac let his shoulders relax some, wincing as tight muscles complained. He'd been so tense for so long, he couldn't remember how it felt to relax. Funny how that was the whole plan behind his vacation to the Shenandoahs.

"Charlie's empathic, too," Noah said into the silence.

• Mac was as unsurprised as Noah had been about the revelation of a secret, psychic division of the FBI. "I kind of figured when you didn't laugh me off the balcony."

"It hasn't been an easy road for her."

"I wish she'd told me. I mean, I'm her friend. Maybe I could have helped . . . somehow."

"It wasn't something she purposely hid. It . . . developed after she witnessed that hit-and-run outside the newspaper."

"Ah." Mac had broken up with her by then, focused on making more money so he could give Jenn the college education he wanted her to have. And Noah had swooped in like the hero Mac could only dream of being. "What about Alex? Also empathic?"

"Yep. It's been worse for her, though," Noah said. "A lot worse."

"I didn't know." Mac thought of how hard Alex and Charlie had pushed him to escape to the mountains of Virginia to get his stress under control. At the same time, Alex had had her own monkey on her back, one she couldn't shake free as easily as Mac had.

Noah finished his coffee. "Alex and Logan are staying with a friend in Lake Avalon. We thought it best to keep her out of sight until we knew exactly what we're dealing with with Sam. What with the cell phone and GPS issues and the request that we borrow someone else's car to avoid a locator device being on both of ours . . . going into hiding seemed a bit of a no-brainer."

"Yeah, it's all very secret agent man, isn't it?"

Noah chuckled, and a minute of silence went by, broken only by the rhythm of the waves. Then he set his empty coffee cup on the table between them. "Sam won't stick around. You know that, right?"

Mac nodded. "Yeah."

"I'm surprised you got her this far."

"She got her memory back overnight and tried to take off this morning. Charlie intercepted her in the hall."

"I imagine she was trying to protect her sisters."

"I know."

"She wants to protect you, too."

Mac raised his head. Really? "Me?"

Noah smirked at him. "You're still an idiot, Hunter. Think you'll ever overcome that handicap?"

Mac couldn't stop himself from grinning in spite of the lingering hurt. Noah had seen something between him and Sam. Maybe he'd gotten another vibe. "Probably not."

"The point is that you're going to have to keep close tabs on her. As soon as she gets another opportunity, she's going to bolt. She made a mistake letting you bring her here."

"She needs her sisters."

"She needs her sisters to be safe, and in her mind, as long as she's around, no one is safe."

"Unless we find a way to take care of the guy after her."

"That's going to take some time. And he might not be alone. He could have the entire might of the federal government behind him."

"I don't know about that. He seems like a lone wolf to me."

"Sam's a psychic spy. You think people like her are easy to come by? The feds might do everything they possibly can to get her back."

"They can't force her to—"

"I'm just warning you that this isn't going to get resolved overnight."

Mac sighed. "And it's already been such a cakewalk."

CHAPTER **FORTY-FOUR**

"Where have you been the past fourteen years, Sam? What's with all the mystery?"

Charlie sounded as exhausted as Sam felt. The fact that Sam was the one who'd exhausted her just made her feel worse. But she had a bigger concern at the moment. "You didn't finish telling me about what's happening with Alex."

Instead of answering, Charlie got up from the sofa and walked into the kitchenette.

Sam swallowed against the anxiety growing in her throat. Disappointment that this couldn't be a happy reunion added to the tension, along with the urgent need to stride the four steps to the hotel room door, open it and walk out. Sad, considering how desperately she'd yearned to come home the past fourteen years. Never once had it occurred to her that maybe home didn't want her anymore.

She swiped a finger at a brimming tear and cursed her inability to control her emotions. She blamed Mac. He'd opened her up when she hadn't remembered the vital importance of remaining closed, when N3's ruthless drugs had taken her memory and her defenses.

Maybe she should blame hormones, too, now that she thought about it.

Resting her head against the back of the club chair, she closed her eyes and concentrated on getting it together. If Charlie couldn't stand to be in the room with her, then she'd deal. She'd dealt with worse over the years. She'd most likely deal with worse in the near future. But, God, it hurt. So much for the unconditional love of family. Not that she begrudged her sister her anger. If the positions had been reversed—

"Here."

Sam snapped her eyes open. Charlie stood beside the chair, a coffee cup in each hand, one extended toward her. "I figure we're both going to need caffeine for this."

Sam knew her eyes shimmered as she accepted the steaming cup, because the fierce lines in Charlie's forehead smoothed out and the compressed line of her lips softened.

"Thank you," Sam said, her voice hitching.

Charlie resettled on the sofa but instead of sitting back, she perched on the front half of the cushions with her elbows braced on her knees and the cup cradled in her hands. "You think I'm not happy to see you."

"Can't say I blame you."

Charlie smiled faintly. "I've been mad at you for a long time."

"Can't blame you for that, either."

"This just isn't how I pictured your homecoming."

"I'm sorry for the way it's happened. It's not fair to any of you."

"Would you be here now if you didn't need help?"

"I lost my memory. I didn't know who to go to for help. And Mac . . . Mac saved my life."

"Woo hoo, Mac." Charlie paused, eyes briefly narrowing then widening as though she'd put two and two together and had come up with Sam and Mac. She quickly got over it, apparently, because she said, "Not an answer, though. Would you be here now?"

Sam worried her bottom lip between her teeth. Charlie always had been a reporter to the core. Dogged with the questions, perceptive as all hell, quick to notice when the key questions were dodged. "No, I wouldn't be here now."

"Where would you be?"

"Dead, probably."

A muscle under Charlie's right eye twitched. "Then I'm glad you're here, regardless of how it happened."

Sam swallowed and nodded. "Me, too."

"Why did you leave? All these years, we've never known."

"Are you deliberately avoiding the subject of our kid sister?"

"I'm thinking I'm entitled to answers first, considering."

She studied Charlie for a long moment, getting a read on her emotions. Wariness. Relief. Curiosity. Resentment. Underlying them all: fear, worry, helplessness. Sam wasn't the only issue churning Charlie's insides. And that churned Sam's even more. Something was seriously wrong with Alex.

If Charlie wanted answers first, then Sam would provide as many as she could. "Dad isn't . . . my biological father."

Instead of disbelief or shock, Charlie seemed to think for a minute, several different emotions—surprise, comprehension, sadness—flitting through her eyes before she sat back, coffee cup resting on her thigh. "Well, that explains a lot."

"Does it?"

"Mom's been a wench our entire lives. I figured it had to be something big." She frowned. "Sad thing is that I kind of thought Dad cheated on her way back when, and that's why he's stuck with her all this time despite her broom-ready personality."

Sam's lips quirked into a sad smile. "So she hasn't changed."

"Nope."

"I'm sorry."

"Not your fault."

"I'm sorry I left you to deal with her alone. My plan, after I found my father and his family, was to come back for you and Alex."

"But things didn't go as expected." It wasn't a question.

"Not even close."

"So how did it go with your dad?"

"*Dad* is my dad. Ben Dillon was the guy who knocked up Mom. I'd known him about a year when he got himself killed during a con gone bad."

"God, Sam."

"He used me. It sucked."

"Understatement."

"Yeah. It wasn't much better for our mother," Sam said. "He bailed on her after she got pregnant. She must have fled her family and changed her name before she met Dad."

"Do you think Dad knows you aren't his?" Charlie asked. "Biologically, I mean."

"If he does, it must not have mattered. He never treated me any differently than he treated you and Alex."

"It's more likely that Mom let him think you were his, and that's why she's so tense all the time. She's terrified we're going to discover her secret."

"You came close the night you found that photo album in her dresser drawer," Sam said. "That must be all that's left of her past."

"That and you."

Sam gave her a rueful smile. "I was the daily reminder of how Ben Dillon screwed her over and dumped her. She might have been relieved to see me go."

Charlie cocked her head, regarding her with searching eyes. "You said he died only a year after you found him. Why didn't you come home after that?"

Sam hesitated as she thought of her years with Flinn Ford and N3. Every detail was classified. "I can't—"

"I know it's bad. I can tell by looking at you."

Sam glanced down at her cup. Ripples in the coffee gave away the tremors in her hands. "Well."

"Don't take that the wrong way," Charlie said quickly. "You're beautiful. Gorgeous. You always have been. But life has been hard on you. Your eyes . . . they look . . . God, Sam, your eyes look old and sad. It kills me that I don't know why, that I can't make it better."

Sam covered her mouth with one hand, swallowing convulsively against the raw emotion clawing up from her chest.

Charlie moved fast, rescuing Sam's wobbling coffee cup and setting it aside before kneeling beside her chair and clasping both hands in a firm, unyielding grip.

They stiffened at the same time, and Sam saw herself through her sister's eyes.

Oh my God, it's Sam! It has to be Sam! She's really here. God, my heart is about to pound right out of my chest.

She looks the same. Older, sure, but the same.

But what the heck is she doing in the hall, looking so . . . stricken? Like she's lost the best friend she's ever had. Could that be Mac?

Wait. Oh, hell. She's leaving. *She came all this way, and now she's running again.*

Damn it. Damn her.

As Sam fell out of Charlie's memory, she took several deep breaths to calm her racing pulse and loosen the tightness banded around her ribs. But it was only temporary. All that coiled anxiety would be back soon enough.

"You're in love with Mac," Charlie said, voice soft.

Sam focused on her sister's gold-flecked eyes as realization shuddered through her. While Sam had taken a trip into Charlie's memory, Charlie had taken a trip into Sam's. "You're empathic," Sam said, her tone filled with wonder. "How? I mean . . . I didn't think you were when I left Lake Avalon."

Charlie sat back on her heels, keeping Sam's hands gripped in hers, as though she feared letting go might encourage her to slip away. "Had a run-in with a cousin Mom never told us about. Maybe you met that side of the family when you found Ben Dillon?"

"No. He was estranged from them. I know next to nothing about them."

After releasing Sam's hands, Charlie reclaimed her spot on the sofa and picked up her coffee. "Long story short: I was touching our cousin when she died, and we think her power mingled with mine to double-charge it."

"Wow."

"That's what I said. After several days of freaking out. So . . . Mac?"

Sam gave her sister a small smile. "I hope that's okay. I know you have a history."

"I'm just . . . aren't you going to leave again?"

Sam winced. "It's complicated."

"I got that when I was in your head."

She couldn't quell her instant apprehension. Did Charlie know about other things? "What else did you get?"

"Nothing much," Charlie said. "My empathy is imprecise. I get a brief flash of something, and that's it. It can be damned confusing, but it's better than what Alex has to deal with."

"She's empathic, too? No wonder Mom's been a basket

case all these years. She was surrounded by daughters who might or might not have been psychic and could have discovered her secrets at any moment."

"Believe it or not, Mom's got the curse. I've never seen her in action, but Alex got a hit off her indicating that when she was a teenager, she used her ability to con people out of money."

"That's what my father did," Sam said. "He told me that his family and Mom's family were part of a band of grifters. More than a decade before I showed up, they started to scatter. By the time I located Ben, he was among only a few left in the area that served as their home base. He said he didn't know why Mom took off, other than he thought she was having an abortion."

"I've got that piece of the puzzle," Charlie said. "Alex flashed on Mom discovering a man right after he'd committed suicide. She'd helped con him out of a bunch of money then felt guilty and tried to return it. She was too late. She must have taken off right after that."

"In search of a better life." Ironic, Sam thought. That's why *she'd* taken off fourteen years ago, determined to find someone more fit than her mother to be family. She'd headed in the completely wrong direction.

Charlie sighed. "Mom found that better life with Dad. It's kind of romantic, when you think about it."

Laughing softly, Sam rubbed at her eyes. "God, I was an idiot to take off like I did."

"If Mom had told us the truth from the start, maybe we wouldn't be having this conversation."

Sam smiled. Leave it to Charlie to bottom-line it, though Sam figured her teen self would still have been determined to meet her biological father.

Leaning forward, Sam retrieved her coffee from the table and inhaled the enticing aroma. Her stomach growled, but she didn't drink. Was it silly to worry about caffeine's effects on an unborn child after all the drugs she'd been given?

"Are you hungry?" Charlie asked suddenly. "I haven't had breakfast."

"There's food in the fridge. Mac's boss set us up very well."

"Simon Walker's my boss, too. Great guy for a billionaire."

As they walked into the kitchenette, Charlie said, "Simon saved the newspaper. Did you know that?"

"Mac told me, yes."

As Sam opened a cupboard and reached for bagels, Charlie whipped open the fridge and peered inside. "Did he also tell you Simon had to swoop in after I defied Dad and single-handedly killed the paper by writing a big story about a crooked advertiser?"

Sam arched her brows. "Nope. Didn't mention that."

Charlie smiled. "God, he was pissed. Mac, I mean. He'd just become managing editor. Dad, believe it or not, was proud of me."

Sam paused, hands full of bagels and eyes filling with tears. "I miss him, Charlie. I miss Dad. I hope he can forgive me."

"Forgive you for what? You went looking for answers. You didn't become a journalist like Alex and I did, but you still went looking for the truth. I bet you stand for truth and justice as vehemently as Alex and I do, just in a different way. It's kind of in our DNA."

Sam didn't respond for a long moment while she liberated the bagels from their packaging and popped one into the toaster. She didn't tell her sister that she didn't know anymore what she stood for. She'd *thought* she worked on the side of truth and justice, but Flinn Ford could have manipulated every aspect of her life for the past fourteen years, rather than just the part where he'd blackmailed her into working for him. And drugged her. And used her. And killed her best friend.

Sam shook the distressing thoughts from her head—she'd deal with all of that soon enough—and watched Charlie pry the lid off a tub of whipped cream cheese.

"Should we yell at the guys to come get something?" Sam asked as she got a knife out of the drawer.

"Nah, I've never known Noah to go hungry. If he wants something, he'll come looking. Mac, too." Charlie started slathering a healthy glob of cream cheese on half of an untoasted bagel. "You know what I miss?"

Sam smiled at the warmth that infused her as she and her sister shared something as mundane as bagel prep. "What?"

"Those omelets you used to make. The ones with the ham and onions and peppers? I haven't had an omelet that good since you left. Do you still make those?"

Sam shook her head. "It's been a long time."

"Do you cook at all like you used to? I swear I haven't eaten a decent meal in fourteen years."

"I gave that up when I left."

"We need to work on that, then. It's just not right to let talent like that go to waste."

Sam swallowed against the renewed tightness of emotion. Charlie talked as though all would be well again. And Sam knew it wouldn't.

CHAPTER **FORTY-FIVE**

Flinn sat in the corner booth of Mama Mo's in downtown Lake Avalon. The diner buzzed with the activity of morning customers as they washed down biscuits and gravy, ham and eggs, bacon and hash browns with copious amounts of coffee and chatter. The Florida sun blazed through the clean windows, casting in sharp relief the differences in the customers. Where the visitors, in shorts and T-shirts, smiled and laughed and planned their excursions for the day, the workday crowd, most in business casual, paged through the newspaper or talked self-importantly on cell phones.

Flinn's own phone chirped, and he pulled it out of his inside jacket pocket. There'd better damn well be some good fucking news coming his way.

"Nat," he said in greeting.

"Good morning, sir."

"What've you got for me?" He wasn't in the mood for chit-chat after the restless night he'd had.

"Got a hit on some guests at the Hotel Sandpiper in St. Petersburg."

He paused to smile. Natalie had disappointed him by admiring Toby's intellect over his own, but Flinn had a forgiving nature, especially when he got what he wanted. "Tell me."

"Simon Walker, CEO of Walker Media, is a regular at the Sandpiper. He also owns the newspaper in Lake Avalon."

Flinn nodded, a renewed eagerness spurting adrenaline into his bloodstream. "Where both Hunter and Charlie work."

"I called Mr. Walker's assistant and posed as the Sandpiper's customer relations manager checking on whether Mr. Walker required anything special for his visit. She said she'd already confirmed that his special requests had been taken care of."

"Special requests?"

"Yes. He asked for some new clothing and other items, for both men and women, to be delivered to his suite." Natalie paused. "There's more." She had a smile in her voice.

"Please continue."

"According to business news reports online, Mr. Walker is in Denver for a media conference this week. He's giving the keynote address this evening."

Flinn began to grin. "It sounds as though we've found our wayward operative, Nat."

"I'm e-mailing you directions from Lake Avalon to the Sandpiper as we speak. It's about a three-hour drive, depending on traffic."

"Nat, you make me proud."

"Thank you, sir."

"Where's Marco? I want him to accompany me."

"He's helping with the setup of the medical facility you requested. He and Dr. Ames secured an abandoned veterinary clinic in a Lake Avalon neighborhood that flooded last summer. They assembled a team of workers and hope to have it ready late this afternoon."

"More excellent news. Give him a call and have him pick me up at my hotel in an hour."

"Will do, sir."

"This is all going to be over very soon, Nat. Do I have to tell you how relieved I am?"

"I can tell by the tone of your voice. Good luck, sir."

"No wishes of luck needed. That's how confident I am."

CHAPTER **FORTY-SIX**

Sam and Charlie refreshed their coffee and took their bagels back into the sitting area. For several moments, neither spoke as they ate, the silence companionable now that the ice between them had thawed. Eventually, though, Sam couldn't stand it anymore and tried again to get Charlie to tell her about their sister.

"So . . . Alex?"

Charlie finished chewing and swallowed, her eyes darkening with anxiety. "It's bad for her, Sam. Really bad." Her hand shook as she paused to sip coffee, as though she needed the extra time to gird herself. When she spoke again, her voice was low. "After she got shot, she coded in the ER, and they had to zap her a couple of times. We think the electric shock supercharged her empathy. So when she touches someone, not only does she relive something traumatic that happened to that person in the past, but she sometimes gets stuck in the moment."

"She gets stuck?"

Charlie nodded. "The flash lasts until the event ends naturally or something happens to knock her out of it."

Sam didn't know of any of her fellow operatives who experienced that particular problem. She herself never had.

"A few months ago," Charlie went on, "a serial killer focused on her. Psycho bastard put her through absolute hell. Every time he touched her, she flashed on some of the sick shit he'd done and some that had been done to him. We almost lost her all over again. She hasn't been the same since."

Sam pressed her lips together to suppress nausea and grief. Poor Alex. The last time she'd seen her kid sister, she hadn't even been aware of boys yet, completely focused on anything

warm and furry and in need of love. The thought of all that
sweet innocence corrupted by a psychopath . . . it was unfath-
omable. And heartbreaking.

"Flash fatigue for her is a bitch," Charlie said.

"Flash fatigue?"

"Don't know about you, but both our brains seem to have a
limit on how often we can flash during a particular window of
time. Too many flashes, and everything goes haywire. Beta
blockers and tranquilizers help line things out when they get
intense. That doesn't happen with you?"

"It has a more scientific name in my world. Synaptic deficit
syndrome. SDS. Which is really just a fancy way of explain-
ing why I get a nasty headache after too many empathic hits."

"SDS sounds way more intimidating than flash fatigue.
And kind of like a sexually transmitted disease."

Sam laughed. "Yeah, it does." The humor didn't last long,
though, as she thought about Alex. She couldn't imagine getting stuck in another person's horrific flashback. Just the few
moments she'd spent in Jake Baldwin's head had been enough
to make her violently ill. He'd been the sickest bastard she'd
encountered in her spy life, and she'd landed in his head only
once. To do that repeatedly and not be able to escape at will . . .
God. She shut her eyes and lowered her head. She needed to
get a grip, damn it. She couldn't lose it now, when every choice
she made in the next few hours would mean the difference
between life and death for the people she loved.

Sam raised her head, determined to be strong. She had no
choice. "I assume Alex has tried to find a way to control her
empathy."

"We've tried everything," Charlie said. "Meditating calms
her down but doesn't prevent flashes from hitting her. She's
had some success with drugs, but she hates those because they
make her fuzzy. She still takes them for work, because being
a photographer and all, she has to shake hands a lot. But the
drugs don't completely stop the flashes. They just mute them.
And as long as she keeps the drugs in her system, she doesn't
get stuck, which is the main thing, I guess." She paused, and

her eyes filled with tears. "Sometimes I fear that one of these flashes is going to kill her. When she encounters someone who's been injured, it's like she experiences a kind of empathic stigmata. Whatever injury the other person sustained happens to Alex. She's gotten black eyes, burns, stab wounds. It's—" She stopped. "This doesn't surprise you."

Sam chose her words carefully. "My . . . boss has done extensive research on empathy."

"Really? This research obviously isn't readily available to the public. I've done searches online, talked to experts, tried to get my hands on everything I can find. All I come up with is a bunch of different names and vague descriptions that sort of sound like what's happening to her but not quite. Clairsentience. Postcognition. Retrocognition. None of the terms seem to cover all aspects of Alex's ability. I don't know why it's so important to put a label on it, but maybe I think that would help us understand it."

"There is no label. It's just what it is." Sam thought of all the training Flinn had put her through, teaching her how to guide and control and maximize her empathy. When things had gone wrong, he had a team of experts, including Toby Ames, to figure it all out. Flinn had chemists to create fancy drug cocktails that enhanced her ability without robbing her of fast reflexes and a clear mind. Alex, however, had no training, no team of experts and no access to drugs or the chemists who created them.

What Sam knew from her years of N3 training could give Alex her life back.

"Who do you work for?" Charlie asked.

Sam blinked up at her, startled out of her thoughts. The moment of truth had arrived. "I can't tell you that."

Charlie's direct gaze didn't flicker. "Try this then: Who are you running from?"

"Charlie—"

"I know you're in trouble. Mac's not a dramatic guy, yet the way he got us here was extremely dramatic. Not to mention the fed who tried to follow us. Noah's got some mad driving skills, by the way." She flashed a grin before she sobered. "I know you're on the run, Sam. It's pretty obvious."

Sam caught her bottom lip between her teeth. "I have unfinished business."

"Is that code for someone's trying to kill you?"

"It's code for there are a lot of people counting on me to do the right thing."

"And what's the right thing? According to Samantha Trudeau."

Sam ignored the edge in Charlie's tone. "The right thing is writing a newspaper story about a crooked advertiser because the public has a right to know, even though you know your defiance is going to piss off a lot of people, including Dad."

"That's hardly on the same scale as the mess you're in."

Sam leaned forward to set her bagel plate on the coffee table. "I have . . . I *had* a friend. Zoe. A really *good* friend, and colleague. She found out our boss isn't a good guy, and he had her killed."

Charlie sucked in a sharp breath. "Oh my God, Sam."

"I'm certain that her sister has no idea she's dead. And when, or *if*, she finds out, she'll never know the truth about what happened."

"So it's up to you to tell her."

Sam nodded. "It's possible that I have other colleagues who are in the same situation Zoe was in before she was killed. I can't sit back and do nothing."

"You can go to the police. The FBI. The federal government—"

"My boss is connected. I don't know how far up the chain of command his corruption goes."

"But risking your life—"

"It could have been me. I could have been Zoe. Wouldn't you have wanted to know what happened to me?"

"Yes, but I wouldn't want someone else to die—"

"Charlie."

Her sister clamped her lips together in a tight line. "I know that look on your face, Sam. I remember it from the day you packed up your stuff and left home. I don't like it."

Sam allowed herself a gentle smile. "Then you know that I'm determined."

"And what about Alex? She needs you. She needs both of us right now to help her get through all this—"

"She has you. She has Mac. And, from what Mac told me, she has a good man in Logan."

"None of us is a substitute for you. And what about Mac? You're just going to leave him? I can tell by the way he looks at you that—"

Sam got to her feet so abruptly that Charlie broke off. Time to go, before her resolve wavered. "I'm counting on you to thank him for me. He saved my life more than once."

Charlie started shaking her head as she pushed herself off the sofa. "No, no, no. Sam, come on. You're not going right now. There's too much to—"

"Someone's waiting for me. Someone who's going to help me work it all out." Sam drew her sister into her arms and hugged her stiff body, her heart breaking at Charlie's refusal to return the embrace. "I'll make sure Alex gets the help she needs. I promise."

Charlie's arms suddenly clamped tight around her. "Sam, God, Sam, don't you think I've noticed you're not promising to come back?"

Sam swallowed hard. "Give me fifteen minutes before you tell Mac I'm gone. If he tries to follow me, he could get hurt."

Charlie buried her face in Sam's neck, a little girl all over again, losing her big sister to something she couldn't understand. "Don't. Please don't do this."

Sam rubbed her sister's back, closing her eyes to savor their hug. She'd feared she would never experience this again.

"I love you, Charlie. I promise."

Mac glanced up from his spiraling dread when the glass door slid open and Charlie, eyes red and puffy, stepped out onto the balcony. Noah rose to meet her. "You okay?"

Charlie gave him a forced smile and a nod. Then she looked at Mac, her eyes flooding with fresh tears. "She's gone."

Mac leapt to his feet and lunged for the door, but Charlie stepped in front of him, hands on his arms. "She left fifteen minutes ago. I'm sorry."

"Fifteen minutes? Are you serious? She could be on the other side of town by now."

"It doesn't matter. You couldn't have stopped her. She wanted to protect you."

"Who's going to protect *her*?" He jerked away from Charlie and turned away, raking his hands through his hair. "Shit. *Shit*."

"I'm sorry, Mac."

Curling the fingers of both hands around the balcony's metal railing, he closed his eyes and shook his head. He fought the burn of anger. And hurt. And betrayal. And grief.

He felt Charlie's hand on his back and would have traded the world for it to be Sam's. "Mac?"

Opening his eyes, he turned to look at her. "She's going to get herself killed."

CHAPTER **FORTY-SEVEN**

Sam huddled in the back corner of the Starbucks and nursed a chai tea. She couldn't stop shivering and knew it had nothing to do with the temperature. Outside, it was seventy degrees and so bright that it appeared the Earth would collide with the sun any second now. If only.

No, this cold came from the inside.

She'd hurt Charlie and Alex all over again. The last thing she'd ever wanted to do.

And Mac. God, Mac.

As much as she was glad she didn't have to see his face when he realized she'd left him again, she wished she could see him just one more time, wished she could trail a fingertip one more time over his adorable dimples, kiss his warm, loving lips.

She closed her eyes and willed away the ache. She wasn't that woman. She never could be. And she certainly couldn't ask him to stick with her while she carried the experimental child of a traitor government agent and mad scientist.

A softly cleared throat snapped her eyes open. Sloan Decker stood before her table, brooding brow cinched in suspicion, dark eyes considering. He wore black jeans and a black T-shirt that had no choice but to conform to sharply honed muscles. His military-cut hair hugged the perfect contours of his skull, thick and dark—and she suspected curly if he were to let it grow.

He didn't wait for an invitation, just slid into the chair across from her and folded his large, calloused hands on the table. "What's up?"

She couldn't help the laugh, edged with hysteria, that escaped her lips. "Not much. You?"

"Heard you're having some trouble."

Sam sipped her chai. "Want some coffee or anything?"

"Enough of the small talk, Sam. What the hell is going on with you? Are you sick?"

"Is that what Flinn told you?"

"Does it matter? I can see plain as day that you look like you've been dragged backward through a hedge."

She cracked a smile. "Is that another of Grandma Decker's sayings?"

"I'm not kidding around. Have you gone rogue?"

"Is that what Flinn's saying?"

He shrugged one noncommittal shoulder. "Maybe."

"That's what he said about Zoe, too."

Sloan shook his head and glanced away. "That was a shitty thing that happened. Some people just can't handle what we do. Zoe wasn't strong enough. I wish I'd seen that before it was too late. I would have tried to help her."

"Flinn's a liar."

"Sam, come on." He reached for her hand on the table, but she pulled back before he could make contact.

"Don't."

He sat back and raised his hands. "Sorry. Just trying to help."

"Reading me won't tell you anything that I'm not already telling you."

"I'm sure you can understand why I'm skeptical. You're sitting there looking like a fucking ghost, Sam. Your hands are shaking. You look like you haven't had a decent meal in months. You look . . ."

"What? Paranoid? Crazy?"

"Scared."

She winced. Damn. She'd called Sloan for a reason. She trusted him, believed that he was her friend regardless of their occupations. Believed that if she could convince anyone of Flinn's duplicity, it'd be Sloan. She just hadn't expected him to be so . . . perceptive. Which was ridiculous, considering it was their job to be observant.

"Talk to me, Sam."

"Flinn had Zoe killed. She was pregnant."

His lips parted, but he didn't say whatever he was about to.

She plowed ahead. "She thought Flinn impregnated her to . . . to breed super spies. Super *psychic* spies."

"Sam—"

She slapped her hand onto the table, palm up. "Fine. Do it. Mine my memories."

He stared at her hand for a long moment, considering but obviously reluctant.

"Come on. Shield yourself so you don't feel it."

He made no move to touch her.

"You were lucky," she said, her voice shaking. "You were already a strong man with a strong sense of self when they got to you. Flinn got to me when I was a kid. He manipulated me, scared the crap out of me, and knew that whatever he threw at me, I'd take it because I thought I didn't have anywhere to go, no one to help me."

"Sam—"

"Out of all of us, all of N3, I was the easiest to control. Gullible and pathetic and . . . *weak*."

"You were *never* weak," he said harshly, then took a moment to regain control. "You're a strong agent. One *hell* of an agent. I trust you to have my back in the field."

"I'm pregnant."

He should have gaped at her, but he didn't. He just watched her with a steady kind of scrutiny and said nothing. Trying to figure the angles, like any good N3 operative.

"This isn't burnout," she said. "It's not grief, either. Or post-traumatic stress disorder. Or paranoia. Or . . . or insanity." But, damn it, she *sounded* crazy. She couldn't help it. This wasn't going the way she'd expected. She'd prepared for denials and disbelief, not this unflinching perusal. He thought she'd been compromised. He thought she'd lost it. And who could blame him? She didn't know what she was doing anymore. She'd lost focus, lost track of her purpose. She was an N3 operative. Sometimes, she helped save the world from bad people like Jake Baldwin and Vince Adler. A man like Mac Hunter had no place in her life, in her heart.

She needed to get a grip. She needed a plan beyond Sloan.

"I want to make a deal with Flinn."

Sloan's dark eyes widened. "You what?"

"That's Plan B."

"Plan B?"

"Plan A was trying to persuade you to help me. That apparently isn't going to happen. So, Plan B."

He tapped a finger against the wooden surface of the table. "Plan A isn't off the table just yet," he said slowly.

"You don't believe me, Sloan. And that's fine. I don't blame you. So let's just—"

"I don't—"

"Let me finish."

He pressed his lips together. "Okay."

"Tell Flinn that I'll come in voluntarily as long as he agrees to leave my family alone." She scooted her chair back and rose. "Thanks for coming down to meet me. I appreciate it."

Before she could turn to leave, he reached out and grasped her elbow. She tensed but didn't try to pull away.

His fingers tightened on her skin, and she swept her gaze to his and watched his eyes lose focus. She knew he'd touched her unexpectedly for a reason. He'd wanted an unvarnished look into her head. That's why he'd refused to take the offer earlier. Smart.

She made no effort to return the favor by jumping into his memories. She just waited until he found what he was looking for.

When his eyes refocused, he dropped his hand. "Please sit down, Sam."

"You saw what you needed to see. There's nothing else to—"

"Please."

She couldn't deny the guttural request, so she sat.

He leaned forward in his chair and clasped his hands on the table. "I had to be sure."

"Sure what?"

"Sure that Flinn isn't trying to flush me out."

She went still. "Flush *you* out?"

"Flinn has been under investigation for months."

She was stunned. "Investigation? Are you serious?"

"About three months ago, Andrea noticed some unusual

notations in the medical files of some of the female N3 operatives, as well as some budgeting shortages that couldn't be
accounted for. She started doing some digging and discovered
that Flinn and Toby had gone off the reservation. Way off."

"Wait. Andrea, Flinn's boss? FBI Assistant Director Andrea
Leigh?"

Sloan nodded. "She put together a team of operatives to
investigate Flinn and Toby. We were getting ready to bring
you and Zoe in on the undercover op when Zoe freaked out.
After Flinn had her taken out, everything with you went to
hell so fast we lost track of you. Since then, we've been trying
to get to you before Flinn does. He's been single-minded,
Sam. You're the only one he has left."

"The only one what?"

"He and Toby impregnated three operatives. You, Zoe and
Mikayla."

Sam jolted at the name of another friend and coworker.
"Wait. He did this to Mik, too? Where is she? Is she okay?"

"We've got her stashed in a safe house. As far as Flinn
knows, she's undercover with black ops in Afghanistan."

"Not an FBI safe house, I hope."

"No. It's in Chicago. Andrea has connections with the
police department there."

Sam let her shoulders sag. "So Mik's safe. That's good."

"Relatively speaking. She didn't know she was pregnant
when we got to her. We don't think any of you were ever supposed to find out."

"I don't get that part. Of course we were going to find out.
I mean—"

"He doesn't want the fetus to come to term, Sam. We don't
know the specifics, but we think he wants to harvest stem
cells from the embryo."

She put a protective hand over her belly. "But that would
kill the . . ."

Sloan didn't give her time to dwell. "There's more, Sam."

She didn't want to hear any more. She wanted to find Mac
and run as far as necessary to escape this insanity. As long as
she had him, the rest of the world didn't matter. Except . . . no,

that wasn't true. Her family mattered. And eventually Flinn would use them against her. The only option was to stop him.

"Flinn is a small cog in a big wheel," Sloan said. "Andrea has evidence that he has partners in other N3 satellite networks in the U.S. and abroad."

"For what purpose?"

"Using N3 operatives' psychic abilities for personal gain."

"Flinn most definitely did that when he blackmailed Arthur Baldwin for research funds."

"He's not alone. There are others just like him. We have to stop them."

She looked away and thought about what Sloan was saying. Stopping Flinn and his cohorts wouldn't be a weeklong mission, or even a month. It would take years, maybe more, depending on the extent of the corruption. But what about Charlie and Alex? She'd missed so much of their lives. They needed her. *She* needed *them*. And what about Mac? And the baby she carried? What about the rest of her *life*?

"I was never meant to be a spy," she said finally.

"Sam—"

"Flinn blackmailed me into it. He took away my choices. Forced me to comply with his demands or die trying. He's used me as a science experiment for the past fourteen years. And now he's trying to use my body for some kind of twisted project."

"None of those things were sanctioned by N3. *None of them*. We need you in this fight. Whatever it takes."

"I don't know. I can't think straight right now. Everything is so—"

He covered the hand she rested on the table and lightly squeezed, an awkward gesture from a man who usually kept his emotions locked down tight. "You don't have to decide right now. The main thing is we need to get you to a safe place so we can figure out our next move."

"Nine o'clock, sir."

Flinn turned his head at Marco's direction and spotted Mac Hunter, Charlie Trudeau and her male friend striding toward the parking lot of the Hotel Sandpiper. He and Marco had arrived in St. Petersburg an hour ago and had parked across the street from the hotel in full view of the front entrance. They'd been discussing their next move, but now that the people in question had arrived on the scene, that plan was shot.

"No Samantha," Flinn murmured. "So either she's in the room alone or they're going to see her now."

"I can check the room."

"Just give it a minute."

Hunter, Charlie and the other man paused in the parking lot for a short discussion before Hunter hugged Charlie, shook the other man's hand then climbed into a new red Mustang.

"Whose—" Flinn broke off as he realized. "Rental car."

Charlie and the man linked hands and started walking toward the beach.

"We can grab the sister now, sir. Use her to flush out Samantha."

Flinn shook his head. "No. Too public. And the gentleman with her is a cop."

"How do you know?"

"Just look at him. And normal men don't know how to drive like he did to lose their tail. Let's follow Hunter. He'll lead us to Samantha."

"Are you sure, sir? What if she's still in the hotel?"

Flinn flashed Marco a smile. "If she were still in the hotel, her sister wouldn't be casually strolling down the beach and Hunter wouldn't be leaving in a rental. They'd stick to her like glue. She's not here."

"What if Hunter doesn't lead us to her?"

"Then we'll use him as bait to bring her to us."

Flinn's heart kicked into a higher gear. He was so close to Samantha. The certainty hummed in his blood like a hive of bees.

CHAPTER **FORTY-EIGHT**

Mac did his best to keep his brain blank as he drove. He put the Mustang's top down and turned the stereo up as loud as his ears could tolerate, hoping the steady noise would drown out the angry, hurt, worried words in his head.

Sam had left him.

Sam didn't trust him to help her.

Sam was going to die.

And he couldn't wrap his brain around Charlie's reasoning to let Sam go without a fight. He got it on one level. Charlie knew her sister would do whatever she wanted to do no matter who argued against it. Sam was wired for hero. When it came down to a choice between friends-family-love and duty-honor-justice . . . well, Sam had fourteen years of duty-honor-justice experience under her belt. Whatever Flinn Ford's objectives, she'd always thought she'd been doing the right thing, fighting the good fight.

The prospect of a life with a man like Mac was not going to change a woman like Sam.

So, yeah, he got it. Sam was wired in a way he would never understand. Charlie understood, though. And, really, when you came right down to it, Charlie had the right to choose between letting Sam go and making her stay. Charlie and Sam shared blood and a childhood. Mac and Sam shared . . . three days on the run and a couple of bouts of mind-altering love-making.

So, Charlie's choice. He just, unfortunately, had to live with it. Thank God Charlie had Noah to help her deal. Mac? He had his journalism career waiting for him at the *Lake Ava-*

lon Gazette. He had good friends. He had a sister to cheer on through college.

Maybe he'd get a dog. Alex probably had a stray or two on her radar. She always did. And a pooch wouldn't bail on him for the greater good.

Yeah, it really helped to make plans for a future he dreaded without the only woman he'd ever loved so deeply his body, heart and soul ached now that she was gone from his life.

In Lake Avalon, he headed for the beach, not ready to go home to his empty house, a pile of mail and . . . silence. He wanted to see Alex anyway. Since he'd learned of how horrible life had been for her lately, he felt compelled to reconnect, to let her know she could count on him, no matter what. Charlie had given him the address for the friend, AnnaCoreen Tesch, who'd insisted Alex and Logan stay with her while Charlie and Noah headed to St. Petersburg.

He glanced at the note Charlie had scribbled: "1237 Sandy Beach Way. Don't judge a book by its cover."

Whatever that meant.

He knew AnnaCoreen had become a staple in Alex's and Charlie's lives shortly after their beloved nana died. He had no idea how they'd met her or why they'd grown so close so quickly, but he looked forward to meeting the mysterious woman.

In the next minute, he knew what Charlie had meant about book-cover judging. The address she'd jotted for him belonged to an ugly, fuchsia hovel that appeared as if the next strong breeze would topple it. Even the three little pigs wouldn't have expected the structure to hold up to a couple of deep big-bad-wolf puffs.

He laughed under his breath at the sign propped against a warped, weather-beaten wall: PSYCHIC READINGS, $10 FOR 10 MINUTES.

A beach psychic. *Now* he got it. Alex and Charlie had sought the counsel of an expert about their own psychic abilities. Made perfect sense.

Based on the shack, Mac decided AnnaCoreen knew how to lower a potential customer's expectations. And judging by the cheerful yellow house visible behind the ramshackle hut, white shutters gleaming in the afternoon sun, the woman did well for herself.

After parking on the street's sandy shoulder, he strode through a lush, fragrant garden to the house. A petite strawberry blonde with model-like cheekbones, sparkling blue eyes and skin so perfect he couldn't guess her age beyond "over forty," answered his knock. A welcoming smile immediately spread across her peach-painted lips.

"Mac Hunter," she said, grasping his hands in both of her cool ones. "Oh, I'm so pleased to meet you, my dear, sweet young man."

The warmth of her greeting—and the fact she knew him on sight—surprised him. "Hello," he said, a bit reserved but already glad he'd come.

Her bright smile fell into an abrupt frown. "You poor thing, please come in and have some iced tea. I have unsweetened, just like you like."

Okaaaay. So Charlie and/or Alex apparently had already had a lot to say about him. Charlie, probably, considering his dick-itude so long ago.

He followed the woman into a bright, homey kitchen. The predominance of white—appliances, floor, cabinets—was set off with accents in bright blues, reds and yellows. "I hope I'm not—"

"Not in the least," she said, gesturing at the white wicker table. "Please sit. Let's talk. Alex is out for a walk on the beach. She's due back in a few minutes."

He sat on a comfy chair with wide arms and a red seat cushion, not sure what he and AnnaCoreen would talk about. The weather, probably. Living on the beach. The sad state of Florida real estate prices.

He was suddenly hungry, realizing he hadn't eaten since breakfast. Even then, he hadn't choked down much, his stomach filled with knots. It was still too knotted, but that didn't stop it from complaining about its emptiness.

AnnaCoreen approached the table with a glass of tea and a plate of scones. "I just made blueberry scones this morning.

Frankly, I'm shocked there are any left after Logan was finished. That giant of a man eats like there's no tomorrow."

Mac chuckled. That did indeed sound like Logan.

"Not that I mind, of course," AnnaCoreen added with a wink as she sat across from him.

She didn't speak again until he'd taken a sip of tea—even more refreshing than he'd anticipated—and a bite of the best blueberry scone ever. He'd have to ask for the recipe and send it to Jenn at Florida State. His sister loved scones. While he munched, he got why people drowned their sorrows in their vices. Comfort food, drugs, alcohol . . . for the few minutes it took to consume them, the bone-deep ache eased just a tiny bit.

AnnaCoreen nudged the plate toward him. "Nothing wrong with an occasional indulgence in sugar, especially when your heart is broken."

He gazed at her with a scone midway to his mouth. The woman had an uncanny ability to respond as if she knew his exact thoughts. Before everything that had happened with Sam, he might have scoffed at the idea that she actually might be psychic. But not now. His formerly closed mind had been flung wide open.

AnnaCoreen gave him a sympathetic smile. "It's all a bit much to take in, isn't it? Charlie and Alex came by their enhanced abilities by accident, and Sam's were prevalent from an early age. Their father's mother—the girls' nana—visited me many moons ago to ensure that her granddaughters would have a place to go if they ever needed . . . support for their abilities. Charlie likes to call me their tech support."

He chuckled. "Nana obviously chose well. Charlie and Alex adore you."

She beamed at him. "You're very kind. I can see why Sam fell so hard for you."

He snorted. "Guess you're not *that* psychic. She blew me off to go chase after . . . whatever she's chasing after."

"Deep down, you know she didn't leave you willy-nilly."

He sat back with a crackle of wicker. "She didn't even bother to say good-bye."

"You're hurt and angry right now. But in time, you'll understand that she did what she thinks is best for you and her family. We can only imagine how difficult that was for her."

Mac offered a polite nod, but he was thinking, How could this woman possibly know that when she didn't even know Sam? Psychic abilities went only so far. He supposed it was likely, though, that Charlie and Alex had talked with Anna-Coreen at length about their sister.

AnnaCoreen reached out and gave his hand a grandmotherly pat. "Sam is a Trudeau girl. Their mother might have struggled, but their father instilled in every one of them an ironclad sense of honor."

Before he could respond, Alex walked into the kitchen in bare feet, denim shorts and a white tank top. Her auburn curls looked windblown, streaked with subtle highlights from the sun. When she saw him, a smile curved her lips. "Oh, hey, Mac."

He rose to greet her, wanting to give her a hug but holding back now that he knew what a simple touch could do to her. "Alex, hi. How was the walk?"

"Perfect way to clear my head."

"I take it Charlie called you with an update."

"Yeah. Said she and Noah are taking care of some stuff before heading back."

AnnaCoreen bustled up from the table. "I'm going to let you two catch up."

"You don't have to leave," Alex said.

"No, no, I know. But I have early dinner plans with my sweetie, and I'm already running late."

Alex grinned. "Tell Richie hi for me."

AnnaCoreen's cheeks flushed slightly. "Hush, you." She turned to Mac. "You will do me a favor, young man." It was more of a demand than a question.

Mac couldn't resist her. "Okay."

"You will not give up on Sam. Trudeaus always do the right thing by the people they love." She grasped his cheeks in cool hands and planted a soft kiss on his forehead. "Everything will work out. I know it will."

Her confidence made his eyes burn. "Thank you."

She smiled into his eyes. "Believe in her, Mac. You won't be disappointed."

And with that, she left them alone.

Mac tried to right his equilibrium before he looked at Alex. "AnnaCoreen has a sweetie?"

"Richie Woods. They've been hot for each other for years and are finally together. It's inspiring. Oh, good, you have tea. I'm dying of thirst."

"This is unsweetened, or I'd hand it over, Ms. Sweet Tooth. Besides, I thought you didn't like tea."

"The way AnnaCoreen brews it changed my mind. It's weird, though. She never makes unsweetened. She must have known you were coming." She grinned, dark brown eyes sparkling with some of their old life. "I swear, it's like the woman is psychic."

They laughed together as Alex went about pouring herself a glass of tea from a second pitcher in the refrigerator. When she leaned back against the counter, the silence stretched a few more moments, until she sighed. "So what's Sam like? I mean, I remember her, of course. I was fourteen when she took off, so I knew the rebel who loved fast cars and motorcycles and ticking off our parents. But what's she like now?"

He gave her a sad smile. What he knew of her sister was likely as close to Sam as Alex was going to get. "Tough. Smart. Strong." His lips quirked. "Pretty much like you and Charlie."

"Charlie said you're in love with her."

Mac laughed, the sound abrupt and not especially amused. "Cut to the chase, why don't you?"

Alex held his gaze for a long moment, her eyes filled with sympathy. "I'm sorry, Mac."

He shrugged and drank more tea. "I'll get over it. That's what I do. Get over stuff." Shit, how pathetic could he sound? "But, hey, I had a great vacation. Shot a guy in the arm."

Alex winced. "Geez, Mac."

He set aside his glass. "You know what? I should go. I just wanted to stop in and say hi. Say thanks for getting me out of town before the stress drove me to drink. You and Charlie are good friends." He went to the door.

"Why don't you stay for dinner? Logan's going to be here as soon as he's off work. Shouldn't be more than an hour."

He shook his head and opened the door, flashing a reassuring smile at her over his shoulder. "In a few days, okay? I need some time to—"

"Mac."

He focused on her face, struck by how quickly she'd gone pale. She was staring past him, her eyes wide.

He turned to see Marco Ricci striding up the walk, gun drawn.

CHAPTER **FORTY-NINE**

Shoulders touching, Mac and Alex knelt side by side on AnnaCoreen's pristine white tile floor while Flinn Ford's muscle, big and menacing and eager to do some damage, hovered behind them with a cocked gun. Mac tried to cast Alex as reassuring a glance as he could manage. She responded with a small shake of her head, as though saying, "Don't do anything stupid."

"Stupid is my middle name," Mac returned with his eyes.

He thought maybe she understood, because she shook her head again. Then Flinn Ford, in all his bald-headed glory, ambled into the kitchen from checking the house for other people.

A vicious tension infused Mac's muscles. Bastard wanted to hurt Sam. If he lunged, even from his knees, he thought maybe he could hurt Ford at least a little before Marco shot him dead. But he fought back the urge. He needed to keep it together so he could protect Alex.

"Flinn, buddy, how you been?" Mac said.

Ford gave him a tight smile. "It's good to see you again, Mr. Hunter."

"Wish I could say the same, but, well, I kind of hate your fucking guts."

Ford hopped up onto a counter and let his long legs dangle like a psychotic little kid. He linked his fingers together and let his forearms rest on his thighs, the posture of a man enjoying his game.

Mac clenched his teeth so hard his jaw ached. He especially hated the speculative look Ford gave Alex, as though considering her many uses.

"So," Mac drawled, determined to keep Flinn's attention away from her. "If you're looking for Sam, she's not here. Afraid I don't know where she is, either. She took off. Left me high and dry. Pissed about it, frankly. So if you happen to see her, could you maybe deliver a message for me?"

"Shut up," the big man growled from behind him.

Mac twisted to look up at the huge man. "Think you could maybe get a Tic-Tac or something? Your breath is—"

He slammed the butt of his pistol against the back of Mac's head.

"No!" Alex shouted.

"Marco," Ford warned.

It took Mac a few moments to get the kitchen's wild spinning under control before he could look up, struggling to suppress a wince. "Yeah, that was rude, *Marco*, seeing as how you're a guest here."

"Mac, please," Alex said softly.

Ford's eyes narrowed, but he smiled. "Yes, Mr. Hunter, please. Your foolishness can't distract me from the knowledge that I've found treasure here: two people for whom Samantha would willingly die."

Mac's stomach threatened to heave. "Like I told you. I don't know where she is. She left. Said she had to meet a friend who could help her out."

"Does this friend have a name?"

"Nope. Sorry." Mac stiffened when he felt the cold barrel of Marco's gun press behind his left ear.

"Marco?" Ford said.

"Yes, sir."

"Give Mr. Hunter a reason to tell me the name of Samantha's friend."

Mac closed his eyes and braced for the blow. He heard a sharp crack, and then Alex crumpled sideways against him. His eyes shot open, and he wrapped his arms around her to steady her, alarmed at the way her head lolled on his shoulder. The bastard had hit her hard enough to knock her unconscious. Rage and adrenaline spurted into his blood.

"What the fuck?" he snarled at Ford.

"We're negotiating, Mr. Hunter. The name of Samantha's friend, please."

"I don't know his name."

"So this friend is a man."

"I don't know. I assumed."

"What else did you assume?"

"Nothing."

"Marco?"

The big man loomed over them, drawing his gun hand back and taking aim at Alex again. "No!" Mac quickly shifted his grip, leaning over her and cradling her close against his chest to shield her.

"The name, Mr. Hunter."

Mac raised his head to peer up at the other man, careful to keep himself between Alex and the brute with the gun. "Look, fine, we're negotiating. I'll give you the name, but you have to leave Alex alone."

"You have no power here, Mr. Hunter. I was being polite when I said we're negotiating."

"I have information you want. You give me something in return, and I'll give you that information."

"What I'm giving you in return is the health of Samantha's sister."

"Fine, then, how about this: Take me with you. You'll have me to use against Sam *and* the name of her helpful friend."

"I could just as easily take you and Alex both to use against her. Why would I agree to such a deal?"

"Because it's the only way you're getting that name. And since you're so desperate for it, I'm assuming you think that's the only way you're going to find Sam. But if Marco touches Alex again, so much as looks at her sideways, I'll die before I tell you anything."

Ford's lips thinned into a vague approximation of a smile. "Marco can torture it out of you."

Mac's heart thudded hard and fast. "Go for it. The more time you waste, the more time Sam has to defeat you."

Ford stared at Mac with squinted eyes. "You realize that I can order Marco to torture Samantha's sister until you tell me."

Yeah, he'd realized that a long time ago. But he had nothing to use as weapons but promises and words. What he wouldn't give for a few of Sam's spy moves. "In that scenario, I'd assume that you plan to kill us both once you have what you want. Why give you information that would also result in Sam's death?"

Ford considered him for a long moment.

Mac didn't have to try hard to appear patient. Alex had mentioned that Logan would be there from work soon. And when the Lake Avalon police detective saw that his beloved had been injured, there'd be some major-league ass-kicking in store for Ford and his brute. If only he could figure out a way to stall without jeopardizing Alex.

As if his thoughts had nudged her, she stirred in his arms, her head shifting against his chest. He tightened his embrace, willing her to understand that he needed her to stay still, even as the awkward position began to cramp the muscles in his back.

Ford hopped off the counter. "We have a deal, Mr. Hunter."

Five minutes later, Mac sat in the backseat of Ford's white rental Impala, hands bound at his lower back by zip restraints. Lake Avalon Beach was behind them, and so was Alex, thank God. As Mac had settled her on AnnaCoreen's white floor, he'd whispered to her to play possum. She'd obeyed, her fingers briefly squeezing his arm to let him know she was okay. He figured that as soon as Ford and Marco had hustled him out the door, she'd gotten up and called Logan. The cop would be on their tail any minute. Assuming he was in the vicinity. And could somehow know he was searching for a white Impala. Shit.

"The name, Mr. Hunter," Ford said from the front seat without turning to look at him.

"John something. Smith, I think. Or maybe it was Joe."

"We can turn around and go back for Alex, if you'd like."

Damn. He was so bad at bluffing. "Sledge. Stupid name, but there you go." He assumed Sam would call the same man she'd thought to call for help when they'd first landed in this mess together. He also hoped like hell that the name meant something to Ford. The last thing he needed was for the bastard to instruct Marco to hang a U-ey.

"Fuck," Ford muttered, and gave a disgusted shake of his head.

Mac relaxed just a tiny bit. So Ford knew the name. Of course, now he'd traded one problem for another. He'd just told Ford how to find Sam. With any luck, maybe he was wrong about this Sledge. Maybe Sam hadn't sought his help at all. And even if she had, maybe there was no way for Ford to find Sledge quickly. If anything, Mac had bought Sam some time. He could hope.

Ford flipped open his cell phone and thumbed a button for speed dial. After a few moments of waiting, he said, "I need you to get a fix on Sloan Decker's transponder."

CHAPTER **FIFTY**

Sam preceded Sloan into the Sarasota safe house, a small one-level home slathered in faded yellow stucco. It didn't stand out in the older neighborhood, surrounded as it was by similar homes amid towering palms and narrow streets with sandy shoulders.

The interior was dim, the kitchen equipped with old beige appliances and an island with sagging cupboard doors. The unmistakable odor of cat urine turned her stomach upside down.

She didn't want to be here, not in a dark, only marginally clean safe house with a man she considered a friend but who was not the man she loved. Exhaustion settled around her shoulders like a heavy cloak, and she continued on into the dining room, intent on finding a bed on which she could take a nap. A small Colonial-style wooden table with four chairs occupied the dining room. An arched doorway to the left led to a living room and the front door, and French doors on the right led to the backyard.

"Hey, Sam?"

She paused and turned to face Sloan, one hand braced on the back of a dining-room chair. At one time she'd thought they might have a shot at romance, but the sparks never flew. Not like they had with Mac. Sloan was far more alpha than Mac, though Mac's alpha came roaring to the forefront when he thought it necessary. Usually to protect her.

Sloan was clearly uncomfortable. "You okay?"

Tears pricked her eyes. This was a man who rarely showed his softer side. He did his job, and he did it well, emotion and entanglements be damned. Yet here he was, peering at her with concern that looked incongruous on his hard features.

"I need a favor. From Andrea, actually."

"I'll see what I can do."

"If something happens to me, I need her to help my sister Alex learn how to control her psychic abilities. I need to know that, no matter what, Alex will get the help she needs."

"I'll make sure that—"

The ring of his cell phone interrupted him, and he clipped it off his belt to answer it. "Decker." After a beat, he cast a quick glance at Sam. "Flinn, what's up?" He listened for a long moment, his eyes narrowing as they met hers.

"What?" she mouthed.

He pulled the phone from his ear and thumbed a button.

"Are we on speaker?" Flinn's voice came through the phone, loud and clear.

"Yes," Sloan said, voice low and grudging. He cast Sam an apologetic look.

"Samantha, are you there?"

"I'm here," she said.

"I'm hosting your lover as a guest, Samantha. I'd like for you to come visit him."

Sam's head went instantly light, and her heart clutched hard in her chest. "Where?"

"You don't need to concern yourself with that, Samantha. All you need to know is that the harder you resist, the harder Marco is going to punish Mr. Hunter. And Marco's quite eager. As you well know, Marco and Mr. Hunter have a rather bloody history already." Flinn chuckled as though he'd just shared a humorous anecdote. "Are you both listening? Sloan?"

"Yes," Sloan said.

"The house is surrounded. I advise you both not to do anything stupid."

Sloan's face flushed dark red. "Son of a bitch."

"I'll come willingly," Sam said. "You don't need Mac Hunter to force me."

"It's too late to negotiate, my dear Samantha, and I'm certain that I require him to ensure that you behave. We'll see you soon."

An audible click indicated he'd disconnected the call.

"Fuck," Sloan said under his breath.

She didn't get a chance to respond. Two camo-clad soldiers busted through the French doors, sending glass flying, and the front door blew inward, admitting two more huge guys. Sloan yanked his Glock nine mil from his shoulder holster and took out the closest men, the two who'd smashed through the glass doors.

Sam dove into the kitchen, scrambling behind the island and pressing her back against the cabinet doors while a volley of gunfire rang in her ears.

Sloan joined her an instant later, swearing under his breath and trailing a stream of blood on the worn off-white tile. He leaned against the island beside her, breathing hard, and reloaded his weapon.

Scanning him, Sam spotted the hole in the left side of his black shirt, just above his hip bone, emitting a steady rush of blood. He knocked her helping hands away and thrust his weapon at her. "Take my Glock and go! I'll try to hold them off as long as I can."

"Without a weapon?" Disbelief made her voice high and squeaky.

"They don't know I don't have one. I've taken half of them out already. They're going to come through the door with more caution now. You need to go. Now!"

"They'll kill you."

"I know that," he growled at her, catching a bloody hand in the front of her shirt and tugging her toward him. Sweat made his unnatural pallor look greasy. "Go and don't look back. Don't stop, don't turn around, don't let them use me to blackmail you into giving yourself up. Got it?"

"No, we can—"

"You're the one he wants, Sam. Whatever happens here, they're going to kill me."

She knew he spoke the truth. She also knew she had no choice but to let them take her. If they didn't, Flinn would kill Mac just to punish her.

She put one hand on Sloan's shoulder and squeezed. "Stay alive. Do your damnedest."

He flashed her a pain-sharp grin, his breath gasping now, his eyes trying to roll back. "You, too."

Sam slipped out the back door, but instead of making a run for it, she eased around the side of the house to the front and maneuvered her way through the front door and over its scattered debris. She could see the two remaining thugs consulting each other in the dining room, using furious hand signals but making no move to rush the kitchen. One, a hulk of a man clad in a tight military-green T-shirt, keyed a radio mounted on his shoulder and spoke into it.

Calling in reinforcements.

Damn it.

She didn't recognize these guys. She'd killed Watson, Deke and Tom, so Flinn had hired some nastier replacements. Mercenaries, more than likely. Not that it mattered. Muscle was muscle. Mean for a buck. Dead for working for the wrong guy.

Feet braced apart under the arch of the dining room door, she aimed Sloan's nine mil at the head of the thug farthest from where she stood. One shot, and he toppled over. The last man standing straightened and whirled toward her, gun ready and waiting. Mexican standoff.

"Hold it," she said in a steady, firm voice. "Nobody else has to get hurt."

His grim, determined expression didn't change. Nor did the grip on his SIG. His camo pants, tucked into combat boots, hugged massive thighs. Muscle indeed.

"Call off the reinforcements," she said.

His lips twitched. He didn't have to say what he was thinking: Not a chance.

"Call them off, and I'll put down my weapon and come with you."

Dark bushy brows furrowed, and he nodded at her gun. "Then drop it."

"Call off your men."

Black eyes narrowed, assessed. Then he shrugged and keyed his radio. "Cancel that last request. Situation is under control."

A disembodied voice responded, "Target is secured?"

"Target is secured and ready for transport."

"Roger that."

Sam tossed the gun so that it landed at his feet, praying Sloan would stay put behind the island and not give himself away. Too much to ask for, probably. When he didn't show himself, she figured that meant he'd passed out from blood loss. That worked, too. As long as help arrived before he bled out.

Lips curving into a hard smile, the soldier shoved her around to face the wall and kicked her feet apart. He roughly patted her down. She gritted her teeth until his hands paused to fondle her breasts, and then she jerked her hips back, trying to bump him back a step but encountering a wall of hard muscle.

His hands got cruel, fingers pinching until she threw back an elbow as hard as she could and caught him in the ribs. "Don't," she hissed.

He grasped her arm and hauled her around. "You and your friend just killed three of my buddies," he said in a gravelly voice, eyes black with hate.

Her heart kicked into her throat. Oh, crap. "Flinn wants me alive," she reminded him.

"He didn't say anything about a few bruises."

He swung a meaty fist at her.

CHAPTER **FIFTY-ONE**

Mac took in as much of the lay of the land as he could as Marco nudged him forward with the barrel of his gun in his lower back. They had parked in the overgrown parking lot of Caring Paws Veterinary Hospital, based on the sign dangling from one corner on the small, dilapidated building.

Last summer, a hurricane had swept through the region, flooding this older, less-affluent area of Lake Avalon and leaving most of its buildings condemned. The city council had been arguing for months about whether to level what was left and help reeling business owners start fresh or just let it all rot. It's not as if the neighborhood drew tourists, and therefore tax revenue, so why bother to hurry with the decisions?

Inside, Marco gave Mac another rough nudge, into a large, open room with counters lining the walls. Storage for vet supplies. The air smelled of mold and must, and grit crunched under their shoes as they traversed the filthy tile floor.

Mac's steps faltered when he saw the shiny new steel table set up in the center of the room, complete with stirrups and restraints. A tray of surgical instruments sat next to it.

"Keep moving, asshole," Marco growled.

"What's with the OR setup?"

"You'll see soon enough."

His stomach twisted, and he strained his wrists yet again against the plastic restraints binding his hands.

Marco said, "Stop."

Mac stopped. His head throbbed where Marco had struck him at AnnaCoreen's. Brutal bastard.

"On your knees."

Mac hesitated. Facing the surgical table? Like it was a stage and he was the audience? "Why?"

Marco's hard first slammed into Mac's ribs. The air burst from his lungs, and as he doubled over, Marco kicked the back of his knee and shoved him down onto his knees.

Mac gasped for breath, tasting blood and seeing stars. "You don't have to be so rough, you know. Odds are good I'm going to do whatever you tell me, what with the gun and all."

"Shut it, shithead."

Mac sat back on his haunches. "Look, I know you're ticked about the shooting-you-in-the-arm thing. But, honestly, I wouldn't have if you hadn't been going after Sam. I was feeling protective."

"Shut the fuck up."

"It's just that . . . well, under different circumstances, I get the sense that we could be friends. You know, beer and football, NASCAR, naked girls and pole-dancing. We just got off on the wrong foot is all."

Marco punched him in the jaw, and while little birdies sang a chirpy tune around his head, Mac spat blood onto the floor.

"I'd listen to him, if I were you, Mr. Hunter," Ford drawled as he ambled over to the surgical table and looked it over with a small smile of approval.

"Are we shooting a scene from *Grey's Anatomy* or something?" Mac asked. The thought of those stirrups made his guts cramp.

Ford grinned at him. "Samantha has something I want."

"Like what? Your balls?"

Ford chuckled as he cast Marco an amused look. "Mr. Hunter seems intent on angering me, does he not?"

Mac feigned a surprised expression. "I thought we were having a conversation."

Marco grunted. "Just give the word, sir, and I'll shut him up."

Ford arched a brow at Mac. "Sounds like Marco's not your biggest fan."

Mac managed a one-shouldered shrug. "I'm sure I can win him over given the time."

Ford sauntered over to where Mac knelt on the dirt-strewn floor. "Samantha is not who you think she is, Mr. Hunter. She's a consummate liar, able to deceive the most rational of men."

Mac snorted. "Do you actually think you're going to turn me against her?"

Ford leaned down and spoke into Mac's ear. "Samantha is pregnant. With my child. Did she tell you that?"

Holy shit. Holy *shit*. "It would have been difficult, considering she's spent the past several days with amnesia."

"You've missed my point, as usual. Is that deliberate?"

"Maybe you just didn't make your point clearly enough."

"Samantha and I have been lovers for years. She's devoted to me and to my cause. Her memory loss was an unfortunate mistake. Now that her memory has returned, I'm going to welcome her back into N3, no strings attached. She'll come willingly. Eagerly. You'll see."

Mac met the other man's stare with a level one of his own. "You're not a very good liar."

Ford straightened. "Soon enough, you'll regret helping her to deceive me."

Mac kept his mouth shut and, instead of freaking out, tried to focus on figuring out a way out of this. But his brain kept circling what Ford had said: *Samantha is pregnant.* Had he really just spent the past three days helping her run from the father of her child?

No. *No.*

He *knew* Sam. Well, maybe not the Sam she was before the memory loss, but he knew the Sam she was deep down, without the trappings of spydom and bad guys with shiny heads. She loved her family, had stayed away to protect them. He *did* know her, damn it. And this bastard had turned her into something that went against her very nature.

Ford's cell phone rang, and Mac watched him answer it.

"Talk to me." A grin bloomed on his too-tan face. "That's excellent news. Did she give you much trouble? . . . I'm sorry to hear that. What's your ETA? . . . Good deal. We'll see you soon."

He lowered the phone and punched in a different number. After a few moments, he said, "We have a go. When can you get here? . . . I need you sooner than that . . . You were the one who insisted time is of the essence . . . I don't care if another hour or two makes no difference. Get your ass over here now."

He disconnected the call and turned toward Mac, his impatience vanishing beneath a beaming smile. "This will all be over soon, Mr. Hunter."

Twenty minutes later, the back door opened, and an even more goon-like goon than Marco walked in, Sam's limp body slung carelessly over his shoulder, her arms and hair swinging.

Mac sucked in a sharp breath. She was unconscious. Which meant that bastard had hurt her. He jerked futilely at his restraints—he needed to get to her, check on her, help her—and ended up doing nothing more than gritting his teeth when the plastic cut into his wrists.

Turned out, he wasn't the only one outraged at Sam's condition.

"What the hell is this?" Ford stalked over to the new guy with murder on his face. "I told you she was not to be harmed."

The thug smirked. "She resisted."

Ford gestured at the shiny table. "Put her over there. If you damaged her . . ." He let the threat mingle with the tension thickening the air.

Mac watched every move as the large man carefully laid Sam on the table, a huge hand cradling her head as he settled her, as though it wasn't too late to handle her with care. Blood trickled from her nose and the corner of her mouth, washing his vision red.

Fucking son of a fucking bitch fucker.

Ford saw the blood, too, and turned a lethal glare on his errant henchman. "Marco," he said without looking away from the object of his anger, "please take Mr. Spellman outside and pay him for his work. We won't be needing his services any longer."

"Yes, sir." Marco all but tapped his heels together. Heil, Hitler.

While the thugs exited out the back door—at least one of them looking slightly concerned—Ford leaned over Sam's still body and pressed two fingers to the side of her neck.

Spots danced before Mac's eyes until some of the stiffness left Ford's shoulders. She was alive. For now, that's all that mattered.

Ford patted the back of his hand lightly against her cheek. "Samantha? Come on now, it's time to wake up."

He sounded for all the world like a concerned lover. Mac wanted to rip his head off. After he ripped off the head of the bastard who'd bloodied her.

Ford kept lightly tapping her cheek. "Samantha, dear, you need to open your eyes now. We have much to talk about."

Nothing.

A gunshot cracked outside, and Mac flinched. *Shit!* And then he glimpsed the smile of satisfaction curving Ford's lips. Evil bastard indeed. And, for once, Mac was in total agreement.

Marco returned from outside, face expressionless as he gave Ford a curt nod.

On the table, Sam's eyelids fluttered.

CHAPTER **FIFTY-TWO**

Sam blinked several times, disoriented, while her eyes tried to adjust to the dim light. Where was she? Why did her head feel as though someone had tried to crack it open with a sledgehammer?

Flinn leaned over her, lips curving into a wide grin. "Samantha! It's wonderful to see you."

Oh, right.

She closed her eyes and touched the tip of her tongue to the blood at the corner of her mouth. That asshole had split her lip. And it was the least of her problems. Ford planned to make her suffer. He made everyone who betrayed him, or disappointed him, suffer.

Then he'd take her baby.

Something deep in her belly coiled, and she had to fight down the grief that clawed its way into her throat. Amazing how quickly she'd grown attached to the idea of life growing inside her. She blamed Mac. If he hadn't made her feel loved, protected . . . human, she'd still be able to shut down her emotions and do what had to be done.

Flinn's hand came to rest on her shoulder. "Why don't we get you up, Samantha? You'll feel better."

She didn't resist as he helped her into a sitting position. The cold table under her puzzled her, but she let that go for now to take in the situation. She didn't let her gaze linger on Marco, not wanting to alert him that she'd already slipped into soldier mode.

The surgical instruments next to the table looked ominous, but then she saw Mac, on his knees and facing her, hands behind his back and jaw smeared with the purple of new bruises.

Her heart jumped as their eyes met . . . and he smiled at her. Gentle and loving, his relief palpable.

Oh, God, he was going to die because of her.

She shifted her attention to Flinn as she slid off the table, nonchalant as could be, hoping to God her legs would hold her.

"What's he doing here?" She tried to sound as derisive as she could.

Flinn chuckled as he took a step back, the gesture granting her permission to roam the room. "Don't bother trying to mislead me, Samantha. I already know your Romeo and Juliet story. Star-crossed lovers indeed."

"I used him. That's what you trained me to do, remember? I needed some time to think, to figure out what I want. He was handy and surprisingly resourceful. But I've made my decision, and I'm here now. You can let him go."

Flinn cocked his head. "Oh, Samantha, don't you know me better than that?"

She let her gaze wander over Marco, a small smile playing at one corner of her mouth as she looked him up and down. His nostrils flared, eyes widening ever so slightly at what he interpreted as sexual interest rather than the weapons check it actually was. Some men were so dense.

She gave him a cute, maybe-later shrug as she turned her attention back to Flinn. "I didn't have to come, Flinn. I could have taken out your last man, but I didn't. I let him bring me to you."

"Ah, but you *did* have to come. I determine the fate of this young man you've apparently grown quite fond of over the past few days. At least, he's grown quite fond of you, judging by the daggers he's shooting at me with his eyes. Of course you had to come."

"I don't want to play games. Just let him go, and we'll get on with . . . whatever it is you want."

He nodded as he hopped up onto the counter across from her and braced his hands on the edge. Like they were teenagers flirting in the kitchen. "You think it's that easy, do you?"

She realized with a jolt that he was stalling. For what? She turned to take in the table that had, she now saw, leather restraints at the middle, for wrists, and on the stirrups, for ankles. The tray of surgical instruments held, among other items, a couple of scalpels, syringes and clamps.

She had to dig for strength before turning to face him. "I'm giving you what you want. I don't understand what isn't easy about it."

"Ah, Samantha. After all these years, you don't know me at all." He paused to smile at her, all shiny white teeth. "I bear a grudge. Mr. Hunter shot one of my men. And he helped you evade me for several days."

"He's an honorable sort. He would have done it for anyone." She felt Mac watching her with an intensity that threatened her composure. They were both dead, but maybe with her last act, she could save him.

"Look, I know you want the baby," she said. "I'll make a deal with you. I'll bear the child and give him or her to you in exchange for letting Mac go."

"Sam, no." Mac struggled anew against his bonds.

Flinn's benevolently dark expression didn't falter. "You assume that you're in a position to negotiate, Samantha."

"You trained me to act like I have the upper hand, whether I have it or not."

"Yes, I did." He nodded with approval. "You've served me very well over the years. I regret that it's come to this."

"May I ask a question?"

"Of course."

"Are we the good guys or the bad guys?"

"We've always been the good guys, my dear Samantha. We've prevented wars and pandemics, terrorist attacks and presidential assassinations. We've gotten to the bottom of financial fraud before it could cost the taxpayers yet more billions of their hard-earned dollars. We've even stopped a mass suicide at a religious commune in Texas. You know all of this."

"And what of people like Arthur Baldwin? What good came of the way you blackmailed him? Wasn't that just a form of revenge on your part?"

"His brother, as you well know, was a serial rapist. You single-handedly put him away, Samantha." He grinned at her arched brow. "Yes, I've known all along that you tipped off the Columbia police. You were the only one who could. Frankly, your honor wouldn't have allowed you to do anything else."

"And Arthur?"

"Arthur helped fund some research."

"Unsanctioned research."

A muscle in his cheek twitched. "Very *important* research."

"Involving impregnating female operatives against their will."

Mac blew out a loud breath. "Son of a *bitch*."

Marco drew back his gun, preparing to strike Mac for his outburst.

"Don't," Sam said quietly but with deadly authority.

Marco lowered the weapon, and the relief that spun through Sam's head made her dizzy.

Flinn raised his chin a notch, looking downright haughty. "You would not have agreed to my experiment."

"So naturally you took away my choice and did it anyway. Why? What's the plan, Flinn?"

"Look at all the good work we've done over the years, Samantha. And with such a small team. Imagine the implications if N3 could grow into a troop of thousands—hundreds of thousands. It would change the way we wage war. No longer could rogue nations hide, or lie about, their weapons of mass destruction. No longer could killers get away with murder or pharmaceutical companies hide the fact that they release drugs they know can harm consumers. No longer could politicians lie to the American people. We're talking about a new way of life, a life in which we all know the *truth*. We're talking about a justice system that would work without fail. Always."

Sam gave an unconvinced snort. "You're trying to tell me that this is all about the greater good?"

"Of course."

"And you would never dream of using such power to further your own agenda."

He smiled gently at her, as though her naivete amused him to no end. "Do you have any idea how much the United States government would pay for a simple way to make its spies empathic, not to mention how much it would pay to keep that capability out of the hands of its enemies? The sky's the limit. So, no, it isn't all about the greater good. It's mostly about money. I learned at a terribly young age that money can have a powerful impact on one's life. The more you have of it, the more power you wield."

She thought of the wrenching moments she'd spent in his past during one of his endless tests of her empathic limits. He'd watched his father kill his mother then himself over the despair of losing his job and reputation to the underhanded dealings of the wealthy Arthur Baldwin. She felt sorry for the child, but not the man. The man had made his choices.

She focused on getting as much information as she could until she figured out a way to disarm Marco and overpower Flinn—without getting Mac hurt further. "How do you plan to turn people who aren't empathic into psychic spies?"

He jumped down from the counter and walked over to her, hands in his pockets. On a leisurely stroll. "The fetus that's growing inside you is the key, Samantha."

She refused to step back, to show her fear, yet she figured he could see the rapid beat of her pulse in her throat. At the same time, she registered his use of the word *"fetus."* Not baby. Not child. Not life. *It* was the key. To her, "it" was a baby. *Her* baby. And no way in hell was he getting anywhere near *her* baby. "How is my child the key?"

He moved his head back as though shocked. *"Your child?"*

"You used my body to create a life. That makes it *my* child. *Mine.* And I'm going to protect that child as any mother would. So answer the question: How is my child the key?"

"Stem cells." His grin returned. "Toby will use them to develop a serum that can be administered by a simple injection that will alter the very DNA of our spies, rendering them psychic."

"And you think this will actually work?"

"The gentleman you helped procure on your last assignment in San Francisco seems to think it will."

"Wait. You told the team he was conducting stem-cell research on living people."

"He was, for Biomedical Research Corp. Instead of going to prison, however, he's helped Toby fill in the blanks in his own research so we can take our project to the next step. Dr. Ames and I are both eager to put our theory to the test."

"People have died—you *killed* Zoe—and you don't even know if such a serum will work?"

"We have to start somewhere, do we not?"

"You're insane. This is insane. You can't possibly think that you'll get away with this."

"My dear, foolish Samantha. Do you think I took on this project alone? N3 has satellite networks all over the world. There are dozens of us pursuing the same goal to ensure that the project *will* be successful."

"None of them are my fellow psychic operatives, though, are they? Otherwise, you'd have them here to lend you a hand. So that means you know this is wrong. You *know* no one in the upper echelons of N3 or even my psychic peers would support what you're doing."

His features hardened, but before he could respond, the back door opened and Dr. Toby Ames walked in.

Flinn didn't look away from her to acknowledge him. "You're late, Toby."

"Fucking beach traffic. I'm here now, so let's get started."

Flinn turned and nodded at Marco. "Secure her."

Marco moved forward, grasped Sam's arm and propelled her toward the surgical table.

Mac jerked desperately at his bonds. "No! Sam!"

"Let him go!" Sam shouted over her shoulder at Ford. "You've gotten what you want."

He waved a dismissive hand at her. "I'm not done with him yet."

Marco yanked on her arm, almost jerking her off her feet.

"Hey!" Mac yelled. "Take it easy!"

Ford moved to stand beside Mac, arms folded over his chest while Marco and Sam wrestled for dominance. When the huge man backhanded her, sending her sprawling against cabinets, Mac nearly dislocated his shoulder fighting his bonds. Sam needed him, and he was so fucking helpless.

"Knock it off!" Words were all he had. Just lame words.

Ford tsked beside him. "She's fiery, isn't she?" His tone spoke of deep admiration as well as regret. "She was always my favorite. Sharp as a razor blade. An incredibly fast learner. Committed and loyal."

"She's not a fucking dog."

"No. She's a consummate N3 operative who exceeded all of my expectations." To Marco, who had Sam cornered, Flinn said, "Any day now, Marco. I'm getting impatient."

Marco bore down on Sam, and Mac had to admire the way she held her own in the fight, no hint of fear in her stony gaze. If the hired gun hadn't outweighed her by at least a hundred pounds—not to mention the mean streak—Mac wouldn't have felt such insane terror for her, certain she could take the guy without breaking a sweat.

She leveled a spinning kick at the big man's head, but he ducked and came up behind her only to pound her down onto the floor with a violent elbow to the kidneys. She lay there, gasping, trying to push herself up on arms that had no strength.

Marco hauled her up by one arm and gave her a rough shove toward the surgical table. She fell to her knees, grabbing onto the edge for support. Mac winced at the way her head fell back before she shook it, as though she had to fight to remain conscious.

When Marco approached, though, she whipped around with deadly force and slammed the heel of her hand under his chin. His head snapped back. But instead of falling, or even looking dazed, he grabbed her up in a bear hug, pinning her arms at her sides.

To Toby, Ford said, "Tranq her, but show some restraint. I need her conscious for a little while longer."

Toby chose a syringe from the tray of surgical instruments.

"Sam!" Mac shouted in warning.

She kicked Marco in the knee, causing a wince-worthy crunch just before Toby nailed her in the arm with the needle.

Marco released her with a pained grunt, and Sam wobbled

on legs that refused to cooperate. As she went down, she threw Mac a desperate look. Her lips formed his name before she sprawled onto the dirty floor. She lay on her back, unmoving, her head lolled to the side, dark hair obscuring her face.

"Sam!"

Ford walked over and stared down at her. "Such a shame." He gestured at Marco. "Get her on the table. Strap her down tight."

"She won't be out for long," Toby said.

"Good. Before you get started, I need to find out if she knows where Mikayla's being hidden."

"I thought Mikayla went undercover in Afghanistan," Toby said.

"I suspect that since Sloan was prepared to take Samantha to a safe house, then Andrea must know something is up. She might also know of Mikayla's involvement."

"If you think Sam will respond to torture, I'll remind you that she's been trained to handle it."

Ford cast a speculative look at Mac. "I'm not going to torture *her* for the information. Not physically."

CHAPTER **FIFTY-THREE**

Sam opened her eyes for the second time in an hour, her mind fuzzy and her senses sluggish. The ceiling tiles overhead looked the same. Water-stained, some missing, revealing tangled wires and rusted pipes.

She knew without trying to move that she was restrained. Arms at her sides, wide leather cuffs snapped around her wrists and secured to the table. Ankles similarly secured with her feet in stirrups, knees slightly spread. She still had her clothes, thank God.

A chill passed through her, raising goose bumps all over her body. Flinn really was going to do this to her. Kill her baby in the name of truth, or at least his twisted idea of truth.

"Samantha."

Flinn's voice, steady and low near her ear, sent the knife's edge of dread through her heart, bleeding off some of the tranquilizer Toby had pumped into her.

She called on years of training and experience to calm her heart rate, slow her panicked breathing and fight the fog of the drug.

Where was Mac? She wanted to look for him, to draw strength from his unwavering love. But she didn't dare give away her desperate need for him. Flinn already knew too much.

"Where's Mikayla?" Flinn asked. His mouth was inches from her ear, his breath warm and moist against her skin.

She closed her eyes and counted to ten, struggled to clear her head. "I don't know."

She felt rather than saw Flinn straighten. "Marco?"

A crack was followed by a pained grunt, and she couldn't

stop herself from turning her head in time to see Marco loom-ing over Mac, who was on his knees and close to pitching forward. Blood dripped in a steady stream from his mouth.

It was enough to break her. Flinn could torture her all he wanted, but it was different when someone else, someone she desperately loved, bore the consequences of her silence.

Flinn shifted to block her view of Mac. "Where's Mikayla?"

"Don't tell him."

She squeezed her eyes shut at the sound of Mac's voice, strained but firm. He didn't even know who Mikayla was, only that the woman had gotten dragged into this the same way Sam had. Maybe it was good that she couldn't see his pain. Maybe that was the only way she would find the strength to resist Flinn's questions.

As if Flinn knew her thoughts, he moved so that all she had to do was shift her head. But she didn't. She stared, reso-lute, at the ceiling. *I'm sorry, Mac. I'm so sorry.*

"He's going to kill me anyway," Mac said. "You know he is."

Flinn grinned down at her. "But the longer you don't tell me what I want to know, the longer it's going to take to kill him. Now, tell me, Samantha: Where's Mikayla?"

She clenched her teeth. "If you had any psychic sidekicks, you could have them here now, mining my memories instead of resorting to brutality. That must really suck for you, not having any of us on your side."

"Marco."

A thud this time, followed by Mac's massive "Oof."

Sam stared hard at the stains on the ceiling tiles. One looked like the Michelin Man. Or perhaps the Stay Puft Marshmal-low Man. Plump with rings of fluffy rust-colored fat.

"We can do this for hours, Samantha," Flinn said, casual and unflustered.

She didn't react.

"Marco."

Another harsh thud. Mac grunted but made no other sound. She knew from experience how much control that took, and she knew from her time with him that he did his damnedest to suppress his reaction to spare her. He'd done *everything* for her. Tears burned her eyes.

"I'm sorry," she said to the ceiling.

"No worries," Mac wheezed. "You're worth it."

A choked sob escaped, and she bit into her lip to stop another from following. If only her head would stop spinning. If only she could focus around the drugs. Maybe there was a way out of this. She was a spy, for God's sake. Trained in situations just like this.

"We're wasting time." Toby this time, impatient—and sounding a bit disgusted. "You should have gotten this done before I got here."

"You can wait outside if you like," Flinn said, not at all perturbed.

"Just get it over with," Toby snapped.

Nothing from Flinn for a long moment, just the scuff of his shoes as he walked to the other side of the bed. "He can't take much more, Samantha. He's hanging on to consciousness by a thread."

"Bullshit," Mac slurred. "I've got a good ten more rounds in me. And if you were any kind of a real villain, you'd come over here and hammer at me yourself instead of making your muscle do all the work."

"Marco."

A thud, and a raw, guttural sound burst through Mac's teeth. Then he swore under his breath. "Fuuuuuuck." He drew the word out, low and raspy, his breaths choppier now, and sounding wet.

Sam recognized the sounds of a punctured lung. Why didn't he just shut up? She knew why: He was trying to deflect the violence away from her with his words, the only weapons he felt he had. But, God, she couldn't listen to him die, punch by punch. She just couldn't. "Mik is in a safe house."

"Be specific," Flinn said.

"Sam, no—"

A loud crack cut off Mac's denial.

"I don't know specifics."

Sam couldn't help herself. She turned her head to see Mac

still on his knees, held up by Marco's grip on the collar of his shirt. His face was a mess of blood and bruises. One eye had already swelled shut.

For a moment, she couldn't breathe through her fear for him. She couldn't lose him. Couldn't live without him. Couldn't—

She refocused on the ceiling and narrowed her eyes. "I'll tell you where Mik is, including who else knows, but you have to let him go."

"No, Sam. Don't." Mac's breath gurgled in his chest. "Please . . . don't."

"I'll spare his life," Flinn said.

"He won't. You . . . know he . . . won't."

"She's in Las Vegas."

"Sam, no."

She met Flinn's flinty gaze with a steady, unflinching glare. His eyes went to annoyed slits. "You can't lie to me, Samantha."

"Sloan had his people take her to Vegas. He told me."

"You're lying!" Flinn backhanded her so suddenly she didn't have time to brace herself. Bursts of light streaked her vision like falling stars. The fresh taste of blood flooded her mouth.

"Bastard," Mac growled. "You fucking bastard!"

Flinn hovered over her. "I want specifics, Samantha. So let's start again. Marco?"

When the blow fell this time, the goon let Mac go, and he dropped onto his side, curling forward around the pain, hands still trapped behind him while he gasped for air.

"He can't take much more, Samantha."

Tears began to roll back into her hair. So unlike her. Crying during a mission gone to hell. Mac's fault. No . . . *her* fault, for letting him in, letting him change her . . . or, rather, rediscover herself. "Chicago."

"Where in Chicago?"

"Safe house affiliated with the police department."

"And who arranged that?"

She carefully thought through the lie that would prevent Flinn from knowing Andrea Leigh was aware of his project.

She had to be more convincing than she'd been when she tried to steer him to Vegas instead of Chicago.

"Sloan," she said finally. "He has a friend who's a cop there."

Flinn regarded her for a long, thoughtful minute.

"I'm telling you the truth," she said, irritated at the way the words slurred. "Please just let him go. You can use me over and over to create all the stem cells you need for this serum."

"I would commend you for that excellent idea, Samantha, if I hadn't already decided that for myself." He flicked a glance at Toby. "You may begin, Dr. Ames."

Mac clung to consciousness by sheer will, determined to be there for Sam. The wet streak of tears tracking from her eye into her hair broke his heart. She'd betrayed a comrade for him. Agreed to be this evil bastard's incubator in a desperate attempt to save him. Even when they both knew he was as good as dead.

Mac watched the man Flinn had called Toby pick up a pair of scissors from the tray of surgical tools and move toward Sam. She fought against the restraints, clamping her knees together and bucking her hips.

"No!" She strained to raise her head, snarling at Ford in her desperation. "Don't do this! You don't have to do this!"

Toby stepped back, annoyance written in the tension of every muscle.

"Hold her, Marco," Ford said.

Marco, standing next to where Mac lay, helpless and enraged, hesitated, shooting a questioning glance at Ford. "Sir?"

"Do it," Ford said, impatiently gesturing Marco over to the table.

Mac's heart started hammering harder now, seeming to rap against broken ribs. What the hell were they going to do to her?

At the table, Marco hesitated again, his lips tight with a squeamish disgust. "Where do you want me?"

"Hold her hips," Toby said.

Marco holstered his gun then leaned over Sam and pinned her to the table with his big, blood-covered hands.

"Don't do this!" Sam cried. "There are other ways to harvest stem cells. You don't have to kill the baby. Please!"

Wincing as though her cries hurt his ears, or irritated the hell out of him, Toby started cutting away her jeans.

Mac strained his wrists against the plastic restraints, gritting his teeth against the grind of agony in his chest. The plastic edges of the cuffs cut into his flesh, but he ignored the pain, ignored the slick wetness of what could only be blood.

Toby dropped the remains of Sam's jeans on the floor. Before he could start on her underwear, Ford snapped, "Cover her. We're not barbarians."

Scowling—and not the least bit amused at the irony of that statement—Toby grabbed a neatly folded white sheet off the cart and, with Marco's help, spread it over her lower half, shielding her from the view of everyone but the doctor.

A moment later, Toby dropped the remains of her underwear on the floor, then reached for what looked to Mac like a metal torture device. Jesus, what was *that*?

Realization sent horror churning up from his gut. He'd never seen a speculum, but judging from Toby's actions, that's what it had to be.

Sam had stopped fighting, exhausted or resigned, he couldn't tell. But she stared at the ceiling, the muscles in her face contracted into a rigid expression of grief and rage.

Mac wet his lips, tasting blood. "Sam."

She must not have heard him, or pretended not to.

"Sam." Louder this time. Commanding.

She looked at him, finally, and Mac tried to offer her a comforting smile, even as his heart jammed hard into his throat. Her eyes were unfocused, drugged. They kept trying to roll back, but she fought to remain conscious. God knew why.

"Hold her knees apart," Toby said.

Marco complied, putting more of his weight on her, and Sam's eyes widened with panic and pain, her teeth sinking into her bottom lip.

"Just keep looking at me, Sam," Mac said, trying to calm

his breathing. Every breath stabbed at him. "Just . . . I'm here, okay? I'm right here."

She gave a small nod, wincing as metal clinked, and then her whole body tensed, and she threw her head back on a serrated sob. "God!"

"Take it easy, Toby," Ford growled from where he did the expectant-father pace far away from the action on the table. "For Christ's sake."

"Shut up and let me work," Toby snapped. "I'm in. Now all I have to do is remove the embryo."

"Please," Sam whimpered, sounding breathless and weak, her pleas slurring. "Please, don't."

"Sam." Mac's voice broke on her name. "Look at me. I'm right here."

Her throat worked as she swallowed, her face wet with sweat and tears and blood. And then she rolled her head to the side, and devastated eyes locked on his.

Mac pushed himself to his knees, fighting dizziness and nausea. "I love you. I'll always love you, Sam."

Her expression twisted into one of grief and pain and love as tears spilled out of her eyes.

Mac jerked against his bonds one last time, and this time he felt a pop followed by some give. Holy shit, he'd busted the plastic cuffs.

Marco was distracted, his back to Mac and his gun right there on his belt, in plain sight. It wasn't even snapped into its holster.

Mac took a broken breath, wincing as bones grated together in his chest. And launched himself at Marco's back with a roar of rage and agony. He had the asshole's gun in his hand before Ford even completed his turn toward Mac, brows arched in surprise.

Marco jerked upright and whirled, face red with fury.

"Idiot!" Ford hissed at the goon.

"But, sir, I—"

"Shut it," Mac snapped. "Both of you." He flicked the gun from one to the other, ignoring the spasms in his chest that accompanied each ragged breath. He could taste blood at the back of his throat, but that meant nothing compared with what had happened to Sam.

"Mac, be careful." Her voice was strong despite a slight waver.

"Step away from her," Mac said to Toby. "Now."

Ford sighed, managing to sound bored. "You're out of your league, Mr. Hunter."

Mac gave him a smile that he knew had to look crazed, considering how crazed he felt. "Shut the fuck up. No matter who makes the first move, you're getting the first bullet, so tell your minions to stand the fuck down."

"Please do as Mr. Hunter asks."

"Hands up," Mac ordered. "All of you."

Ford, Marco and Toby all obeyed.

Mac gestured at Toby with the gun. "You. Remove that—"

All hell broke loose then, soldiers bursting in from all sides, shouting orders: "Everybody down on the floor! Face-down! *Now!*"

Mac dropped Marco's gun and did as he was told, groaning at the screaming pain in his chest. He couldn't see what was happening, but he kept his eyes on Sam, watched her yank and twist against her restraints, the cords in her neck standing out with her desperate efforts. While her situation was horrific, at least the way the gurney was positioned kept her from being displayed to the whole room. But, Jesus, still.

"Hang on, Sam," he called to her. "Just hang on!"

A shadow fell across him, followed by a voice: "Christ, Mac, are you okay?"

Mac looked up into the concerned face of Noah Lassiter.

"Thank God," Mac said. He pushed to his feet with Noah's help, gritting his teeth against the pain but concerned about only one thing: "Sam."

Noah followed close on Mac's heels as he dodged gun-wielding soldiers to make it to the surgical table. Mac was peripherally aware of a soldier cuffing Marco and hauling him to his feet, but he ignored the bastard. He had only one objective.

"Aw, fuck," Noah muttered when they got to Sam's side.

Mac knew the other man didn't have to see anything other

than the sheet covering her knees and the stirrups to know that Ford and Toby had had gruesome plans for her.

Mac put his hand on top of her head and looked down into her frantic eyes, the pupils so dilated only a thin band of blue iris encircled them. Panic bled off her like waves of Florida heat at the height of summer. He wanted to touch her, wanted to use the warmth of skin-on-skin contact to help bring her down from the terror high, to focus her around the drugs. But he feared sending her into his head and forcing her to psychically endure what Marco had done to him.

"It's okay, baby, it's okay. I've got you. Cavalry is here."

"Get it out of me," she moaned, straining against her bonds. "Please get it out."

Mac looked at Noah, who glanced down toward her sheet-covered knees and appeared just as horror-stricken as Mac felt. "Get her wrists," Mac said.

Noah bent over the buckle on her right wrist and squeezed her shoulder with a gentle hand. "It's okay, Sam. You're safe now. We'll have you out of here in no time."

Mac went to the end of the table, his heart slamming harder and harder at the terror of what he would find. Had Toby finished what he'd started? *Please, God, please.*

The speculum was still in place, and Mac winced at the absolute horror of what Toby and Ford had forced on her. "Son of a bitch," he muttered under his breath. "Son of a *fucking* bitch."

"Please, get it out," Sam begged. "Get it out."

Mac hesitated, as terrified of touching her skin-on-skin as letting her violation continue another instant.

"Use gloves," Noah told him. "There, on the tray."

Mac got it right away. Gloves would shield her from an empathic flash. He snatched up a pair and shoved a shaking hand into one. *Hurry, hurry, hurry.*

When he had both gloves on, his stomach pitched as he fumbled with the release on the metal device, conscious that every clumsy second he wasted extended Sam's suffering. "I'm sorry, I'm sorry, I'm sorry."

Finally, he hit the release and the blasted thing collapsed on itself. Mac removed it as gently as he could and dropped it on the floor before going to work on the straps around her ankles. Frustration ate at him as his fingers fumbled. Impotent rage vibrated in every cell for what those assholes had done to her. "Almost there. We're almost there."

He had to fight the growing fury as he freed her right ankle, revealing the raw skin where she'd fought the bonds.

Once he released her other ankle and Noah popped her remaining wrist free, she immediately curled onto her side and drew her knees, sheet and all, up to her chest.

"Thanks," Mac said to Noah, voice low and shaking as he rested a hand on Sam's side. He didn't know what to do for her, didn't know what to say. He just knew she needed to feel his presence. The trembling of her body under his palm just added to his fury. Those *bastards*. Those *fucking* bastards.

Noah exchanged a long look with him, his expression painfully concerned. "What the hell were they—"

Mac choked up. "Not now."

"You gonna make it?" Noah asked softly, so Sam wouldn't hear.

"I'm fine," Mac ground out. Praying his knees wouldn't betray him, he tightened his fingers on Sam's quaking hip. *I'm here, baby. I'm right here.*

She wasn't crying, but the tremors shuddering through her worried the hell out of him. Probably shock. Even so, she peered intently at him, her fingers grasping the hem of his shirt as if she feared he would slip away from her. Worry for him shone through her distress and the haze of drugs in her eyes. "Are you—"

"I'm fine, Sam. I promise."

Paramedics bustled in then, laden with medical equipment. As they swarmed around Sam, pushing Mac and Noah aside, another man in riot gear approached. He held his automatic weapon with both hands, crossways close to his torso. A trained soldier.

"Area is secured, Mr. Lassiter," he said. "We're getting ready to clear out."

"Thanks for everything," Noah said. "Your men did good work."

Mac watched the medics quietly talking to Sam. His worry eased at her answering nods, sluggish as they were. By the time the guy talking to Noah walked away, the paramedics had wrapped her in a blanket and slipped an oxygen mask over her face.

Mac, gaze still fixed on Sam, asked Noah, "Who are these guys?"

Noah, also watching the medics with Sam, rubbed at the back of his neck. "They're part of an FBI tactical team called in by Andrea Leigh. A friend with the feds put me in contact with her. Charlie and I were meeting with her in Lake Avalon when an N3 operative named Sloan Decker called and tipped her off that Sam had been taken. Decker had been shot during the confrontation, but he's going to be fine. Meanwhile, Leigh had already tracked down Flinn Ford's operation here. One of his people used Ford's American Express to pay for a plane ticket to Fort Myers for his suspected partner, Dr. Toby Ames. Leigh put some agents on Ames who tracked him to the makeshift clinic. It's been under surveillance since yesterday."

"What took you guys so long to come in? Sam could have used some rescuing a little earlier, don't you think?"

"The surveillance was handled by two tech guys. They needed to mobilize a tactical team for the rescue. I kind of insisted on helping out. Logan's here, too, somewhere. Hopefully kicking the shit out of that fuckhole Ford."

At the mention of Logan, Mac flinched. "Oh, God, *Alex*. Is she okay?"

"She's good. She called Logan as soon as Ford left Anna-Coreen's with you."

Mac released a sigh of relief. Now he could focus on venting his building rage. "Speaking of that fuckhole Ford, where is he?"

"Outside."

"Will you keep an eye on Sam for a sec?"

Noah nodded sharply. "I won't budge."

Mac gave her one last long look, satisfied she was in good hands, before turning on his heel and striding outside into a gray, rainy day. He no longer felt any pain—only fury—as he spotted Flinn Ford standing next to a federal-looking black Suburban. His hands were cuffed behind his back, his lips set in a grim line as raindrops dribbled over the smooth skin of his scalp. Toby stood next to him, looking as pissed as a drenched cat.

Mac reached the two men in three long strides and threw the two biggest punches of his life.

CHAPTER **FIFTY-FOUR**

Sam surfaced, groggy and confused, to an incessant, steady beep. She blinked against the light and tried to get oriented. Pain flared in various areas of her body, most prominently in her jaw and head. She moistened her lips and swallowed against her dry throat. She knew she was no longer in that dingy excuse for a medical facility. The bed she lay on was soft, warm blankets tucked all around her.

Mac.

The last time she'd seen him, he'd been bloody and choking on a punctured lung. The beeping started to race.

"Hey."

She had to turn her head to the side to see Mac, wearing a hospital gown, struggle up out of the chair by the bed, grabbing hold of the IV pole that snaked a slim tube into the back of his hand. He perched on the bed beside her and rested his hand on her covered shoulder and squeezed. "It's okay. You're safe."

She smiled up at him and didn't bother to tell him she hadn't feared for *her* safety.

He was a mess. One eye was swollen shut. The whole left side of his face was black and blue. And he held himself as if every breath hurt. He was absolutely beautiful.

"Hi," she replied.

She lifted her hand off the bed, intending to wrap her fingers around his forearm where his hand rested on her shoulder. She wanted to feel his warm skin, feel for herself that he lived and breathed.

Before she could touch him, he tensed and drew back. "You probably shouldn't do that."

She didn't understand what he meant at first, but then she

smiled, loving him all the more. "It's okay. I can block your memories."

"You can? Really?"

She nodded. "Really."

A smile spread across his face, and he leaned down to cup her face with one hand while he kissed her, gently and tenderly. Afterward, he nuzzled his nose alongside hers.

"I love you," she whispered. "More than anything. Kind of amazing, considering we just met."

She felt his grin against her cheek. "And we can't even say it was love at first sight, considering how badly you wanted to kick my ass."

She laughed softly, sifting her fingers through the hair at his nape, reluctant to release him. "Are you okay?"

"Yep," he said as he eased back. "Worst thing is a busted rib. It punctured a lung. I've got a super sexy chest tube sticking out of my side. In fact, the doctor's irked that I insisted on sitting in here with you, but he was no match for my alpha tendencies."

She smiled as she tangled her fingers with his. "So you're risking your life all over again for me?"

"Like I said, you're worth it."

Tears burned her eyes. She loved hearing him say that. If only it were true.

He cocked his head, expression turning serious, as though he'd read her mind. "You believe me, don't you? You believe that you're worth it?"

"I've spent most of my life messing up."

"Join the crowd."

"I hurt my family."

"They're the forgiving kind. Trust me. In fact, Charlie and Alex have been pacing the waiting room since we got here."

"Alex is here?"

He nodded. "Your mom and dad, too. It's a Trudeau family reunion out there."

A warmth she'd missed for more than a dozen years flowed through her.

Mac's fingers tightened around hers. "Sam."

She focused on his serious, green-tinged brown eyes, and her heart thudded.

He took a steadying breath. "The baby's okay. The doctor— Toby—didn't get far enough to do any damage. You're eight weeks pregnant."

She pressed her lips together to suppress the surge of relief and emotion. Worry at his reaction joined the chaos churning inside her, and she couldn't say anything for fear of bursting into tears. *Eight weeks.*

He swallowed, his tension transmitting itself through his grip on her hand. "I know you haven't had much time to even think about what you're going to do . . . but I . . . well, I just want you to know that whatever you decide, I love you. No matter what." He lifted her hand to his lips and kissed her knuckles. "You can count on me for whatever you need."

The thudding of her heart eased—he loved her no matter what. How amazing was that? She swiped at her eyes with her free hand, wanting to see his face unblurred. "The baby needs a daddy."

One brow arched, and a smile tugged at the corners of his mouth, threatening to send that adorable dimple of his into sharp relief once again. "Yeah?"

She nodded, happiness expanding the muscles around her heart, because she could tell by the light in his eyes that he was thrilled with the idea. "You said I could count on you for whatever I need."

"Did I mention that there are strings attached?"

"I don't remember anything about strings."

"String, actually. Singular."

"I suppose we can negotiate, if you insist."

"I insist." Grinning, he took her hand into both of his and gazed into her eyes for a long, long moment. "Samantha Trudeau, will you marry me?"

Tears spilled over before she could stop them, and laughing and crying at the same time, she nodded, blurting out a soggy, "Yes," before he kissed her, long and deep and wet.

When they parted, he thumbed away her tears and said, "You'll have to wait for a ring. The hospital gift shop is all out."

"I don't need a ring. I just need you."

They kissed again, and it was sweet and breathless and warm.

Afterward, they sat together for a long time while Sam drifted in and out of sleep. It felt good to sleep while Mac watched over her.

And safe.

Funny that a man who didn't know rule one about handling firearms could make her feel that way.

CHAPTER **FIFTY-FIVE**

19 months later

Sam dropped large gobs of vanilla cream cheese frosting onto the double-layer white cake and began distributing it with a spreader. Her hands held a slight tremble, and she paused to shake them out, berating herself for the nerves. Sure, she was anxious about hosting her entire family for the first time. But dinner—citrus-grilled grouper, Cuban black beans and rice and Mojitos—had gone even better than she'd hoped. Now, if she could just finish frosting the cake for dessert.

The chatter of voices in the dining room grew louder, and she glanced over her shoulder as her mother pushed open the swinging door into the kitchen, an uncertain smile curving her lips. That smile surprised Sam. Her mother, who'd been as serious as a shark attack since the beginning of time, or at least since Sam's earliest memories, was *smiling*?

Elise's gaze darted around the kitchen, as though searching for eavesdroppers, or enemy combatants, before stepping farther into the kitchen and letting the door swing shut behind her. She wore her customary pearls and sunshine yellow dress, her dark brown hair in an elegant French twist. Sam felt dowdy in bare feet, denim shorts, a red T-shirt and a loose ponytail, but she also felt comfortable. And happy. God, she was happy.

"Do you need any help?" Elise asked.

Sam returned her attention to the cake, a bit perplexed at the unexpected question. "Thanks, but I think I've got it."

Elise lingered behind her, and Sam could practically hear her mother's thought gears grinding. Sam cast her a questioning look. "Did you need something?"

Elise clasped her hands in front of her, diamond rings glittering in the kitchen light. "I, uh, there's something I've been wanting to say to you."

Sam's nerves twanged, but she set down the spreader and turned fully toward her. "Okay."

They hadn't talked beyond formal pleasantries since Sam had returned to Lake Avalon, so this nervous, let's-talk demeanor was new from her normally tight-lipped, I-have-no-emotions mother.

A burst of laughter from the other room filled the silence before Elise took a shaky breath. "I'm sorry."

Sam widened her eyes. *Huh?*

Elise rushed on, "I was . . . a terrible mother. I wasted so much time on fear of what the future would bring and what would happen if . . . if . . . and now I see you with your own child, with that sweet, adorable little boy, and it breaks my heart that I squandered so much time with my own girls. I don't know what my problem was . . . *is* . . . and that's not true, I do know, but I'm trying to work it out, trying to find a way to become the woman I want to be and I just want you to know that . . . I want you to know that I—" Her dark eyes began to shimmer. "You've shown me how to do that, Samantha."

Sam stared at her for a long moment, lips parted in shock. She'd never heard Elise Trudeau talk like this, about emotions and mistakes and the past.

While Sam tried to think of something to say, Elise stepped forward and clasped her hands in both of hers. Closing her eyes, Elise shuddered in a way that told Sam that she was having an empathic flash into Sam's past. The realization unsettled her at first, because it was the first time she'd known her mother to acknowledge, and use, her own psychic ability. At the same time, she feared what her mother would think of what she saw.

In turn, Elise's uncertainty and regret washed over Sam in

a wave so intense that grief tightened the muscles around her heart. She couldn't imagine living an entire life feeling such fear and guilt every instant of every day. No wonder their mother had been so inaccessible when she and her sisters were children. Fear had all but immobilized her.

When Elise opened her eyes, tears slipped down her cheeks. "What you've been through, my dear child, and it's all my fault. If I hadn't been so—" She broke off, grasping for the appropriate word.

Sam squeezed her mother's hands and smiled through the tears blurring her own eyes. In this moment, she understood her mother in a way that she never had. "You were afraid, Mom. Fear is a great motivator."

"I should have been stronger. Mothers are *supposed* to be stronger than their children. They're supposed to be the ones who teach their children how to love and nurture and be loved. Yet you and your sisters are the ones who've shown me those things the past two years. And while you all have every reason to shun me, to *hate* me, you haven't. I don't understand why you—"

Sam cupped her mother's cheek with one hand. "Because you're Mom, and we're a family. Dad gets some credit, too."

Pink flushed Elise's face and neck. "I asked him last night why he puts up with me. Do you know what he said?"

"He loves you."

Elise nodded, forehead wrinkling as if in disbelief. "After all the ways I've hurt him and you girls."

Sam cocked her head. "Does he know about me? That I'm not—"

"You *are* his," Elise said fiercely, with such emotion that Sam felt it in her heart. "In every way that counts. But, yes, he knows. I told him when you returned to us last year. It was long past time." She paused, and her lips curved into a small, shaky smile. "Your father . . . is an amazing man. I don't know why he still loves me, but—"

"Love isn't conditional."

"I realize that now. And seeing you with Mac and how he is with Little Reed . . . I wish I had made different choices."

Sam took her mother's shoulders and looked into her red-rimmed eyes. "Listen to me, Mom. The best choice you ever made was leaving Ben Dillon. He was not a good man."

Elise's damp eyes widened. "He *was* . . . does that mean . . ."

Sam nodded. "I'm sorry, yes. He died after he tried to con the wrong man. You spared yourself, and me, what undoubtedly would have been a terrible, violent life when you left him and found Dad."

Elise pulled Sam into her arms and hugged her close. "I'm so proud of you, Sam. What an incredible woman you've become."

Sam hugged her back, surprised, and pleased, that her mother had finally called her "Sam" instead of "Samantha." Not to mention the "I'm so proud of you" comment. Who knew?

Elise drew away first, laughing softly as she swiped at her eyes. "All right then. I should let you get back to that cake. And I need to fix my makeup before your father realizes he hasn't used the video camera in the past half hour."

When Sam was alone with the cake again, she laughed and shook her head in amazement. The ice inside Elise Trudeau was finally melting.

She finished up the frosting, then picked up the single blue candle on the counter and placed it in the center of the cake. She fumbled with the matches, swearing under her breath when the first couple of attempts to strike one failed to produce flame.

The door behind her swung open again, letting the laughter of her family into the kitchen. Mac slipped his arms around her waist and rested his chin on her shoulder. "How's it going, Mrs. Hunter?"

She leaned her head against the side of his and savored the scent of chocolate on his breath. "Almost there, Mr. Hunter."

"That looks like a really good birthday cake for a kid who's turning only a year old."

When he swiped a fingertip through some of the frosting near the base, she lightly slapped his hand. "Stop it."

Chuckling, he kissed the side of her neck. "I love you, you know."

She grinned sideways at him. "Love you, too." She struck a match, and this time the flame burst into life. "Finally."

Before she could touch flame to wick, though, Mac blew it out.

"Hey! What the—"

He turned her to face him and kissed her, the caress of his lips and the slide of his tongue along her bottom lip making her forget where they were and what she'd been doing.

He drew back too soon, and when she chased his mouth with hers, wanting more, wanting him, he slid a thick envelope into her hand, gave her one last, quick kiss, then stepped back and graced her with an expectant smile, dimples winking at her.

She glanced down at the long white envelope, and her heart kicked when she recognized the return address. Florida Department of Children and Families.

"It arrived in the mail this morning," he said. "The adoption is official. Reed is my son. I mean, he has been all along, but now he's legally mine." His hazel eyes glimmered with the same kind of helpless wonder that had been there the day she'd labored to bring Reed into the world. "I'm officially his father."

Sam threw her arms around his neck, laughing and crying at the same time. They held each other close for a long moment, kissing and nuzzling and looking forward to the future.

Sam extricated herself from his arms only when the embrace began to veer into territory that was inappropriate when guests waited for cake in the next room.

"Later," Sam promised, with one last, lingering kiss.

He grinned and swatted her on the rear as she turned back to the matches.

With the single candle lit, she picked up the cake and Mac pushed open the door into the dining room for her, where the entire Trudeau family, along with AnnaCoreen and her new husband, Richie Woods, sat around the table, happily chattering.

Charlie and Noah took turns describing the hotel in Jamaica, where they'd spent their honeymoon. They'd gotten married two weeks ago in their backyard, surrounded by a blooming garden that would have made the sisters' grand-mother proud.

Alex and Logan took notes, planning for their own honeymoon after their knot-tying ceremony scheduled for six months from now. Alex reached out and grabbed Charlie's hand as they talked, and the lack of hesitation in the gesture pleased Sam. It had taken months of work and training, but her kid sister finally had a handle on her empathy. She and Charlie both could block their abilities at will, no drugs required.

Sam's parents sat at one end of the long table. The senior Reed, in full-on grandpa mode, bounced his namesake on his knee, teasing the rapt boy with the I've-got-your-nose game, while Elise watched, quiet but amused, reserved once again.

Charlie started singing "Happy Birthday" as Sam set the cake in front of Little Reed, and everyone chimed in. Sam helped the boy blow out the single candle, then Charlie set about cutting the cake.

Alex got up and tugged Sam into the kitchen by the hand. "I've been dying to ask you something. Charlie told me the boss of that rat bastard Flinn Ford called you this week, trying to get you to go back to the FBI. Is that something you think you might do?"

"Nope. I'm here, I'm committed, and you can't get rid of me."

Alex grinned. "And that's cool with you? I mean, you're not having any twinges about missing the spy life?"

"Not one twinge." Being Mac's wife and Reed's mother provided all the excitement she could ever desire. Once Reed started preschool, she planned her own educational foray, into the culinary arts.

She had confidence that her former N3 colleagues could handle the rogue satellite networks, especially with Andrea Leigh and Sloan Decker involved. She could also rest assured that Zoe Harris' sister would soon know at least some details about what had happened to Zoe: Sloan had promised that he would inform the woman, in person.

Alex gave Sam a quick hug. "I know I've said it before, but thank you for giving me my life back. I don't know what I would have done without my big sister showing me the way."

"You're doing the meditation every day?"

"Never miss a minute. I've gotten to where I can reach for that calm place inside me automatically before I touch someone or they touch me. The intense focus doesn't work a hundred percent of the time, but I'm getting better at it the longer I do it."

Choking up, Sam hugged her sister again. Maybe that's what all those years with N3 had been about—giving her the resources to help Alex learn to control the more violent aspects of her ability.

Flinn Ford—may he rest in prison for the remaining years of his life—had blackmailed her and used her and manipulated her. But his maniacal greed had also given her and Mac a son. She would never know who Reed's biological father was, but she knew as well as anyone that biology meant nothing when it came to being a good father. And Mac had that role down as if he'd prepared for it his whole life.

As if her thoughts summoned him, Mac stuck his head in the kitchen door and said, "Hey, think you might want to see this."

Sam took his extended hand and let him draw her back into the dining room. The first thing she noticed was Charlie swiping away a tear. Heart in her throat, Sam looked in the direction Charlie was gazing, and froze.

Prim and proper Elise Trudeau sat with Little Reed on her lap, offering him a fingerful of frosting. His tiny hand grasped her finger, lifted it to his mouth and shoved it in. His blue eyes widened at the sweet taste, and he grinned around her finger, all gums and happy drool. In the next instant, he reached for his grandmother's plate of cake on the table and plunged both hands right into it.

Sam started forward to rescue her mother from the impending mess, but Mac held her back. "Wait a sec."

Frosting landed with a silent plop on Elise's linen pant leg. Reed leaned forward and smeared it around, releasing one of those high-pitched baby laughs that makes everything wrong in the world fall away.

Sam held her breath, noticing she wasn't alone. Her two

sisters watched the scene with growing apprehension. Any second now, Elise Trudeau, the woman who never left the house with a hair out of place or a wrinkle in her impeccable clothing, would have a fit that the baby had just ruined her expensive slacks.

When Elise lifted the baby under the arms, Sam reached out to take him, but instead of handing him over, Elise folded him into her arms and hugged him to her with a delighted laugh. "He's just the dearest little thing."

Sam exchanged a disbelieving look with her sisters. Their uptight mother was *laughing* about sticky baby fingers smearing frosting into her fancy clothing.

Charlie shrugged and relaxed against Noah's side with a wide smile.

Alex looped her arm through Logan's and giggled like a little kid.

Sam looked at Mac to find him grinning at her, a flat-broke guy who'd just won the emotional lottery. She smiled back with tears in her eyes.

This was her family.

Wrapping his arms around her, Mac whispered in her ear, "Welcome home."